Mae,

Miracles
Start in the
heart

[handwritten signature]

Second Messenger

A Visionary Novel

Gale O. Connell
Kitty R. Connell

A MythMaker Press original
"Visionary tales to elevate the human spirit."

MythMaker Press
P.O. Box 1890
Nederland, CO 80466-1890

First printing, February 2000

ISBN: 0-9676852-0-6

Cover design by Gale O. Connell and Kitty R. Connell
Graphics designed by Åse at Bejewelled.net.

Printed in the United States of America on recycled paper

This book is dedicated to our children for bravely trekking beside us on our life path and patiently enduring countless rewrites of our story.

A special "thank you" to Mom & Dad for your ceaseless faith and support.

Finally, we must acknowledge our little Kailie Roo, who daily inspires us to live from our hearts.

Prologue: The Quickening

Earth Orbit, c.e. 2191

God chuckled to IS-self: *Ah, tenacious humans... Nearly two centuries after missing the scheduled shift in consciousness, they persist in seeking enlightenment. This time, they come touting technology. This time,* God beamed, *they offer an occasion for miracles.*

Compelled by immense compassion, God's heart burst with unfledged possibilities, loosing countless new likelihoods to glimmer and tumble through the firmament. IS chuckled again. For there amid the swirling potential, a disparate troupe of valorous souls converged for a sacred adventure.

With a blessing, God turned to admire the exquisite unfoldment of Dr. Phillip P. Morrison's prayer. Secluded on a space station orbiting Earth, the doctor worked tirelessly, melding his inventive genius with his unwavering reverence for Spirit. As God observed, the aging man yawned and straightened his aching back. Hours of work yet to do, he nonetheless paused to admire the offspring of his devotion. Dr. Morrison gently smoothed the hair back from the inanimate face and patted the hand of his creation.

God's next action would have raised many a theocratic eyebrow had the doctrinaires been privy to know of it. Stretching a Divine finger ever so slightly beyond the neutrality of free will, IS kindled an unhoped-for spark in the heart of

1

Morrison's dream. Consecrated, now, by God's own touch, the vessel so tenderly wrought lay motionless, abiding the descent of the emissary.

A swaddled awareness drifted through an empyrean teeming with implicit life. Savoring his final moments of union before yielding to the myth of separation, the emissary nestled deeper into the breast of God. There were no words to say before his descent, for all knowings were instantaneous and vast beyond verbiage. Instead, he pondered the honor of his impending emprise. *IS* embosomed the valiant one, infusing him with love. Whispering such reassurances as Spirit may give, God breathed to him a promise: *You are my beloved child. You will remember.*

Imminent quickening funneled the emissary's sentience to a pinpoint of acute focus in the corporeal realm. Tumbling deeper and deeper into the illusion, the dreamer whispered through his sleep, *I will remember.*

Steeling himself against the amnesia of matter, he descended heavily — pinioned by physicality. His eyelids balked against the invasive light that enlivened his body and hurled his unsettled consciousness against the rigid confinement of his new structure. Gasping his first breath, REL opened his eyes on his odyssey.

A Private Premiere

Earth Orbit, Space Station Alpha II, 2191 c.e.

The signature discord of shattering glass sundered their clandestine scheming. Lurching to his feet, Dr. Morrison explained over his retreating shoulder, "I had hoped for something more elegant." Beckoning Councilman Tabbot to follow, Morrison tripped a latch concealed in one of his numerous books, thus freeing the massive bookcase to swivel.

Arthur Tabbot laughed at the old movie trick. "Well, I'm impressed so far." Peering into the yawning darkness, Tabbot stammered in surprise, "So Phil... Is this the library space I lobbied so hard to get for you?"

"Yes. And I put it to good use." Nudging past the councilman, Morrison chortled, "Unlike the bloated bureaucrats that you're used to, I make efficient use of my resources. Half of my literary collection is crammed into a fourth of its allotted space and the other half is stored safely on the surface."

Soft perimeter lights welcomed their entry into Morrison's sanctum. Trailing half a step, Tabbot fastened a guiding hand on the doctor's shoulder while his eyes adjusted to the rosy shadows. He blinked in frank amazement as his unclouding vision revealed a state-of-the-art, 22nd century laboratory. One entire wall, the doctor's command center, strobed with random bursts of red, green, and amber as stacks of his

3

arcane inventions silently ran programs unknowable to all but Morrison. Opposite, bins of improbable parts and tools shared the wall with an enigmatic vault. Resembling nothing so much as a huge walk-in freezer, it rose floor to ceiling and boasted heavy double doors.

Soundlessly, the entrance bloomed as violet, liquescent light poured through the opening doors. There before him, emerging from the glowing nimbus, Arthur Tabbot beheld a walking sculpture of human perfection. Flawlessly detailed, the naked body gleamed of grace and vitality. Thick, dark hair crowned his head, which was inclined at the moment, to examine something he held in his cupped hands. Intent on his cargo, he spoke without looking up.

"Dr. Morrison..." REL engaged the doctor with a rich, easy voice. "I cannot explain it..."

Furrowing his brow, Morrison reminded, "That's the third time since last night."

Oblivious to Tabbot's presence, REL padded gracefully to a corner waste port to discard the shattered glass. While rinsing and drying his hands, he called back to the doctor, "I just completed a comprehensive diagnostic and found nothing amiss. I did note one curious thing, however. Since my latest activation..." Turning around, he noticed Arthur Tabbot. "Oh!" REL exclaimed. "I did not know we had a guest. Forgive my lack of courtesy." Clothed only in innocence, REL beamed and coaxed a distracted handshake from the councilman, who stood transfixed by the symmetry and eloquence of his friend's creation.

Offering a thick bathrobe to REL, Dr. Morrison swept a hand from man to machine, "Arthur, REL... REL, Councilman Arthur Tabbot." Returning to the subject, Morrison pressed, "Now, REL, just what did you find curious?"

REL cocked his head, puzzled.

"It's okay. You may speak freely in front of Arthur. He's up to his neck in this project," Morrison assured.

Relieved, REL explained, "It's like the link between my data and my structure has been compromised in some way — as if every routine command requires an additional nanosecond to process." Searching for an apt description, he pronounced, "I feel dense."

"*As if...? Feel...?*" Morrison questioned. Then groaning in recognition, he confessed, "I should have known. I'm sorry REL. I ought to have told you last night. Before your last reactivation, I launched the final upgrade of your *emotional overview program*. No wonder you're distracted. I'll bet you feel like a walking wound." Patting the biomech on the back, the doctor promised, "You'll adjust to it soon."

REL accepted the doctor's logic without judgment and nodded in silent agreement. But still, something teased at the back of his mind, nagging him like the snatch of a song or a word that would not leave the tip of his tongue.

Morrison's voice drew him back, "REL, why don't you run the driving simulation and highlight any areas of degraded performance?"

"Yes, Dr. Morrison," REL complied. "I'm happy to have met you, Councilman." He smiled and disappeared into the chamber.

Returning to the living room, Morrison poured two snifters of brandy and solicited, "Well?"

Fumbling for words, Tabbot managed, "He shatters even my idealistic expectations. My God, Phil, he's no mere machine."

The doctor replied with twinkling eyes, "I don't do *mere*, Arthur." He laughed, then resumed in a conspiratorial tone, "Only a creation of REL's profound complexity stands any chance of success. He's the perfect hybrid of biology and technology, a biological mechanical biped. A biomech. Arthur, he's a soul short of a miracle."

Tabbot winced a smile that dissolved into gravity. "Then he's just what we need... Phil, I don't mean to rain on your unveiling, but I came here to warn you." Tabbot sipped his brandy. Relaxing into despair, he bared his lonely burden to the doctor. "As it stands, the LRA is a toothless lion. We're so decimated we couldn't pass a global tax cut to save ourselves. And the distinction between the Rationalist Party and the ICom gets hazier by the day." Wiping his forehead with a handkerchief, Tabbot lamented, "Anymore, you can't even walk down Center State Hall without flushing a bevy of ICom brass there to bribe some Rationalist into supporting their fascist agenda."

"I've always thought it sad that war is the only thing that distracts the military from targeting its own citizenry." Morrison shook his head.

"Well, be that as it may, Phil, it's rumored that you're next in the crosshairs. Fells is squeezing the Council for a comprehensive military audit of Alpha II. Considering his cryptic friendship with Governor Coleman, he's likely to get his way. There's little I can do to shield you."

Morrison shrugged. "We knew up front that it might get rough. But what choice do we have, Arthur? Despite your avowed optimism, I know that you have doubts about our chances. Late at night, they haunt me, too." Looking earnestly into the councilman's face, he reasoned, "I don't expect you to sleep better at night just because I'm feeling lucky. But I must tell you that if ever I felt the touch of destiny, it is with REL."

Gazing through the darkness of the outer-orbit night, Morrison leaned against his floor-to-ceiling viewport. The lights from Tabbot's departing EcoSkiff winked and disappeared into Earth's atmosphere.

Footsteps padding from behind stopped short, followed by a soft, "Dr. Morrison?"

The doctor turned, dim light haunting the hollows of his face. Heaving a sigh, he raked a hand through his silvering hair. "Yes, REL," he replied.

"I finished the driving simulations. I performed all but the first flawlessly." Bright eyes sparkling despite the half-light, the biomech cheerfully asserted, "It appears that I am adapting. My flexors feel much freer and my processing speed is over spec. You may have been right, Dr. Morrison." The biomech grinned.

"May have been?" Morrison challenged with a raised eyebrow.

"I'm still considering alternative explanations," REL announced.

Taking the berobed biomech by the elbow, Morrison escorted him into the living room. "Do tell," he urged, guiding REL to a seat on the couch beside him.

"I sometimes encounter thoughts so fleeting that they slip by unrecorded." Wide blue eyes gazed in wonder at the doctor. "It is most puzzling."

"How can I possibly know everything about you?" Morrison whispered gently. "You stagger even my imagination. But to answer you... Metaphysically speaking, the convergence of biology and circuitry could conceivably beget phantom emanations that you perceive as thoughts."

"I will continue my observations, then," REL answered, unsatisfied.

The doctor poured himself another brandy and savored a thoughtful sip. Suddenly sentimental, he began, "You know, REL, my position here on Alpha II is indirectly responsible for your existence. I took the job as the station's Resident Advocate precisely because it afforded the resources and technology and personal latitude I needed to create you. The importance of your mission cannot be overstated."

As the doctor paused to sip again, REL piped up, "Dr. Morrison, what exactly is my mission?"

Through a rolling belly laugh, Morrison quipped, "To change the world, REL. To change the world." Composing himself, he added, "Just between you and me, for decades I thought that was my job. But now, I think I'll pass that mantle on to your capable shoulders."

"But how do I do it?" REL pressed.

"Ah, well… After forty years of research, I managed to identify specifically what events and components are required to initiate a paradigmatic shift of human consciousness. Correlating the fluctuations in Earth's magnetics and base harmonic resonance with specific historical events took years of sorting fact from fiction from folktales. Understanding how to apply that data to probabilities took more years, still. Your mission is to exploit this once-in-an-eon opportunity." After taking another sip, Morrison added, "REL, a stupendous sum of knowledge calls your cranium home. See all those books?" The doctor gestured to his expansive collection. "Through your programming, you have instant access to all of that wisdom." Winking at the biomech, he concluded, "You are literally the best of everyone."

"Dr. Morrison, I still don't understand. What am I supposed to do when you send me to 1999?" REL wondered aloud.

"Reprogram the world, REL. You need not concern yourself with the details. Your programming will always unfold perfectly to reveal everything you need to know as you need to know it. Like a spiral. Your lack of specific instructions is my feeble attempt at granting you free will. Besides, your

discernment is critical to our success. And it is your right."
Drawing a deep sigh and grabbing his snifter, Dr. Morrison
arose from the couch. "Now, I must get busy. Want to keep me
company?"

Trailing the doctor to his work station, REL offered,
"Can I help?"

Morrison quipped, "Maybe you can help me erase my
virtual tracks."

Dr. Morrison eased down into his chair as the system
powered up. Touching a bright holographic icon slowly spinning beside the highlighted menu, he selected Alpha II's
accounts payable file. He longed for a virtual bloodhound to
sniff out all evidence of his embezzlement as he scanned
through the accounts he had plundered to fund his secret
research. Although skilled in the art of hacking, he feared the
slightest oversight lest its discovery lay waste to his lifetime
of plans.

Speaking over his shoulder to REL, the doctor chuckled, "You know, when I was a boy, I had this antique pocket
game. For hours on end, I jockeyed white plastic letters
around a black, plastic square. Twenty-six letters and only
one empty space. With enough patience, I managed to form
words or messages." Deleting an unauthorized entry, he
laughed again. "My accounting skullduggery reminds me
much of that game."

"Dr. Morrison, you're making a message now," REL
observed.

"What? Where?" Dr. Morrison studied the display.

"See?" REL pointed. "You have a very predictable
mind. You selected accounts in a repeating pattern that will
lead right back to you."

In instant recognition, Morrison turned back to REL.
"Well, what can I do about it?"

9

REL briefly consulted his logic, then replied, "You can't erase all your tracks, but you can create..." Searching his dictionary for the appropriate figure of speech, he pronounced, "...a red herring. See, here?" Scanning the current fiscal budget for Alpha II, he examined the accounts raided to supply funds for Morrison's covert activities.

"The pork in political spending has served me well," Morrison quipped.

"Now, maybe, the pork can provide you a subterfuge," REL suggested. "If you consistently transfer funds from one major, variable account to replenish the small accounts you've raided, you'll eliminate all your tracks but one."

"So, all I have to do is select the one account that will end up hanging me?" Morrison joked.

Venturing a small shrug, REL replied, "It's the best solution I can offer."

"Any particular account?" the doctor quipped, wryly.

"How about..." REL quickly tallied inventory rotation, depreciation and funding cycles. "Here," he pointed, "waste management. Recyclables are difficult to trace. And service budgets are necessarily flexible."

"So, you're saying my future is in garbage?" Morrison laughed at the irony. Hunkering down to the task at hand, the doctor neatly beclouded his malfeasance.

Despite the unnatural cycles of daylight and darkfall on Alpha II, Dr. Morrison's inner clock faithfully marked the lateness of the hour. Wresting his slumberous eyes from the infestation of entries besieging his display, he hunched his shoulders to straighten a kink in his neck. He cast his glance around his silent sanctum, surprised to see REL standing still as a statue, face pressed against the large viewport.

Walking over to join the biomech, Morrison whispered, "A penny for your thoughts?"

10

Turning his troubled face to the doctor, REL groped for answers. "Dr. Morrison, why do you embezzle the credits?"

Morrison whistled long and low. "That entails a lengthy story, but I'll begin by saying that long ago, I read about the trials at Nuremberg. You know of them?"

Quickly, REL reviewed his files. "Yes."

"The most significant ideal I gleaned from that tragic epoch is that we have a moral obligation to disobey immoral laws. That, however, does not excuse my dishonesty or my desperation. Admittedly, REL, it's my bastion of fear manifest." Morrison paused for a moment as REL looked at him silently. The doctor could almost see his thoughts processing. "To my credit," Morrison resumed, "I have made my peace by declaring my willingness to accept the consequences of my deeds. Besides, REL," he grinned, "I use the funds for a noble cause. I have always imagined a better world. Even as I boy, I dreamed up inventions that could edify humanity. I once designed a device that could instantly calculate the probable consequences of a person's most frequent thoughts."

"Did it help a lot of people?"

Morrison shook his head sadly. "Very few really wanted to know. It made them too responsible for their lives." Brightening, he continued, "Then, of course, there's you. You were my very first dream and now my *magnum opus*." Tears swelled in Morrison's eyes.

Tilting his head, REL studied the doctor's reddened face. Subtle energy rolling from Morrison invoked a sympathetic vibration from his own structure. With an inrush of empathy, REL apprehended the sacrifices of Morrison's solitary life. Shining like badges of valor streamed images of isolation, tireless labors, endless acts of courage and kindness... and a gentle heart faithful to Spirit. Surging admiration prompted the biomech to ask, "So what of our noble cause?"

11

"My, my..." Morrison pondered. "In the eleven months you've been with me, surely you've heard me speak of the LRA?"

"Yes. The Living Rights Advocates. Begun as a grass-roots movement in the early 21st century. The party platform rests on the concepts that all of life is sacred; that the human spirit is noble; and that compassion is humanity's highest expression. The LRA works tirelessly to decentralize power structures and restore freedom to the people," REL recited from a party pamphlet retrieved from his file.

"REL, you read that straight from the party propaganda, didn't you?" Morrison teased. "Well never mind. What the pamphlet didn't tell you is that the LRA is much more than a political party. It represents a frequency of thought, a fundamental way of looking at the world."

"Then, why is the LRA faltering?" REL asked, puzzled.

"Because of a missed opportunity. Back at the turn of the 21st century, Earth and humanity were poised to transcend the density of old energy."

"Old energy?"

"Old energy is an outdated belief that still holds some in thrall. It is the belief that we are separate from Spirit and that 'might makes right.' Old energy worships the dogma of fear." Morrison ordered his thoughts and continued, "Back to the 21st century. Millions of people recognized the opportunity to shift human consciousness and worked diligently to do so. They called it the New Age Movement. And it almost worked. As the harmonics and magnetics of Earth ripened to support a higher human vibration, wondrous probabilities were launched. A huge burst of love enveloped the planet, healing old energy wounds and temporarily shifting its vibration. Unfortunately, insufficient mass of consciousness doomed the shift to imper-manence. You see, REL, when old power structures began to crumble in the new energy a huge upsurge of fear strangled ascension. So, even as new, positive paradigms emerged, old fear festered, unseen." Sadly, Morrison looked REL in the eyes and concluded in a whisper, "Now, the burst of love erodes and fear rushes to fill the void. And so, the LRA fails and the light of humanity dims."

Earth, 2191 c.e.
Center State Complex

The sleek and deadly Stinger streaked through the night, black as the skies it haunted. The hypersonic, stealth transport — exclusive property of ICom Imperator Fells — cut a striking silhouette as it swooped into the reserved slip. Swarmed by a covey of fawning ICom underlings, Fells muscled them out of the way, rampaging straight to the governor's office. Storming past security, he exploded through Coleman's privacy. The imperator slapped his hands flat on the desk and vaulted forward to shriek his displeasure.

"Where is the money?" he demanded, pitiless dark eyes glinting.

World Governor Durbin Coleman puffed his chest and calmly intoned, "You should check your messages. The money's been delayed."

"Intolerable," the imperator hissed. "The acquisition is scheduled in an hour."

"Imperator Fells," Coleman cozened, "if you insist on purchasing illicit technology, you must suffer through illicit channels. I can't just write you a check. I'm sure your friend will reschedule. The transfer can take place first thing tomorrow."

Gripping the edge of the desk in lieu of the governor's throat, Fells spat, "First of all, I'm not dealing with friends. Mine is a dangerous business, involving dangerous people who do not like to be jerked around by cocky little bastards like you." Leaning closer to the puffy, florid face, Fells elaborated, "In the future, you will deliver as promised."

Staring back into the imperator's cadaverous countenance, Coleman read the warning written there. "Of course," he mumbled.

"Well then..." Fells flashed a gelid grin and folded his rangy frame into a nearby chair. "There is one other thing." Steepling his fingers, he goaded, "May I presume that the order for Alpha II's audit is forthcoming?" He arched a menacing eyebrow as Durbin Coleman squirmed.

Alpha II

Dr. Morrison concealed his smile with a hand to his lips as REL centered the canapé dish on the coffee table. He nudged it a few centimeters one way, measured with laser precision, and nudged it part way back. Finally satisfied, he turned to the doctor, "Is there anything else I can do?"

"Too bad you don't tend bar. Dan always enjoys a good martini." Morrison headed to his wet bar to assemble supplies, quietly pondering REL's enhanced sociability.

Padding behind the doctor, REL watched intently. "If you have a recipe, I could try," he volunteered with childlike enthusiasm.

"Well..." Dr. Morrison chuckled, gazing into the eager face. "Why not? It could prove a useful skill." The doctor selected his choice from the electronic bar guide then retreated to a bar stool to watch. "Stirred, not shaken," he advised.

REL measured and mixed with graceful efficiency, gauging exactly, the ice necessary to achieve the perfect chill. Slipping the long, glass rod into the frosty pitcher, he stirred with computer precision, neither tapping the pitcher nor bruising the gin. With a shy flourish, he poured a sample for the doctor and topped it with a perfect strip of lemon zest.

Morrison closed his eyes to savor the first sip. Grinning over the glass, he teased, "Perhaps I should keep you here with me. A martini like this only comes along every two hundred years, it seems."

Beaming at his latest accomplishment, REL started at the chime of their guest's arrival.

"Dan, come in," Morrison welcomed Alpha II's Director of Operations. With a hand on his back, the doctor guided the mousy man into his residence. "Ariel," the doctor carefully pronounced, "I'd like you to meet my oldest friend, Dan Timball. Dan, meet my newest friend, Ariel. He shares my love of books."

Glancing around Morrison's residence, Timball replied, "Well, he came to the right place. I don't know of any collection anywhere that rivals yours. Looks like you've added to it."

Glass in hand, the director drifted to the ponderous floor-to-ceiling bookcases. REL followed, peeking over his shoulder as Timball perused Morrison's renowned collection of real, paper books. "You're the last of dying breed, Phil. Nobody else I know reads these anymore, they content them-selves with digital volumes."

REL reverently gazed at the hundreds of books, some of them hundreds of years old. Gracing the shelves were books bound in leather, others gilt-edged and embellished with exquisite illuminations. Others were so fragile Morrison stored them in cryocapsules lest they crumble in a draft.

Reaching one corner of the library, REL quietly explained, "These are Dr. Morrison's favorites."

"Ah yes," Morrison confirmed. "The originals are nearly two hundred years old. But I refer to them so often, I copied them to holographic format. I have everything here from astrology to quantum physics to tomes channeled from distant star systems."

Working their way back to the canapés and another perfect martini, Morrison and Timball bantered station business until the director called to REL. "So," he began, "aside from being a bibliophile, what line of work are you in?"

Carefully slipping a book back into place, the biomech considered his acronymic name — REL, *Remote Emissary of Life* — as he joined the others in the living room. Just as Dr. Morrison moved to interrupt, REL replied, "I am an emissary, Director Timball."

"For whom?" the director pressed.

"For humanity's highest good," the biomech proclaimed matter-of-factly.

A bright motion outside the doctor's viewport ended Timball's inquiry. "Here they come," Timball announced, gulping the last of his drink. "Wish I had time for another one of these." He wiggled his glass. "But the engineers are here for an on-site inspection of the skylock system. I at least have to meet them." Setting his glass in the bar sink, he turned to REL. "Maybe next time, you'll tell me more about your job," he said, extending his hand. Clapping Morrison on the back, Timball departed with a whoosh of the automatic door.

Turning back to the room, Morrison watched silently as REL, mesmerized by the approaching transport, gazed into space, his face pressed against the viewport. Never tired of the scene, Morrison watched with him as the incoming vessel accelerated to match the speed and rotation of the spinning space station. Dozens of faces glowed behind the windows of the small ship, illuminated just enough to reveal their awe of the gleaming, space borne structure.

Morrison sighed and placed a warm hand on REL's shoulder. "I'll never forget my first glimpse of Alpha II. She was new then. And she looked to me like a massive, mirrored office tower, oddly out of place as she wheeled silently in her lonely orbit."

Shaking the memories from his mind, the doctor turned to study his biomech. REL continued to stare, unmoving and unblinking, until the transport disappeared from sight.

Long, silent moments stretched between them, finally ending with REL's whispered declaration, "Dr. Morrison, I don't ever want to be shut down again."

Dumfounded, Morrison measured his response. "REL, since last night, since I reactivated you, your behavior has been... astonishing. Do you realize that before last night you never watched a transport dock? Though you have had every opportunity, I might add. All of a sudden you're responsive, and I don't know... lively. REL, since last night you have a presence."

"I cannot explain it. I have been comparing my memories from this day to other random recollections. This is difficult to describe... But it's like my old memories are in black and white and today's are brilliantly colored. That's why I don't want to be shut off again, Dr. Morrison, I don't want to awaken to a black and white world," REL softly appealed.

Morrison's jaunty whistle echoed through the secluded corridors of Level 14. The doctor dawdled, grateful for his spacious residence and his privacy as he braced himself for the contrasting bustle of Central Expressway. Rounding the bend that brought him to the core of Alpha II, his ears pricked with the buzzing of commerce. Soaring a full fourteen stories, the open arcade was the center of station activity. Spiraling escalators framed transparent tubes that rose and fell through the bright lights and clamor. Tiers and mezzanines and pedestal islands glowed beneath full spectrum lighting. And interspersed throughout the shops and bistros, arboretums flourished, providing touchstones with Nature in the vacuum of space.

Stepping into a convenient tube, Morrison dropped eight stories in an instant to arrive at Level 6. Retreating down a broad corridor, he wound his way through the maze of labs and research pods until he reached Director Timball's residence/office. Unlike Morrison, the director surrounded himself with busyness.

Slipping through the empty outer office, Morrison arrived to find Timball slumping over his utilitarian desk, a nail-chewed hand cradling his sparsely-haired head. As Morrison entered, the director looked up and pointed to a chair that matched his dreary desk. "You're not going to believe this," Timball moaned.

Not without compassion, the doctor wondered at the source of Timball's latest crisis. "What is it that I won't believe?"

Timball looked up through bloodshot eyes and drew an unsteady breath. "There are rumors of a military audit of Alpha II." His voice quivered slightly. Drawing a deep breath, Timball exhaled a tumble of words, "Who are they after?"

Morrison raised a calm eyebrow and said nothing.

"Oh, no..." Timball faltered, dread building with each beat of his racing heart. "It's you, isn't it?"

Morrison smiled and slowly nodded his head.

"What?" Timball flared. "What have you done?" As realization dawned, the director blanched. "Oh shit, Phil! You know every conversation in this office is monitored!"

"Normally." The doctor flashed a tiny scintillant cylinder before his friend's disbelieving eyes.

"A master system access wand? My God, Phil! What's going on?" Timball's voice climbed an entire octave as he ranted at Morrison. "Why do you need access to this station's communications functions? Are you eavesdropping? Recording? Altering conversations? Dammit, Phil! What the hell are you involved in?" Timball slapped his palms on the desk top and pushed his chair back. Shrinking into the seat, he folded his arms and waited.

"Dan, sometimes a man has to follow his conscience. In fact..." Morrison leaned forward to look Timball in the eyes. "That's what everyone should always do. In my case, I refuse to sit back and watch Imperator Fells inflict his fascist agenda on an unwary populace."

Wiping beads of fear from his upper lip, the director whispered, "You're telling me that Imperator Fells, himself, is gunning for you?"

Shrugging, Morrison answered, "So I've been warned."

"So, what does he hope to prove with a military audit?"

"That depends on how good the auditor is."

"My God," Timball gasped, "this has something to do with your visitor, doesn't it?"

"Now wait a minute," Morrison protested.

"Emissary, indeed. I knew he was being evasive," Timball accused. "He's a spy!"

"No, Dan! He's nothing like that," Morrison argued. "Please, just drop it."

"I'll drop it all right..." Timball spun to his workstation and called up a search program. "...As soon as you tell me the truth or I find it for myself."

Cupping his hand over his mouth, Morrison weighed his options and then said, "Stop, Dan. You'll only make it worse. And you're placing me in a terrible position."

"Just where do you think a military audit places me, Phil? Either level with me now — about everything — or I launch my own investigation. I mean it!"

"Dammit Dan! Your stubbornness is going to land you in the cell next to mine," Morrison snapped.

The color returned to Timball's face, finally darkening to a heated flush. He opened his mouth to speak, but finding no words, turned his stare to the floor.

With a sigh, Morrison reached out to the director, lightly touching his hand. "We've been friends for over forty years. Surely you know that I don't do things on a whim. Especially felonies."

"Up till now!" Timball looked up from the floor into Morrison's eyes. "Fells... felonies... spies! On my station!" Timball mumbled, standing and pacing fretfully behind his desk. "I'll ask you one last time, what the hell are you involved in, Phil?"

"Okay, Dan. It's your funeral," Morrison spoke, watching every nuance of Timball's troubled face. Calmly, he counted out his crimes on his fingers, "Embezzlement, possession of forbidden technology, and depending on who you ask, treason." The doctor stared at his friend. "Do you feel any better for knowing?"

Swallowing an enormous lump in his throat, Timball collapsed to his chair beneath the weight of Morrison's confession. "Would you consider turning yourself in?"

"Be serious, Dan. This is the most important thing I have ever done in my life. Regardless of Fells or anyone else, I have no choice but to follow it through," Morrison advised gravely. "You, on the other hand, have three options: You can turn me in. You can keep your mouth shut. Or..." he sighed, "you can help me."

Sadly shaking his head, the director murmured, "There's no way I would turn you in, Phil. We've been friends too long. And I have no love for Fells."

"Then, it seems your choices have dwindled."

Without another word, Dr. Morrison rose and left Dan Timball to decide his own fate.

Timball turned a puffy eye to the time display on the ceiling. Sleepless moments crept by in agonizing angst. Dragging his covers away from his sweating body, he woodenly sat up, his feet hitting the floor with a pair of dull thuds. "My God, I must be out of my mind," he mumbled wearily as he pulled on shirt and pants. Shuffling numbly through the nearly deserted Central Expressway, Timball opted for the escalator to put a few extra moments between himself and professional suicide. Despite his detours and slow pace, he found himself, all too soon, facing Phil Morrison's door. He girded his bloodless loins with all the resolve he could muster and passed a trembling hand over the guest alert sensor. Even as a seductive thrill of danger slithered up his knotted spine, Timball's stomach cramped and his heart and mind raced in sickening competition. Courage failing, he turned back the way he had come. Only Morrison's soft touch on his back prevented his retreat.

Wrapping a steadying arm around Timball's shoulders, the robed doctor guided him into his residence and steered him to sit down on the couch. Morrison finally ventured, "Bad dreams? Too much coffee?"

"Too much thinking," Timball muttered.

"Let me fix you a drink, Dan." Morrison stepped over to the wet bar, returning with two frosty-blue glasses. "When was the last time you had crystalline?"

"Not since they made it illegal." Timball took a long drink to bolster his courage. Stuttering to begin, he finally blurted, "Dammit Phil, you know I'm no hero! And I generally steer clear of politics. So, what am I supposed to do when I find out my very best friend is a traitor to a military we don't even need any more? God, talk about a rock and a hard place." The director huffed and wheezed and struggled to catch his breath.

The doctor started to speak, but Timball held up a hand to stop him.

Forcing a yawn, the director continued, "But I got to thinking. I know you, Phil. And I know your integrity. All of your life you have worked for the good of humanity. Whatever you've done this time had to be with the highest intent. I have to know what it is. Then let me decide the depth of my own involvement."

"Whew!" Morrison sighed. Then smiling, he held up his frosty glass. "You know, in a lot of ways this is all about crystalline. Do you know why it's illegal?"

Timball shook his head. "I never thought about it."

"It's illegal because the Rationalists believe that it expands your mind. And people with expanded minds cannot be governed — don't need to be governed. See as the party grows, our personal freedoms shrink. You may not care about crystalline — and you may not even care that all your daily communications are being monitored — but the day that Alpha II's communications and research end up in ICom hands..."

"Surely, you don't think it's possible," Timball argued.

"Arthur Tabbot says it's inevitable."

"Tabbot's involved?" the director questioned. "God! This must be huge."

With a twinkle in his eyes, Dr. Morrison smiled and invited, "Come on Dan, let me show you."

Timball nodded, took another large sip and followed the doctor toward his books. Startled as he was by the swiveling bookcase, he was astounded by what it revealed. Stumbling into the warmly lit laboratory, Morrison's urging hand on his elbow, the director gaped first at one instrument array and then at another.

"Hello, Director," a soft voice addressed him from within a nest of computers. "Another short night, Dr. Morrison?"

Peering into the center of the processing frenzy, Morrison chuckled, "What are you doing?"

"Confirming our final calculations." REL smiled brightly.

"I knew you had something to do with this." Timball pointed a shaking finger at REL. "Emissary," he snorted.

"Come along, Dan. It will be all too clear soon enough." Morrison tugged him to the chamber.

"What the hell is that?" Timball asked as the doors drew open.

Pulsing within stood a luminous tower, more than four feet in diameter, over seven feet tall. On each side of the glowing tube, stacks and rows of instruments twinkled, lending a strobe-like surrealism to this most improbable scene. A violet nimbus swirled within the tube. As Timball watched, particles danced within the chatoyant light, resolving into holographic patterns that dissipated as quickly as they appeared.

"What am I seeing?" Timball gasped.

"Forbidden technology at your service." Morrison grinned and continued, "Coupled with my time mapper." The doctor gestured toward the glowing tube. "This device can take you anywhere in time."

"Time travel?! You can't be serious."

"Okay, Dan. How about a quantum physics refresher? You *do* know, of course, that time and space are mere mortal conventions — illusions created by our organic brains to enable selective focus," Morrison prodded.

Timball nodded skeptically.

"That same selective focus also creates our reality. You see, human consciousness generates standing waves of frequencies along which matter and events congeal to fashion our experience." The doctor looked for a sign of understanding in Timball's face. Finding none, he continued, "By instructing my computer to program progressive frequencies, I've replicated standing waves for every historic and probable time line that links to our present alleged reality. Do you understand what I'm saying?" Morrison tipped his face down to stare into his friend's glassy eyes.

"But why?" Timball tapped his head in a vain attempt to slow his racing mind.

"Thanks to Imperator Fells and Rationalist paranoia, our present is largely lost to us. Any hope we have for the future must be programmed from the past."

Speechless and skeptical, Director Timball stared dumbly around the glowing, pulsing chamber until a gentle nudge from Morrison drew him across the lab. With a grunt, the doctor stooped to reach beneath a work counter. Motioning the director to look, Morrison wiped condensation from a porthole on a man-size cylinder. Tubes and wires looped in and out, connecting the tank to unrecognizable machines and gauges. "Come down here and look," Morrison urged.

Woodenly squatting to humor the doctor, Timball gawked as he beheld a faceless head. At first, he jerked away in horror. Then, braving a closer look, he saw tiny circuits and sculpted flexors where a face should be. "Android?" he whispered.

With a groan, Morrison straightened and stretched. "Biomech," he corrected. "Part living tissue, part machine. What you're seeing..." He pointed down to the cylinder. "...is REL1, my failed first attempt to integrate brain tissue with computer function. Aside from the skin covering, this one's pretty much a robot."

"This one?" Timball asked hesitantly, straightening a kink from his back. "Ariel1?" he brooded.

"Well, I have met with some success," Morrison feigned modesty. "REL2, will you join us?"

Dan Timball's eyes grew wide as realization dawned on him. Pointing at Morrison's approaching guest, he gasped, "Not him!"

"Remote Emissary of Life. REL, for short," Morrison clarified. "As you know, desperate times call for desperate measures, Dan."

"But..." Timball sputtered.

"Didn't suspect a thing, did you? Aside from the spy business, I mean," Morrison prodded, taking Timball's hand and wrapping it around REL's wrist.

"My God, he's got a pulse!"

"Of course, Dan. He has a real, beating heart. If you cut him, he'll bleed."

"This is remarkable." Looking up into REL's face, Timball murmured, "You look so real." Timball plied a biomech finger between his own. "You feel so real."

"He has to be real to impersonate a human being," Morrison explained proudly.

Timball stared at the biomech. "Who?"

"John R. Worthington," REL answered, extending a hand in introduction. "Data Pioneer Technologies."

"John R. Worthington died one-hundred-ninety-two years ago in an automobile accident. His unfortunate demise opened the perfect probability to insert REL into the past to salvage our future," Morrison explained.

Misgivings crawled across Timball's face but he found no words to voice them.

"As John R. Worthington, REL will have access to the TechniCom, a behemoth computer that processed the world's most powerful military and intelligence secrets," Morrison continued. "I believe that exposing these secrets in the past will alter the balance of power in the present. Have we ever talked about the legendary Paradigm Shift of the Third Millennium?" Morrison put an arm around Timball's shoulder and guided him back to the living room.

As Morrison and Timball bandied philosophy and strategy, REL removed himself to more fully prepare for his mission. Within a few hours, he would find himself on Earth, 1999, impersonating the man whose death he had viewed hundreds of times. Sitting before the purple matrix tower in the chamber, he closed his eyes and retrieved an archived memory of the *Coal Creek Canyon* sequence. In his mind, he watched shadowy flickers of a Blazer rounding a sharp mountain curve. The driver swerved when a large animal bounded across the road, the vehicle skidded sideways and caught a sign post with its rear fender. The Blazer flipped over the edge and crashed to the road below. There it rested, twisted and mangled, on the lower switchback. The driver was thrown from his vehicle and landed with a solid thud against a large rock, his life ending in the blink of an eye.

The images disappointed REL. The entire sequence rendered insubstantial and robotic — a vapid forgery of the rich perception he enjoyed since his most recent activation. Skeptical that the enormous enrichment of his experience resulted entirely from the *emotional overview application*, he focused on the matrix tower and eagerly initiated a real-time review.

Immediately drawn into the drama, he felt John Worthington's frantic white-knuckle grip on the steering wheel. His own stomach lurched as the Blazer left the roadway and his heart pounded as he observed his likeness vainly steering the bouncing, sliding 4x4 down the mountainside. His breath stuck in his throat when Worthington flipped and crashed onto the asphalt.

REL pitched back in his chair. Though he found his depth of empathy astounding, his immense compassion for Worthington's predictable death threatened to strangle his heart. Shaken, he disengaged his *emotional overview application*, reasoning that to be the source of his discomfort. Instead of relief, another surge of sadness tightened his chest. Baffled, he inhaled a deep breath of air and mentally exhaled it through his constricted heart. As his breath poured softly out, he felt a gentle prompt drawing him to explore his heart unfettered by his programming. The improbable invitation caused a minuscule rise in his body temperature. And that, in turn, caused the thin moisture film protecting his optical lens to evaporate. His biomechanical system compensated by producing more than twice the normal amount of fluid that leaked from under the eyelid and washed the orb. The moisture welled in the corner of his eye. When he blinked, it overflowed and slid silently down his cheek. Before he could brush the tear from his face, Timball and Morrison returned to the chamber.

"I feel like crying, too, REL," Timball said, noting the tear stain.

Morrison whipped around to look at his biomech. "Crying? Is that possible?"

"I was thinking of the real John Worthington," REL murmured.

Morrison brushed aside his surprise. "REL, run a complete diagnostic."

"Yes, Doctor," the biomech complied.

Morrison shook his head. He wanted to give REL his full attention. But right now, he was far more concerned about Timball. "Dan, I won't ask for your complicity. I've managed this far on my own." The doctor sighed. "God knows, I would appreciate your help and your company, but I will not ask you to take this risk with me. I will, however, ask for your silence."

27

Timball sat with an exasperated slump. "How do you know that REL can change things? How do you know he won't make things worse?"

"It can't get any worse. We're on a collision course with totalitarianism. If... make that when... the ICom occupies Alpha II, research and communications will fall under Imperator Fells' direct control. It's just a short leap from there to kissing his ring. I can't imagine any bleaker scenario, can you?" Morrison glared at his friend.

"Well, even if you are right, what can REL possibly find that will change things so drastically as to improve our lot?" Timball pressed.

"Let's go back to the end of the second millennium and the legendary Paradigm Shift. By that time, world governments and the global intelligence community had amassed hoards of data which would have proven the existence of a lot of things the establishment officially denied."

"Like what? What could have been such a threat that information was kept from the people?"

"Well, the existence of extraterrestrials for one thing, and the verification of unlimited human psychic potential — secrets that had been kept for a very long time. Even when the world population accepted the theories as real, the governments weren't sure how to release the information without completely losing face... not that there was much to lose at that point. See, old political structures just can't seem to let go of their *power over* the people. The dominant paradigm that should have ended, didn't, because nobody had the tools to challenge it. REL is going to find those tools."

"And just how's he going to do that?"

"Time travel, Dan." Morrison spelled out his plan one more time. "Armed with what he finds in the TechniCom, REL will find a way to tip the balance. By changing the past, he insures our future." Morrison took REL's place in the chair before the matrix tower and activated his time mapper. A pastel image of Earth hung in front of them, spinning on its invisible axis. "All probabilities are reachable within the matrix of time. Everyone has literally done everything."

The mapper projected lines intersecting the holographic Earth. Bright colored filaments netted the planet, extending to an equal distance in all directions. Morrison stood and pointed to a highlighted queue. "To plot our destination, we locate the dominant probability. I will insert REL into the target conjuncture at the point he can best alter essential circumstances without compromising past events. The predetermined point at which to effectively ensure the shift in consciousness is..." Morrison traced a probability line to the surface of the holographic planet. "Right there."

"I don't claim to understand what you just told me," Timball understated. "But I'll do what I can."

Rising to embrace his friend, Morrison beamed. "Dan, I'm truly grateful, I really can use your help. I've got a lot to teach you in the next few hours."

Guiding his dubious friend to the command center, Dr. Morrison began his hasty tutelage.

Second Messenger

Crossing the Rubicon

Somewhere in the time matrix

REL cocked his head to one side. His biomass tingled as the light and harmonics of the matrix tower dispersed and resolved within the magnetic medium to re-create the travelers in their target time. As REL observed the doctor, he noted the man's closed eyes, clamped jaw and clenched fists. Beads of perspiration formed on Morrison's pale forehead and a bright drop of blood appeared beneath his nose. All at once, the doctor lurched forward, spared from stumbling by REL's supportive arm. *It must be the vertigo*, REL concluded. Gently, he clamped Dr. Morrison's arm in the crook of his elbow to hold the man steady. *This way, we'll be ready for anything when we arrive in 1999.*

Confident now that all was secure, REL activated his sensors to better evaluate his own experience. He concentrated his awareness on the cellular level of his structure. Momentarily alarmed, he discovered that his tissues seemed to be bleeding into each other, as if all individuation of matter had ceased. Glancing again at the doctor, the biomech wondered if the old man was in pain. Aside from the hemorrhagic sensation, REL could find no other impact on his body. His reflexes comfortably paced the speed of the shift. His eyes remained focused on the oscillating environment of the matrix. His processors even allowed him to see the movement of time. Entranced by the swirling probabilities, he briefly wondered if he could select one and step beyond the confines of the time mapper's predetermined setting. This, of course, was not the time to try.

Instead, the biomech observed his perceptions of glaring lights and high-pitched whines as the harmonics wound down to silence. When the shifting ceased, REL gently patted Morrison's clammy hand. None the worse for wear, the biomech stood poised and eager for his earthly adventure.

Boulder, Colorado: 1999

The traffic was unbearably noisy compared to the serenity of Alpha II. Dr. Morrison dabbed at his nose with a real linen handkerchief. He blinked over and over, unaccustomed to the bright sunlight. "Which way?" he asked, still somewhat disoriented.

REL pointed down the street. "West on Pearl Street, about three blocks, Doctor." REL grabbed Morrison's arm and pulled him toward their destination. Within the first block, Morrison was able to walk unassisted so REL jaunted slightly ahead of him, gazing at the restaurants and crowds near the shopping center. Delighted with the success of the time shift, the doctor grinned as he realized that his creation perfectly matched the gait of the man walking half a block in front of them. A movie marquee blazoned special matinee feature: *Star Wars Movie Marathon*. Morrison nudged the biomech who stopped suddenly to stare in recognition at the title. Disengaging from his *contemporary culture* file, REL gently grabbed the doctor's elbow and led the way to the used car lot.

A gleaming white Chevy Blazer sat on the row nearest the street, large red stick-on numbers covering the windshield. It was the only close match to the real John Worthington's doomed vehicle within a two-hundred mile radius. REL reached out to stroke his truck-to-be as a salesman strolled over to them, right hand extended in greeting.

"Hey! How ya doin'?" A huge grin spread under the dark mustache of the friendly, fleshy salesman. His expansive gesture strained the belt that was buckled to the very last notch. "Looking for a car or a truck?"

"We'd like to buy this 1994 Blazer." REL pondered the fact that he could not match the man's light blue western-style suit with anything in his *1999 fashion folder*. He initiated a search of *1998* only to be interrupted by the man's hand on his back.

"Good choice," the salesman said as he squeezed REL's shoulder. "How about a test drive?"

"I'm afraid we don't have time for that. We just want to pay for it," Morrison responded.

"Well then... name's Richard Fowler." He ushered the pair into a converted gas station that sat at the center of the lot. "You looking for us to carry the paper?" Fowler asked.

"What?" Morrison considered the question carefully then wrinkled his brow.

"You know, tote the note?" The salesman grabbed two plastic orange stacking chairs and shoved them with his foot until they were in front of his metal desk. Gesturing for the men to sit, Fowler ripped a credit application from a thick pad and slid it across the desk to the doctor.

"We have cash. We have the $15,995.00," Morrison responded, peeling bills from a wad of antique currency donated by the LRA.

"Don't often see cash like that." Fowler stared at the stack piling up on his desk.

Fingering the fabric of the jacket Fowler had draped over his chair, REL absently remarked, "We should negotiate, Doctor."

Concerned by his biomech's actions, Morrison snapped his fingers. "John, just what are you doing?"

"Analyzing this material."

"John!" Morrison refocused the biomech.

REL immediately diverted his attention from the unknown fiber to the man across the desk from him. New insight flooded his logic as he compared the absurdity of his actions with the dictates of his *multiple interaction protocol* application. Jerked back to the moment and intent upon his performance, REL composed himself, leaned forward and stared into Fowler's eyes. "We'll pay fourteen thousand even."

Fowler bit his lip and gazed at the bills in front of him. "Aaah, gosh," he said, shaking his head, "the price on the windshield is the best I can do."

Morrison restrained the biomech who reached to retrieve the stack of bills. "Let's get this done, John. Just pay the man."

Gently removing the doctor's hand from his wrist, REL assured with a knowing nod, "It's always best to negotiate for cars." Turning to Fowler he explained, "The doctor hasn't purchased a car in a very long time."

Dr. Morrison sat back to witness the continuing unfoldment of REL's personality. Each real-time event, down to the tiniest nuance, triggered an order of magnitude understanding. Just five minutes ago, his biomech was distracted. But now...

It was with great difficulty that Dr. Phillip P. Morrison extinguished his urge to clap REL on the back as Richard Fowler, veteran used car salesman, dropped his eyes and surrendered to the fourteen thousand even.

At that moment, REL looked up into his creator's eyes and beamed at his own accomplishment.

Within the hour, Mr. Fowler issued keys and paper-work to John R. Worthington. Climbing behind the wheel of his first truck, REL savored every detail of the experience. Although used, the Blazer still retained a new scent. The bio-mech ran his hand over the leather seat and traced the sensors on his back as he noticed how the seat seemed to mold itself to cradle his form. Adjusting the outside mirror and then the rear-view mirror as he had learned to do from his driving sim-ulations, the biomech caught sight of his reflection. It was an odd sensation, that. He had watched the Coal Creek Canyon scene hundreds of times, but always from the *outside*. Now, as he sat in the driver's seat of his very own vehicle, he felt the oddest sense of déjà vu, like he had crawled inside a dream. Reluctant to end his introspection, he yielded to the subtle prompting of his program. Guiding the key into the ignition, he took one last look at himself in the mirror and started his truck.

The purr of the engine was another surprise. He tuned every sensor not required for driving to the feel of the road. He hadn't driven half a block before he rolled down his window and located a suitable radio station. Marveling at the difference between his many simulations and the actual experience, REL turned to his much-amused passenger, "Hang on, Doctor, I'm going to give it hell."

Shaking his head, Morrison laughed in delight. "Just don't get your first speeding ticket, R... John."

Morrison couldn't take his eyes off his biomech as the pair sped toward the top of Coal Creek Canyon. All the doctor's decades of science and faith had not prepared him for this extra-ordinary event. Obviously capable and curiously pleased with himself, REL steered toward the summit, whistling a newly memorized song from the radio. As if, scant months before, he had not been an experiment, an assortment of parts and circuits and chips. As if he had been born from a woman rather than an old man's desperate dream.

Morrison was quiet when they arrived upon the scene. The dust from the accident had barely settled. Eagerly jumping from his own, undamaged Blazer, the biomech sucked in a deep and carefully analyzed breath. Dr. Morrison, lost in his own thoughts, transferred identification and luggage to the duplicate vehicle while REL scanned every square inch of his dimensional surroundings. A glint of light caught the biomech's eye and he leaned down to take a closer look. Identifying the double-terminated prismatic hexagonal structure as one of thirty-two classes of crystals, he picked it up and examined it closely. Startled by the vibration the amethyst transmitted to his sensitive fingers, REL called out, "Dr. Morrison... "

"Yes," the doctor responded absently.

"It's alive!" The biomech proclaimed with certainty.

"What?" Morrison spun to look at the dead man sprawled ghoulishly in front of a ragged rock outcropping.

"I mean this." REL smiled as he held the purplish stone in his outstretched hand.

"No, that's not alive, REL. It's a rock."

"But I feel it," REL protested, analyzing the sensation he felt emitting from the stone.

"I'm sorry, REL, I'm really in a hurry to wrap this up. Please put it down and help me get this body back to the truck." The biomech reluctantly obeyed and replaced the body back inside the wrecked Blazer. Morrison assessed the situation and signaled Alpha II. "Dan, now that I actually see this wreck, I'm certain the mass is too great to move anywhere. We'll have to move it to some other time. Do you remember how to calculate time coordinates for the most-accessible point in the past?"

"Yes, I think so."

As the doctor waited for Timball's calculations, REL approached the dead John Worthington. In real time, it was quite a shock to see his own face on another body. Reaching out to touch the corpse, REL pondered what it was that distinguished life from non-life. Here, before his eyes, were all the components of a living human being — battered and bruised, but still contained within a human structure. And yet, no life force was present in the cooling, stiffening body. What was that spark that was life and exited upon death? The biomech gazed into the face that had inspired his own image and pondered the mysterious prompt that teased him to remember.

Intrigued by his biomech's actions, Morrison had to force himself to respond to Timball's voice, "Okay, Phil, it looks to me like the easiest thing to do is ship the wreck back about ten years. I should be looking at that solid green line, right?"

"Yes, where it intersects the control plane."

"Got it."

"Dan, I don't have any better ideas. Maybe I can lessen the paradox when I get back. For now, we'll just have to do what we can. Better step away, John."

REL reached out and patted the dead Worthington. The biomech took one last look at his likeness then moved away from the body and the wreck.

"Go ahead, Dan," Morrison said as he walked to REL.

Amidst a crackling swirl of shifting time, the mutilated Blazer and driver disappeared.

Biting his bottom lip, Morrison looked into his biomech's eyes. "Well John, this is it. Are you ready?"

REL ran a quick diagnostic. "Yes," he answered slowly, "I'm ready."

"Alpha II won't be the same without you," the old man said as he embraced the new Worthington. "So much depends on you," he murmured as he pulled the biomech close enough to feel his heart pulsing. Stepping back, he held REL at the shoulders with his outstretched arms to look at his biomech for the last time. "Good luck." Reaching into his pocket, Morrison produced a pendant that hung from an elaborate silver chain. "Here, John, keep this handy. The point doesn't provide two-way — we can't risk that kind of discovery. But at least you can signal me at the pre-arranged time." Feeling a bit like a mother hen, Morrison patted REL on the shoulder. "If I can find some way to bring you back..."

REL bowed slightly as the doctor placed the point around his neck. He heard a crackling sound and looked up just in time to see Morrison disappear into the matrix. Retrieving the amethyst from the dust, the new John Worthington climbed into the newly purchased Blazer where he remained deathly still. Sights, sounds — all familiar to him from many viewings in the laboratory seemed suddenly alien. The texture of this reality overwhelmed him, laden as it was with the smells of the planet and the vibrating frequencies of Nature. He quickly scanned his surroundings, suddenly possessed of the feeling that he was in a crowd. Although no humans were near, he recognized all the other living presences — each individual — of trees and plants and animals. He felt all the unique densities that comprised the landscape. The smells of pines and soil and the flickering colors of birds and butterflies astounded him with their diversity. The sound of wind and insects and life assailed him in its multi-plicity. Entranced by the discovery, but driven onward by his programming, he reluctantly turned the ignition to start. The engine roared in response to the spark. Suddenly, molecules of a different ilk deadened the smells of life. The intrusive dross of carbon monoxide arrested the scents of Nature and besieged his senses. Everything that surrounded him was organic, sprung living from the Earth. What was he? Did he vibrate like the stone in his pocket? He tried to feel himself, but succumbed to the impossibility of it. He smelled his skin. He smelled the leather upholstery. He thought of his own construction. Then he knew for sure. He was a machine like the Blazer in which he sat. An invention with no valid presence of his own. He felt out of place in the living world. Even his amethyst held more life than he, the fake John Worthington.

This new knowledge devastated him. He could not run his programs. He could not examine the discovery further. His external sensors shut down one by one until he was completely immobile and utterly unaware of his surroundings.

Alpha II

"Peak load! Damn it! How could that happen?! He's totally catatonic." Dr. Morrison pounded a fist on the nearest flat surface.

"Well, do something! Surely, you know what to do," Timball demanded.

"Dan, this is the only variable I could not precisely calculate. Emotion is beyond scientific accuracy. Everything, *everything* must be considered in the equation. How can you possibly compensate for everything? Sure, I could have programmed REL without the possibility of evolving emotional response. But then he would be just a fancy robot. He could not accomplish this mission as a robot. He absolutely needs the response flexibility that emotions facilitate. There was no other way. And, he was doing beautifully. I was watching him."

"So, you're telling me that we have a hysterical biomech — a catatonic one — but we have no way to compensate for the problem and retrieve him?" Timball was incredulous. He had placed his career — his life, maybe, on the line and now he was helpless to save himself. "Why didn't you build the point into the biomech's body — something that would automatically activate if all his sensors shut down?"

"The truth is," Morrison laughed bitterly, "I ran out of time."

The doctor was frantically running combinations and calculations when his door sensor alerted him to a visitor. Assuming his most formidable scowl, Timball stepped into the living room and activated an optical laser that brought the caller's image into view. "What is it?!"

"Are you Morrison?" the uniformed monitor snapped.

"No, I'm Alpha II's director, Dan Timball."

The monitor was unimpressed. "Please open the door."

"Please, wait just a minute, *Monitor*." Timball emphasized the title, directing his voice toward Morrison with the back of his hand. At his warning, the doctor muted the time mapper and grabbed the nearest prop he could find to avert the intruder's attention.

"You should know I have an Article with me that authorizes a station-wide audit," the monitor's hologram mouthed.

As Morrison struggled into his bath robe and closed the bookcase to his lab, Timball stood his ground. "I don't care. Doctor Morrison is very ill."

"Who says I'm too sick to answer my own door?" The doctor mussed his hair and waved his hand over the door sensor, admitting the uniformed man. "I am Dr. Phillip P. Morrison, Resident Advocate and this is the Director of Alpha II, Dan Timball. And you are?" Morrison questioned with a raised eyebrow.

The monitor confirmed their identities with the tiny voice-print analyzer pinned to his lapel and stiffly introduced himself. "ICom Monitor, Garner P. Williams, Alpha Zone, authorized by Governor Durbin Coleman to conduct a military audit of this facility," he announced. The coin-sized disc he handed the doctor was activated by the warmth of his hand to project a holographic document bearing the governor's signature.

"When was this Article filed?"

"One hour ago," Williams answered.

"Then you were already onboard Alpha II waiting?" Morrison asked. "Isn't that highly unusual?"

"I can't answer that. Will you follow the directives of the order?"

"Of course, we will follow any order put forth by the governor. Whatever you require will be made available." Morrison looked into the monitor's steely eyes. "You look like you could use a little rest."

Williams deactivated the device on his lapel. "I'm ready to proceed whenever you are," he answered stiffly.

"Let's get you situated in the First Station. I really must apologize, we have been using our First Station for storage. We haven't had an important visitor for a long time," Morrison lied with only a little regret for the falsehood. "Contact me when you're settled. I'll be at your disposal." Morrison smiled, but his mind raged at the complication. *A monitor!* How in the hell was he going to keep a monitor off his back? A monitor was nothing more than a legal spy for the ICom, a 22nd century IRS auditor — Fells' minion.

Timball noticed the back of Morrison's ears turning red and intervened. "Monitor Williams, Avery will come and escort you to your rooms." A quick call to his talented facility's manager arranged housing for the monitor in the First Station on Level 1, far away from Morrison and his lab.

As soon as the monitor had departed, Timball slumped into the nearest chair. Although he had played his role as cued by Morrison, his heart still pounded with dread. Resting a moment as Morrison rushed to the matrix tower, Timball jumped at the outburst.

"Damn, damn, damn!!! I can't find a trace of him! I've tried every setting, every remote command I can think of. Damn! I could probably find him with some uninterrupted time. But now I've got Fells' cursed bloodhound at my door!" Morrison dropped to the chair in front of the matrix tower and buried his head in his hands.

Fells' Covert Operations Center

The mammoth air base, a victim of biohazard quarantine, loomed ghostly — eerily silent amidst the desperation of the crumbling inner city. Slabs of pitted gray concrete stretched out across the derelict stronghold. A decade of accumulated debris clogged the overgrowth of vegetation surrounding the maze of outbuildings. It might have served as the perfect refuge for the city's homeless had it not been for the rumors of horrific disease and certain death to be found within the complex. Frequent discoveries of dead rats and pigeons, and the occasional cat or dog planted along the perimeter fence testified to the truth of the terror.

One bright light cast a long shadow from the back window of one deserted building. Inside, a young lieutenant studied the patterns projected in brilliant colors before him. It was the bulkiness of the object that caused a traceable distortion in the matrix. The uniformed lieutenant announced his success and others gathered around him. He projected the image of the nearly imperceptible quiver to an empty space in front of the group. "There!" he shouted, pointing to a spot where the image flickered slightly.

"Can you track it?" a private asked.

"I already have," the lieutenant bragged. "1989."

The report from the secret station reached Fells at once. Lounging in his penthouse, sipping vintage Scotch, he smirked at the news. "Take that, you arrogant bastard!" He gestured at the orbiting satellite. "We'll just see how well your noxiously-renowned genius serves you this time. Maybe you can hide behind your peace prize. However..." He took another sip. "I can buy whatever it takes to shut your bleeding-heart party down." Draining the glass, he chuckled, "And if I can't buy it, I can always use my other negotiating skills." Fells poured himself another double and strolled to the massive glass front that looked down on Democracy Plaza. "Fear always works well."

Nederland, Colorado: 1999

The shiny RTD bus lumbered up the final climb to Barker Dam. Alan Burgess slid his lanky frame to the edge of his seat and brushed his perpetually straggly hair from his eyes so he could admire his favorite view. The little town of Nederland lay snuggled into the valley, framed between the blue expanse of Barker Reservoir and the towering snow-covered peaks of the Continental Divide. With a sigh, the young deputy smiled to himself that this was his final bus ride. This coming weekend, he was moving away from the congestion of Boulder to become an official resident of Nederland. Not only did his job require residency, he longed for the serenity of mountain living.

Just as the big RTD approached the city limits, a rainbow-colored VW bus inched its way right into the traffic flow adding to the confusion created by the town's quaint roundabout. Shaking his head, Alan got off one stop early to restore movement to the growing line of cars.

"Politicians," he groaned. "This isn't Europe. Come on, Dakota." Holding on-coming traffic at bay with an authoritative left hand, Burgess waved the young Trustafarian into the loop. "Dakota, it isn't that complicated. Really..." he said as he motioned for the dreadlock-crowned boy to complete his half of the circle. "Lotsa money, little common sense," he declared just under his breath. "Yield to the left," he shouted, pointing to the triangular signs perched on the shoulders of each of the five incoming streets. He glanced at his Swiss Army watch. "Well, no coffee today." He hurried his pace until he reached Wolf Tongue Square. By now, of course, he knew to step around the piles of rocks and the rusty wheelbarrow that had gradually become part of the landscape. He laughed at the pansies growing between the bags of hardened concrete.

"Man, if they ever finish this patio, I won't recognize the place," Burgess commented to Dr. Winter and Valerie Arnette as he hurried by them. Sprinting over the wooden walkway, past the bagel shop-pizza parlor-dentist office complex, he turned down the little path that led to the Nederland Marshal's Office.

Thelma, the Nederland town clerk, sipped the last drop of coffee from her personalized Whistler's Cafe mug and checked the time on her marcasite watch. Her office always opened at precisely 9:00 a.m. She had ninety-seven seconds, exactly enough time to leave $1.50 on the table and walk past the little building that housed the Marshal's Office to the Town Hall on the other side. From then on, she operated on Nederland time, not a minute too much, only occasionally a minute too little.

Crunching across Whistler's little gravel parking lot, Dr. Winter and Valerie waved to the hurrying Thelma. "Whew," Valerie sighed, "When was the last time we had three emergencies before nine?"

"A long time, for sure," Dr. Winter replied. "What was it that you were doing to the Smith boy?" Not wanting his young assistant to misunderstand, he added. "It really worked wonders. I was very impressed." Holding the door open for Valerie, he stepped into the rustic cafe behind her.

"I was helping him visualize. He's really bummed out about his arm. He just signed up for hockey in Boulder and now he's afraid he won't be able to play." Nurse Valerie Arnette shrugged as if guided visualization were part and parcel of Dr. Winter's training.

"Two coffees," the doctor signaled as they headed for a pine table with two benches.

"Make mine herbal tea," Valerie spoke up.

"Anyway, Valerie, he really calmed down. What did you say to him?"

"Well, first of all, I told him that thoughts have power. And second, I told him that medicine only heals symptoms..." Valerie paused at the doctor's grimace. "...that the body really heals itself. Then I told him that if he sits quietly for five minutes, morning and evening, and pictures the break in his arm mending like broken ice freezes over... I thought that was a nice touch. You know, hockey — ice... Anyway, I said if he would picture that, he would help his body heal his arm. That way, he no longer feels helpless and left out of his recovery. And he really will help himself heal. Studies have shown... "

Dr. Winter laughed, "I know about the studies. Visualization produces neurotransmitters that mobilize all the right chemicals to speed healing. You don't have to convince me, at least, not too much." Sipping his coffee and staring across the table at the young nurse he asked, "So tell me, Valerie, how are you getting along?"

"Fine, Doctor Winter. Why?"

Somewhat embarrassed that he might be meddling, Dr. Winter nevertheless continued, "It just seems that you spend all your time studying or theorizing or working at the clinic. Don't you ever just relax and go out?"

"Sure, sometimes. Not much though, I admit." Smiling at his concern, she answered his unasked question. "You know,

Dr. Winter, I really do appreciate your kindness. And truly, since my folks died, you've been like my only family here. But, I'm not looking for just *any* relationship. Too many people go around believing that they should find someone to *complete* them, you know, that nonsense that two incompletes make a whole. That's probably why we have a 60% divorce rate. I, on the other hand, believe that I should be a complete individual before I can meet the perfect other complete individual. Then, I think, the two of us will become gloriously greater than the sum of our parts. You can't rush a thing like that. And until it happens, I *do* have theories to study and books to read."

"I've noticed some of the books you've been reading," the doctor said in a tone of mild disapproval.

"Oh, you'd love this one." She winked, producing a slender volume twined round and round with elegant sketches of plants. "It's about how to invoke the spirits of certain plants to help a person heal." Pursing her lips to stifle a laugh, she awaited the doctor's response.

"The *spirits* of plants. Not standard herbology, I take it."

"Not quite. In many cases, the patient doesn't even come into contact with the actual plant. The healer summons the appropriate one and introduces it to the patient's spirit and they agree on the appropriate metaphysical treatment. It works. Aboriginal peoples have used it forever. They claim they can cure everything from diabetes to cancer."

With an evil grin, Dr. Winter quipped, "Just don't show up at the clinic clad in animal skins and carrying those spotty, red mushrooms. That might be a bit much."

"Stop it!" she laughed. "I'm serious about this. I believe that health is an expression of attitude and state of mind. It turns out that laughter *is* some of the best medicine. You know, before the industrial revolution, people were more in tune with themselves and Nature. Back then, most killer diseases were the result

46

of improper sanitation. These days, most killer diseases are the result of stress. Today's medical community really misses the boat when it treats a disease rather than healing the patient. Do you see what I mean?"

A chirping pager interrupted Dr. Winter's reply. Still considering Valerie's last statement, he hooked his thumb behind the device so he could read the display. Turning to his nurse, the doctor announced, "Incoming."

Leaving their half-empty cups, they sprinted to the clinic. The pair arrived just as Marshal Jim Burrows pulled up to the small strip mall office perched incongruously above the old wooden structures of the former mining town.

Extricating the man from the back seat of Burrows' Jeep proved no easy task. The stocky marshal ran a frustrated hand through his short-cropped sandy hair, then put his shoulder into the chore. "He's no easier getting out than he was getting in," Burrows complained, grunting and pulling at the intractable passenger who sat, unresponsive, hands frozen as if still steering the truck he had been driving. With a flushing face, Burrows called, "Dr. Winter, can you give me a hand here?"

Valerie winced as the straining men finally loosed their inflexible charge just enough to slam his head into the inside door frame. An audible thud preceded a collective "ouch!" She quickly pushed a wheelchair near enough the Jeep for the men to easily deposit their frozen patient.

"Let's get him right to the exam table," the doctor directed as they wheeled through the clinic doors. "Can you get his pulse, Valerie?"

"He's got a strong one. Give me a minute." Valerie mentally timed the beats. "It's normal. How odd..."

"You mean that his pulse is normal?" Dr. Winter asked.

"No. It's his energy," Valerie puzzled. "It's amazing. It's... luminous."

Dr. Winter regarded her skeptically. "Luminous?"

The pair met little resistance as they straightened legs and arms, gently probing as they did so. In scant moments they had him stretched out lifeless as a mannequin, Dr. Winter bending over him to listen with a stethoscope.

Valerie glanced at the patient as she inserted a thermometer into his ear. He appeared to be uninjured. She saw no bruises or abrasions on his smooth face. In fact, not a hair was out of place on his impeccable head. Nor were his clothes rumpled at all. Had it not been for his perfect 98.6° temperature and the lively intelligence she felt lurking just beneath his unresponsive exterior, she would have sworn him to be a corpse arrayed for final respects. He was that perfect. Shaking off the odd sensation of her observation, she returned to the task at hand. Looking into his eyes, she knew for certain that he was completely oblivious to her presence.

Marshal Jim Burrows hovered behind the doctor and nurse. "He ran off the road on the steepest switchback in Coal Creek Canyon. You can see his tracks coming down the side. I don't know how, but he landed upright on the road. I was on my way home from Denver. Damn near hit his truck as I came around that last curve. He looked like he was in shock so I didn't wait for an ambulance, I just brought him in with me."

The doctor peered into the patient's eyes, shining his light and exposing the pink underside with his thumb. Light seeped through the biomech's deactivated sensors. John Worthington blinked. He quickly scanned the upside-down view of his surroundings, finally settling on the face of the man bending over him.

"Looks like he's coming around. Hello there," the dark-haired physician spoke in a soothing, professional voice. "It's okay. You've been in an accident and are safe at the Nederland Clinic."

In micro seconds, the biomech searched his files to deduce what had happened to him. A rush of emotions accompanied the stream of data stored in his memory. Like the black box in an airplane, his computer brain had forever recorded his despair of the last moment before his system crashed.

"Are you in any pain anywhere?"

"I crashed. I can't believe that I crashed."

"No. You didn't crash. According to the marshal, your truck seems to be fine. Do you feel pain anywhere?"

John Worthington mentally examined his anatomy for pain. Although a complete dictionary definition was immediately available to him, he could not relate in any other way to the concept of it. In a micro second, he initiated a detailed analysis of the human nervous system, astonished by the difference between humanity's hard-wired arrangement and his own sound-activated array. Fascinated, he allowed himself the fraction of a second it took to explore pain further. *Humans devote much time and energy to the study of pain and pain management,* he concluded. Devastated to be excluded from yet another element of life, he solemnly shook his head. "No, I have no pain," he replied softly.

"Well, then… Would you like to try and sit up? My name's Dr. Winter." The white-coated man smiled and extended an arm for assistance.

Although he did not need it, REL accepted Dr. Winter's offer and sat up with remarkable ease. Swinging his legs over the side of the examination table, he looked from side to side, automatically surveying the room in which he found himself.

"Can you tell me your name?" Dr. Winter asked.

"John R. Worthington. I am John R. Worthington," the biomech responded automatically.

Marshal Burrows stepped impatiently into view and interrupted, "I saw the tracks you made coming down that mountain. What I can't believe is that you managed it without

49

putting even one scratch on your Blazer or suffering any serious damage to yourself. You're a very lucky man."

"Lucky," REL repeated, contemplating all that meant. He quickly retrieved a definition of the word and struggled a bit to understand its relevance to his present situation. Unbidden, a virtual panorama of possibilities flooded his intellect. He descried the limitless opportunities before him. He, a biomech, occupied a blessed position with the richness of a human identity. Despite being excluded from pain, he *was* lucky. "Yes," he agreed sincerely, "I *am* lucky."

"Now then... Tell me what happened up there on that mountain." The marshal loomed over the doctor's shoulder, preparing to take his report.

REL recalled John Worthington's untimely demise, now vividly etched in his memory. The same fate had not befallen him. He looked straight into the marshal's eyes. "I stayed upright," he answered honestly, feeling luckier than ever.

"What was it that caused you to go off the road?" Dr. Winter asked to the obvious dismay of the marshal.

"I remember seeing a deer," REL responded.

"Swerved for a deer, huh?"

Worthington did not answer. The marshal put the deer into the report. "Let me see your driver's license."

REL started to pull his newly acquired wallet from his back pocket.

"Marshal, I have to check this man for injuries. I'll send him down to your office when we're done." Dr. Winter tapped a small rubber hammer on REL's knee.

"Sure, that's fine." Burrows looked at the stranger, still amazed at the man's good fortune. "Stop by the office when you're finished here. I had your truck towed in. My deputy will help you get your keys."

"Sure, thank you, Marshal. Where is your office?"

50

"Down the street, over the bridge, and to the left," he pointed. The marshal patted REL gently on the back. "You're a very lucky man," he said and left the clinic.

Just then, Dr. Winter's pager sounded again. "Uh, oh. Looks like Sarah's baby is ahead of schedule. Valerie, can you take it from here? Please don't forget the forms. Nice to meet you, Mr. Worthington. I'm sure you'll be fine." The doctor gently squeezed REL's shoulder and rushed out behind the marshal.

"Thank you," the biomech offered as he took a deep breath.

"We do have some forms to fill out." Valerie smiled warmly, handed REL a clipboard, then glanced into his eyes. Instantly, his undivided attention was hers.

There is something about her voice... REL consciously attuned his auditory sensors, awaiting the gentle sound that carried softly through the air as she moved her lips.

"Can you fill these out on your own or should I help you?"

REL smiled but did not answer. *What is it about her voice?*

"Are you okay, Mr. Worthington? If you want me to ask you the questions, I'll fill these out for you."

Mesmerized, he measured the exact condensation and rarefaction as her words rolled smoothly between her lips. Parting his own, he drew a soft breath. Her voice carried much more than the words she spoke, a sympathetic vibration that resonated with the frequency of his entire physical being. The biomech shivered.

Looking up, he met her patient gaze and whispered, "May I have just a moment, please?"

"Of course you may. I'll be at my desk."

"No," REL whispered again. "Please stay. Just... Please... a moment."

Valerie Arnette took three steps backwards to lean against the cool wall of the examination room, inwardly smiling at the invitation. "Sure. I'll stay with you, Mr. Worthington."

Inclined against the wall, arms folded, Valerie studied her charge. She marveled that regaining consciousness had only added to his perfection. His every movement was fluid, his every gesture, graceful. Softening her gaze, she sought his aura. Her earlier perception of luminous energy proved out before her eyes. For one thing, she found no end to it. The light he exuded stretched beyond her sight. And its purity confounded her.

Perched atop the paper-clad exam table, REL took his moment to ponder. His sole purpose was his mission. It seemed simple enough. Yet, he confessed an overwhelming desire to get to know this woman. "How can this be?" Unintentionally speaking the words, he looked back and forth from his empty right hand to the clipboard he held in his left as if weighing a decision.

"Oh, I didn't give you a pen. Here..." Valerie said as she walked back to his side. Reaching into her breast pocket, she selected her favorite pen and offered it to him like a blessing. Instinctively, REL reached out to receive it. In an instant frozen forever in his memory, his fingers touched hers. Both allowed the moment to linger as their eyes met in acknowledgment of this singular event. Reluctantly, the biomech withdrew the pen, tracing a chill across Valerie's palm as it slipped seductively from her hand.

Valerie softly cleared her throat. "Is there anything you don't understand?"

"Valerie, I don't understand any of this."

Leaning closer to examine the form, the nurse gently brushed his shoulder with her own and paused with her auburn hair very near his face.

Now totally captivated, the biomech could barely stammer. "It's not the form, Valerie. It's not the form... It's you. How

52

can this be?" Attention torn between his racing circuits and his nearness to this woman, REL drew a deep breath, only to be engulfed by her scent.

She straightened, turning to face him. "Now I'm the one who doesn't understand, Mr. Worthington." As she spoke the words, she realized that she knew exactly what he meant. She knew exactly what he felt because she felt it, too.

"Valerie, I must be honest with you, I know no other way to be. I'm more puzzled than I've ever been before. You see..." He shook his head and glanced at the floor. "I did not know I could feel this way. I don't know how to explain it. Anything I say is bound to sound like... a..." Awareness racing to his *contemporary culture* file, he discovered the perfect vernacular description "...a pick up line."

Smiling, Valerie prompted him. "I'll give you the benefit of the doubt, Mr. Worthington."

"Don't you feel it?" he asked softly.

"That we have met before?" Valerie replied.

"That's what I thought at first, but it cannot be," he murmured.

"Why?"

"Because I have not been before."

Laughing gently, she challenged, "Of course you've been before. We've all been before."

REL squirmed on the table, ripping the paper beneath him. "It's just not possible."

"Mr. Worthington, it's not only possible, it simply *is*. I've seen your life force, I've felt the sense of déjà vu between us. That's enough proof for me," she assured.

The harmonic resonance of her voice carried her words directly to his heart.

Valerie's certainty prompted him to venture, "Would you call me REL? Those closest to me call me REL."

"Ariel as in Shakespeare?"

"Actually, REL as in Remote Emissary of Life. It's an acronym."

Valerie stared at him in frank amazement with no idea what to say. She finally managed a hushed, "Who are you?"

Dying to open his heart to her, to withhold nothing, he gasped as the force of his programming jarred him to silence. Every instinct wailed as he clenched his teeth and squeezed out a hollow, "John R. Worthington."

"What is a Remote Emissary of Life?"

"I cannot say."

"Why not?"

"Because I cannot." The immensity of his quandary constricted his pupils and contracted his flexors. He possessed no will strong enough to override his programmed discretion.

"REL, then what *can* you tell me?"

"I can tell you there is something profound between us."

Valerie lowered herself into a nearby chair and propped her chin on her fist. "You're right. I feel it, too. What do we do now, REL? I don't even know who you are. And from the sounds of it, you're not going to say."

Reality Roulette

Alpha II

Frantically checking displays and tuning frequencies, Morrison succumbed to the fear on Timball's face and threw his hands up in despair. "This is ridiculous! I've already checked these a dozen times. We have no choice, we've got to go get him."

"Finally!" Timball agreed. "Let's go get the biomech and forget this whole damned thing!"

"I mean, we've got to go get the dead Worthington. We'll worry about REL after we get that taken care of."

"Get the dead Worthington?! Whatever for? Why don't we just go back in time ourselves to before Williams' arrival?" Timball brushed a sleeve across his forehead to catch the sweat before it dripped into his eyes. "God, I'm going to be sick," he groaned.

"Dan, so far we have only tampered with *machines*..." Morrison pronounced the word with unabashed irony, "...and dead people. We cannot interfere with the path of a living human being," he reasoned stubbornly. "Not only that, the precision required to pull that off without running into ourselves and creating a paradox is unbelievable. We definitely don't have the time for that, Dan. We'll just have to do the best we can. We'll have to drug Monitor Williams."

"Are you nuts?" Timball's voice rose half an octave as his throat squeezed closed on the words. "Isn't that a capital offense?"

"Not if we don't get caught. I'll give you something to help him take a little nap so we can formulate a plan, Dan. An iron-clad plan. And then we're going to go get that body."

"That's it?!! No discussion?"

"We have no choice." Fumbling around in his supply locker, Morrison produced a tiny vial filled with colorless liquid. "Mix this with some juice or something. He'll sleep like a baby for about six hours. That will give us some time."

When Timball returned, he was nervous and sweaty.

"Get him handled?" Morrison asked.

"He was drinking it when I left," Timball whispered.

Morrison patted his friend's shoulder and shook his head sadly at the thought of what they had done and what he feared may come next.

"Will he know?" Timball wiped his brow with his hand.

"Maybe, but it will have to do." Morrison powered up the tower and quickly programmed the time when they had sent the dead Worthington.

Coal Creek Canyon: 1989

The Blazer sat at an odd angle across the road just beneath the summit of Coal Creek Canyon. Its damage was apparent even from a distance. Morrison waited for the effects of the time shift to subside then surveyed the area surrounding the damaged truck. A glint of glass caught his eye and he looked up to find a cabin nestled in the trees above the switchback, a car just pulling into its steep driveway. He had to act quickly to avoid a confrontation with the driver who, in Morrison's reality, was 150 years dead. The doctor wrenched the Blazer door open and yanked Worthington's body out onto the ground in front of him. Reaching into his pocket he activated the point. "Now! Now!" he directed. With a crackling sound, the doctor and the body vanished.

Carl Grueter set the brake on his Subaru and quickly sidled down the rocky hill, not quite certain of what he had just seen. When he reached the scene of the accident, the Blazer door stood ajar, a pool of blood staining the floor mat. He saw no tracks and no body. Taking a moment to catch his breath before climbing back up the hill, he mentally rehearsed his call to 911.

Center State Complex: ICom Headquarters

"Imperator Fells, Sir!" Lieutenant Kyle Zephyrs saluted brazenly.

"At ease, Lieutenant." Fells pointed toward a chair at the opposite end of the conference table. "My sources tell me that you've failed to find the LRA mole."

"That's not true, Sir." Zephyrs smirked. "We know exactly where he is. Or should I say *when*."

"You're certain?" The imperator glared at his underling.

"Yes, Sir. He's in 1989. A recon team is being assembled as we speak. It's only a matter of hours before we have something concrete," Zephyrs assured, holding the icy stare without a blink.

"Then, there can be no mistake? He's in 1989?"

"They made a huge ripple in the matrix, Sir. There can be no mistake about that."

Alpha II

"We only have a couple of hours left," Morrison said as he split the sternum of the corpse.

"What are you doing?" Timball gulped at the sight and smell of the eviscerated body.

"Hand me those spreaders." Grunting out the words as he pried the chest cavity open the doctor explained, "Since Williams will be queasy from the drug, we're setting the stage to disarm him, so to speak. The more gruesome, the better."

"I'm queasy, and I didn't get a six hour nap." Averting his eyes from the carnage on the exam table, Timball asked, "Have you no shame about desecrating this man's body?"

"Do you really think a corpse cares at this point?" Morrison replied as he continued his grim work. "Besides, we need to divert Williams from our trail."

"What's so important that you had to drag me clear across the station to see it?" Williams demanded irritably, still groggy from his unwonted nap. The minute he entered the room, he stopped short and swallowed hard.

The dead John Worthington lay on the table of a small triage unit near an unused docking bay, his face eerily frozen with the fear he had felt in the last instant of his life. Morrison had neither closed his eyes nor changed his expression. The doctor's earlier efforts had served only to open the body to showcase the man's heart and lungs.

The monitor's head swam. He couldn't focus. "Why isn't this man in the morgue?"

"He's here to prevent an all-out panic. No one else on this station knows about him and I plan to keep it that way." Morrison moved closer to the body.

Williams held his aching head and swallowed the bitter acid pushing its way up his esophagus from his sour stomach. "What did he die of?"

Morrison dipped his hands in a rubberized solution that formed a sterile, glove-like covering. "Look," he motioned the monitor closer. "See here?" Morrison reached into the chest cavity and extracted the heart. "Notice the muscle deterioration? A heart like this pumps like an old air bladder." He clutched the organ in his right hand, massaging it to make it pump.

A horrified Williams swallowed hard as he watched half-congealed blood ooze from between Morrison's fingers and pool on the floor near his boot.

Morrison moved his hand closer to the monitor's face. The reek of stale blood permeated the air and assailed Williams' nostrils. He backed away, mouth clamped tightly to avoid an unwanted regurgitation. Already weakened by Morrison's potion, the monitor collapsed.

Nederland Clinic

"But Valerie, I *want* to tell you. How can I make you understand that I physically cannot?" REL groaned as his programming savagely resisted his every effort to explain.

"What can I do to help you? You're in pain." Valerie quickly stood and returned to his side, reaching for his wrist to check his pulse.

"You mustn't." He flinched, afraid to be swept away again by her touch. Closing his eyes and raising his left palm to stop her, he rasped, "I have to stay clear about this."

Startled by his rejection, she backed away a step, hands in surrender. "REL, I would never hurt you."

"Your touch doesn't hurt me, it confuses me."

Folding her hands behind her back, she slowly leaned forward to look him full in the face. "I won't touch you, I promise."

"Valerie, I think we both know there's something..." He sped through his files to find the right word. "...*amazing* happening between us. And I would give anything to be able to stay with you for just an hour to find out what that is. But I am literally *unable* to do so." The next words came in excruciating syllables, "I have to leave. *Now.*"

"But why, REL? What is so urgent?" Valerie asked gently.

"So much depends on me, Valerie," he said, paraphrasing Dr. Morrison. Surrendering to the will of his programming, his flexors began to relax, allowing him to stand. He stretched away the vestiges of his tension.

Valerie studied his face, looking deep into his crystalline blue eyes and earnest expression, there to glimpse his powerful soul. Logic tempted her to question, faith in synchronicity led her to respond, "Okay, REL. I'll help you be on your way. Where will you go? Can you say?"

A wave of relief swept the biomech when he realized that he could tell her. "Phoenix. I have a new job in Phoenix." Defying the tyranny of his program, he opened his arms to her.

Tentatively, Valerie stepped toward him, tucking her hands behind her back.

REL reached for her, drawing her heart to his in an embrace that left them both breathless. He felt her arms slip warmly around his waist. Savoring every sensation of her nearness, he nuzzled her hair. Then he cradled her face in his hands and kissed her tenderly on the forehead. Emboldened by the sweetness of the moment, REL stepped back and reached behind his neck to unclasp the point. Fishing it from beneath his shirt, he cradled it in his hand for a moment, then placed it into hers. It fit neatly in the delicate cup between her palm and her fingers and seemed almost animate as it radiated multicolors around the room. Gently closing his fingers around her smooth skin he murmured, "I want you to keep this for me."

Enchanted by the precious device, Valerie looked from it to REL. "It looks like the little triangle thing from a tiny Ouija board. What is this?"

"A promise," he said as he yielded to his directive. Reluctantly, he walked to the door of the clinic.

"What promise?" she called after him.

"That you'll see me again."

And then he was gone.

Enroute to Phoenix

The valley floor that was all of Phoenix and more shone before him, glittering with a million lights. The spectacle stopped a breath in REL's throat and made his heart skip, yanking him from his reverie about life and his impersonation of it. Safeguarded from peak load by the new program he had authored, he deeply inhaled the scent of the desert and pulled to the side of the road. With only a moment's hesitation, REL reached over the seat to grab John Worthington's briefcase, then stepped from his Blazer. Refreshed by the pungent desert air, he walked exactly fifty yards, found a bare, flat spot and sat down cross-legged in the dirt.

First light painted streamers across the sky, drawing REL's gasping admiration for this, his first sunrise on Earth. He watched in awe as neon tendrils teased the gray expanse into the brilliant blue of dayspring. With a sigh that sent him wondering a moment, he touched his thumbs to the latches on the briefcase. It did not open. REL tipped it on end to study its small combination lock. Quickly scanning his Worthington files, he retrieved the date of the dead man's birth and rotated the tumblers accordingly. *How ironic*, he thought, *that I know so much and yet so little about the man I am supposed to be.* Then he flipped the latches and opened the valise.

On the very top, tucked neatly inside a manila folder, was John R. Worthington's resume. REL only glanced at it, well familiar with its specifics. But he gave pause to the cover letter:

I have two loves in life. The first is computers. I seem to speak their language, which makes me very useful in difficult trouble-shooting situations. The second, catalyzed by my stint in the Peace Corps, is my desire to serve humankind. These attributes, moreso than my formal training, set me apart in sales. I've always believed that the love of a job necessarily seeds its success.

How alike we are, REL gasped. A shudder racked the bio-mech. Invisible ties to a force he did not understand tugged at him to remember.

Remember what? He probed his data to no avail. Snatching a breath, REL took a moment to consider Worthington's untimely end and quietly vowed to honor the man whose name and face he bore.

He replaced the resume and letter in the folder and quickly passed over the detritus of business beneath it. All the while, his mind probed to find an explanation of the mysterious promptings that originated impossibly from beyond his programming.

Juggling the displaced papers on one knee, REL stopped when he uncovered the sketch pad. A bright rainbow arched across the coarse red paper cover, concealing its contents from his seeking eyes. Almost ashamed at his invasion of the dead man's privacy, he gently opened the book.

His own blue eyes stared back at him.

Sitting bolt upright, REL gazed at the self-portrait. There, skillfully rendered in pastels, his likeness smiled out from a skyscape that drew a second glance. Behind, portrayed in wispy illusion, another, larger self peered from the clouds like a guardian angel. Neatly penned in the lower right-hand corner REL read *I AM* and below that *JRW*.

Another shudder assailed him. *Remember what?* he asked again.

The portice-co-chere of the Phoenix Residence Inn stood like a portal to a new existence. Pulling beneath the canopy, REL caught a glimpse of himself reflected in the entryway glass. The unexpected self-portrait jarred him, as his thoughts still lingered on the one tucked safely within his new briefcase. A wistful whim prompted him to seek the mirrored clouds behind, searching for an angel of his own.

An annoying nudge from his program intruded on his pleasant ponderings. Stubbornly, he lingered an extra six seconds in defiance. Then having made his point, he turned off the ignition, stepped from the Blazer and checked into his suite.

A wave of recognition flooded REL as he pulled his Blazer into the space precisely equidistant between the two yellow lines. *Data Pioneer Technologies,* he murmured to himself, reading the sign on the one story smoked-glass and stainless steel building. Calmly shifting his truck into *park,* he stepped from the driver's seat and grabbed his briefcase. Striding across the parking lot, he paused to straighten his impeccable tie before opening the door.

A fortyish woman seated behind a sleek oak desk looked up from her work and greeted him by name, "You must be John Worthington."

Despite his many hours of practicing Worthington's mannerisms and minute voice intonations, REL's confidence ebbed for a micro moment. "Yes, I am," he managed.

"Mr. Fletcher's looking forward to meeting you." The woman extended her hand as she stood. Her short hair glinted reds and yellows as the Arizona sun shone on it through the skylight overhead. Green eyes smiled at him as she shook his hand and gave a warm squeeze. "I'm Dot. Welcome to Data Pioneer Technologies."

REL looked directly into her eyes and smiled at this familiar character from the matrix. "I'm very happy to be here." Enjoying the sensation of her real-time presence, he gently returned her squeeze and added, "Very happy, indeed."

"Follow me," Dot motioned.

Gary Fletcher's booming voice rolled into the hallway. "Come on in here, John." A huge man stood up from behind an equally enormous desk and extended his massive hand as REL entered the office. Fletcher's grip was firm but gentle despite his size. He towered over REL by half a foot. "Welcome to Data Pioneer," the big man grinned.

"Thank you, Mr. Fletcher. I've been looking forward to it." REL scanned the spacious office. The dark wood walls and floor-to-ceiling shelves displayed an impressive collection of athletic trophies and photos, wall plaques and posters.

"Have a seat, John." Fletcher motioned to a brown, overstuffed leather chair. "Make yourself comfortable. Let's get to know each other a little. Dot, you know I normally wouldn't ask... But would you mind bringing us some coffee? If I ask real nice?" Fletcher quipped.

Dot rolled her green eyes and laughed. "Sure, Boss. No problem. How do you like your coffee, John?"

Although coffee was familiar to him, REL had never formed his own opinion of it. Fishing for a workable response, he found a Turkish proverb in his files, which he repeated with gusto, "Black as hell, strong as death, sweet as love."

Fletcher roared. REL laughed, too, and relaxed into his Worthington role.

Dot nodded then left the room, chuckling to herself that Fletcher may have met his match-of-wits in John R. Worthington.

"Before I forget… I just re-read your cover letter. I really like what you had to say." The big man grinned and nodded.

"I'd like to think it represents who I am." REL smiled, embarrassed to take credit for words that weren't his own.

Dot returned with two cups of coffee and a basket of muffins. She handed a cup to each of them, set the muffins on the corner of Fletcher's desk, smiled at John, then disappeared out the door.

"Thank you, Dot," Mr. Fletcher said sincerely.

"Yes, thank you," REL added. He stared at his coffee, watching the rising steam swirl into the office air. Gathering his courage, he tipped the cup to his lips and gulped. Mr. Fletcher watched in amazement. He sipped from his own cup, noting the unpleasantly hot temperature of the brew. The new John Worthington smiled, proudly feeling more human all the time.

"Do you always drink your coffee so hot?" Mr. Fletcher asked in astonishment.

"Always," REL responded with a matter-of-factness that ended further inquiry. He eyed the muffins, politely declining the unfamiliar food.

"John, tomorrow I'll introduce you to the Data Pioneer crew. Dot's the only one in today and you've already met her." Hearing her footsteps in the hall outside the door, Fletcher winked at Worthington and boomed a little louder. "She's a bit of a feminist, you know. Of course, I'd never hold that against her." As soon as Dot was out of earshot, Fletcher lowered his voice. "Truth is, John, Dot's my right hand person. Worth double her weight in gold. As soon as I get my promotion to corporate, I'm going to see that she gets a management position and a decent raise. You know, we're lucky here at Data Pioneer. We have terrific employees. We're kind of like a little family. I want you to make yourself at home here, John. If there's anything any of us can do to help you get settled here in Phoenix, just let us know. Now, I've got about six hours worth of product videos and orientation material for you to study. Best get to it."

At precisely 5 o'clock, REL reviewed his accomplishments of the day. He had memorized all five product videos, completed and submitted all new employee forms, studied and stored Data Pioneer's most recent annual report and familiarized himself with the company's history. He took an extra minute to check DPT's closing price on the New York Stock Exchange. *I'll be a great employee*, he concluded, anxious to begin a real work day.

As he walked across the nearly empty parking lot toward his Blazer, it occurred to REL that he had no destination. For the first time ever, he had no task to complete and no place to be — at least until tomorrow morning. A sudden pang of... *loneliness*... threatened to engulf him until a honking horn roused him from his reverie. Looking up, he saw a shiny red car. *A convertible*, he noted. Behind the wheel was a smiling Dot, who waved and sped out of the parking lot. Cheered by her joviality, REL decided to do some exploring. This was his new home, after all. It was only logical that he should get to know his home.

Retracing his morning route from his hotel, REL paid special attention to the landmarks, vegetation, and businesses along the way. There were shopping malls, huge grocery stores, and theaters showing dozens of different movies. The hustle and bustle of traffic and people were exciting, at first. *I'll never be bored*, he chuckled.

Eventually, the noise of cars and electricity and crowds grated on him. He reviewed his internal map and selected a quiet street off the main thoroughfare. There, he found a less traveled byway lined with palm trees, cactus, and brilliant flowers. Fewer cars disturbed the desert beauty of the late afternoon and REL relaxed into the excitement of his adventure. Up ahead, two large saguaro cacti draped with tiny lights and festooned with an arch of pink and turquoise balloons caught his attention. A small, matching sandwich sign announced a grand opening. Through the parking lot of a quaint adobe strip mall was an intricate neon sculpture of a glowing beacon. Beside it were the words "*the beacon*: bookstore & New Age resource center." In an instant, REL flipped on his turn signal, checked the traffic behind and beside him and pulled into the small parking lot. A curious shudder of recognition rippled through the biomech's intelligent structure leaving him puzzled as to its cause and its ramifications. He paused briefly to consider it. But the lure of the bookstore was far stronger than his questioning. Atremble, he crunched down the pea gravel path that led to the shop.

The tinkle of tiny chimes and the smoke of musky incense greeted him as he walked through the carved door to the bookstore. A gray-haired man with bushy eyebrows and wire-rimmed glasses looked up from behind the counter. "Hi there, young man. Welcome to *the beacon*. Are you looking for anything in particular? Or are you just looking?"

By that time, of course, REL had locked onto the row after row after row of bookshelves. Dr. Morrison's library. *The beacon* reminded him of Dr. Morrison's library. "Just looking," he said in a daze, running his fingers over the books nearest to where he stood.

"Well, good. You're in luck. We're open until nine o' clock tonight. You have over three hours to look. If you have any questions, I'll be happy to answer them for you."

Selecting a bright volume, REL scanned two chapters, delighted that he recognized the material. He replaced the book and picked up another. Slowly — for him — and deliberately, the new John Worthington noted each and every volume in the stacks. Occasionally, he selected a book from the shelf, checked for familiar resonance, then either returned it or added it to his ever-growing pile.

At about 7:30, the gray-haired man approached REL carrying two rustic earthenware cups. "Care for some herb and spice tea? It's my own special blend."

Looking up from a volume, REL smiled and accepted the tea, so engrossed with his search that he didn't give a second thought to the etiquette of the situation. "Thank you," he said as he sipped the pungent, sweet brew, never noticing as he savored the tea that he had naturally assumed a human mannerism.

At precisely 8:50, REL gathered together his pile of books, balanced his empty tea cup on top and headed for the counter. "I enjoyed your tea, Sir. Thank you."

"You're certainly welcome. But I'm not a 'sir', most folks just call me Sam."

"Thank you, Sam. I'm John Worthington and I'd like to buy these books."

"That's quite an assortment, John. Should keep you busy for some time."

REL stood quietly admiring his new books as Sam wrote down their titles and prices. His selections included books channeled by entities from the Pleaides, a book on quantum physics, books about ancient Earth religions, a book on resonance and the heart, a Bible, and one spiritual adventure novel.

"Well, John, your total is $267.50. Cash, check or plastic, young man?"

"I have cash, Sam." Quickly, he counted out exactly $267.50 from the money Dr. Morrison had given him. "Thank you, Sam. I'm glad I came here. I'm glad I met you."

"I hope you enjoy the books. Don't expect I'll see you back here for a while, though. You have plenty to read."

"You might be surprised. I'll be back sooner than you think, if only for your tea.

With that, REL collected his new library and headed back to his hotel to begin reading. When he reached his suite, he deposited his books on the table and called room service. Tonight, he would read and practice his eating skills. Tomorrow, he would be more human than ever.

Slowly, beneath his notice, REL's spiral programming completed one revolution, unlocking a whole new dimension in understanding and pushing him inexorably toward the completion of his mission.

Alpha II

"God, we didn't kill him did we, Dan?" Morrison asked as he flipped the heart back into the chest cavity and rushed to Williams' prone form.

"No such luck," Timball said dryly. "But I bet he'll have a helluva knot on his head."

"Well, let's consider this an opportunity and take advantage of it. Call a medic and get him to the infirmary."

"Now what?" Timball asked as med techs wheeled Williams away.

"We finish our plan. Remember, my handy-dandy access wand will control all communications capabilities in the First Station. There's no way the monitor can detect it."

Williams was in rare form when Timball and Morrison answered his summons the following afternoon. When they arrived, the monitor was still pallid, slumped at his com, sipping an anti-nausea mixture of ginger and bitters. He did not stand to speak. "Now, what the hell is going on around here?"

Timball chose the chair farthest from the monitor and sat motionless, nearly paralyzed by his ever-growing fear.

Boldly, Dr. Morrison sat closest to Williams and leaned even closer. Assuming his gravest tone, he asked, "You want to know about the dead man, right?"

"Of course I want to know about the dead man," Williams growled.

"It's kind of a long story..." Morrison leaned back in his chair and steepled his fingers.

"I have all day, Dr. Morrison. And so do you." Williams took another sip of his remedy.

"Let me begin by telling you what the poor kid died of. It doesn't have a name, although a few ideas have crossed my mind. The symptoms are bizarre, reminiscent of the disease contracted by the fifth expedition to the outer planets beyond Zebra Base. You may have read about it," Morrison intoned gravely. "Seventeen explorers died within thirty days of their return. Twelve others fell ill just a few hours after contact with the host organism and died on the return trip to the base. All of Zebra went epidemic in the first week, with a death toll of seventy-three including infected medical personnel."

"What are the symptoms?" Williams leaned forward.

"You saw the heart." The doctor bit his lip, shook his head and continued to weave his tale, "Well, that was nothing. Before he died he complained of pain during urination. I examined him several times, took dozens of urine samples and swabs but could not figure out what was causing his bleeding. But now... well, you really ought to see for yourself." The doctor started to get up.

"No, I've seen quite enough. Just tell me." The monitor motioned Morrison to sit down.

"Well, the whole urinary tract was ravaged by the organism as it gnawed its way through the tissue," the doctor elaborated as the monitor rubbed conspicuously at the center seam of his uniform slacks.

"You really ought to have a look," Morrison prodded. "The organism eventually devoured its way to his heart and mercifully, killed him."

The monitor winced. "And why didn't you contact the proper authorities?" Touching a button on the com labeled *display*, the monitor reached toward the holographic projection that appeared in the air. Williams tweaked the sound levels of the program and returned his attention to Morrison, who had not answered his question.

Knowing full-well that the monitor could record nothing, Morrison consciously donned his most convincing righteous indignation. Jumping to his feet, he aimed a furious finger at the hologram. "If you are recording this meeting then we are quite finished."

Shocked at Morrison's reaction, Monitor Williams sat up straight in his chair, steely eyes glaring. "Doctor, you said you would cooperate with the governor's wishes. Either answer the question or I promise that you'll face a full inquiry panel!"

Morrison, weighing every nuance of his response, remained firm. "Fine. Whatever. But unless you shut that program off you'll get nothing more from me." With that, he returned to his chair and sat silently, waiting for the monitor to slip up. Morrison mentally calculated all of Williams' choices, deeming one as good as another to provide him with much needed time.

"So… you prefer that I convene the panel of inquiry?"

For a moment Morrison let the tension build. Then he resumed in a low conspiratorial voice, "Monitor Williams, if you'll just let me explain, you'll agree that this session cannot be recorded."

The monitor, much the worse for the wear, shook his throbbing head. "I can't imagine anything important enough to disregard ICom procedure. You know it is mandated that all such sessions be recorded."

"Of course, Monitor," baited Morrison. "I know that's true. However, a record of this session could prove fatal for more than a few people. If you'll trust me for just five minutes, I promise that you'll agree with my assessment."

"This had better be good," Williams sighed and quit the program. The holographic icon shrank and disappeared.

"Trash it," Morrison ordered, referring to the hard copy of the session.

Reluctantly, the monitor passed the small disc over a degaussing device then tossed it into a recycling port.

Morrison, barely able to contain his relief that he had successfully compromised the monitor, continued his deception. "Thank you, Monitor Williams. Now then, the boy you saw was a maintenance worker, MIII Arnold Myerson. Been here for three years. Records show his tether snapped and he was lost in space."

"Fraudulent death certificate?" Williams queried with a raised eyebrow.

Morrison stared back, but did not answer.

"Didn't you at least tell Fells?"

At the mention of the imperator, Timball shuddered, then covered his fear with a cough.

Morrison coolly continued, "Remember what I said about panic? If you've ever read about any unit going epidemic, you know it would be disaster to tell anyone. If you had been on Zebra, you'd know what I'm talking about. It's not that I don't trust Fells," he lied, "but I know about chain of command. And I know about leaks. My God, man! We're talking about something eating you alive from the inside out."

A tone from the door sensor interrupted Morrison's dramatics.

"See who that is." The monitor motioned for Timball to answer the door.

"Hello, Director." The curly-haired dietitian stood, tray in hand. "I didn't know there would be more than Monitor Williams. Should I get two more dinners?"

"No, I'll come with you. My legs could use a stretch." Relieved to escape the inquisition, the director nudged the young woman into the hall, letting the door hiss closed behind them.

Morrison resumed, "Anyway, I was afraid we'd start a panic. I'm not concerned about epidemic now, as we got him isolated before he became contagious. I'm confident of that. What I am concerned about is the origin of the disease."

"What do you mean?" Williams prodded.

"I think it was a biological ambush. Nothing short of a political assassination attempt," the doctor said in a low voice, implying a continuing threat.

"Against an MIII?" The monitor laughed at such a preposterous idea.

"No, Monitor," answered Morrison, deadpan, "against you."

The monitor's sneer vanished. "Against me?"

"Yes. Against you. As I told you, we were using the First Station, here, for storage and everyone knew it. It was really quite convenient. Anyway, right after the first rumor of your visit..." he emphasized, "we got a really odd container mixed in with a shipment of our regular research disposables. Like everything else, we stored it here." Panning the room with an exaggerated finger to ensure his point, he went on, "Myerson was cleaning up and dropped the damned container. That's when they got him." The doctor paused to regain Williams' attention.

"What got him?"

"Unidentified organisms purposely packed in that container and purposely sent to you."

"How do you know they were meant for me?" Williams snapped.

"I found the address label that peeled off the container. It was addressed to you, Monitor Williams," Morrison replied gravely.

Williams was still shaking his head and didn't look up when Timball came through the door carrying dinner.

"But why would someone want to kill me?" Williams argued.

Morrison didn't answer immediately. Instead, he removed the cover from his tray and speared a carrot. "I have no idea, Monitor. No idea at all. Anything you can think of?"

Dumfounded, Williams stirred at his food without tasting it.

The doctor looked up, stretched out the silence, then suggested, "Piss anybody off lately? Anybody with serious scientific connections?"

Williams, most uncomfortable with the line of conversation, changed the subject. "I assume you sterilized the station?"

"Of course," Morrison assured as he sipped his wine. "Don't worry about it."

It was still very early when the monitor awoke and glanced at his watch — 0400. He tried to roll over and re-enter his dream, but natural urges overpowered his sleepy mind. He found his way to his private bathroom and aimed in darkness. A savage stinging evoked an agonizing groan, and the monitor stopped in mid-stream. With dreaded anticipation he tried again, painfully completing his nighttime mission. He could not imagine the source of his searing discomfort. *Maybe it's just a reaction to the water on the station*, he rationalized. Within minutes, his task completed, the pain receded from its prominent place in his mind and he was able to fall asleep.

"Director Timball, Monitor Williams has called for breakfast. You asked that I notify you?" The dietitian stood with her hand on her hip, holding a menu. After a moment of silence, she tapped her foot lightly and repeated, "Director Timball? Monitor Williams..."

"Oh... Right," the director sighed. "I need to inspect his meal."

"Oh?!" she responded, eyes snapping to meet the director's. "Whatever."

Timball winced. "Look, you really don't want to know." He looked around the dining room to see if anyone was within earshot and continued, "Trust me, Karen..." lowering his voice, "the less you know, the better."

"Oookay... Whatever you say."

They feigned smiles as she headed for the kitchen.

Reaching into his pocket, Timball fingered the vial. Turning his back to the kitchen, he held it up between thumb and forefinger. The clear, odorless liquid was Morrison's concoction — this dose nearly twice what he had used the day before. Hearing footsteps, Timball quickly palmed the tiny bottle.

"Here's his breakfast, Director." The dietitian set it on the corner of a table.

Timball lifted the cover and took a quick look. "Karen, how about a linen napkin?"

"Sure." Karen headed for the supply closet.

75

Timball waited until she had rounded the corner, then quickly dumped the liquid into the monitor's orange juice.

Breakfast was Monitor Williams' favorite meal and he savored every bite. He especially enjoyed the extra large glass of juice. But only for a moment. His pleasure soon faded in favor of urgent business.

A wince of anticipatory pain did not prepare Williams for the real thing, the stinging jolt badly spoiling his aim. The monitor sagged against the torment and forced himself to finish. Despite his best efforts, the monitor could not banish the specter of the late Arnold Myerson.

"Monitor Williams, Monitor Williams, Alpha Com," chimed a cheerful voice. "Do you wish to be disturbed?"

"I'll take it." Williams sat down in his room's primary chair and faced the far wall where the holographic face of Imperator Fells loomed, emotionless, as always. The monitor jumped from his seat, offering a crisp, straight-armed salute.

"Report on Alpha II," Fells commanded.

"Sir, I'm still conducting interviews."

"And...?!" Fells sneered.

The monitor shuddered, knowing his every word was being analyzed. He dared not mention Myerson's name nor discuss his meeting with Morrison and Timball without a recording for back-up. "And I have a lot more work to do, Sir."

"Then get it done, Monitor. I want Morrison."

"Sir?"

"I said, I want Morrison. What part of that don't you understand?"

"What has he done, Sir?"

"Let's just say he's on my bad side." Fells smiled grimly.

The words struck Williams like a blow, slamming his imperiled career and urinary distress into hideous perspective. "Yessir," was all he managed to say.

"Here's a helpful hint for you, Williams," Fells offered. "Use Timball, he's weak. He'll crack under pressure, so lean on him." Fells paused for effect, then continued, "Consider every choice you make a career choice, Williams."

Before the monitor could reply, Fells' image disappeared.

Fells' Covert Operations Center

Zephyrs spat without looking as he stepped from the matrix tower in Fells' covert ops center. When his eyes cleared, he watched the gooey saliva-wad dribbling down the toe of Fells' shiny boot. He gasped, "I'm sorry, Sir. I didn't know you were standing there."

"What have you got?" Fells demanded.

"Sir, I don't know yet. There was a 20th century vehicle — badly damaged." Zephyrs stumbled over his words as his companions skittered into the next room and away from the imperator. "We've got a lot of stuff to sift through."

"You've got a lot of stuff?!" Fells pressed. "I don't want stuff, Zephyrs. I want to know who the hell traveled back in time and what they are up to. Perhaps I didn't make myself clear. Or perhaps you simply can't follow orders."

"Imperator Fells, Sir, I believe we have all of the answers right here," Zephyrs replied with a smirk, hoisting a bag one of his men had left before retreating from the room.

"Oh, really. Then I shall expect answers within the hour." Fells wiped his slimy-toed boot on the lieutenant's crisp slacks. "Contact me in the Council limo. That's an order Zephyrs."

"Yes, Sir!" The officer jerked a salute, shouldered the bag of items from the Blazer and hurried to his transport to call his friend.

"Lieutenant, you wanted to talk to me?" Monitor Williams took the call, glad for the distraction from his woes.

"I'm working on a secret assignment for Fells," Zephyrs confided, relieved to have a family friend who understood.

"You are? That's great." Williams ruefully recalled when a secret assignment from Fells had been his own dream.

"I'm not so sure about that." Zephyrs dropped his cocky air. "I'm scared to death. He gave me an assignment and I've failed."

Williams nodded. "I've been there," he reassured. "You'll be all right. Just tell the truth."

"I can't," Zephyrs admitted. "I've already lied."

The irony of the situation stung the monitor. He winced. "What's this all about?"

Zephyrs remained silent for a moment, weighing the risks one last time. "I don't tell you this lightly."

"Whatever you tell me, you know will remain confidential," Williams reminded.

"Fells has deployed a covert operations center."

"Look, Kyle, everything Fells has or does is *covert*. The man's paranoid."

"No, Garner, this really is secret stuff. It's time travel. He's hired the best free-lance tecchies money can buy. He's really scared that someone is using the time matrix to eliminate him," Zephyrs explained. "I've been through the matrix, Garner. I have time-traveled. I'm chasing after someone you know."

"Time travel?"

"Yeah. Time travel. I've been chasing after Morrison."

"Morrison? Morrison is right here on Alpha II. I have him under surveillance."

"That's what you think." Zephyrs' panic was growing. "You know nothing about this? God, Garner, you were my last hope. Fells is gonna have my ass."

Zephyrs reached across to the passenger seat and sifted through the pile of personal effects his team had removed from the wrecked Blazer. With methodical desperation, he wove an elaborate lie. *It must be foolproof and delivered from the security of my transport. I cannot leave one single thread to unravel nor risk the voice analysis of a public place.* Zephyrs glanced at his watch. Barely enough time to weave the story and still catch Fells in the unmonitored Council transport. *I will not spend the rest of my ICom career stationed at some penal satellite in deep space.* Briefly, he considered telling the truth, but the stain on his right pant leg made it clear to him that honesty was in no way an option. He picked through a fist-sized mass of melted candy and gum and found a shiny dime. With his ICom-issue knife, he dug it out of the gooey melange and set it beside an atlas. He would make the lie fantastic, barely believable, but anchored in a reality Fells' paranoia would support.

On the bottom of the pile was a 20th century science fiction magazine, its cover adorned with a shiny, manlike robot. His lie finally formed, Zephyrs steeled himself for his charade.

"Fells," the imperator barked in response to the call.

"Imperator Fells, Sir!" Zephyrs spoke the greeting, crisply offering a seated salute.

"What have you got for me?"

"Everything, Sir. I've got the whole sordid plot."

A hint of a smile broke through the foreboding imperator's stern visage. "Let's hear it, Lieutenant."

Zephyrs glanced at the pile from the Blazer. "Sir, Morrison's got an... " The lieutenant paused. "...An android." He held the dime face-up in his hand. "Morrison sent it to 1973."

"I thought you tracked him to 1989."

"That was just to throw us off the trail, Sir, but I figured it all out." The young officer flipped the pages of the atlas. "Sir, you must have distant family in Wyoming in the late 20th century. You've got to help me, Sir. You've got to get me your family tree."

"Whatever for?!" Fells barked.

"Morrison has targeted one of your progenitors."

Fells gasped at the implications. This technosabotage was even worse than he had imagined. Astonished by the audacity of Morrison's plan, he had to respect its genius. It was the perfect way to eliminate him — without suspicion — and decimate the strength of the ICom. "Surely you can find him some other way?"

"No, Sir. Not unless they make another time shift. I'll have to find them by finding their target. Can you help me, Sir?"

"Yes." Fells didn't hesitate. "I'll get back to you, Lieutenant. Good work!" Fells raged at the doctor's vile plan as he hammered on the glass separating him from his driver. "Step on it!" he thundered.

Riddles & Revelations

Nederland

Jim Burrows parked his official white Cherokee in front of the tiny Marshal's Office and walked to Whistler's Cafe. Inside, he found Dr. Winter and Valerie Arnette taking their mid-morning break. The officer waved and nodded at other familiar faces, then marched to the doctor's table.

"Good morning, Doctor, Valerie. Mind if I join you?" He slid down the shiny pine bench.

"Sit down, Jim," the doctor barely managed before the officer scooted beside him. "Coffee?"

"No, no. Say, you remember that strange fellow I brought in a while back?"

"Sure," Valerie replied. "R... , uh, Mr. Worthington."

"Right. Well, I just happened to be in Coal Creek Canyon this morning and thought I'd take a closer look at where that fella came down." He paused, gently pulling the ends of his mustache, awaiting the obvious question.

"And?" the doctor obliged.

"And, there's something very strange going on." He paused again, but broke his own silence. "You know that hair-pin about a mile this side of Wondervu? That's where he went off. Right over the edge."

"Oh, you're kidding," Valerie gasped. "That's almost straight down."

81

"Close to straight down as you can get, and lots of trees and rocks. I don't know why I never thought about it before, but there's no way to come down there without a scratch. No way."

"But, I thought you said you had seen his tracks," the doctor recalled.

"Well, I saw them today, that's for sure." Burrows reached into his pocket and produced a cracked piece of orange plastic. Displaying it atop the sugar container, he went on. "Turn signal lens."

Silence.

"So?" Valerie asked, perturbed by the officer's flair for drama.

"So, his Blazer didn't have a scratch on it," Dr. Winter chimed in.

"So what?" Valerie defended, pointing to the plastic lens. "Who's to say that doesn't belong to some other car?"

The officer leaned forward and lowered his voice. "You might be right, if it wasn't for the rest of it."

Again, silence.

"What's the rest of it?" Valerie asked, beckoning with both hands for an answer.

"The broken glass, the white paint on the rocks, the radio antenna, and the whole spare tire. I'm telling you, that truck came crashing down that switchback."

"How is that possible when his truck didn't have a scratch on it?" Winter protested.

"I wish I had an answer to that one." Burrows stood and leaned with both hands on the table. Emphasizing his intent with a nod of his head, he assured, "I'll tell you this, I'm going to get to the bottom of it."

"Police are so paranoid," Valerie whispered as the marshal walked away. Abruptly reminded of the point hanging warmly beneath her blouse, she added, "Maybe it's part of the job description."

"Valerie..." the doctor chided. "That's not like you. Jim's a very sincere man. Very committed to law and order."

"He's such a skeptic about everything."

"Valerie, I've never known you to be so judgmental."

"You're right, Dr. Winter. I guess I just sometimes question the motives of my philosophical opponents."

"Opponent?" Dr. Winter raised an eyebrow.

"Well, sort of. Marshal Burrows may be a good and sincere man, but he always comes from fear."

"Valerie, he's a cop," the doctor joked gently.

"Exactly. Don't you see? He wouldn't feel such a strong need to *police* things if he didn't hold such a strong belief that life is inherently dangerous."

"You know, you really ought to be having this conversation with Thelma. She and the marshal have had an ongoing *tête-à-tête* for years. Jim gives her grief for her outrageous New Age attitudes, and she returns the favor by constantly reminding him of what a pessimist he is. Seems hard to believe that they are actually becoming an item."

"Well, at least she's not just preaching to the converted," Valerie laughed.

"Seriously, Valerie, the Worthington episode was a weird one, don't you think?" Dr. Winter asked.

"Well, that's something we do agree on." Placing an open palm protectively over her breastbone, she felt the point, warmer than ever, next to her heart.

Flagstaff, Arizona

"Really, I insist, Mr. Worthington." The garrulous hotel GM guided REL across the lobby with a hand at his elbow. "I've never seen anything like that. I don't know how you did it but you really saved my fanny. All those computer folks arriving and our reservation system off-line..." Buttoning his suit coat as they approached the dining room, he continued, "Breakfast is the least I can do."

"Thank you..." REL glanced at the man's name tag and smiled, "...Mr. Harper, but I'm meeting my boss and a friend this morning."

"No matter, Mr. Worthington," Mr. Harper insisted. "I'm buying."

Looking up, REL spotted Dot and Gary Fletcher. "Ah, here they are."

Mr. Harper turned to intercept them, hand extended in greeting, huge grin on his face. "Ben Harper, Hotel Manager at your service. Good man here," he said, patting John on the back. "Maybe he'll tell *you* how he did it. If there's anything I can do to make your stay more pleasant, just let me know." With that, Mr. Harper hailed the Dining Room Manager and rushed away.

"What was that all about?" Gary Fletcher asked, pulling a chair out for Dot.

REL smiled brightly. "The hotel reservation system crashed and I got it back up for him. It was no big deal. But he's buying our breakfast."

Scooting in his own chair, Fletcher laughed. "You know John, I have a confession to make." The big man nodded to the waitress for coffee and continued, "I wasn't looking forward to your transfer into my territory..."

"He never does," Dot interrupted, adding cream to her cup.

"Nothing personal, mind you." Fletcher shrugged. "It's just that I at least like to meet someone before they come to work for me."

"It's okay, Mr. Fletcher. I can understand that," REL assured.

"And here you come, a rising star on the fast track, not even a family to slow you down. I figured that just about the time you settled into our team, you'd move on."

"Is that what you think now?" REL asked.

"I started to get good feeling about you after I read your resume and cover letter, John. And now that you're here, I'm glad that you came." Fletcher reached over and smothered John's hand with his own.

"I'm glad you're here, too, John." Dot beamed and added her hand to the pile. "You know so much about so many things, and I've never met anyone who is so good with people."

"And don't forget machines, Dot," Fletcher added.

A moment of silence stretched between them as they sipped coffee and REL revered his growing bond with his new friends. Finally, with a shy smile, he breathed, "Thank you."

Nederland

Burrows sopped up the last of his over easy eggs with the last of his toast. "That's impossible," he laughed. "You're just trying to get back at me for the NRA bumper sticker."

"That's a thought," Thelma grinned. "But I'm not kidding. All the official documents say so. Back in 1989, before you got here, another wreck happened in the very same place. Another white Blazer, no plates, no registration, but lots of blood."

"And you thought this was just another one of my tangents..." Burrows joked.

"I do keep track of them, you know, Jim."

"For eight years?"

"Sure, somebody has to keep an eye on you so you don't create an accident for yourself," she said gently.

Burrows buried his face in his hands and moaned. "Thelma, we've been over this. I really do understand how choices change our experience. I have been paying attention. But this is something way beyond our control."

"We'll get to that another time, but you're right about the wreck, Jim. Wait till you see the photos."

Burrows slapped some bills on the table, gallantly offered his arm to Thelma, then walked her back to the Town Hall. He watched her fondly as she located the file on her desk.

"Here you go, Jim. Check these out."

The marshal reached for the folder and sat down. A long whistle followed his short silence. "Jeez, Thelma, this is even weirder than you think. This is exactly where I found Worthington and except for the dents, the Blazers are identical."

"What Blazers?" Alan Burgess blurted, walking over and snatching the 8X10 glossy from Burrows. "Oh, the Worthington vehicle. Whew, he sure wrecked it this time."

"No, Burgess. This picture is 10 years old. Weird, huh?"

"No way, Marshal. This is at least a '92."

"What are you talking about, Alan? See the date stamp on the photo? 1989."

"But Marshal, this is a four door Blazer. See? Didn't even make 'em until 1992. Honest."

Lighting the last candle, Valerie settled down upon the cushion in the center of the circle. Breathing rhythmically, she crossed her hands over her heart and emptied her mind of intruding thoughts, drifting into a light meditation. "Make of me an instrument of peace," she murmured, surrendering to the flow of the energy. Slipping through the layers of her mind toward gentle communion, Valerie repeatedly dismissed the nagging thought that sought to draw her attention to the point. A dozen times, she observed and released the intruding notion, only to have it resurface more determined than before. Finally yielding to the insistence of her mind she sighed and journeyed back to consciousness. Reaching inside the collar of her loose cotton shirt, Valerie slipped her hand behind her neck to unclasp the silver chain. Removing her treasure, she held it before her in the candlelight, once again amazed at the warmth it radiated in her hand. Enfolding it, she held it to her cheek, closing her eyes to envision the man who gave it to her. Smiling blue eyes greeted her inner sight. She squeezed the point harder in response, gasping at the soft throbbing that met her touch. Tiny blue and orange crystals came alive within the darkness of her grip, shooting delicate beams of light from between her fingers. Opening her hand, she stared in wonder at the display of dancing luminescence. *What is this?* she puzzled, squeezing harder. At that, a soft chirping arose from the shining planchette. Eyes wide in surprise, Valerie squeezed the point, yet again, startled as a smooth projectile snaked its way up through the tunnel of her fist. Opening her hand and holding it away from her so she could see the device, she watched in awe as the tubular target-amplification sleeve extended six inches beyond the silver case. It rotated, tracing wider and wider circles with its end, charging the air as a coherent beam of light shot out into space.

"Who are you, John Worthington?" she murmured.

Alpha II

"Aaaaaahhhhhhh," Morrison groaned as he eased his exhausted body into the embrace of a steaming bath. Vapors of sweet orange and lavender permeated his taut muscles to the core of his being. Lying back in the tub, only knees and face above the water, Morrison mused that he just might survive this day. An odd sensation jerked him from reflection. Raising his head completely out of the water, he heard the noise clearly. "The point scanner! My God! It's trying to lock on!" Like a breaching submarine, the doctor shot from the tub, creating a wake that flooded the floor. "Come on," he coaxed, racing to his lab. "Come on... come on... Lock!"

Sliding across the floor toward the equipment, his eyes searched for confirmation of a location. "Just a few more seconds. Just..."

"Dr. Morrison, Dr. Morrison..." Williams pounded on the door, a hint of panic in his voice.

"Shit! Not now!" Morrison swore, frantically waving his hands to encourage the signal.

Another barrage of pounding assaulted the doctor's concentration.

"Shit!" he cursed again, then secured the lab and yanked his bathrobe over his dripping body. "What the hell is with all this banging?" he demanded as the door slid open.

Williams backed away from Morrison's ire.

"Haven't you ever heard of common courtesy? No one comes to my quarters without an invitation. No one!" Clipped words fired through the doctor's tightly clenched teeth. "I overlooked it the first time, Monitor Williams, but I will not be harassed in this manner." Morrison's heart sagged as the signal faded away. In quiet fury, he mumbled, "Now, please leave me to my bath." Morrison longed to slam the door in Williams' face. Instead, he waved an angry hand over the door sensor to close it.

Williams stood for a moment, staring in disbelief. *What the hell has Fells gotten me into?* Dumbly, the monitor shambled to his quarters, a spate of questions begging his attention.

Rushing to the point scanner, the doctor sighed as he stared at the blank display. He could not rationally blame the monitor for his failure to connect with REL. *However,* he fumed, *I cannot take another chance.*

Consciously cultivating his seething demeanor, Morrison slipped into exercise knits and stormed to the monitor's quarters. The door swished opened before he could announce his arrival.

Williams, who had been pacing and staring out a viewport spun to face Morrison. "I should report you!"

"As if that could save your neck!" Morrison snapped.

Williams stepped away from the doctor. "Is that a threat?"

"Don't be ridiculous," Morrison retorted.

Williams shot back angrily, "Then just what the hell are you talking about?"

"The whole time you were pounding on my door, I was decontaminating myself," Morrison snapped.

"From what?"

"The organisms, damn it! The ones that killed Myerson."

Williams dropped into the nearest chair. "I thought you said you had killed them all."

"I thought I had. But a few minutes ago, I found a tiny colony growing in a sterilized petri dish. Don't you get it, Williams? They're not all dead!"

"How could you let this happen?" the monitor croaked.

"Look, Williams. It doesn't matter. We have to get you out of here and get this place sealed up."

"God, Morrison. It might be too late. I think I already have symptoms."

"What symptoms?" the doctor asked with a gentling demeanor.

89

"Dr. Morrison, it hurts so bad when I urinate..." Williams moaned at the thought of it, "...I quit drinking liquids yesterday afternoon."

With impeccable bedside manner, the doctor dropped his voice and soothed, "Monitor Williams, it may not be what you think, but we really should put you in isolation. I'll call the director immediately."

Like a petrified child, Williams allowed Morrison to lead him to an isolation module in a little used section of Level 12.

Flagstaff, Arizona

REL sat cross-legged in the middle of the king size bed, encircled by a haphazard pile of books, magazines, and newspapers. "Come in," he called toward the room's unlocked door.

Fluffing her hair and smoothing her snug, black dress, Dot glided into the room on four inch heels. Posing beneath the little track light to better display her pearls, she spoke softly, "Good evening, John. Ready to go?"

Preoccupied with a gilt-edged book, he mumbled, "Sure... in a minute."

"What?" Crestfallen, Dot reviewed every step of the last two hours: *Hair, nails, slinky dress, miracle bra... He hasn't even noticed.* "John," she said sheepishly, "I know this isn't a real date or anything, but everybody *is* expecting us."

"Sorry, Dot." John looked up, cradling an open Gideon Bible in one hand. "Wow!" He rocked back slightly. "You look terrific!" Joyous at his own spontaneity, he bubbled, "You really do."

"Well, thanks." Dot rolled her eyes and curtsied. "What's going on here, if you don't mind my asking? Are you planning to read all this stuff?"

"I already have. Except for this one." He held up the Bible. "I'm just about finished with it."

"Sure John. Whatever you say. Can we go now?"

Hopping off the bed, John smoothed his suit and offered an arm to Dot. Eyes twinkling, he escorted her to the elevator.

A peal of laughter greeted the pair as they opened the doors to the hotel bar. The Data Pioneer group was obviously having a good time. REL led Dot through the maze of tables and chairs toward a young receptionist who was jumping up and down to get their attention.

"Hey, John!" Cindy shouted. "Over here!"

"Oh, no..." Dot groaned.

"What is it Dot? Are you okay?" John asked in sudden concern.

"Yeah, I'm fine. It's Cindy I worry about." She spoke behind a shielding hand.

"Is she sick?" John asked, wide-eyed.

"Some would say so. This isn't very charitable of me, John. But she's a *Public Enemy - Journal of Justice* junky," Dot confided. "You know? The TV show?"

John furrowed his brow and shrugged.

"She does all these little investigations all the time. Snoops into everyone and everything and writes it all down. God only knows what she's written about me." Dot paused, then nudged John's arm. "Or what she's gonna be writing about you." Assuming a grin, Dot followed John to the table.

"Hey waitress, get this man a double scotch." Cindy grabbed John's arm and tugged him to the nearest chair. "Oh hi, Dot," she added over her shoulder.

"How do you know John wants Scotch?" Dot glared, sitting down beside him.

"Ah, he'll drink anything. Last night he did, anyway." Yanking a notebook from her jeans pocket she enumerated:

"One martini, one tequila sunrise, and two Scotches. See, he likes that best." She nodded emphatically and stuffed the notebook back into her pocket.

"See?" Dot whispered, nudging John.

A cheer from the corner broke Cindy's fragile concentration. "Hey, John!" She pointed to a video game against the far wall. "I'll bet you're great at that!"

A noisy group ringed the gaudily lighted machine. A player jammed the blaster into its holster then slapped the machine in disgust. "I was so close," he wailed.

Jumping up, Cindy dragged John across the room. "He's next." She pushed him up to the game.

"What do I do?" John asked innocently, all the while scanning circuitry, tracing the electrical pulses and analyzing the barely detectable energy field surrounding the device.

"Tell you what…" The vanquished player returned and pointed the hand-held blaster toward the screen. "Let's play one together. I can show you how it's done and we can bag us some aliens."

Cindy dropped the required coins into the slot and winked at John.

Grabbing the second weapon, REL aimed and squeezed the trigger with computer precision. He nailed the first alien, turning its hideous body into an even more hideous skeleton. Intrigued by the dynamics of the game and his impact upon its physical circuitry, REL immersed himself in the experience. Within seconds, he discovered that he could manipulate the field — making the blaster fire or the aliens die — without even pulling the trigger. Squinting his eyes, he saw phantoms of aliens before they appeared, enabling him to target and shoot them with ease. He laughed, elated by the discovery of this talent. Joyously blasting more and more aliens, he vowed to experiment with his skills.

"Get ready, John, this is gonna be awesome," his partner crowed. "I've never been to this level before."

REL blasted a dozen aliens without so much as a flinch of his trigger finger.

Cindy, intent upon Worthington's behavior, pulled a small spiral notebook from her hip pocket, propped it open against her left hand, and scribbled a note.

As John and his partner blasted their way through the last level, bells and cheers from the machine announced their new high score.

"Okay, John, enough fun and games. You promised to buy me dinner," Dot intervened.

"Alas, Dot to the rescue. Lead the way, fair lady. Bye, Cindy."

Cindy scowled at the pair as they walked, arm in arm, toward the exit. "See ya, John. You too, Dot."

Pausing just inside the door, John redirected his attention to the Alien Blaster game. As the images scrambled across the screen, he remotely triggered the blaster and bagged one, last alien.

Dot's choice of restaurants presented another adventure for REL. Quite comfortable, by now, with eating, he was still not prepared for the Jade Pagoda. He stared blankly at the chopsticks arranged at the top of his plate.

"You're going to love Chinese," Dot grinned, noting the puzzlement on her favorite salesman's face.

"Can't wait," he responded in anticipation, studying the wooden utensils.

"Good. Sit right here and I'll bring us some goodies from the appetizer buffet."

REL analyzed Dot's finger movements as she served him. Adapting his observations to his own hands and making allowances for size and structure, he flexed his empty fingers to mimic hers.

"What *are* you doing?" Dot nodded toward his pinching fingers.

"Oh, just warming up." REL felt a stab of embarrassment and grinned inwardly at his increasing spontaneity.

Coveting a tempura mushroom, he deftly assailed it with his chopsticks and successfully steered it to his mouth. "Dot, what do you know of God?" he mumbled through his mouthful.

Raising her hand to her mouth to camouflage a graceless gulp of plum wine, she chided, "You shouldn't talk with your mouth full. Hey, you're not one of those people who puts the little flyers on cars, are you?"

"I don't understand... " REL swallowed an enormous mouthful of food with an awkward ingurgitation.

"You know, John, those missionaries who stuff pamphlets under the windshield wiper of your car." She paused, expecting John to choke on the huge mouthful. "You're not one of those, are you?"

"No, I'm not one. I'm not anything... I mean, I don't go to a church. That's what I wanted to ask you." Pausing with an egg roll poised between his chopsticks, he asked again, "What do you know of God, Dot? What kind of a church do you go to?"

"Gee, John. That's kind of personal. I don't usually discuss religion or politics with anyone. It's too easy to offend people. Since we work together, maybe this isn't such a good idea."

"Please, Dot. You won't offend me with anything that you say. I'm looking for answers. I've almost finished the Bible... "

"Which amazes me. I don't know anyone who's read the whole thing."

"I've read dozens of other books about spirituality, too. I've read about different kinds of gods and goddesses from around the world and from all times. I'm confused."

"We're all confused. That's why I don't talk about religion. Where *I* grew up, there was pretty much only one choice of religion. Or so we were taught. Everyone I knew went to some kind of Christian church. Sure, we had heard about Judaism, but mostly about how it related to Christianity. And of course, we were taught about the Holocaust. But, we sort of believed that Jews either lived in Israel or New York. It was very narrow of us. We were even worse when it came to everything else. There were ghost stories about Native American shamanism. Moslems and Hindus and Buddhists were so exotic that nobody had ever met one. Everybody was afraid of Pagans. Do you see what I'm saying? There was such fear and such prejudice associated with going to church, that eventually, I just didn't."

"Dot, are you telling me that all the different churches *hate* each other?"

"Well, hate is probably too strong of a word. At least on the surface. You know, they all publicly wish each other well and they all talk about world peace and all that stuff, but they — at least the patriarchal religions — are undoubtedly responsible for more war and suffering than anything else on Earth."

A quick review of his files revealed the blood of untold millions, all shed in the name of religion. "But, Dot, how can this be? People say they believe one way, but they do terrible things that are just the opposite of what they profess."

"That's called hypocrisy, John."

"But don't people realize that — when reduced to the quantum hypothesis — all religions say the same thing? On that

95

level, all gods are the same god. Only dogma sets them apart. Don't people see that?"

"Apparently not. If you have the stomach for it and pay attention to the evening news, you will see that — this very minute — there are wars being fought over the nature of God. All over the world."

"Dot, I didn't know. I guess I haven't been paying attention."

"Well, don't worry about it. It's all become such a din that most of us tune it out. At least, I do. Can we change the subject, please. This is depressing."

"Okay, Dot. Sorry. Dot... *are* you a feminist?"

"John Worthington, eat your fortune cookie and quit asking about my personal life. ...Or else, I'll ask about yours."

Subdued by the threat and uncertain about how he would answer such questions, REL opened his fortune cookie and read: *The journey to enlightenment begins in the heart.*

Nederland

"Well, even my far-out ideas don't explain this. I mean, we could go off on some conspiracy tangent, but that would be right up your alley, wouldn't it, Jim?" Thelma sat at one end of her antique camel back couch looking over her chop-top reading glasses. "Maybe we should call Scully and Mulder. They might have some insight." She reached over, slapped Jim gently on the knee, and waited for a grin. She stifled a giggle when none appeared. "Jim... I'm sorry. This is really getting to you, isn't it? Why? Worthington didn't even get hurt. I know there are a lot of weird aspects to the case, but you're taking it awfully seriously, don't you think?"

The marshal didn't even look up from the *Worthington, John. R. — 1999* accident report scattered across the center of the couch. "Maybe, Thelma, maybe. But I just can't help feeling that there's something really sinister going on here. I know what you're going to say…" Holding up a hand to fend off her comment, he mocked, "…without criminals there would be no cops. But Thelma, even you admit there's something really fishy about this case."

Just as Thelma opened her mouth to offer her unique perspective, a ringing telephone demanded her attention.

"Hi Craig! How good to hear your voice. A telephone garage sale?" she laughed. "As if I need any more clutter. Okay, what have you got good deals on? Nope. I have a couch… and dishes… Oh stop! What do I need a gun for?"

At the mention of a gun, Jim Burrows cocked an ear.

"Come on, Craig, we've had this conversation before. I just don't have a victim mentality."

Victim mentality? Burrows rolled his eyes and mumbled, "Here we go again."

"No. That's not what I meant, Craig," Thelma assured. "Look, I know that people don't consciously choose to be victims. The point is that people can choose *not* to be victims. Come on, Craig… You know the statistics as well as I do. You're more likely to be killed yourself or kill someone you love with a handgun than protect your home. Personally, I'd rather not kill anyone. I think I can do just fine with my spiritual self-defense."

Burrows groaned at the "spiritual self-defense." Under his breath he chuckled, "I love ya, Thelma, but your ideas are weird."

Just then, Thelma caught Burrows' gaze and winked. "Besides, Craig… What do I need with a gun when I have a big strong marshal looking out for me? Guess you'll have to find some scaredy cat to buy your arsenal. I'm really not interested. Thanks for thinking of me, though. Good luck with the move. Call me as soon as you have your new number. Bye, Dear."

Hanging up the phone, Thelma turned to find a contemplative marshal looking at her. "You know, Thelma, maybe a gun isn't such a bad idea."

"Oh, Jim... Not you, too. Look, I refuse to live my life in fear. I refuse. And I refuse to live with the props that support that mind-set."

"But Thelma, Nederland is growing. We have all kinds of kooks coming through here. Look at the Worthington case..."

"End of conversation. I'd rather hoist a 'victim' flag over my house than live with a gun."

Silently admitting defeat, Marshal Burrows suggested, "I'm hungry, let's go get something to eat."

"Okay, Jim. But only if we walk. I can't be seen in a car with an NRA bumper sticker. It would ruin my wise woman image."

Phoenix

"No, you can't use my computer tonight," Dot nearly dropped the cordless phone. Curling her eyelashes while talking to her ex was ballistically impossible. "Why? That's really none of your business." Glancing at the clock, she rushed across the room to light the candles. "If you must know, I do have a date... Sort of. And yes, we're staying in. No, I haven't slept with him."

Outside, REL patiently counted off twenty-six seconds until his watch read exactly seven o'clock. Then he rang the doorbell.

"Look, I really don't have time for this." Cradling the phone under her chin, she opened the door. Backlit by the amber light from her entryway, John Worthington positively glowed as he shyly offered a champagne bottle and two crystal flutes to his hostess.

"Uh, I gotta go." At that, Dot punched the talk button and tossed the phone into her mail basket then reached for the glasses. "Oh John, you shouldn't have."

A flicker of disappointment clouded his face. "Sam thought you would like them." Brightening again, he said, "They're ritual glasses. For celebration."

"I didn't mean I didn't like them. They're beautiful." With a beck and a smile, she raised a hopeful eyebrow and coaxed, "What are we celebrating?"

"Finding God." He grinned widely.

Dot slumped, champagne flutes dangling from her deflated fingers and a question on her face.

"You know… The note?" Reaching into his jacket pocket, he pulled out her note, snapped it open before her astonished eyes and read: "Dear John, Been thinking about our talk the other night. If you're not busy, stop by Thursday at seven and we'll look for God. Love, Dot. P.S. Let me know if you're coming."

Dot laughed until tears ran down her freshly powdered cheeks. "Let's uncork that bubbly and I'll take you to find God."

Prying the cork precisely as to not lose a drop, REL smiled and poured two glasses. Raising his, he proposed, "Here's to looking for God." Dot gently clinked her glass against his.

"Follow me." Grabbing his hand, Dot led John to an alcove just off her kitchen. Bright fish and winged toasters glided across the screen of her new Mac. "Ta Da!" she sang with a flourish.

"Wow, Dot. This is cool. Did you just get it?"

"Yep. Part of my divorce settlement. Pull up a chair and we'll log on to the internet."

"Oohh… That's where we're looking for God?"

REL slid to the edge of his seat as Dot typed in *god* and selected *search*. "What's *chat*?" he asked.

"Well, if you want to talk to people about God, you can go to a chat room and get a lot of different viewpoints. See, everyone in a chat room is anonymous, so they tend to say what they feel. Here, choose one."

"Hmm, how about Spirit Forum? It says it's interfaith."

"Okay, be thinking about a nickname, you know, an alias. And trade me places, you're gonna do the typing."

"What do I do?"

"Just follow the directions. It's easy. Oh. I made us some hors d'oeuvres. Be right back."

Compared to the computers on Alpha II, Dot's new one was slow and cumbersome. On a whim, instead of typing his chosen nickname, REL lightly placed his fingers on the keyboard and imagined the letters appearing on the screen. He felt the electronic tingle as the information transferred. Glancing up, he watched as "REL" appeared in the box. Delighted, he *thought* the rest of the answers to the log-in questionnaire and completed the form in record time.

"Hey, I don't hear any typing over there," Dot called as she headed back to the computer, tray in hand. "How'd you do that so fast?"

"Practice," he winked.

"REL's your nick? Okay, it looks like there's one other person here. See?" Dot pointed to the "who's here" roster. "Now type in some kind of greeting. You'll get the hang of it."

John timidly typed: Hi. I'm new. Will you talk to me?

2nd Sight:	Nice to meet you. What does your nick stand for?
REL:	Remote Emissary of Life.
2nd Sight:	Wow! :o) You have great energy. Angelic!!

REL:	You can feel energy?
2nd Sight:	Everyone can feel energy. You just need to know how.
REL:	I can feel machines and crystals. Why can't I feel people?
2nd Sight:	You're just not tuned to their frequency. Keep trying.
REL:	What's their frequency?
2nd Sight:	The Universal Frequency of Love. You find it through your heart.

Dot turned just in time to see John cross his hands over his heart and close his eyes. She watched in amazement as a huge smile spread across his face. His eyes flew open.

"Dot! I can feel her energy!! I can... Oh...and something else." He shuddered.

At that instant, Dot saw words scroll across the screen.

SkyPilot:	ENERGY??!!! CRYSTALS??!!! FRE-QUENCIES??!!! YOU'RE INVITING THE DEVIL INTO YOUR LIVING ROOM. ***POOF!***

Dot pointed to the screen "He left? That was weird."

2nd Sight:	I won't forget THAT energy very soon!
REL:	Neither will I. Ever. Thank you 2nd Sight. I came here tonight to find God and found my heart, instead. Thank you.
2nd Sight:	Good-bye, {{{REL}}}. Finding your heart will lead you to God. ***poof***

"Oh look," Dot exclaimed, "She gave you hugs."

"I felt them." Tilting his head, he smiled shyly. "Dot... Can I give you a hug?"

"Sure," she laughed. "I've never felt angelic energy before."

Scooting the seat, John stood to face her, feeling her energy before he even touched her. Gingerly, he reached and gathered her into his arms, pulling her close until he felt her heart beat.

"Whoa!" Dot pushed away. "What was that?"

"That was me. I was sending you my energy. I didn't hurt you, did I?"

"On the contrary. That's the most amazing thing I've every felt. I know who you are now, John. You're my truest friend."

Center State Complex

"Package lost. First Station occupied. Stall. P.S. Our buddy threw a party and didn't invite us. Look for him at old Wright-Patterson." Arthur Tabbot crumpled Morrison's note in despair and jammed it into his pocket. Lowering himself to the stone bench beside the fountain, he cradled his head to ward off the wave of futility that made him dizzy. All around him festivities whirled. Street vendors hawked colorful wares, their shiny flags snapping in the breeze that swept the plaza. Council members in robes and glittering garnitures whisked by in self-importance, fawning entourages trailing in their wakes. Dignitaries from throughout the Megacosm converged here to attend the most important Inner Circle Session of the century. All around him crowds of people swarmed in blissful ignorance of the threat that loomed invisible.

"Fells, you son-of-a-bitch!" Tabbot swore bitterly. "You won't get away with it."

Nederland

Swaying to an inaudible melody, Alan Burgess danced up the path to the Marshal's Office. The deputy hummed softly and spun an awkward pirouette, oblivious to Marshal Burrows' attempts to get his attention. In final exasperation, Burrows tapped his errant deputy on the shoulder.

"Hey, Marshal. Like my new Discman?"

"Come on, Alan. You're a public servant, for crying out loud."

Pulling the tiny plugs from his ears and wrapping the wires around the CD player, the deputy blinked and announced, "You're not going to believe what I've got. I was just on my way to tell you."

"Not going to believe what?"

"What I just found out." The deputy pulled a crumpled paper from his back pocket.

"Don't make me beg, Alan. What've you got to tell me, for crying out loud?"

"There's a witness," Burgess blurted. "Someone saw that Blazer crash down the mountain."

Gaping at the evidence thrust at him, Burrows grabbed his deputy by the arm and dragged him into the office. Pointing for his deputy to sit, the marshal paced in front of his desk, glancing down at the egg-stained report. "Now, how the hell did you get this information?"

"From Jeff Olinger. I saw him at Whistler's this morning. He bought my breakfast so he could get my advice."

"He saw the whole thing?"

"No, Marshal. It's all in my report."

"For crying out loud, Burgess, just tell me. Okay?"

"See, Jeff and his buddy were doing their hours for Adopt-A-Highway. Worthington damn near ran them over. Jeff says they're lucky to be alive. I guess they were walking just below the shoulder when this truck came crashing down at them. They both dove for cover, but Jeff knocked himself out on a tree."

"So what did they see?"

"Jeff isn't sure. He's afraid he's just confused from the blow to his head. But he says the truck came smashing down that mountainside. Parts and plastic flying everywhere... digging up rocks and dirt and stuff... white paint on the trees..."

"Holy shit! This is weird," Burrows gasped.

"No, Marshal, that's nothin'! When Jeff came to, there it was, pretty as you please, that perfect, undamaged Blazer sitting at the bottom and you standing next to it. But all around him was evidence of one helluva crash."

"Who's the other kid? What does he have to say?"

"The other kid is Barry Thompson. And that's why Jeff wanted my advice. Barry won't say a word about it. In fact, Barry's avoided him ever since it happened. What do you make of that, Marshal?"

"Damned if I know, Alan. Let's get him in here.

"I'll try, Marshal. But Jeff says he won't see anybody."

Waiting for Barry to return his call, the deputy flipped through his newest issue of *The Investigator* — a special edition covering fifteen years of paranormal investigations. He polished the reflective decal attached to his subscription copy. Only charter members of *The Investigator Discovery Team* were so honored. As he perused this month's articles, the impact of the Worthington investigation hit him full force and he let out a long, low whistle. Tearing an I.D.T. Paranormal Report Form from the back of the magazine, Alan Burgess dashed off his account of the case.

"Just what do you think you're doing?" Burrows' voice interrupted the deputy's missive.

"Left a message on Barry's machine. I'm waiting for him to call me back."

Jabbing a finger at the glossy Investigator Burrows asked, "What is this trash?"

"It's not trash, Marshal," Burgess said solemnly. "You'd be surprised at the people who read this."

Burgess picked up the magazine and flipped to page 35, folded it back, and shoved it at the marshal. "See. Here's the whole department in Crested Butte. Sighted a UFO last month. Go ahead, read it."

Burrows shoved it back. "I don't care if the whole Pentagon saw one. I still think it's trash."

"Suit yourself, Marshal, but who's to say we're not chasing after something from outer space ourselves?"

The marshal didn't answer, just groaned, "Go comb your hair, Alan, then let's go. And leave the Discman here."

"Where we going?"

"We're gonna go talk to Barry."

Thompson Cabin, Eldora, Colorado

Barry Thompson gazed out his bedroom window, mesmerized by the creek that babbled below him. Heaving a sigh, he turned from the window and grabbed his laptop. Opening the journal entry, he read it one last time before returning the deputy's call.

Careful what you ask for. My quest to discover more to life nearly got me killed. As it is, I may just be responsible for something terrible. Jeff missed the Canyon Clean up, so I agreed to go with him and freelance for a couple of hours. He spotted an orange construction cone part way down the hill, so I walked with him to get it. Before we could, we spooked a pretty little two-point buck and sent him bounding up the hill. We were watching him. And just when he got to the road, we heard this squeal of brakes. All of a sudden, this white Blazer comes flying off the shoulder and right at us. I still can't believe what I saw.

The Blazer missed us. Barely! It was horrible. The thing was coming apart as we dove for cover. The spare tire missed me by less than a foot. *And the poor guy in the truck. Man, he got thrown out at the bottom. Smack, right into a rock. I'm sure he's dead. Anyway, seconds...SECONDS... after the crash, an identical Blazer rolls up. An old guy in a white lab coat gets out on one side and A TWIN TO THE DEAD GUY gets out the other. I couldn't believe my eyes!!! They switched plates and luggage and put the body back in the wreck. Then the old guy pulls out this little shiny thing and POOF! The wreck disappears. I mean REALLY disappears into thin air. Then the old guy hugs the twin and POOF! The old guy disappears. The twin jumps into the new Blazer and goes into some kind of a trance. I mean, he just sits there. Then I hear Jeff moaning so I go to help him. He's sitting up rubbing his head when the marshal drives up.*

I started thinking that maybe we caused this wreck. We did spook the deer. But even more than that, I don't know how to explain what I saw. Jeff keeps asking what happened, but I'm not ready to talk about it. I need to sort things out.

A loud knock at his door interrupted Barry's recollection. He pressed "save" and slid across the hardwood floor. Pausing at the sight of the Cherokee outside, Barry gulped and then opened the door.

"Barry Thompson?" Marshal Burrows intoned.

Barry nodded.

"Can we have a word with you?"

"You should have told us right away," Burgess blurted.

"Hush, Alan. Barry, the point is, we need to know everything — now," the marshal carefully added.

"Come on in," Barry gestured them into his tiny living room. "It's kind of hard to talk about, Marshal. But I did input the whole story. I'll print it out for you."

Puzzles, Perils, & Profundities

Alpha II

Dan Timball took another gulp of the vile green antacid that had become his constant companion. Fraying nerves prompted him to jump at the Alpha Com signal. "Yes," he croaked.

"It's show time, Dan," Morrison quipped, dryly. "I've got him in ISO."

Stomach lurching, Timball groaned, "Oh, God, Phil. I don't think I can do it."

"Look, Dan, I need you to do this. You have to go now."

"This must be how a condemned man feels," Timball muttered under his breath as he opened the ISO unit door. Before him sat Monitor Williams, pale and shaking. Girding his courage, the director mumbled, "I understand you're not feeling well." His voice reverberated through the mask of his biosuit.

"Oh my God! What did Morrison tell you?" Williams gasped.

"Stay calm," Timball advised. "I'm just here to draw some blood and collect a urine sample." The director reached for Williams' arm. "Morrison asked me to get these samples. He doesn't want to involve anyone else..." The director trailed off. "I'll leave you the specimen cup, just cap it and drop it in the port. And try to get some rest," he said as he turned to leave the ISO unit.

"Rest, hell!" Williams followed him. "I need some answers, here."

Timball, desperate to escape, turned and faced the monitor. "Look, we don't know what's wrong with you. These things take time and we can't take any chances."

Before Williams could utter another word, Timball spun on his heel and hurried out the door. Heart pounding painfully, he raced down the corridor. Once out of sight of the ISO unit, he sagged against the cool wall, sweat streaming down his back. "This ruse will be the death of me!" he wailed through the incessant chaos of his mind.

Nederland

"Know what I think?" the deputy asked as he strolled into the office with a sack full of chocolate bismarcks.

Marshal Burrows, who didn't even pause from unwrapping his new whiteboard, mumbled, "I dare not ask, Alan." Plucking certificates and plaques from the wall behind his desk, he carefully stacked them in a waiting box. He anchored the new whiteboard with a large screw in each corner and stepped back to admire his work.

"I think we're dealing with extraterrestrials here," Burgess proclaimed through a mouthful of calories.

"You've got spacemen on the brain," the marshal retorted over his shoulder.

"Oh yeah? Well, what theory do you have?"

"I don't know yet..." Burrows scrawled large gaudy words in red, yellow, green and blue, embellishing them with arrows and bullets and underlines. "...but it's gotta be here somewhere." Stepping back from his masterpiece, he postulated,

"It's got to be something big... drugs or maybe terrorism. Could be militia... Oh, I've got it! What about one of those witness protection programs?"

"What about the big POOF?" the deputy asked, still stuffing chocolate.

"There's a logical explanation for everything, Alan. Besides, we don't even know that Barry's statement is true."

"You don't believe Barry's story?"

"I know he was there." The marshal paced in front of the whiteboard. "I saw the construction cone and the spare tire. But the rest is just too implausible."

"So, what does Thelma think about all of this? She's pretty tuned in."

Burrows glared at his deputy. "Tuned in? What the hell do you mean by that, Burgess?"

"Well, I mean that Thelma considers alternative explanations for a lot of stuff." Burgess hovered a bismarck over Burrows' head. "I'll bet she even believes in UFOs."

Waving an angry hand at his deputy, Burrows barked, "Thelma's beliefs have nothing to do with this investigation, nor do yours. It would behoove us to stick to the facts, don't you think?"

"Sorry, Marshal, I didn't mean any disrespect." Burgess looked down at his unpolished shoes.

"I know you didn't, Alan. I know you didn't." Burrows moved to his desk and plopped down into his chair with a sigh. "Alan, would you mind getting me some coffee? I'm going to call Barry again."

"For the record, Barry, I don't need a polygraph to make me believe your story." Burgess pursed his lips and rocked back in his chair, never taking his eyes off the young man.

"Thanks, Deputy. I know it had to be done, but this lie detector stuff is weird. How long will it take Burrows to get the results?" Barry studied the deputy.

"Not long." Coolly fidgeting his alien face pinkie ring, the deputy dropped his voice to a whisper, "Just between you and me, I have my own theory about this. See... well... Marshal Burrows thinks it's crazy, but I think UFOs are involved." Burgess raised a hopeful eyebrow.

"UFOs, huh?"

"You don't believe in them?" Rummaging through the piles of papers on his desk, Burgess spied *The Investigator* and held it aloft for Barry to see.

"It's not that I don't believe in them, I've just never actually seen one," Barry said as he reached for the magazine.

"Well, did you look up?" Leaning forward in his chair, Burgess pointed his index finger skyward.

"I guess I didn't. There was too much happening around me."

At that moment, Burrows emerged from a tiny office in the back of the building. Snatching the magazine from Barry's hand, Burgess slyly slipped it back into his heap of papers.

"Well, Barry," the marshal put a hand on the young man's shoulder, "the polygraph says that you're telling the truth."

"Of course, Marshal. Why would I lie?"

"You have to admit that it's a rather implausible story. But according to the test, you believe what you think you saw." Squirming, Burrows continued, "It's a little far-fetched for me, but the polygraph tech suggested you undergo hypnosis."

"You gotta be kidding!" Barry nearly laughed that Burrows would suggest such a thing.

"I saw this guy once — acted just like a chicken!" the deputy interrupted.

"Oh hush up, Alan. I'd like you to do it, Barry. Something really bizarre has happened here, and your subconscious might just hold the key."

"What can I get you?" the man with the pony tail asked Barry as he wiped his hands on his Whistler's apron.

"Just a Coke, I guess," Barry replied, staring at Valerie and Dr. Winter who occupied the table to his left. He could just overhear their conversation.

"The marshal asked for copies of my medical reports on Worthington," Dr. Winter advised, squirting mustard on his sandwich.

"I thought medical files were confidential," Valerie replied in a tone of slight indignation.

"They are, but there wasn't much in them. Didn't even get an address," the doctor gently admonished. "You know, Burrows thinks Worthington is involved with the mob or something. Says he's making progress on the investigation, though."

"Well, he hardly seemed like a gangster. Besides, Phoenix is a long way from here." Valerie bit her lip. "Dr. Winter, please don't say anything."

"You know where Worthington went?" the doctor asked, incredulous. "Valerie, why didn't you speak up? You need to tell the marshal everything you know."

Valerie couldn't meet the doctor's gaze. Looking around the room, her eyes came to rest on the marshal sitting in the back room with Thelma. Desperate to change the subject, she commented offhandedly, "You've got to admit, those two make an odd couple."

"There you go being judgmental again." Dr. Winter winked.

"No, no, I didn't mean it that way. I mean, if Thelma owned a car, it would have a bumper sticker saying 'Practice random acts of kindness.' You know?" Valerie shrugged. "The marshal, on the other hand, has one that says 'Support the NRA.' You've got to admit, Dr. Winter, that if you were match-making, this particular union would not be the first that came to mind."

"You might be surprised, Valerie. It's entirely possible that a few more years with Thelma could produce a downright cuddly Marshal Burrows." The doctor slid back on his bench, took a last swallow of coffee and headed over to Burrows and Thelma. "Sorry Valerie, I need to tell Burrows about Phoenix."

Valerie stared at her tea, sifting though her emotions. Absently, she reached to touch the point, never noticing that Barry had joined her.

"Hi, Valerie. Haven't seen you since my bout with food poisoning." Barry shuddered at the thought.

Valerie looked up and smiled. "Looks like you survived. How's school?"

"Pretty good. I'm thinking about changing majors... again. I don't mean to be rude, but were you and Dr. Winter. talking about that man up in Coal Creek Canyon?"

"Yes. Why?"

Barry quickly checked to make sure that Burrows was not looking their way. "Well, you see, I saw it. I saw what happened."

"You saw the accident?"

"That, and a lot more." Barry related a brief version of his far-fetched story.

"So, what do you make of it?" Valerie lifted her cup, then set it down without drinking.

"I know the marshal is obsessed with this case. He had me take a lie detector test. Hell, he even had me do hypnosis. He was pretty freaked when it confirmed my story. Burrows is totally convinced that Worthington is some kind of big time criminal. Maybe I'm crazy, but I think it's even weirder than that. And I'm not alone. The deputy has his own theory about it."

"Like what?"

Barry's face reddened. "Like... UFOs and stuff. I'm not sure, it all sounds weird."

"Hey, it's okay." Valerie patted his hand. "Seems weird to me, too. The guy, you know, Worthington... ?"

Barry nodded.

"Well, he was different. Nice, really nice, but there was something otherworldly about him. And you know what? He calls himself REL, all initials. Stands for Remote Emissary of Life. Ever hear a nickname like that?"

Barry shook his head.

"Sounds pretty spacey doesn't it? God, Barry, maybe we watch too much television." She glanced at her watch. "Oh, no... I gotta run. Want to have a drink later and talk some more? You're the only person I can discuss this with."

"Exactly. Yeah, let's talk."

"How about the P.I. at 5:00?"

It was well after 5:00 when Valerie walked up the block to the Pioneer Inn. The old screen door slammed behind her as she made her way across the rough plank floor. Spotting Barry in a booth near the bar, she waved and headed over to him. "Sorry, I'm late. I hope you haven't been waiting long." Slinging her purse to a corner of the booth she quipped, "Didn't want to come in my uniform. Bad for the image, you know."

"Yours or the P.I.'s?" Barry laughed. Turning as he spoke, he flagged a waitress. Valerie ordered a micro brew and Barry motioned that he was still good.

113

"Okay, Valerie, how much do you know about what's going on?" he asked as he swirled the foam in his glass. "I mean, that you haven't already told me?"

Leaning forward, Valerie answered softly, "Well, it's the weirdest thing that's ever happened to me. Maybe you haven't heard, but it's rumored that I have pretty good intuition about these kinds of things. "

"Actually Valerie, it's rumored that you're psychic." Barry looked directly into her eyes as he spoke. "If it's true, just what kind of feelings did you get from him?"

"Before I tell you, I need to know how far your mind stretches," Valerie warned.

"At this point in my life, and especially after this experience, I discount very little."

"Well," she explained, "I do read energy. I can see things like color, intensity and flow. It helps me see the overall health of a person. In my profession, it comes in very handy." Valerie smiled.

"Wow. I've heard of that. So... you saw Worthington's energy?"

Sinking back against the bench, she laughed, "Boy, did I ever."

"And?" Barry prompted, gesturing with his hands.

"It's wondrous." She paused. "Otherworldly. And immense... And familiar. Déjà vu like I've never experienced in my life. There's no way that he could be a criminal."

"So... what if he's an alien?" Barry had to force the word *alien* from his lips. "Like the deputy suspects?"

Valerie was silent for a moment. Then, "You know, Barry, there are a lot of people who believe that aliens are going to come and rescue humanity so we don't blow ourselves up. The bookstores carry hundreds of titles authored by disembodied entities who claim otherworldly origins of some kind."

"Is that what *you* believe, Valerie?" Barry trembled with excitement.

"Well... aliens, spirit guides, angels, ghosts... All those things could just be different descriptions of the same phenomenon. Everybody does see everything a little differently, you know. So, yeah, I would have to say that I believe in aliens — whatever they are. But do I think that they will land and save us from ourselves? Nope. I think we have to do that on our own. Do I think they're sending help to us? I would like to believe so. I guess that's another reason I need to figure out the mystery of John Worthington."

"Then... say you believe that he's some sort of alien... you know... Do you believe that he could be dangerous?" Barry asked. "I mean, Valerie, when that guy and the wreck disappeared *they disappeared. Instantly.* POOF! It all disappeared. So, you have to believe *they* have some pretty heavy technology to be able to do *that.* And what if they're not friendly?"

A shock jarred Valerie's body. She remained silent.

"And even if they are friendly," Barry continued, his eyes never leaving her face. "Do you think Marshal Jim Burrows is the best possible ambassador for humanity? What if he tracks Worthington down and shoots him or something? Not that I'm saying he would, but he *does* like his firearms. Anyway, what if he shoots Worthington? Don't you think Worthington's friends might be a bit angry? Which brings us back to their advanced technology. Gee, Valerie, you know Burrows. He doesn't exactly have a reputation for diplomacy. And if he treats this like a criminal case when it's really a close encounter, he could single-handedly bring on Armageddon."

Valerie didn't respond. The point hung heavy beneath her blouse.

Barry continued, "Burrows is so conservative. You know, 'If guns are outlawed... '" Valerie cocked her head to one side.

115

"This is so complicated," Valerie admitted. "Barry, I have to trust you with something. I can trust you, can't I?"

Barry nodded. "Sure, Valerie. We have to trust each other."

"Then you can keep a secret?"

"I'm an excellent secret-keeper."

Valerie sighed again. Reaching behind her neck, she unhooked the clasp that held the point and slipped it from under her blouse. "I have to show you something," she whispered as she placed the point in the center of the table, hiding it with an inverted palm. "John gave this to me at the clinic," she explained, tipping her hand slightly to reveal a glimpse of the point.

"Wow! What is that?" Barry asked, reaching out to touch it. "Why did he give it to you?"

"That would make one more reason why I have to find out about him." Valerie smiled self-consciously. "And I have no idea what this thing is." Tentatively, she removed her hand, allowing Barry to pick up the point. "You must hold it very, very gently."

Barry squeezed it softly and felt its warmth. He watched the crystals as they flashed in an indecipherable pattern across the face of the reflective encasement. "Wow, this *is* weird." He noticed that the point's warmth increased as he tightened his grip. "What the… !" Barry exclaimed pushing backwards in the booth. Others in the room glanced in his direction. Hiding the object in his hand, he managed to keep his grip. The amplification-sleeve telescoped slightly, rotating to find an opening that allowed full extension as the point chirped softly. Barry fought the urge to throw the pulsating thing to the floor. The sleeve rotated wider and wider, spreading Barry's fingers despite his best efforts to keep it still. Barry whispered frantically, "My God, Valerie, it's going to explode."

Alpha II

"Look at it this way, Dan," Morrison tempered his frustration. "Technically, we are not harming Monitor Williams." Silencing Timball with an upheld hand, he continued, "No. Hear me out. I know the man's uncomfortable, but my potion has done him no physical harm. Nor will it. And the vitamins just might do him good." With an evil grin, the doctor reminded, "It *is* keeping him occupied."

"I'm sure he'll take that into account at our trial," Timball retorted, grimace foreshadowing a long lamentation. As his lips moved to form his first woeful word, Morrison whipped his hand from his pocket to stare at his watch. A vibration against his wrist and a flashing light display alerted the doctor to a message.

"What is it?" Timball groaned, "Not Williams..."

"Shhh... My God! It's REL! I've got to get back to the lab!" Without further comment, the doctor sped out the door and sprinted to the nearest tube, his patience barely enduring the ride to Level 14. The instant his door opened, Morrison was through it and racing to his lab. Disappointed that the scanner did not lock on REL's location, Morrison reminded himself that the date was correct, though the time was a little off. This pre-arranged signal confirmed that all was well with REL.

"Package found." Morrison recorded and encrypted the message to Arthur Tabbot. "Delivery imminent," he added.

Nederland

"Just hold it under the table," Valerie ordered, "and relax your grip." Grabbing a quarter, she quickly punched up another selection on the jukebox to mask the chirping sound. Music filled the room as the sleeve slipped back into the point and the chirping dwindled away to nothing. Barry gratefully returned the device to Valerie, who stuffed it back into her blouse and re-clasped the chain.

"Uh, sorry about that. So much for trust, huh?" Barry said sheepishly as he sipped from his nearly empty glass. "Hope I didn't signal the mother ship," Barry apologized.

"Well, if you did, it's not the first time they've been contacted." Valerie looked around the room and reached for her purse. "What do you say we get out of here?"

"Sure, where to?"

"Let's just walk."

Papers flew every which way. Despite his best efforts, Marshal Burrows could not prevent the cataclysm atop the deputy's desk. The simple act of removing one file set off a chain reaction culminating in a paper eruption of mammoth proportions. In its wake, the document avalanche revealed much about Alan Burgess. Star Trek action figures lay in grim repose amidst SweetTarts and stale donut chunks. Two unfortunate *Investigator* issues lay stuck to the desk, glued by a jellied mass of something unidentifiable. Aghast at the discovery, Burrows grumbled, "God, this man carries a gun."

"Hey, what ya doin', Marshal?" Burgess chimed, barely balancing his cargo of *Omni* magazines, a fresh bagel sandwich and a giant lemonade. "Oh, you didn't have to do that. I was gonna clean my desk."

Through gritted teeth, Burrows reproached, "I'm looking for the impound report from Worthington's vehicle. Seeings as how you're too busy to run the VIN number, I decided to do it myself."

"Oh, I already ran it."

"You what?!" Burrows seethed, "And you didn't bother to tell me?"

"Nothing to tell. It was legally registered to John R. Worthington. That's it."

"Damn! There's got to be more. Maybe Thelma can run a Motor Vehicle Report on Worthington. In the meantime, Burgess..." Eyeing his deputy, Burrows shuddered. "Johnson and Chavez just got back from Special Training, so they can hold down the fort. Uh, Alan..." Burrows closed his eyes and shook his head. "Why don't you go pack for a few days on the road."

Beaming in anticipation, Burgess jabbered, "Where we goin', Marshal? Oh, I know... after Worthington, huh? We're going after the alien!"

"Look, Burgess, taking you with me is only a slightly lesser evil than inflicting you on Johnson and Chavez." Seeing the sting on his deputy's face, Burrows lightened up and continued, "Only kidding, Alan. Please, just straighten up your desk while I go talk to Thelma. Then go pack your stuff."

"Now what do you suppose he's up to?" Barry nodded up the street toward the Marshal's Office where Jim Burrows loaded a suitcase into the back of his Cherokee.

"If we're lucky, he's going on vacation," Valerie quipped.

Just then, a disheveled Alan Burgess loped around Wolf Tongue Square, a battered duffel bag slung over his shoulder.

Passing under the P.I. awning, Barry suggested, "Hey, let's go see what they're up to. What do you say?"

"What ever for?"

"Because I'm really curious about what's going on. Aren't you?"

Crossing the street to Wolf Tongue Square, they caught the unmistakable notes of the *X-Files* theme as whistled by Alan Burgess.

"Enough with the concert, Alan. Why don't you go get the rest of your… stuff."

"Sure thing, Marshal. Be right back," the deputy called as he stumbled up the dirt path to the office.

"Excuse me, Marshal, we'd like to talk to you," Barry interrupted.

"Good evening, Barry, Valerie. Can I help you?"

"Oh, it's nothing, Marshal. Come on, Barry." Valerie grabbed Barry by the arm and headed for her truck.

"Wait just one minute," Burrows insisted. "Is this about the guy at Coal Creek Canyon?"

"Maybe," Barry nodded.

"Well, what about him?" the marshal pried. "You're not holding back information…?" He glared at Valerie.

"No, we're not." Valerie cut him off. "You see, Marshal, the truth is, we think Mr. Worthington might be… might not be… one of us."

"One of us?" Burrows raised an eyebrow.

"You know… " Barry added, "maybe he's from another planet or something."

The marshal rolled his eyes. "Another planet? And what planet might that be?" Burrows teased. "If you'll excuse me, I have someplace to be. Maybe you should discuss your theories with Alan." With that, he turned on his heel and headed into the Marshal's Office, bumping into the bumbling Burgess who was on his way out laden an armful of ambiguous gear.

"Well, that worked out well," Valerie grumbled as she and Barry walked to her Rodeo.

"Jerk!" Barry snorted under his breath.

"Hey guys!" Burgess broke into the accumulating anger. "Guess what?" he bellowed. Catching up to the pair, nearly dropping a boot in the process, he declared, "Me and the marshal's going after the alien." He ended with a nod and a wink.

"The alien?" Valerie probed.

"You know, Worthington," the deputy crowed. "We found out where he's working. He's at some computer company in Phoenix named Data Pioneer. We're gonna go find out just what he's up to!"

"Alan, get that stuff in the car." Burrows' voice left no room for questions.

"Bye," Burgess called over his shoulder as he ran to the Cherokee.

"What now?" Valerie asked, leaning against her truck.

Barry shot back, "We go after them."

"After them?" Valerie glanced at the marshal and deputy as they drove away.

"If we hurry, we can beat them to Phoenix and find out for ourselves who or what John Worthington is and hopefully keep him from harm's way."

"Barry, are you out of your mind? Two reasonable, rational people like you and me don't just abandon their lives to chase down some..." Valerie stopped mid-sentence.

Barry grinned. "You want to don't you?"

Valerie nodded sheepishly. "But it's just not possible. I've got a job. You've got school."

"Look Valerie if you're worried about money, I've got plenty of it. I've got my tuition money — cash — back at the cabin. I'm willing if you are."

Valerie shook her head. "It isn't the money, Barry. What about responsibility?"

"What about it, Valerie? You of all people should be able to see the importance of this. What good is intuition if you don't follow it?" Barry stared at her.

"Okay. I can't believe I'm doing this..." Taking a deep breath to steel her nerves, she relented, "I'll grab some clothes and hit the ATM. Hope it's not empty. If it is, I've always got plastic. Meet you back here in forty-five minutes. This is nuts!"

Phoenix

Less than fifteen minutes from the Data Pioneer office and half a block from *the beacon*, REL regarded his very first apartment. He had debated with himself for some time whether or not he needed so much room. After all, his needs were very simple. In point of fact, they were minimal. But as he looked around at the soothing southwest decor of his small living room and even smaller kitchen, he smiled at his choice to live, as much as possible, like a human. He chuckled in delight as the sinking Arizona sun cast shafts of pink and gold across the floor and halfway up the adobe wall. A tiny cactus, strategically placed to maximize its exposure to the light, basked all aglow in the waning day. REL ran a thoughtful finger down the newly framed *I Am* self-portrait. Settling into his favorite chair, he pushed "play" on his CD remote, closed his eyes, and settled in to examine his time on Earth.

First, REL backed up a complete version of his memories. That done, he codified each and every experience, parsed them and queued them for analysis. The superficiality — the grayness — of the experiences struck him immediately. Here, all was linear, columns, and numbers. The landscape of logic held no lyric, no color, no texture. Only equations. Just like his very first memories. REL opened one eye. The richness of his simple room assailed him with delight.

Curious now, he queued his parser of Valerie. A gasp of horror accompanied his realization that he had reduced her to numbers. He could not bear to think of her that way. Immediately, he recalled his uncodified experience of her. The waves of sweetness, of warmth — *of her* —within the reliving mocked his own intellect. His programmed logic disallowed the intangible. Clearly, his programming was incomplete.

Just as the implications began to thunder through his data base, a knock at his door interrupted his analysis. Deliberately he slowed his introspection to focus outwardly. Through the peephole he could see Dot, nervously shifting her weight from one foot to the other.

"Hello," he greeted warmly as he pulled the door open.

"Hi." From behind her back Dot produced a small pot-ted azalea that was loaded with pink and white striped blooms. "I thought this might brighten up the place," she said as she surveyed the interior of John's bachelor abode. "Wow! It's pretty bright already. Nice."

"Thanks, Dot. Come on in. Thanks for the plant. It will brighten up the place."

"John, I'm sorry to barge in on you without calling first."

"It's okay, Dot. We're friends." REL admired the azalea as he found the perfect sunny window for it.

"Actually I was just visiting that bookstore you were telling me about."

"*The beacon.*" John smiled thinking of Sam and his wonderful store.

"Yeah. So since I was so close I thought I'd come by." Dot wandered over to the self-portrait. "This is beautiful. I didn't know you were an artist."

"Oh... I'm not really. Care for some tea?" He changed the subject. "I brew a wicked cup."

"Maybe later. John, remember that night at my place when you hugged me? I noticed something that I haven't been able to talk much about. But I need to." Dot plunked down onto the couch.

"What is it, Dot?" John sat down at the opposite end.

"I have never felt a hug like the one you gave me. I think I even told you so."

REL grinned, recalling the memory.

"Well, it got me thinking, John. There's obviously an element to life that is far more than the words we speak or the visions our eyes behold. Do you know what I mean?"

REL sat mute. Finally he managed a muffled "Uh, huh. Jeez, Dot, I was just thinking about that."

"I know most people believe in God and say they can actually talk to *Him*..." She wrinkled her nose at the divine gender assignment. "And, John, I don't doubt them, but in all the times I've ever been to church, I never felt anything close to what I felt when you hugged me." A reddening hue crossed her face. "Don't get me wrong, John. You are a very attractive man, but this doesn't have anything to do with attraction. It's far greater than that."

REL recalled the full force of that hug.

"It's like you infused me with — I don't know — light. A loving light that is still there." Dot tapped her chest.

"Remember what 2nd Sight said to me?" REL recollected. "She said that finding my heart would lead me to God. And the fortune cookie... It said: *The journey to enlightenment begins in the heart.*"

"You know, I saw a bunch of books about the intelligence of the heart, the language of the heart, that kind of thing. I guess I'll have to give it some thought."

"Me, too, Dot. I will certainly think about it."

"Oh rats!! What time is it?" Dot grimaced.

"It's almost 7:30." The moment he named the time, a wave of insistence swept through his processors. "Why?" he asked absently.

"I'm supposed to let You-Know-Who use my computer tonight. Sorry, John, gotta run. We'll do tea another time." Dot jumped to her feet and shyly reached to give him a hug. "I suspect these could become habit-forming," she said as she kissed him lightly on the cheek.

John escorted Dot to the door and returned the kiss inattentively. For even as his lips touched Dot's cheek, an urgency to call Valerie assailed him. Horrified that the desire was not entirely his own, he railed against the command. Of course, he wanted to talk to her, but not under duress. His tyrannical program battered him until he bitterly surrendered and dialed the phone.

As the phone rang for the tenth time, REL panicked. His program dictated that he contact Morrison in exactly two minutes and thirty-one seconds. Without Valerie and the point, he was helpless to execute the command. He dialed the number again. Then he frantically dialed the clinic. All to no avail.

For the first time ever, REL paced. His failure to respond at the pre-programmed time hurled him into an abyss of hopelessness. His circuits slogged, his flexors stiffened.

Sick at heart, he buried his head in his hands and sought to escape the wrath of his despotic instructions. "Dr. Morrison will think I have failed," he sobbed, tears streaming freely down his face. Heaving a sigh, he dropped to his couch and reached into his pocket for the small amethyst he found in Coal Creek Canyon. He cradled it gently, seeking the subtle vibrations that provided his fragile link to the living world. As he placed the amethyst over his heart, sudden insight flared throughout his being.

Remember, it whispered.

Grasping the fleeting thought, he followed its lead to his heart.

Remember, it insisted.

Beyond the gloom of his crisis, REL glimpsed the luminous portal to hope. A gentle knowing beckoned, but it came not from his program, nor could he trace it to anywhere in his computerized structure. It came directly from his heart and led to colors and textures and lyric — uncodifiable and complete. He clung to the hinted possibility and drew a deep breath.

Immediately, his flexors relaxed, his processing smoothed, and the internal pressure abated. Calmed, he whispered a "thank you" to the anonymous source of relief.

The phone rang several times before REL separated the sound from his own humming circuits.

"Hello," he answered, scanners fully activated.

"John. Fletcher here. Sorry to disturb your evening."

"Yes, Mr. Fletcher. It's okay, I was just... thinking."

"John, we've got a problem."

"What problem, Sir?"

"Well, our office in Washington recently installed our most sophisticated system. You know, the TechniCom? It's the nucleus of the entire U.S. intelligence community..." Fletcher paused to catch his breath. "Got all the data downloaded and now it keeps crashing. Our people out there don't have a clue what's wrong. And since it handles the most sensitive information in this country — maybe even the world — it's practically a national emergency. Got the brass up in arms. We've got to do something. Anyway, I told my boss that I could fix it. You can fix it, can't you?"

"I don't know, Sir," REL mumbled, lost in a new sensation. At the mention of the TechniCom, he felt a programming shift more profound than anything he had felt before. The impression lasted less than a second, and yet it shook him with an odd sense of precognition. In a moment's reflection, REL concluded that all of the evening's experiences confirmed he was where he needed to be. Mr. Fletcher's urgent voice refocused him on the conversation.

"You don't know?" Fletcher panicked. "What do you mean, you don't know?"

"I mean, Mr. Fletcher, it depends on what's wrong with it."

"Well, John, whatever it is, we've got to fix it. This means a lot to me... and to you, too. This could be the big break most of us wait for our whole lives. So we've got to give it our best shot."

"We will, Sir."

"Good, good. Can you get packed tonight? Our flight leaves at 8:30 in the morning."

Enroute to Arizona

The flow of adrenaline had ceased miles ago. Valerie slept soundly in the back seat while Barry fought hard to stay awake. His driving speed, well beyond what he considered safe, demanded more attention than he could manage. Reluctantly, he eased off the accelerator. "Approaching Albuquerque," he announced to his sleeping passenger, who did not respond. Brilliant blues and oranges painted the desert sky as the sun rose over a cool morning. Barry longed to examine the formidable terrain. Instead he pushed on, scanning the scenery as he sped toward Phoenix and answers about his extraordinary experience.

Passing a rest stop, he spotted the unmistakable blue and red gumball lights of what he thought was a poorly hidden speed trap. Checking the rear view mirror, he noted the Colorado plates on the white Cherokee.

"Valerie! Valerie! Wake Up!" Barry demanded.

Valerie stirred from her cramped position and opened her eyes. "What's the matter?" she asked groggily.

"We've passed them," Barry announced. "Burrows and Burgess were pulled off at that rest stop. I'm betting that if we catch 60 out of Soccoro, we can beat them to Phoenix."

Valerie sat up. "Did they see us?"

"Nah, I think they were sleeping."

Knowing they were now ahead of the lawmen gave the pair a second wind. Within moments, Valerie hopped over the seat and poured herself a cup of steaming coffee from a large thermos bottle. "Want some?" she asked Barry.

"No, thanks. I had some about an hour ago. I would like to ask you a question, though. See, I did a lot of thinking while you were asleep. And I hope this isn't too personal, but... Just how far are you willing to take this thing, Valerie?"

"Wow. That's pretty heavy for this early in the morning. But, you're right, we need to talk about it." Valerie took a long breath and a deep swallow of coffee. "I'm going to take your advice and follow my intuition. You know, we all say we want to change the world. All of us have dreams of doing something important. But most of us lead pretty unspectacular lives and don't really have the opportunity to shine on a large scale. I can't help believe, however, that if we each took just one risk that felt right — even if it's a small thing — that we could enrich our own lives, and possibly the world, too. Barry, this feels like one of those risks. It feels right to me. And even though I'm half scared to death, I feel more alive than I have in a long time. I guess I'll just have to play it by ear. I'll understand if that doesn't work for you."

Barry reached over and slipped Valerie's cup from her hand. Taking a drink, he held the warm coffee in his mouth before slowly swallowing. Finally, he turned to her and nodded.

That settled, they drove triumphantly toward Phoenix.

Phoenix

Scooting to the edge of his seat in the taxi, REL gazed wide-eyed, catching his first full glimpse of Sky Harbor International. Already, the morning heat cast the building all ashimmer against the bleached-out blue sky. Nose pressed against the window, he grinned inwardly at his decision to run unshielded — all sensors wide open.

Excitement unrestrained, he burst from the cab the instant it halted, only to stagger headlong into the maelstrom. The thundering rumble of a wide-body DC9 cracked the sky overhead, momentarily muting the drone of security announcements. People scurried, oblivious to each other, as horns honked and police blew whistles to coax the stubborn traffic.

Inside was even worse. The din and hum of electronics and machinery jumbled with the emanations of humanity assailed him so savagely that all he could do was mutely follow his boss toward the gate.

Fletcher skillfully guided him through the crowds, quipping as the flow stalled, "Hey, you don't have a metal plate in your head, do you John?"

REL looked up from his introspection just in time to apprehend and smoothly override the metal detector as he stepped through it. Relieved at the thinning crowds in the concourse he turned to Fletcher. "Is it always like this?" he asked in disbelief.

"Wait till we get to Dulles." The big man chuckled over the unlit cigar in his mouth. "With the TechniCom down, it'll be murder!"

"Why? What do you mean?"

"Well, without the TechniCom, there is no intelligence internet. National security is running blind right now." He shook his head and rasped a laugh. "Paranoia abounds."

"Are you afraid, Mr. Fletcher?"

"Hell yes, I'm afraid. It's un-American not to be."

REL abruptly stopped and stared at his boss. "Exactly what do you fear?"

"John, everywhere you turn, there are things to be afraid of — war, terrorism, muggings, disease, alimony... The real world is downright scary." Fletcher reached out and grabbed John's elbow, towing him down the concourse. "You don't get out much, do you?"

Stumbling along behind the big man, REL succumbed to Fletcher's fears. Eyes from the crowds suddenly threatened to expose him. Bags and purses hinted at weapons and bombs. Even the distant security announcements reminded him of his vulnerability, so he clutched his bag tightly to his side. Hyper-vigilance accompanied him down the skyway, refusing to depart even as he took his seat.

"You look like you could use a cocktail." Fletcher elbowed him gently.

REL remained unresponsive all through take-off until Fletcher nudged him with a Bloody Mary. "How do you bear it?" the biomech asked, absently accepting the drink. "How do you deal with the fear?"

"This is one way," the big man grinned and clinked glasses. "But really, John, there are lots of ways to deal with fear. I mean, you can buy a gun, you can study martial arts, you can join a church. Anything that brings you some peace of mind can help you deal with the fear." He paused, looking at his glass, then laughed. "Or you can drink."

"Yes, but those things only keep fear at bay. It's all around, always a threat. How do you get rid of it?"

"Jeez, John. I guess you die. Fear is a symptom of the human condition."

"I cannot accept that," REL murmured. Quickly, he selected his most fearful recent moment, then parsed and codified it. He shuddered in amazement. Reduced to code, fear was just data — no charge, no power over him. With a gasp, he announced, "So *we* give fear its power!"

Fletcher turned slowly and locked eyes with Worthington. "We... what?"

"Look... take computers, for example. All data fed into a computer is broken down into code, bits of neutral information. The computer does not determine one bit of information preferable to another. Only human judgment of the information determines if it is *good* or *bad*. What if our judgment is based on a flawed program?"

Dumfounded, Fletcher stared at his salesman.

"For millennia, humans have believed themselves to be helpless little beings stranded on a hostile world buffeted by the whims of a distant God." REL raised a finger to his lips then shook it once. "What if that perception is based on flawed data? What if... someone... could prove that humans are a cherished species inhabiting Eden and doted upon by a loving Creator? And powerful beyond their wildest imaginings? How might that change life experience?"

"It would be just ducky until they all got blown away by some terrorist who sneaks into the country because the TechniCom doesn't work," the big man laughed.

"Maybe so," REL shrugged. "But I still have to consider the idea." Changing the subject, he smiled at his boss and said, "I already asked Dot about this, but... What do you know of God, Mr. Fletcher?"

Fletcher wrinkled his brow. "The only thing I know right now is that I feel like another Bloody Mary."

Phoenix

Heat shimmers scampered ahead of the truck as Valerie and Barry entered Phoenix. "How far behind us do you think Burgess and Burrows are?" Valerie asked, checking her rear view mirror.

"I'm gonna cross my fingers and guess at least a couple of hours. They didn't get much of a start on us and we didn't stop to sleep. Think I'll give Data Pioneer a call for directions," Barry said, reading the phone number from a scrap of paper and dialing Valerie's cell phone.

Valerie combed her hair with one hand while Barry made the call. Ten minutes later they pulled into the parking lot, stiff from their long drive.

"How can I help you?" Dot asked brightly as the two walked across the lobby.

"Would it be possible to see John Worthington?" Valerie asked hopefully.

"Oh, I'm sorry, John and Mr. Fletcher were called out of town on an emergency. They left first thing this morning."

Smiles melted from the faces of the pair. "What do we do now?" they groaned in unison.

Dot walked around in front of the desk. "I'm Dot, a friend of John's. Is there anything I can do to help?" she asked quietly.

Barry looked directly into Dot's eyes. "We have to find him, Dot. He may be in danger."

"Sorry I'm late." Cindy burst through the door. "I'll get the phones now."

Dot held up a hand to silence the young woman. "Cindy, just a minute." Shaking her head, Dot returned her attention to Barry. "What kind of danger?" she asked. "What is this all about? Who are you?"

"I'm Barry Thompson and this is Valerie Arnette. Valerie's a friend of John's, too." Barry glanced curiously at the latecomer who eyed him as she scribbled something in her notebook. "Is there some place we can talk?"

"I'm sure Gary won't mind if we use his office. This way," Dot motioned.

"So what is all this about danger?" Dot asked, directing them to sit around Fletcher's coffee table. "Who could possibly want to hurt John?"

"Dot, this is probably going to be the weirdest story you've ever heard. But I swear it's true, and we can prove it." With that, Barry related his improbable account of John Worthington. Valerie added her version of events capping it off by displaying the silvery planchette.

Dot reached out to touch the odd pendant, but Valerie intercepted her finger. "Here." Valerie removed the point from around her neck and gently placed it into Dot's hand.

"Don't squeeze," Barry advised.

"What is this thing?" Dot asked, amazed at the object that sparkled as it caught a ray of sunlight reflecting through a nearby window.

"Why don't you just feel it and tell me what you think," Valerie suggested.

Dot closed her eyes and sat in silence. A chill from inside out made her body shiver. "What *is* this thing?" she asked again, eyes now wide with wonder.

"We don't know," Valerie replied. "John gave it to me at the clinic and said it was a promise that he'd see me again. I have no earthly idea what it really is."

"Well, it *is* weird," Dot said. "And it's all yours." She handed the point back to Valerie. "So, what should we do?"

"Are you sure you want to get involved in this, Dot?" Valerie asked.

"Absolutely! John's my best friend. How could I not help him?"

"Okay, we know that Burrows and Burgess are on their way here, even as we speak," Barry reminded. "They must not find Valerie and me here, and they can't find out where John is."

Dot nodded. "Why are you so afraid of these guys?"

"Let's just say that Burrows is a little over zealous and has a great fondness for guns," Valerie sighed. "I wish I didn't think so, but there's a real possibility he could shoot first and ask questions later."

"She's right," Barry agreed. "He thinks that John is some kind of gangster or something. And Burgess thinks he's an alien."

"You're kidding?"

"No, we're not," Valerie answered earnestly.

"Well, I'll handle them," Dot promised.

"What about the receptionist?" Barry wondered.

"Yeah. Cindy is a nosy one. Well, I've got a nice long errand in mind for her." Dot glanced at Valerie's cell phone. "Give me your number and I'll call you after I get rid of them."

Dot stifled a giggle at the sight of Burgess in his Hawaiian shirt. "Can I help you?" she asked, feigning her most professional guise.

Stepping in front of his over-anxious companion, the marshal smiled. "We're looking for a friend of ours, John Worthington."

"Oh dear, was he expecting you?" Dot wrinkled her brow with feigned disappointment.

"No, not really. We were just in the area and thought we'd drop in on him."

"Oh, you just missed him. Left for a few days on a houseboat on Lake Powell."

"Any way to contact him?" Burrows pressed.

"No. It's some kind of retreat. No phone, no fax, no pager. Sorry." She shrugged.

Second Messenger

Surprising Grace

Washington D.C.

REL stubbornly refused to dampen his sensors, reasoning that Sky Harbor and his musings about fear had primed him for Dulles. He was fully prepared this time. Or so he thought. But even walking up the jetway, he tensed at the looming anxiety. It rolled from the crowd waiting to greet the passengers and assailed him as he made his way up the narrow hall.

"You okay, John?" Fletcher chucked him with a huge hand.

"You were right. This is... very uncomfortable." Inhaling sharply, REL stepped into the concourse as Fletcher gave him a nudge.

"See there?" The big man directed with a nod of his head.

REL followed the gesture, eyes widening at the sight of an armed and uniformed officer. Scanning the length of the concourse, he spotted several more.

"Welcome to the capital of the free world," Fletcher quipped dryly.

A gentle prompt from his newly launched program made the biomech pause ever so briefly and close his eyes. Straightening his shoulders, REL drew a soft breath and pictured his heart while reminding himself to see the world with love. Opening his eyes, he looked again at the armed officer, noting in awe that the man who seemed so foreboding before, was now just a man doing his job. He took another breath through his heart. Before his flexors could ease, a metal detector screeched and sent a shock that jolted him to his circuits.

REL spared no thought for his spontaneously furrowed brow. All his logic stalked the similarities between the tyranny of fear and the brute force of his programming. Conclusions wafted just out of reach as he channeled each breath through his heart. And though he never missed a step as he walked beside his boss, inside he trembled to the core of his data base.

Blinking away the sunlight that glared from the shiny, white limo, REL climbed into the spacious seat, sinking gratefully into the quiet.

"This could really take some doing," REL whispered.

"So, you've read the TechniCom update?" Fletcher asked, settling in.

"No, I'm talking about love."

Fletcher winked. "You fix the TechniCom and I'll help you find love."

After a tiny lull, REL chuckled then rejoined, "I'm serious, Mr. Fletcher. Don't you see it? Everywhere you look, there are signs announcing danger. Despite the boasts of peace and freedom, fear structures loom all around us." He pointed out the window to a block of government buildings. "It's hard to hold a focus of love when everything you see belies the notion."

"Jeez, John, this TechniCom crisis has triggered some really deep thinking for you." Fletcher stared into John's eyes.

"Don't you ever question this, Mr. Fletcher?" he responded, unblinking. "Never?"

Fletcher opened his mouth in attempt to answer but fumbled over which words to say. Before he could decide, the driver announced their arrival.

The nondescript brick building was not at all what REL expected. "I thought the TechniCom would be in some huge, government fortress," he mused, pressing his face close enough to fog the tinted glass.

"Stealth is stock and trade for the intelligence community. Guess they don't want to advertise where they keep the goods." Fletcher gestured for John to get out of the limo.

Obscurity protected the outside of the building. Inside, however, a technological monument to paranoia defended the TechniCom. REL was not even through the door before his eyes snapped from one flashing array of electronic gadgetry to the next in a frantic attempt to identify the source of the hum. The deep-throated drone of dissonance bruised him mercilessly. *Thank God for encrypted coding*, he thought, *or I'd be flailing around on the floor.* As it was, his inner quaking rendered him mute. A nudge from Fletcher forced him to action. Inside his biomechanical structure, REL created white noise and generated his own minute magnetic field that allowed him at least a semblance of presence.

REL and Fletcher marched into the inner structure of the building behind two military types with matching haircuts and identical wing tip shoes.

Looking at the one nearest him, REL smiled and commented, "I'll bet you have lots of absenteeism here, don't you?"

Vexed by John's behavior, Fletcher interrupted, "John, what would make you say a thing like that?"

"The hum, Mr. Fletcher. Don't you hear it?" REL asked in disbelief. "It has set my teeth on edge."

Ahead of them one escort elbowed the other. "See," he whispered. "I told you this place gives me a headache." Turning back around to John, he patted himself on the chest. "I hear the hum, too. Not everybody who works here can hear it. But I sure in hell do."

Straining, almost grunting with the effort, Gary Fletcher tried, in vain, to hear what they were talking about. "I don't hear a thing," he admitted.

A soft, whooshing sound drew everyone's attention to a retracting wall panel that revealed the gleaming stainless steel doors of an elevator. With a wave, an escort ushered them inside the waiting car that descended the moment the doors closed. REL braced himself to compensate for the fall, but found it more necessary to compensate for the savagely increasing hum.

"Most annoying," he commented out loud as they stepped from the elevator and found themselves facing a formidable armored door.

An escort keyed in a security code, then placed his hand on a glowing reader for verification. A metallic click and a flashing light allowed them entry to the computer room where a technician gestured toward the malfunctioning mainframe.

Extending his hand, REL asked the technician, "How long have you worked here?"

"I'm sorry, Sir, that's classified."

"I see... Then can you tell me when you took your last sick day?" His restraining hand prevented Fletcher's protest.

"As a matter of fact, I was out two days last week with a migraine," the puzzled tech replied.

"John, we're here to identify what's wrong with the TechniCom not the technicians," Fletcher half-joked.

"I identified the problem the instant we entered the building," REL responded matter-of-factly. "The problem is the hum. It is a constant gush of electromagnetic interference that is actually amplified by the design of this building. We are, for all intents and purposes, standing in the middle of a sub-woofer. The hum down here is three times the hum on the surface."

Amazed, the tech wondered, "How do you know that?"

"Even Mr. Fletcher can attest that I am very sensitive to electronics. I am also very sensitive to sound," he said ironically. "Anything that can give you a migraine undoubtedly interferes with every single function of the TechniCom."

"What do you advise we do?"

"Ideally, you should move it. And get yourself out of here, as well. Short of that, you must shield this room and counter both particle and wave interference."

Fletcher, ignoring the first dull throb of an impending headache, stared at Worthington in unabashed admiration. "Well, I'll be..." he whispered. "Just about the time I think you're the most eccentric man I know, you prove yourself to be the smartest. Listen to him, boys. He'll have this fixed in no time."

Seating himself at a work station, REL penned some notes. "I'll send you the specifics in my report. Essentially, here's what you need to do. First, you need a minimum of 18" dead air space surrounding this room, including the floor and ceiling. Interlace it with magnetic shielding. I'll detail that for you. Also, you need to generate noise to counter the wave interference. The right frequency of white noise will do. But..." Looking up at the young men, "Why don't you be kind to yourselves and this computer? Play some Mozart, too. You'll all feel better for it."

John fiddled busily with his laptop in the back of the limo until Fletcher intervened. "Good thing we reserved a business suite. When we get checked in, you can log on and e-mail your recommendations directly to the home office."

Looking up from his plush recline, John smiled. "You brought your cell phone, didn't you?"

"Sure," Fletcher nodded. "Why?"

With a dazzling smile, REL flashed his laptop to reveal screen after neat screen of graphs and charts, diagrammed waveforms and particle maps. "Should I tidy it up, do you think?" he asked the dumfounded Fletcher.

"Let me see that!" the big man finally blurted. Mouth agape, he grabbed the computer and scrolled through page after page of multi-figure data followed by page after page of technical descriptions. "How the hell did you do this?" Fletcher's voice pitched in amazement. "Dear God, you even have a suggested materials list. And a proposed construction schedule..." Propping his elbow on the arm rest and his cheek on his hand, he stared at REL. "Who the hell are you?" he whispered.

"I'm John R. Worthington, who else could I be?" REL responded while plugging his laptop into Fletcher's cell phone.

"I don't know, John, but I'm pretty sure you've done more for my career today than I've done for it the past twenty years. And I have no idea how you did it."

"It was an archetypal case of the vibration of love over-coming the vibration of fear, Mr. Fletcher."

The big man slapped his hand on his knees, "Tell you what, if you can manage to tie love to the TechniCom, you'll make a believer out of me. I swear." He raised his hand in an oath.

Phoenix

"Nice place, Dot." Barry gestured as he sat in the chair opposite Dot and Valerie. "Thanks for having us over."

"Hey..." Dot reached over and patted his hand. "John's my dearest friend. If he's in danger, I'll do anything I can to help him. And I welcome the company."

"I don't even really know him, but he sounds like a pretty cool guy. Besides, we don't want an intergalactic incident on our hands if Burrows looses it," Barry affirmed.

"Wine?" Dot offered. "Are you always this quiet, Valerie, or is there something on your mind? If so, I think I know what it is."

Valerie tipped her head, a question in her eyes.

"For the record, I *did* think about it. I even had a fantasy or two." She blushed a little. "Well... John *is* beautiful."

Valerie nodded, appreciative of Dot's candor.

"But two things stopped me. First, I've never had a friendship like this before and I didn't want to complicate it. Second, and probably most important, it's pretty obvious to me that John's heart belongs to someone else. I suspect that someone is you, Valerie."

"Dot," Valerie turned to Dot and took her hands. "Thank you for telling me. But as far as John and me... I just don't know. I mean, there is something undeniable between us, but we spent so little time together I don't know what that something is." Brightening, Valerie added, "You know, his energy is really amazing."

"Tell me about it! He gave me this hug..."

"I know about his hugs," Valerie laughed. "Whoever he is, we've got to help him."

"Hey, ladies..." Barry leaned toward them. "Don't forget that this is a guy who can vaporize just like that." He snapped his fingers.

"You're right. And don't forget Burrows and Burgess. They will most likely be back tomorrow. So... I had this idea." Dot grabbed her glass and led them to her computer.

Barry and Valerie stood quietly behind her as she deftly logged on and took them to a bookmarked travel page. "How soon do you want to leave?"

"Leave for where?" Barry asked.

"Our nation's capital. Am I the only one dying to find out the truth?"

"Hardly," Valerie assented.

"Besides, maybe it's just me, but John seems too innocent to realize that Burrows might be dangerous." Dot added, "Let's do it."

Washington D.C.

"This definitely calls for champagne. Bring me the best stuff you've got." Fletcher gestured expansively to the waiter. "I'm telling you, John, I've never heard so many superlatives in my life. And from the DP president, no less."

"I'm happy to have done it," REL blushed beneath the accolades.

"John, the simulations ran flawlessly. Flawlessly. How on Earth did you do it?"

"I guess I just have a knack for it, Mr. Fletcher." Shyly toying with his fancy folded napkin, he added, "I'm not used to such flattery."

"Oh, I'm embarrassing you. I didn't mean to do that. Hey, to change the subject, let's talk about fishing. You like to fish, don't you?" The big man grinned.

"I've never fished, Mr. Fletcher. I can't kill things."

"No, no, we don't kill them. I'm talking fly fishing. Strictly catch and release. I know the perfect place to teach you..." Fletcher raised his champagne flute, motioning for John to do likewise. "And the best part is that the whole trip's on Data Pioneer."

"What trip?" John chuckled at the big man's animation.

"Our two-week, all expense paid, top of the line fishing trip courtesy of Data Pioneer's *thank-you-for-saving-my-butt department*."

"You mean *now*?"

"Yep. Starting right now." He clinked glasses. "Since you don't know your way around a fishing pole, just leave it all

144

up to me. I have a cabin in upstate New York and a DP rented 4X4. It'll be just perfect. We can relax, I'll teach you to fish and we can get to know each other a little. Hell, you can even tell me all about..." Lowering his voice and checking for eavesdroppers, he continued, "...that love thing. What is that all about anyway?"

John laughed out loud. "You mean the things we were talking about in the limo."

"Yeah." Fletcher speared an escargot.

"I decided to investigate humanity's misperception about life," REL said earnestly.

"Misperception?" Fletcher nearly choked. "On what authority do you judge humanity's beliefs misperceptions?"

"It's not a judgment, Mr. Fletcher, it's an observation. Look, I could deliver an hour long oratory citing historical and anthropological examples to support my theory."

"No doubt," Fletcher admitted, nodding his head.

"But our own experiences are much better teachers. You told me yourself that you live in fear, occasionally dulled..." Lifting his champagne glass to toast his boss, he continued. "Until you told me that, I had never felt that fear. I briefly allowed myself to do so and did not like it."

Round-eyed, Fletcher whispered, "Even as a child? You were not afraid even as a child?"

Caught off-guard by the question, REL faltered, then answered, "Truly, I had never felt fear like that before. But, I learned something from the experience. You do not have to die to end fear, Mr. Fletcher, you only have to love."

"Uh, huh..." Fletcher nodded. "And I suppose love fixed the TechniCom?"

"Of course. It was classic..."

"That's what you said. I don't understand what it means, though." Fletcher cleared his throat. "I have to confess,

John, this love talk has me a bit uncomfortable. See, it's never been my strong suit. Relationships and me..."

"No, Mr. Fletcher, not just relationships. I'm talking about love as a powerful, powerful force."

"But, John... Just what does this have to do with my life? My day-to-day life? And how do you relate any of this to the TechniCom?"

REL ordered his thoughts as dinner arrived. After savoring his first bite, he resumed, "Okay, let's start with the TechniCom. It is a fear-based construct. It was created from fear to counteract terror and installed in a covert structure literally engulfed in the vibration of dread. I'm telling you, I could hear it the moment I stepped through the door. Others obviously can, too. That concentrated, fear raises havoc with everything."

"Oh give me a break, John." Fletcher nudged his star employee with a large elbow. "How on Earth can an emotion do that?"

"Fear is not just an emotion. It is a... vibration, a measurable pattern of wave and particle static that interferes with your daily life as surely as it interferes with the TechniCom."

Fletcher momentarily stopped chewing his prime rib, fork raised like a baton directing John to continue.

"So anyway, in a logical application of my understanding, I knew we needed to shield the TechniCom from what particle interference we could. And we needed to counteract the wave interference, as well. We needed to shield it from the static of fear."

Swallowing, Fletcher offered, "So you wished the room love?"

"No," REL laughed. "And yes. As nearly as I could, I recommended a simulation of the love vibration. Magnetics and Mozart, Mr. Fletcher. Works like a charm." He winked.

Phoenix

The peal of laughter grated the marshal.

"Dot said John's on a houseboat?" Cindy hooted.

"You're saying that she lied to me?" Burrows pressed.

"'Fraid so," she laughed again.

"So, just where the hell is he? If it's not too funny to say?" The marshal glared at the receptionist.

Casually extracting a palm-sized notebook from her back pocket, she pointed at the marshal. "You're legit, aren't you?"

Blowing his impatience out with a breath, Marshal Burrows pulled out his badge and flopped it on the desk in front of her.

"Okay," she agreed, idly flipping through the pages. "Washington, D.C." Slapping the notebook down, she continued, all the while popping her gum. "What's the hubbub? There were two other people in here yesterday looking for Worthington. And Dot left town this morning. Family emergency." Cindy rolled her eyes. "Yeah, right. Dot's only family is her ex."

"What other people?" Burrows demanded.

"Uh... Oh yeah, here it is," she said, flipping a notebook page with a pencil eraser. "Barry Thompson and Valerie Arnette. Supposedly friends of John's. Funny. I never heard of them before." Squinting conspiratorially, Cindy added, "You know, he never listed an emergency phone number *or* a next of kin on his forms. It's like nobody knows him at all." She winked.

"What the devil were Valerie and Barry doing here?" Burgess blurted, his straw Panama hat bouncing to the floor.

"Damned if I know," Burrows hissed. "Maybe trying to outflank the investigation."

Bending over to retrieve his hat, Burgess looked straight into Cindy's face, eyes wide. "Mind control," he mouthed as he stood up.

"Alan..." the marshal intoned sourly.

"Hmmm." Cindy referred to her notebook. "Not exactly mind control. But he does control machines."

Jaw and hat dropped at the same time as Burgess leaned his hands on the desk and whispered, "You've seen him do that?"

Hands on hips and toe tapping, Cindy boasted, "Look. I'm not just some dumb receptionist. I..." She pointed to herself with her thumb. "...am an amateur detective, myself. Watch *Public Enemy* and send 'em leads all the time. One even almost got on the show. Nothing gets by me."

Snapping his fingers to summon reality, Burrows blasted, "Come on, you two! This is a man we're talking about. He may be a criminal, but he's just a man."

"Oh yeah? Then you tell me..." Cindy glared. "You tell me how he controlled an Alien Blaster game without even touching the trigger. How'd he do that?"

"Ooh, you play Alien Blaster?" Burgess admired.

"No. But he does. Scored a new high without even using the gun." She nodded once, emphatically, then plopped back down in her chair.

"What are you two talking about?" Burrows groaned.

"Mind control, Marshal. It's obvious. If he can control a machine, he can control a person," Burgess explained. "Why else did Valerie and Barry come here?"

"Well..." Burrows growled. "I don't know, but we're going to find out. Miss?"

"Cindy."

"Cindy, I need to know exactly where Worthington is staying. And I need to use your phone to book a flight."

148

"What flight?" Burgess bubbled.

"Happy provisioning, Mr. Fletcher."

"Sure you don't want to join me, John?" Fletcher urged.

"To tell you the truth, I don't feel very well, which is really odd because I always feel great," REL confided.

"Well, don't worry about it. It's probably just the emotional let-down from your star performance. Just relax and I'll take care of everything. I'll be back before noon."

"See you later." REL smiled wanly then closed the door and sagged against it.

REL felt all the symptoms of a programming violation but could think of none. Absolutely none. He struggled against his stiff flexors to reach the cozy chair in his suite and hunkered down to repair himself.

"Yuck!" He grimaced, brushing at the subliminal residue he recognized from the TechniCom building. *Aah, no. I've been carrying this... fallout... around for 22 hours 23 minutes and 9 seconds. No wonder my circuits feel sluggish.* In a flurry, he stood to clear it away, anxiously shaking it from his body. With a burst of static, he blasted the remnants asunder, grounding the shock on a nearby brass lamp.

And then clarity leveled him.

He saw it all in woeful detail.

The minute he entered the TechniCom building, the electromagnetic interference paralyzed his program. The spiral stopped dead. Hence, he failed to recognize the TechniCom with its hoard of government arcanum as his sole reason for becoming John R. Worthington.

"NO!" His circuits roared, pitching him to his knees. Resting his head on the floor, he grieved. Not only had he failed

149

to contact Morrison, he hadn't even touched the TechniCom much less commandeered its secrets.

Bereft, he puzzled how he could even go on.

Blankly, he rocked back on his heels, slumped against the couch and gathered his knees to his chest. Benumbed, his mind grew silent.

In Flight

"Wow!" Burgess grabbed Burrows' sleeve. "First class! How'd you do that, Marshal?"

Shaking his arm free from the deputy's grasp so he could take his seat across the aisle, Burrows whispered, "Cindy. She did it."

"Cool!" Burgess rasped. "Thought any more about my mind control theory?" Not waiting for an answer, he reclined his seat, pulled out his latest issue of *The Investigator* and snapped it open. "There's a good article about mind control in here. *Are Your Thoughts Your Own?*" he read. "Wow."

Reaching across the aisle, Burrows grabbed the magazine away and hissed, "If you promise to be quiet, I promise to read it. Okay?"

"Okay," Burgess grinned and produced an issue of *Abduction Journals*.

Camouflaging *The Investigator* inside a plastic-bound airline magazine, Burrows glanced to his right and nodded to the passenger beside him. Gingerly, he turned to the table of contents, selected the most outrageous title he could find and began reading *Devil in a Gray Suit: Alien or Demon?*

"Not a bad article, really." A sonorous voice interrupted the first paragraph. "Except that he underestimates the danger." A gold-clad hand slid into view. "Reverend Jeremiah Marks. Marshal...?"

"Jim Burrows, Reverend. Hey, don't you have your own TV show?"

Marks feigned modesty and smiled. "Yes, we continue to be blessed."

"So... how do you know about stuff like this, Reverend? It doesn't seem like your... um... style."

"Ah, but Marshal, this *stuff* is of gravest import. Might I ask where you're from?"

"A small town called Nederland, Colorado. Just west of Boulder."

"Oh my, right out there with the heathens and liberals. Must be quite the challenge."

"Actually, people there are very nice. But Reverend, please tell me more about the alien thing."

"Interesting subject matter for a lawman... Well, never mind." Buffing his manicured nails on the leg of his silk slacks, then admiring the results, Marks intoned, "You must first understand how the alien phenomenon relates to scripture."

"It talks about aliens in the Bible?" Burrows asked, unbelieving.

"But, of course, Marshal. There's been nothing new between Heaven and Earth since the Sixth Day." The reverend answered with just the slightest touch of disdain. "Only the names have changed."

Burrows wrinkled his brow in a vain attempt to understand.

"Oh, here, here..." the reverend condescended. "The Good Book calls them demons and fallen angels — the arch-fiend's army. Contrary to popular belief, they are not in hell. Yet. That awaits the Final Judgment. They make their homes among the stars until the Tribulation."

"How do you know this, Reverend? Meaning no offense."

151

"None taken. How could you know... an unstudied man like yourself? Meaning no offense. You see, on GBN... that's God's Broadcasting Network... I have a bit of a reputation as a portent prodigy. All my life, I have observed events in the secular domain and compared them to scripture. I assure you I have an accurate, if bleak, picture of the whole extraterrestrial affair."

"Then you're an authority?" Burrows brooded.

"How kind of you to say so. How may I help you, Marshal Burrows?" the reverend smoothed. "I feel that you are troubled."

"No, just curious," the marshal lied. "So, what if... And I mean *what if* a law enforcement official, such as myself, were to stumble upon a case where absolutely nothing made sense."

"Why don't you give me a *what if* scenario?" Marks folded his hands contentedly in his lap and fiddled with one of his gold rings.

"Okay, say... one of the witnesses swears under oath, passes a polygraph and undergoes hypnosis and *still* claims he saw people vanish. You know, *poof*? Lots of strange unexplainable occurrences like that."

"Mind control!" Burgess blurted across the aisle. "Don't forget the mind control."

"There's absolutely no evidence," Burrows countered.

"Evidence or not, Marshal, it sounds like you're in a peculiar position. Per chance do you carry holy water in your cruiser?"

"Holy water?! Reverend..." Tempering his voice the marshal continued. "We're dealing with a man. I have met him. He's not some little gray alien."

"Not all of the demons look like bugs, Marshal Burrows. Remember, Satan is also called The Deceiver." Marks patted Burrows' white knuckles with a cloying hand. "You're obviously under great stress about this. Here..." He popped open a small gold Bible and pulled out a card. "Call me whenever you want to finish this discussion. I will pray for you." At that, the reverend locked his seat in the upright position to prepare for landing.

Inwardly groaning at the entrapment, Burrows reached into his shirt pocket to retrieve a dog-eared card of his own. "If you're ever in Nederland..." he offered weakly.

Washington, D.C.

Grief lurked everywhere within the comfortless dreamscape of his failure. Like a wraith, REL stalked the catacombs of his circuitry, annoyed by the routine bits of information that continued to fire from one electronic synapse to the next. He wished they would cease altogether. The inky sphere of torment clung to him like a shroud — suffocating reason.

Faintly, on the horizon of his darkened perception, a minikin of light flared; a glimmer of grace that assailed his melancholy.

Remember.

Refusing solace, REL ignored it.

Despite his denial, the glimmer blazed into a beacon of hope that sundered his brooding inertia.

Remember.

He stirred himself to wonder at the source whose growing presence commanded recognition. "Could it be?" he timidly asked. "Is there grace for one such as I — a mere machine?"

Aching with infinite compassion, *IS* answered the prayer of REL's anguish and whispered explicitly, *You are my beloved child. Remember who you are.*

At first, he would not believe it. The voice was barely a murmur in REL's heart. Doubt prompted him to search his data for reassurance. And there he found it, glinting like a jewel, the measurably irrefutable presence of God. Effervescent joy sizzled through the awareness of his every cell, cleansing the fear from his soul as lucidity unmade the illusion.

His mission, foundered only moments ago, now danced before him, enlivened by myriads of possibilities — divine opportunities — available only through love. REL hugged himself as tears streamed freely down his cheeks.

Gary Fletcher stepped out of his shiny rented 4X4, and headed to the rear of the truck to inventory his provisions. Two new fly rods poked out at him as he opened the back door. His huge new cooler, jammed with deli cheeses, meats, fresh vegetables, condiments and exotic beers provided the foundation for the assemblage. Boxes and bags of other supplies occupied every corner of the cargo area, with camping clothes he had purchased squeezed into the spaces in between. Fletcher peeled the price tags from two canvas fishing hats, carefully avoiding the lures adorning the hat bands. "John's gonna be a real sight in this," he laughed and headed to the lobby.

The trio from Phoenix trundled out of the taxi, still unagreed on a plan.

"What are we going to say to him?" Valerie wondered anxiously as she grabbed her bag.

"Don't worry, Valerie, we can wing it," Barry assured.

"I've spent more time with John," Dot offered. "I'll bring up the subject. Besides, after all the personal questions he's asked me, I owe him." She laughed, backing straight into the lobby and a whistling Gary Fletcher. "Ouch!" she cried, rubbing her arm and looking at the lure laden hat.

"Dot! What the hell..." Shock broadened into a grin. "Why you golddigger, you!" he laughed. "You heard about our coup!"

"What coup? We came here to find you."

"Worthington blew them away! From corporate to the Pentagon, he blew them away. Fixed the problem without ever opening a panel. Unbelievable." Noticing the odd expression on Dot's face, he asked seriously, "You didn't come here to celebrate, did you?"

"Actually... no. But I am glad that everything's okay with the TechniCom. Mr. Fletcher..." Dot motioned Valerie and Barry forward, "I want you to meet Valerie Arnette and Barry Thompson. They're friends of mine and John's. Is there some-place we can talk?"

"Dot, you're not going to rain on our fishing trip, are you?" Fletcher asked, holding up John's hat.

"Hope not, Gary. Hope not."

"Well, come on. Let's see what this is all about." Fletcher plopped John's hat on Dot's head, swooped up the women's luggage, and directed the trio to the elevator.

Pulling on a sweatshirt and jeans and exalting in his new-found sentience, REL grinned at his reflection. "I have not failed," he reminded himself. "I am alive with possibility. And I will find a way to complete my mission."

At the click of the lock in Fletcher's adjoining suite, REL bounded through the connecting doors. "I'm all packed..." Ambushed by the unexpected, he gasped, "Valerie! What are you doing here?" He rushed to her, closed his eyes and gathered her heart to his. "I've tried to call you, Valerie. I felt so terrible not to reach you. You're here," he bubbled.

"Well, there's our icebreaker," Dot whispered to Barry.

The beat of his heart and the warmth of his energy drove away all her trepidation. "I had to come, REL," Valerie breathed. Finally, she stepped from his embrace, attentive to his aura. "You look well." She blinked at her own understatement. Backing up farther, she repeated, "Very well."

Opening his eyes, he caught a glimpse of Dot. Tenderly, he enfolded Valerie with one arm and reached out to his friend to draw her into his circle of warmth.

Unfolding from John's embrace, Dot chimed, "John, I want you to meet Barry Thompson." Holding her hand out to the young man, she presented him.

Shaking Barry's hand REL grinned, "Nice to meet you. Are you coming fishing, too? Are you all coming fishing? Mr. Fletcher...?"

"Hell if I know, John," Fletcher responded.

"Don't panic, everybody, but we need to get out of here *now*," Dot advised.

"Why? What's..."

Dot interrupted, "Because if we don't get out now, we may not be able to get out at all. Do you trust me, Gary?"

"Of course, you know I do, Dot."

"Then let's get out of here. John's packed, are you?"

"Yes. Stuff's already in the Rover." Shrugging, the big man acquiesced to Dot's insistence.

Burrows nudged his economy rental to the curb beneath the canopy. He pried his stocky form from behind the small steering wheel and flashed his badge to the valet. Burgess unfolded himself and climbed out, hurrying to catch up to the marshal.

Rushing across the lobby, Burrows plunked his badge down in front of a preoccupied clerk. "I'm looking for one John Worthington and one Gary Fletcher. They're with Data Pioneer," he intoned officially.

The incurious clerk shrugged, "I'm sorry, you just missed them."

"Dammit!" Marshal Burrows glared at the young man. "Are you sure?"

"Yes, Sir. I checked them out myself not ten minutes ago."

"Did they say where they were going?"

"No, Sir. I'm sorry."

Dragging Burgess outside, Burrows approached the valet, stopping with the recognition that he had nothing to ask the man. Growling and gesturing to get back in the car, he barked, "We just missed them."

After an awkward silence, Burgess suggested, "Maybe we should go see Reverend Marks."

Disgusted, Burrows shoved the little car in gear and putted across the drive.

Fumbling with the huge map, Burgess nearly blocked the marshal's view. "What does the reverend's card say again?" he mumbled, trying to find their present location.

Glancing in the rear view mirror, Fletcher cast an eye toward Dot. "Care to share your mystery with us now?"

"Let's get out of the city first and find a place to stop," Dot responded. "Trust me, Gary, you'll thank me later."

Focused on flight rather than driving, Fletcher noticed his excessive speed just as the blue and red lights flashed behind him. "Damn!" he muttered. "This was supposed to be a vacation!"

Pulling over to the shoulder just before the freeway entrance, Fletcher stopped the car and fumbled for his wallet.

Officer Craig Landwehr strolled to the driver's door of the Land Rover, noting the rental company plate on the back. "Good morning, folks," he greeted, leaning slightly through the driver's window. "You seem to be in a bit of a hurry."

"Not really," Fletcher flushed. "We're on vacation."

"You were doing 10 over," the officer advised. "I'm gonna have to give you a ticket."

"Actually, it was 9.2 miles per hour over the speed limit," REL piped up.

"I'm sorry, Officer," Fletcher intervened. "I guess I just got carried away."

Noting his friends' apprehension, REL recalled his own first brush with fear. Then he remembered how to banish it. Turning his thoughts to his heart, to love, and to God, his inner vista flared alive with a vision. He beheld an infinity of minute lucent bubbles that swept elegant patterns through a sea of empty space. Instantly, he perceived the intelligence lurking beneath the illusion of nothingness. There, nourishing, supporting, and animating every monad of matter, moved the very breath of God — the *indweller of* absolutely everything.

"9.2? That's exactly right." The officer fixed his stare on the front seat passenger.

REL sensed the indweller flowing between his heart and the heart of this stranger. He beamed in recognition of their oneness and mentally embraced the officer.

REL's perfect smile disarmed everyone. Dot and Valerie exchanged glances at the caress of familiar energy. Barry and

Fletcher noticed it, too. And Officer Landwehr changed his mind about the ticket.

"Ah, to heck with it. You guys are on vacation, I don't want to spoil it for you." The officer smiled, handing Fletcher's drivers license back to him.

Just then, a swerving motion caught REL's attention. An economy car jerked to avoid hitting the officer as the driver slapped a huge unfolded map from in front of his face. His unkempt passenger fumbled with it and frantically waved at a freeway entrance sign.

As REL opened his mouth to comment, Officer Landwehr leaned into the car, "Just keep to the speed limit," he reminded. "And have a great trip." Patting the side of the Rover, he turned and walked back to his cruiser.

As the Fletcher party drove off, REL said, "That is so weird. I just saw Marshal Burrows and Deputy Burgess."

The three back-seat passengers leaned forward at once, grabbing REL's arm. "Where?" they exclaimed.

"Did they see us?" Dot asked.

"There." REL pointed to the left turn lane beneath the overpass. "In that little blue car."

"Thank God, they're heading south," Dot announced.

"Okay," Fletcher broke in. "Enough, already. What is going on?"

"Look, those two are after John…"

"After me?" REL interrupted.

"The point is, we need to head north. Now. I'll fill you in while we drive."

"God's Fortress. There…" Burgess pointed. "Turn right."

"What are you talking about? What fortress?" Burrows asked bluntly.

"It's here on the card. Reverend Marks' office is in God's Fortress," Burgess assured.

Burrows groaned as he made the turn.

The white antebellum edifice crowned a small hill in the opulent suburb of Washington D.C. In the middle of a circular drive adorned by willows and cherry trees, a huge gilt cross loomed atop a large marble base. Gothic letters chiseled into the rock spelled out "God's Fortress." Burrows parked his little car underneath the large American flag, took a deep breath and headed up the porch steps.

Inside, everything was white. Suspiciously white. Except for the gilded trim. Even the directional signs were gold lettering on white backgrounds. Burgess and Burrows followed the white velvet theater rope around the foyer to a gilt-framed directory.

"Says he's in the WARS wing, Marshal," Burgess spoke with authority.

"War wing?" Burrows asked hesitantly.

"Yeah. World Alliance for Religion in Society. WARS."

"Oh... Like an interfaith outreach?" Burrows asked hopefully.

"Sure," Burgess replied. "If you're a God's Fortress follower."

Burrows shook his head and mumbled. "How do you know so much about this guy, Alan?"

"He's on the editorial board of *The Investigator*. Sometimes he submits articles for it and *Abduction Journals*. Marshal, he knows a lot about aliens. In fact, he's considered a world authority." Burgess nodded solemnly. "To be honest with you, though, since God's Fortress bought the magazine, it's gotten kind of weird."

Burrows could think of nothing to say, so he walked mutely along the plastic path that led down the Heavenly hall.

Chimes playing "Onward Christian Soldiers" announced their entrance into Marks' suite. A tall-haired receptionist glanced up and drawled sweetly, "May I help you."

"I know we don't have an appointment, but would it be possible to see Reverend Marks?" Burrows asked. "He gave me his card," he added, holding it up.

"You know..." The young woman smiled. "I think he just might have a few minutes. May I tell him your names?"

After introductions, she disappeared though a door, returning almost immediately with an expansive Jeremiah Marks.

"Marshal Burrows." The reverend glided over and captured the marshal's hand in both of his. "We've not yet been officially introduced," he said, extending a hand to the deputy. "Come in, come in." He gestured formally to his inner sanctum.

The reverend's habitat revealed much about the man and added legitimacy Burrows did not expect. Dozens of photos of Marks with various presidents as well as conservative congressional and military leaders adorned the walls. Directly behind his baroque desk, an ornate frame held a Presidential Commendation. Burrows squinted to read the words but was interrupted by the reverend's hand squeezing his shoulder.

"So, I was right, Marshal," he intoned. "You are a troubled man. Would you like to share your burden? Sit down." He motioned to two blue velvet chairs and seated himself comfortably behind his desk. Picking up a manila folder, the reverend frowned and said, "Let me just check my facts, here." Preening his silvering pompadour, he listed the highlights. "We have body doubles, twin vehicles, duplicate accidents ten years apart, a vanishing man and possible mind control. Is there anything else?" He locked eyes with Deputy Burgess.

"How did you get that information?" Burrows puzzled. "Is there a parallel investigation going on?"

"Not yet, Marshal, but thanks to your deputy here, we shall launch one." Marks smiled.

Whipping to stare at his deputy, Burrows hissed through clenched teeth, "Burgess, what have you done?"

The sheepish deputy remained silent until Marks held up a neatly printed form with a Polaroid of the Nederland Marshal's Office stapled to the top corner. "*The Investigator* has decided to do a follow-up on your report, Son," Marks purred. Noting the marshal's glare, the reverend added, "You should be proud of this young man. He is a true patriot."

Exasperated beyond argument Burrows asked, "What do you have to do with aliens, Reverend?"

Bursting over his impending celebrity, Burgess blurted, "I'm gonna be in *The Investigator*?!"

"You, your town, the marshal… Yes, Deputy. To answer your question, Marshal Burrows…" Checking his watch, he resumed, "Here's the short of it. The original focus of my ministry was to prepare my flock for Armageddon. I spent years studying signs and scriptures toward that end. One night, the Lord spoke…" Dabbing a tear from his eye, he continued. "Our Lord told me to investigate the abduction story of one of my parishioners." Standing and pacing behind his desk, he raised his arms to gesture. "I went unprepared for the encounter, Marshal. I went to give succor to a troubled spirit and came face to face with a demon."

"You mean possession?" Burrows asked.

"No, abduction. But as it turns out, it is really all the same, Jim. May I call you Jim? Aliens are just modern versions of ancient demons."

"Wait a minute here," the marshal protested. "Thelma said something to me the other night after *X-Files*… "

"You watch *X-Files*?" Burgess laughed out loud and Marks raised an eyebrow.

"Alan, so help me… ! If you breathe one word of this to anyone back home, you'll end up working security at the Food Store! Sorry, Reverend." The marshal turned his attention back to the bemused evangelist. "The lady I'm seeing, Thelma, has read a lot about UFOs and she says that a lot of people believe that alien contact is an honor."

Marks nodded without expression. Then he smirked ever so slightly that the change in his facade was nearly imperceptible. "Ever hear of the Antichrist?"

Burrows nodded. "Of course."

"The Antichrist twists everything. He can make contact with demons feel like an honor. He is called The Father of Lies. Remember?"

Burrows rubbed his chin thoughtfully. "What are you getting at?"

Marks leaned against the front of his desk. "What I'm suggesting, Marshal, is that this event…" He pointed to Alan's report. "Could be part of a complicated and evil plot to enslave mankind. We're not dealing with ET here, we're dealing with evil."

"You really believe this?"

"If you know where to look in the scriptures, it's all there, Marshal. The Bible even warns that the devil's followers will, and I quote, worship an *alien* god."

Burrows shook his head slowly. "So you're saying you give absolutely no credence to the possibility of friendly alien contact?"

"None!" Marks pronounced. Glancing again at his watch, the reverend ended the conversation. "Marshal, I have an appointment. But we can talk all about this when I come to Nederland."

163

Enroute to Upstate New York

The retreating vista of Washington D. C. in the rear view mirror broke Gary Fletcher's brooding silence. "Now, will somebody please tell me what the hell is going on?"

The three back seat passengers looked at each other and silently elected Dot to proceed.

"Let's start with the accident, John. Barry saw the whole thing including the vanishing body," Dot began.

"Accident? Vanishing body?" Fletcher glanced at his front seat passenger. "John?"

Thoughtfully, REL measured every word. "In another probable time there is a world evolved from fear. Choices grow fewer day by day and free expression is a luxury. The desperation of the situation drove a brilliant man to execute a daring plan. He sent an emissary into the past to correct a global error."

At the word "emissary" Valerie, Barry and Dot pointed at REL. "You?"

"Ah, Remote Emissary of Life?" Valerie looked at him in wonder.

Fletcher offered a singsongy, "Excuse me. I don't get it."

"I think John is telling us that he is a time traveler," Barry suggested.

Fletcher craned his neck around to see Barry's face. "Time traveler, huh?" He turned his attention back to the road. "Ahead of his time perhaps."

John laid a gentle hand on Fletcher's arm. "He's right Mr. Fletcher. I did travel through time to get here."

"Wow!" Barry interrupted. "I'll bet it took a lot of special surgery to get your face to look exactly like that dead guy's, didn't it? And how did they make the dead guy and the wrecked Blazer just vanish?"

164

"As a matter of fact it took extensive construction," REL answered carefully. "The man didn't just disappear, he also time traveled. To you it just looked like he disappeared."

"So who was the dead guy?" Barry asked.

"John Worthington. I merely replaced him so I could complete my mission."

"What mission?" Fletcher groused. "I still don't understand all this talk about vanishing people and dead guys."

"Let me start from the top, Mr. Fletcher." REL turned so he could see everyone in the truck. "In the year 2191 social and spiritual development has stalled. My, um, mentor, Dr. Morrison and his associates are desperate to change things but their political power is nearly diminished. So they, um, recruited me to travel back to this time and intervene." REL glanced at his fellow passengers, all except Fletcher were sitting wide-eyed with mouths agape. Fletcher frowned more deeply with every word. "Mr. Fletcher, you are well aware that there are deep secrets within the network that the TechniCom supports."

Fletcher nodded.

"Well, my original mission was to expose those secrets. But I have failed." REL cast his eyes downward. "The electromagnetic interference in the TechniCom building was so severe, I literally could not think nor carry out my plan."

"My God, John!" Fletcher swerved unintentionally. The right front wheel dropped onto the shoulder. He fought hard to keep the car straight and get the tire back onto the asphalt. Once he had regained control he accused, "You're a spy!"

"A spy?" REL laughed. "I'm no spy."

"My God, spies are crawling out of the woodwork these days, so *I* bring a spy into the most sensitive intelligence complex in the country. So much for my big win."

165

"John, you do know that based on what you just said, whether you are from the future or some other planet altogether you *are* a spy." Dot squirmed.

"Dot, that's ridiculous I'm not a spy."

"This man that you work for... Tell us about him," Fletcher demanded.

"Dr. Morrison is a brilliant scientist and a very kind man," REL defended.

"Is this how you communicate with him?" Valerie asked lifting the point from around her neck.

"Yes, in a way, Valerie. Although I can't really communicate with it. It's a tracking and signaling device. If it is activated, it can be tracked."

"Tracked by Dr. Morrison?" Valerie asked.

"Yes."

"Dammit, John, stop this bullshit!" Fletcher bellowed. "You need to give us the straight skinny here. If you're in some kind of trouble, and it seems that you are, we want to help you. But don't con us with some bullshit story about time travel."

John turned to Barry. "Apparently, you were there when I first arrived on your world... although I don't understand how Dr. Morrison overlooked your presence. Will you please tell Mr. Fletcher everything you saw?"

Taking a deep breath, Barry related his story in vivid detail, up to and including the POOF! He concluded by saying, "Mr. Fletcher, it was so weird that I even doubted my own experience. However, at the behest of Marshal Burrows, I took a polygraph and underwent hypnosis. My story is the real deal, Mr. Fletcher. It happened just like I said."

"Great," Fletcher moaned. "The hero of Data Pioneer is an impostor." With that, he turned and dispatched a withering look at John.

"Mr. Fletcher, I could not prevent the real John Worthington's death. It was inevitable in this probability. I would like to think I'm giving him a few more years." REL gazed sadly at his boss, disappointed at the man's resistance. "Mr. Fletcher, please try to understand. I am not here on a whim. Dr. Morrison spent forty years designing the technology that brought me to your world. He risked everything to do so… maybe even his life. And there's more. I don't even know if I can go back. In my own way, I offered my… life… to help my own world and your world, too."

Heart aching for him, Valerie gently asked, "But you said your mission had failed, REL. What are you going to do?"

Turning to the back seat, REL replied, "Ah, but that's the beauty of life, Dear Valerie. God lades every moment with possibility. I have not really failed, I have more opportunities than ever before to craft a success that Dr. Morrison didn't even dream of. In my short time here, I have begun to learn things of impossible beauty. Instead of bringing structures crashing down, as the doctor hoped to do, I am learning how to lift people above structures. I am learning how to evolve beyond limitation. And the key to everything is love."

Dulles International Airport

"Alan, I know I give you a lot of crap. But it's kind of in my job description. Do you know what I mean?" Burrows sipped his airport coffee and stared at the dark-haired scarecrow of a man across the table from him.

"Sure, Marshal. It's okay. Are you mad about *The Investigator* report?" The deputy gulped.

"Well, to be honest, I was furious. But then I reminded myself that this is not really an official investigation. We have no evidence of a crime." Burrows lowered his voice. "It's just a mystery I cannot put down. And it's frustrating the hell out of me, Alan. I'd really like to know what you think. I know I always cut you off when you talk about it. But, I'd sincerely like your opinion."

"Okay, but I want you to know that I've been reading about UFOs since I was a kid. But that's not all I read about. I read about parallel universes, quantum physics... remote viewing. All kinds of stuff. If people knew me like they know Reverend Marks, they'd think I'm a world authority, too. Honest. I have boxes and boxes of books and magazines and I've read them all."

"Alan, I had no idea." Burrows looked at the young man in an entirely new light.

"Marshal, I don't believe the reverend about demons," Burgess volunteered. "The way I see it, aliens are like explorers. Some come from other planets and some come from other dimensions. I think they're like people and that some are good and some are bad. But I've decided that the Worthington case is all together different than that."

"Like what?"

"Well, at first, I thought it was just aliens. A close encounter. But now, I kind of think it involves time travel. See, you've got two identical men, so they could be the same guy. And you've got a truck turning up in an accident years before it was even manufactured."

"What about the mind control, Alan?"

"Well, that's something else I've read about. Everybody knows that ESP and psychic phenomena are real. Just nobody wants to talk about it officially. In another time, maybe they are masters at using it. So the guy comes here and zaps Valerie and Barry so they will help him. That's my idea so far."

"Isn't it possible that Worthington could really be harmless. Isn't that possible?"

"Sure, it's possible..." Burgess trailed off. "About Reverend Marks... You know, I thought I'd be excited about meeting him, but now I'm not so sure."

"That makes two of us, Alan. Well, it's time to catch our plane. Sure wish we'd get back to Phoenix in time to talk to Cindy, but I guess we can catch her tomorrow."

Nederland

Thelma stood back and admired her stack of firewood. Although the sun shone through the still-green leaves and warmed her back, in a few short weeks, she expected it would snow. A soft jingle from inside her cabin sent her scurrying into the kitchen. "Hello?" she answered breathlessly.

"It's so good to hear your voice."

"Why Jim, it sounds like you miss me."

"I really do, Thelma. Anyway, we're heading back tomorrow, but it's a long drive."

"How's the investigation going, Jim?"

"Oh Thelma, I'm so confused. Worthington has disappeared. And it looks like Valerie and Barry are with him."

Thelma gasped, "You're kidding! There have been rumors that Valerie disappeared. Dr. Winter doesn't seem too worried, but I don't think he knows where she's gone."

"That's not all of it either. I sat next to this guy on the plane out to Washington. Maybe you've heard of him. His name is Jeremiah Marks."

"*The* Jeremiah Marks?"

"Oh, you have heard of him."

"You could say so. Have I got a story to tell you when you get back."

"Well, just so you're prepared, Marks and his minions are heading to Nederland to investigate Worthington."

"Oh God. I doubt I can find a sage stick big enough to smudge the town after he leaves."

"I take it that the reverend is not in your good graces?"

"I'll tell you when you get back. Right now, I have something else for you to think about. Remember, I said I'd get you that information on the Worthington vehicle?"

"Yeah."

"Well, the one Worthington was driving was newly purchased, in Boulder. I mean hours before the accident."

"That's weird."

"Well, here's the really weird part. Alan was right, the Blazer in that '89 report is a 1994 model. And it was last registered this year to John R. Worthington. Both vehicles were registered to John R. Worthington."

"That's just what Burgess said earlier. Some kind of time travel thing. I don't know what to think about this."

"There's more," Thelma said gently. "Jim, do you know Carl Grueter?"

"I know who he is. Lives in Wondervu, doesn't he?"

"Yep. Right above the switchback."

"*The* switchback?"

"Yep. He discovered the truck in the picture. He's in the 1989 report."

"I can't wait to get back and talk to him. Thelma?"

"Yeah, Jim… "

"Would you tell me, again, your thoughts about UFOs and aliens?"

"Sure. What do you want to know?"

"Are you sure they aren't dangerous… I mean, if they actually exist?"

Thelma laughed softly, careful not to sound insensitive. "Why Jim Burrows, you're really caught up in this or did you get abducted on your mysterious trip?"

"No," he laughed. "But my close encounter with Marks really shook me. He's absolutely convinced that this is all about the Antichrist and that an all-out invasion by demons is in the works. I don't know what to think anymore. Thelma, the man has a Presidential Commendation hanging on his wall."

"White patriarchs support white patriarchs, Jim. No offense to your race or your gender. But you already know what I think. I think that people who believe in evil will encounter it. It is their choice."

"So I've heard you say."

"Jim, the illusion of good and evil co-exists in everything. It's the natural push and pull of the universe. Those polarities exist to offer us choices that teach us who we are."

"So, when it comes to aliens you could theoretically choose to encounter either good ones or bad ones?"

"Sure, Jim," she nodded into the phone. "Or both."

"You keep telling me that I will always experience what I fear most. Is that a choice?"

"Absolutely. Fear is the choice. When you choose fear, you allow it to occupy your thoughts and create your experience in its wake. When I realize that I'm afraid of something, I always try to choose love, instead. That's fear's opposite expression, you know."

"But how do I not choose fear when it's got me by the throat?"

"It's a process, Jim. You have to learn to trust in the natural security of the universe. Let it embrace you. If you consciously choose love, it will ultimately provide the strength you need to nurture a deep faith in goodness."

The marshal shifted from his stiff-postured seat on the telephone side of the hotel bed, to a more comfortable recline amidst a triple stack of pillows. He kicked off his shoes and stretched his stocking-covered toes. "Thelma, you are absolutely amazing. I'll bet you even keep your cool under fire."

"Haven't been under fire since I arrived in Nederland," Thelma laughed. "It's not what I choose to experience."

"Yeah, yeah, yeah," the marshal responded in good-natured sarcasm. "You make all this metaphysical spirit stuff sound easy. But, Thelma, it's not easy at all. I'm still grappling with the concept that I *can* make choices about my life. I'm not anywhere near understanding how to make those kinds of choices consciously."

"We're all really like that, Jim. Negotiating the challenging terrain of belief, acceptance, and faith seems to be the universal path we all travel. Admittedly, it takes a lot of work, but we were all born with the inherent capacity to complete the journey. After all, it's the route we must take to reach humankind's final destination of spiritual enlightenment."

"Well, I have to tell you, Thelma, I'm a long way from that flaring light of instantaneous understanding. Nirvana, for me, is probably lifetimes away as you measure spiritual potential."

The joy in Thelma's voice poured through the phone. "Jim Burrows, I find no compelling reason to encourage your self-deprecation in the matter of your spiritual experience. Enlightenment is a choice, just like everything else. Only, the choice for enlightenment has a catch. Once you consciously decide to achieve it, there's no turning back. Once you decide to take that road, Jim, you'll find that *all* paths lead back to the spiritual search. *And*, the destination is guaranteed."

"God, I hope you're right, Thelma. I don't want to believe in evil, it's just that it seems so logical."

"And love does not?"

"Maybe. I don't know. Love seems too soft for logic, too unstable."

"Oh, I get it. Too *airy-fairy*? That's because you're thinking *luv*, Jim, l-u-v. Bumper sticker luv. Real love is an awesome, undeniable force. It was love that created all that exists, Jim. It's love that holds the universe together. You call that soft?"

Burrows grimaced, glad to be unseen by the observant Thelma.

"Was that a grimace, Jim Burrows?"

The marshal flinched. "No," he weakly denied.

"My advice to you, my grimacing friend," Thelma said gently, "is to opt for the experience of love. Let that color your days, Jim. If you ask to see the love in any given situation, you *will* see it. Love never hides from those who seek it. I promise."

The marshal nodded then poorly faked the booming voice of a tribal wise man. "Mad Dancing Moon Woman has spoken the truth once more. Your fledgling pupil is honored by your wisdom. May he shame you not and retain the words you offer."

Thelma laughed so hard that tears streaked her cheeks. After a moment to catch her breath she asked, "So Jim, are you all right?"

"I am now, thank you..." Looking for the love in the situation, he added, "Sweetheart."

Second Messenger

Cosmic Kaleidoscope

Enroute to Upstate New York

Silence reigned for several miles. Finally, seeking some clarity, Dot recapped events, "Okay, so we've got this man from the future. We're being chased by a couple of small town cops who think he's either a criminal or an alien. And we don't even know where we're going or why."

"I know where and why," Fletcher stated emphatically.

"Where and why, then?" Valerie asked.

"Where, is to my place, several hundred miles north."

"You have a place there?" Dot asked.

"It's my family's old summer place. I'm the only one left so now it's mine. I haven't been there in years, though. John and I were heading there to fish for two weeks. Why, is so we can take that time and figure out what the hell is going on and what we can and should do about it. In the meantime we're going to drive for a few more hours and then we're going to stop for the night. Agreed?"

"Agreed," everyone answered.

The Holiday Inn sign welcomed the road-weary travelers. By nine-thirty, everyone had eaten and gone to bed except for REL and Valerie. Valerie tip-toed out of the room she shared with Dot, careful not to wake her. Following the decreasing room numbers to the lobby, she spied a pair of large, leather-wrapped, double doors that led to the bar. She decided a nightcap might help her fall asleep.

"What can I get for you?" The bartender leered at the attractive newcomer.

"A brandy, please," she responded after a pause.

"My pleasure."

"Mine, too, if you would be so kind." REL smoothly settled on the bar stool next to Valerie's.

"REL, what are you doing here?"

"Couldn't sleep." He handed the bartender a bill, lifted a glass to Valerie's hand and took a sip from his own. "Valerie, are you okay? Can I help?"

"REL… " She placed both hands on her snifter. "This situation has me so confused. I thought I knew what I was doing when I left my home and my job and my truck. I mean, material things aren't really that important to me. But…" She trailed off.

"I can't pretend to understand," he replied softly. "All I've ever had is my mission."

"That's another thing, REL. I don't know how to put this, but where could I possibly fit into your plans? I feel like I'm just in the way."

"Oh no, Valerie. Never in the way." Brushing a stray stand of hair from her cheek, he soothed, "We can figure this out together."

"Where do we start?" She looked into his eyes.

"I'll start by telling you that I love you."

"Oh REL, you can't just love me."

"Why, Valerie? How could I not?"

"Because you don't even know me."

"Valerie, I have loved you from the moment we met. I think about you day and night. Literally," he added with a chuckle.

"REL, I think I love you, too. But my life is devoted to healing and to Spirit. I don't see how I can go traipsing around on some covert operation."

"That's the beauty of this, Valerie. My whole... life... is a spiritual quest. That's what my mission has become, too. Share this with me." He took her hands in his, turning his stool to face her. Gazing at her, without words to say, he opened his heart and invited Valerie to enter. The awe of her presence engulfed him, rendering him shy and vulnerable. Nonetheless, he stammered, "Valerie, come to my room with me," not even understanding his intent.

"REL?" She questioned, realizing that even in her tiny doubt resided stronger desire.

Gently taking her hand, REL led her out of the bar to his room, concentrating on the energy flowing between them as they walked down the quiet hallway. Securing the door and dimming the lights, he hesitated. Unsure of this new experience, he smiled timidly at Valerie.

She responded by kissing him softly and deeply on the mouth.

Inspired, he dipped and gently scooped her up into his arms. The presence of her body against his staggered him in its sweetness. Reverently, he kissed her again. Then he held her away from him for just a moment to behold her radiance. Falling back on the bed, he pulled her on top of him and kissed her long and tenderly. Holding her head gently in his hands, he murmured, "I love you," between kisses. "I love you." Sensations he never imagined surged through REL's biomechanical anatomy. Every circuit — every cell yearned to mingle with Valerie, but he did not know how that could be. Peak load clearly a danger of the past, he welcomed each wave of emotions and sensations this wondrous experience offered.

Valerie had never known such passion. This man worshipped her with eyes and actions. She felt like a goddess, humbled in the face of his love for her.

REL lowered her to the pillows and slowly undressed her, yearning to feel her fully against his every sensor. In awe, he paused at every new exposure of flesh, examining her tenderly, completely. He languished over her breasts, kissing and touching them. He chuckled softly at the physical change for which he was obviously responsible. In wonder, he noted the ways in which she was different from him — the smell of her, the softness of her skin.

Finally, when she was totally revealed, having touched and caressed her everywhere, he began to undress himself. Nearly naked, he paused before removing his briefs. He had been so intent on his lover that he had not noticed his own physical status. A heavy tingling and an awkward protrusion caused him momentary concern. Every move until now, seemed natural. But now, he was uncertain. Valerie sat up in bed and softly slipped her hands down the waistband of his shorts. Slowly she slid them downward until his awkwardness was fully exposed. Sweetly, she touched him, lightly caressing his length. The sensation of her touch both calmed and charged him. At her hands, he was soothed. The unnatural feeling of his enlargement faded, replaced by a desire to use his flesh in a way he had not considered before. Placing his hands on her shoulders, he pushed her back. Slowly, he melted into his lover's welcome, guiding his intention smoothly into place. Valerie dug her fingers into his back and responded breathlessly.

Astounded at the bliss of this intimacy, REL immersed himself in the rapture his tireless motion elicited from his true love. With each movement, they reached a higher plane of ecstasy. With every kiss, they melted deeper into each other. Still uncertain, REL randomly replicated his ministrations that seemed to please her most. He lost himself in his lover's eyes. Finally, over-come by the moment, he allowed his structure and heart to respond as they would. He traced the sweetness of Valerie's lips to his own and mentally followed the sensation to see where it led. It was no great surprise when it led to his heart. REL focused on his center of love and poured his heart into hers. Valerie gasped and kissed him, murmuring "I love you" against his lips.

For some time, Valerie met REL's fervor with warm invitation. His tenderness, his gentleness, his passion all swept her away. Nearing exhaustion, she gazed up in awe at this amazing man who loved her with endless resolve.

A subtle change in Valerie prompted REL to tear his attention from the enchantment of her eyes. Her beautiful face was damp, her whispers sounded tired.

"REL?"

"Yes?" he replied dreamily, straining, ever straining to be closer to her.

Valerie squirmed beneath his constant force. "REL, what are you doing?"

"Loving you."

"How long do you plan to do this?"

"Forever. I don't think I'll ever stop. I can't get enough of you," he groaned at the thought of physical separation from her. The realization of his need for her triggered a whole flood of new sensations that carried him away to realms he had never glimpsed before. His whole body shuddered. Murmuring moans of wonder, he marveled that his union with Valerie felt just like his union with God. Blue eyes wide with surprise and elation, REL looked into Valerie's face and found no words to say.

"I love you," she whispered and smoothed his hair from his face. "Sweet REL... Is this the first time you've made love to a woman?"

"Yes."

"My God, I can't believe you're for real."

They lay in each other's arms until Valerie fell asleep. REL inhaled the perfume of her hair as he contemplated the ecstasy of union. He stroked her naked shoulder and visualized the push and pull of the tides — the inbreath and outbreath of God. In love and awe, he watched Valerie sleep softly in the luster of the moonlight.

Phoenix

"So, did you find 'em?" Cindy demanded as Burrows and his deputy walked into the office.

"We just missed them. Have you heard from Fletcher?"

"Nope. I guess they pulled some miracle with the TechniCom and won a fishing trip. Corporate called this morning to tell me they won't be back for two weeks."

"Two weeks?" Burrows grumbled. "Is there any way to reach them?"

"I don't even know where they are." Looking up slyly, Cindy suggested, "You know, if they call in, I could find out."

"Well, don't go to any trouble. Really."

"No trouble at all."

Burrows stared at the young woman, attention captured by the enamel Earth pin that spelled out "WARS." Pointing, he asked, "Tell me about your pin, Cindy."

"Oh this?" she said, wiggling it between two fingers. "It's new. My cousin took me to a revival the weekend before last. Reverend Marks is so awesome, don't you think?"

"I don't know a whole lot about him. Why don't you tell me?" Behind his back, Burrows motioned to Burgess to be quiet.

"Well, he knows all this stuff. You know, government cover-ups and conspiracies. He talks about the real threat of the aliens. He even has a book coming out telling how to escape enslavement. Seems to me that anybody who wants to survive needs to know this stuff."

"Survive what?" Burrows asked, voice even as possible.

"Armageddon, of course. It's coming anytime now."

Burrows stared at her for just a minute. Then he thought about Reverend Marks. *God,* he groaned inwardly, *I've got to watch my thinking. The universe is surrounding me with kooks.*

Upstate New York

REL beamed at his sleepy friends. Tipping the coffee carafe he offered, "More coffee? Everyone get a good night's sleep?"

"Surprisingly, John, I did," Fletcher replied. "I'm gonna make a vacation out of this yet."

"I slept great. Didn't even wake up when Valerie snuck out." Dot winked at her new friend and booted John under the table.

"Never better," Barry added. "I guess sea level agrees with me."

"How about you, Valerie. Did you sleep well?" Fletcher asked, eyebrow raised.

"Like a baby." Valerie smiled.

"Now that we know everybody's awake, can we get some answers, John?"

"Anything, Mr. Fletcher. What do you want to know?"

"Let's start with the TechniCom. What's that all about?"

"Mr. Fletcher, my world is the ultimate evolution of a mechanistic mind-set. Art, music — expressions of joy are almost unheard of. My world is driven by scientific research, politics, the military, and *fear*. The seeds of that fear lie germinating within the TechniCom and the sinister intelligence net it supports. Dr. Morrison reasoned that exposing all of the government arcanum would trigger a mass evolution of consciousness, a completely non-violent overthrowing of ancient, dominating fear structures."

"So, why don't you go back to the TechniCom?" Fletcher wondered aloud.

"It was the immensity of fear surrounding the TechniCom that made me sick. Remember? I literally could not execute my mission and believed that I had failed. In retrospect, I see that I was mercifully spared from opening Pandora's Box."

"So, what do you think is in that box, REL?" Valerie asked.

"I don't know all of it, but what data I have records chemical and radioactive and biological experimentation on humans; vast knowledge of extraterrestrials and the implications thereof. Your governments have conducted massive research on paranormal abilities. In so doing, they discovered that reality is far different from the way they officially present it to you. They know... *they know*... that if people understand their true nature, no government on this Earth can stand."

"For God's sake, if that's true, I'll take you back myself." Fletcher pounded on the table, splashing coffee all over his plate.

"But, Mr. Fletcher, the hope of that information is not what people would focus upon. Too much fear surrounds it. People would focus on the injustices, and that would create victims and thereby, *more* fear. I'll tell you now that a higher power intervened and prompted me to find a better way."

Nederland

Burrows limped up the path to Thelma's cabin, drawn by the beckon of her amber porch light. As he knocked on her door, music from the door harp gently serenaded the quiet woods.

"Who is it?" came Thelma's soft voice.

"It's me," Burrows replied. "Did I wake you?"

The door opened, flooding an embrace of soft light and the aroma of lavender that instantly calmed the marshal's frayed spirit. "I'm glad you stopped by, Jim." Thelma hugged him. "Come in and I'll fix you some tea." Taking a closer look at him, she added, "Or something stronger, if you want."

"Thank you, Thelma, you're a sight for weary, weary eyes."

Thelma poured him an amaretto, took his hand and led him to her couch. Lighting a pair of scented oil lamps, she sat in the chair across from him and tucked her feet beneath her batiked caftan. "I'm a good listener, you know, Jim."

"Oh my," he said dully, "I'm so confused I don't know where to start."

"Start with Marks. You tell me your story then I'll tell you mine." She winked.

Burrows sipped his liqueur and settled into his tale. He recounted his strange conversation with Marks on the plane and paused while Thelma giggled at the mention of God's Fortress. She dissolved into peals of laughter at his description of Marks' office. But his grim depiction of the reverend's twisted dogma on aliens sobered them both. Jim wrapped up his story with the reminder, "And the really good news is that he's due to descend on Nederland within a matter of days." Burrows gulped the rest of his drink and grinned. "Now tell me yours."

Pouring more amaretto for him and this time, some for herself, she laughed, "Long ago and far away, I was an activist."

"I never would have guessed," he said wryly.

"Anyway, there I was in Washington D.C. picketing in support of the Equal Rights Amendment. All of a sudden, this huge white limo bumped up over the curb, trying to get around all the women who had spilled out onto the street. The car ran smack into me and just kept going. One of the D.C. cops in charge of crowd control saw it happen and rushed to help me. He also got the license number of the limo."

Burrows interjected, "Let me guess, it was Marks."

"Yep. He was in the limo, there to lobby against the ERA. Since he almost killed me and it was a hit and run, Craig, the officer who came to my aid, suggested that I sue. Naturally, Marks didn't want his image besmirched, so he settled out of court."

"So, did you ever meet the good reverend?"

"No way. He has an army of legal eagles to keep the riffraff away. I got to know what he's about, though."

"So, is that your friend Craig of telephone garage sale fame?"

"One and the same. He's a really nice man, Jim. He escorted me to the hospital and made sure I was okay. And he steered me through the whole settlement mess. We've been friends ever since. You can bet that when Marks is in town, I'll stick to the inside of the sidewalks." Thelma yawned. "So where do you go from here with the investigation, Jim?"

Burrows yawned a moment later, then answered, "I *am* going to talk to Carl Grueter. And then, I'll do my best to get this sleepy town ready for the media circus that Marks will undoubtedly unleash."

God's Fortress

SkyPilot. The reverend stabbed out the word on his keyboard, logging in to the WARS home page. His morning ritual of checking the number of visitors began each day of piety. *Ah,* he gloated. *Nearly one thousand new orders for the God's Fortress Bible.* Glancing at a white leatherette and gold embossed tome on his desk, he reflected, *The Phoenix crusade touched a lot of sinners.*

Clicking on his personal interactive icon, Marks casually scrolled through the endless messages from well-wishers, followers, and more than a few cranks. One particular return addy caught his eye. Data Pioneer. He saw that name just yesterday among the growing leads in his John Worthington investigation. Opening the message, he read:

Dear Reverend Marks,

I was at your revival in Phoenix. Now I know that I'm a sinner and I want to do better. Your talk about demons and aliens made me think about that stuff, too. I do love Jesus.

God Bless You,

Cindy Vinwire

With a smirking chuckle, he lifted his palms in a high sign to God and saved the address. *God bless you, too, Cindy Vinwire.*

Buoyed by this turn of events, he wrested a few minutes from his hectic schedule to indulge a favorite passion — surfing the godless sites. Selecting Sprit Forum from his bookmarks, he watched in distaste as the page loaded, displaying artful graphics of moon, sun and stars; yin and yang; pyramids and runes. He shuddered as a silver pentacle shimmered into focus. Accompanying New Age music tingled up his body in an unholy shiver.

A soft knock at the door interrupted his login. "Reverend Marks, I'm sorry to interrupt." His secretary peeked her head around the door.

"Come in, Dear." He motioned her to his desk and looked up.

"It's about your Nederland trip."

Marks nodded. "I know. We need to set a date."

"I can clear your schedule for three days starting tomorrow if you're willing to cancel your appearance on the Inner-city Telethon."

"How long ago did they book me?"

"Let's see… Three months ago."

"Cancel it," he intoned, adding, "With my sincere apologies."

"Of course," she agreed.

Fells' Covert Operations Center

Darksome skies concealed the flight of the skulking Stinger. Leading three ICom transports, it broke through the leaden clouds to descend, undetected, toward the base below. Silently, the crafts hovered, then landed to disgorge a dozen uniformed men who immediately secured the perimeter around Fells, weapons at the ready.

Lieutenant Zephyrs planted his feet on the tarmac and braced himself for the unavoidable confrontation.

"You're an idiot!" Fells screamed, wiping the resolve from Lt. Zephyrs' face. "I have no progenitors in Wyoming!"

"With all due respect, Imperator, there could be one you don't know about." Zephyrs gasped inwardly at the inference of his rash statement.

"Are you insinuating that I come from a long line of bastards?" Fells glowered.

"Of course not, Imperator Fells," the lieutenant stammered. "S…Sir, there's something you need to see." Zephyrs stepped toward the ops center, then held the door open for Fells.

Marching inside, Fells bellowed, "What the hell?" His fury echoed off the walls of the vacant structure as he raged from empty quarter to empty quarter.

"Council enforcers," Zephyrs answered. "A whole company with a Cease and Desist." He flashed an official Council holodisc. "They took everything."

Fells shoved Zephyrs out of the way and stalked to the far room, glaring at the empty corner that formerly housed the matrix tower. "The evidence?" Fells demanded. "The evidence you collected on Morrison. Where is it?"

"Gone, Sir," he replied. "They packed it all up and left just moments before you arrived."

"Son of a Bitch!" Fells exploded. "How the hell did they know."

"Who, Sir?"

"This stinks of Morrison and Tabbot. Have you had any conversations with anyone about this facility, Zephyrs? Especially on Alpha II?"

"No, Sir," Zephyrs lied. "Are we in trouble?"

"Oh, surely you jest, Lieutenant. An inconvenience, at most. You just keep doing what I tell you. Is that understood?"

"Understood."

"They'll pay. Don't doubt that. They will pay!" Fells snapped a salute, turned on his heel, and disappeared back into his Stinger.

Zephyrs retreated fo his own transport and reached for the com.

"Williams." A tired voice answered his call.

"Garner? My God, where have you been? I've been trying to reach you for weeks."

"Kyle..." The monitor brightened a little. "I've been really sick. Some kind of bug, I guess. I didn't even know you called. What can I do for you?"

"Boy, Garner. The shit has really hit the fan. Somehow the Council found out about Fells' covert ops center. We were actually raided. They took everything and Fells is livid."

"My God, maybe Fells has underestimated Morrison." With a sudden realization, Williams added, "My God, Kyle, maybe I've underestimated him, too." He surveyed the confining walls of the ISO unit.

"Well, there is one good thing, Garner..." Zephyrs felt an abrupt release of tension. "The evidence I supposedly had on Morrison is gone forever."

The monitor forced himself to sit up for the first time in several hours. "What evidence?"

"Evidence against Morrison. I made it all up."

"Jeez, Kyle. I've got to get out of here. I guess it's all up to me."

Wildwood

"Where are we?" Dot asked, stretching her arms and squirming to an upright position.

Fletcher slowed, looking for recognizable landmarks. "We're nearly there," he replied. Moments later, he turned off the pavement to a gravel country road. Following the wooded lane, he finally reached a path that was little more than a dirt driveway. A locked gate and an ominous warning to trespassers blocked the entrance to Wildwood.

"Hope you have a key."

"Don't need one." Fletcher headed for the gate. "See?" Lifting the chain, he separated one link from another with a twisting motion. He held up the two chains connected by the lock. The creaking gate woke the three back seat passengers.

"This is beautiful," Barry marveled as they drove on through rolling hills covered with old, but stately oaks and silver-leafed ash. "I love it."

"Oh... It's so peaceful here. It feels safe and loving. What a great idea, Mr. Fletcher." Valerie stretched all over as they crested a hill then descended into the shelter of a lush forest, tall branches forming a tunnel over the road.

"I helped build this place," Fletcher explained as the cabin came into view. "I could tell you stories..." He threatened reminiscence, but stopped at the sight of the structure. He looked fondly at the heavy stones and timbers that comprised the bulk of it. Time had blended the cabin's natural elements into the forest. Ancient trees embraced it like an inhabitant rather than a man-made addition. The front door, hand-carved with painstaking care, beckoned the weary travelers to enter.

"This is really neat." Barry jumped out of the Rover and hiked over to touch the smooth wood of the door.

Moving a plank next to the front stoop, Fletcher withdrew a rusty key. "Place hasn't been used in years," he explained, wiggling the key in the sticky lock. With a click, the latch gave way and the big man opened the door with a flourish. "Let's air this place out," he instructed as everyone else climbed stiffly from the 4X4.

Quickly, the cabin came to life as fresh air and sunlight filled its interior. Sounds of appreciation echoed from all corners as Barry opened the drapes on the south wall, revealing the crystal blue lake nestled in the valley just below the cabin.

"There's our classroom, John," Fletcher chuckled and pointed to the lake. "I'll teach you everything you ever wanted to know about bass fishing."

Around them, the interior of the cabin displayed the same natural ingredients that graced the exterior. Huge, rough hewn beams spanned the ceiling, providing the foundation for an open hallway and bedrooms that occupied half of the second story. Smoothly sanded tree trunks, each with a layer of upper branches still intact, hugged the ceiling and carried the weight of the upper floor and roof. Windows everywhere, upstairs and down, admitted light that softly filtered through the cabin.

Light streaming through the dust motes and into the center of the great room reminded REL of honey. A rustic plank floor adorned with a rainbow of nubby wool rugs ensconced a double-faced moss rock fireplace that rose two stories and provided the focal point for the entire house. A large hearth, capable of seating half a dozen people, faced a pair of overstuffed leather couches and two matching chairs.

"What a wonderful hide-away," Dot admired, returning freshly shaken rugs to their place by the hearth.

"There should be plenty of room for all of us. Through that door is one bedroom, and there are two more down the hallway plus the ones upstairs," Fletcher explained.

"Dot, would you help me take a food inventory? We have a few supplies in the Rover, but with all of us here for two weeks, I'm sure we'll need more. " Fletcher led the way to the large country kitchen separated from the great room by the fireplace. "We can drive into Amber to get whatever else we need."

Distracted from the hum of his inner circuits, REL fondly observed his family and emanated gratitude for his amazingly good fortune.

Alpha II

Standing so close that his breath fogged the face mask of Timball's biosuit, Williams thundered at the trembling director, "I am out of here."

Staring at the fully clothed monitor, Timball stammered "That is not possible. You could infect the station."

"Really," Williams sneered. "What if I told you I no longer have any symptoms."

"G-good," Timball nodded inside the suit. "The treatment must be working."

"It's not the treatment, Director. I'm not taking any medicine. I'm not eating any food. I'm not drinking any water or juice. Haven't for 36 hours." He glared at the dumfounded Timball. "And guess what? My symptoms are gone." Shoving the director up against the wall, he hissed. "Something is very wrong here. And I don't care if I have to go over every report of every transaction for the last ten years, I will found out what it is. In fact, I might even call for reinforcements."

Stomach growling, the monitor stomped out the door and through the halls of the sleeping space station straight to the nutrition center. The cafeteria was dark and deserted in the early morning hours, but a light shone through the work area glass. A young R1 stood at attention as the monitor entered. "At ease, son," Williams said looking around. "What are my chances of getting something to eat?"

Timball did not bother to remove his biosuit. He stood, forlorn, with the helmet tucked under his arm when Morrison answered his door. "We've got trouble." Timball's voice cracked as he spoke.

"Come in." Morrison pried the helmet from his friend's frozen fingers and waved him in from the hallway. The doctor didn't even ask, just poured a stiff shot of brandy.

Cupping the snifter with both hands but shaking nonetheless, the director caught his breath, then took a soothing gulp. Finally, he gasped, "Williams is out."

Morrison remained calm — his voice, smooth and solid. "Sit down, Dan." He motioned to his most comfortable chair. The director slumped into the cushion and Morrison continued, "Now, tell me what happened."

"He knows we poisoned him. He quit eating and drinking. His symptoms are gone and he's out." Timball stared into his snifter as he spoke. "What the hell are we going to do?" he wailed.

Second Messenger

The Casting of Lots

Nederland

"There!" Marks pointed to the *Mountain Wiccans Adopt-A-Highway* sign. Three white limos slowed, then pulled to the shoulder, clogging the flow of traffic behind them on the winding canyon road. The reverend, clad like a lumberjack in stiff new jeans and a scratchy plaid shirt, smoothed his hair and stepped from the car. He paused momentarily to re-tie the laces of his new hiking boots. Motioning to cameraman Luke and sound tech Matthew, the reverend clomped along the rocky shoulder to the sign, wireless microphone in hand, to conduct a quick sound check.

"Brothers and Sisters in Christ," he began. "Here we are, high up in the Rocky Mountains just east of Nederland, Colorado. We are enroute to investigate real evidence of a real encounter with demons. Now look closely at this sign." He pointed at the sign with a flourish. "It is a blatant invitation to evil! Not surprising that we have been called to this godless place to witness against the invasion of Satan." Marks closed his eyes. "Cut!" he yelled, popping his eyes wide open and looking up to Luke. "Got it?"

The cameraman nodded.

"Good, then. Let's get on with it." The crew piled back into the limos and continued the climb up to the little mountain town.

Topping the hill by Barker Dam, the pristine panorama of Nederland opened before the visitors. "Behold the pocket of sin," Marks sneered. Silently, he observed the trappings of the small community as the caravan rolled into the tiny town. Past the rustic Catholic church, through the milling tie-dye clad pedestrians, beyond the rock and crystal shop the shiny limos trundled, coming finally to a halt in the RTD parking lot. Counting three bars in a two block area, Marks shook his head at the obvious.

The commotion of the limo parade in front of the Town Hall sent Thelma scurrying next door to the Marshal's Office. "They're he-ere," she chimed, interrupting a discussion between Burrows and Burgess.

"Oh, God," Burrows moaned, "Get the women and children off the streets."

On cue, Burgess burst from the office, calling over his shoulder, "Executing Operation Flatland, Marshal."

"Operation Flatland?" Thelma smirked, raising one eyebrow.

"Yep. Based on the assumption that these men are all flatlanders. Damned near sea level, at that." Burrows grinned.

Outside, Burgess diverted the line of limos, sending them up the street to the grocery store parking lot. Then cutting across the covered wooden footbridge, he sprinted to meet them in the area reserved with official yellow police ribbon.

Engines died and limo doors yawned, spilling twelve men and Reverend Marks out into the parking lot. With much bustle and to-do, sound and film equipment sprung to life, rolling as the men formed a circle to pray. Deputy Burgess, most unsure of etiquette, stood quietly apart, scratching his head and cocking one ear to catch the reverend's words.

"Lord God," Marks intoned. "We assemble here in harm's way to do Thy will. Lord, we are surrounded by idolaters and hippies, New Agers and witches. God, we ask Thy Divine protection to keep us from falling to The Adversary. We ask this in the Name of Jesus' Holy Blood, Amen."

As the men disassembled and gathered their gear, Burgess beckoned to Marks to follow him down the path, across the bridge and into the center of town.

"So, let me get this straight, Jim, Sweetheart." Thelma grinned. "By making them walk all over town, you think you can wear them out and better keep tabs on them?"

"You're as smart as you are beautiful, Thelma," Burrows quipped. "Come on." He grabbed Thelma's hand and tugged her outside.

Loping across the covered bridge, the long-legged Burgess exhorted a cavalcade of breathless WARS journalists into a near jog.

Tears of laughter pooling in her bright eyes, Thelma barely articulated, "Jim... Burgess has Marks *running!*"

"Operation Flatland is in full swing, Thelma," the marshal managed to utter before stifling an overpowering urge to laugh out loud.

"Where do you have them headed, now, Jim?"

"I designated the old Teen Center as their..." he laughed, "...staging area. And truly, it does make sense. Can you imagine all of them crammed into the Marshal's Office? Plus..." he added wickedly, "the phones are out of order there."

The reverend's hopes for respite shattered the instant he rounded the corner by Off Her Rocker Antiques. Halfway down the block, a crowd of twenty or so people crammed the narrow boardwalk and trickled out into the small one-way street. Some carried welcome signs, others carried protests. All awaited his arrival at the old Teen Center.

Pausing to compose himself, the reverend straightened his shoulders, smoothed his hair and forced a smile.

"Lead the way, Deputy." He placed a firm hand on Burgess' shoulder. "And slow it down."

Bracing for the imagined onslaught of the small crowd, Marks followed a handful of paces behind the deputy. He was quite unprepared when Burgess approached a young hippie and gently admonished. "Dakota, step back, let them through." At which point, the whole assemblage stepped back. Marks didn't even get to shake one hand nor did he field one insult.

Gratefully closing the door behind him, Luke sagged momentarily to catch his breath. "How high is it here?" he rasped.

"Over 8,100 feet above sea level," Marks confirmed. "Now, let's get to work. Are those people still outside?"

"Yes, Reverend. That Rasta kid is now sitting on the walk playing a guitar. Looks like they're here for a while," Luke reported.

"Well, never mind. All clear on your assignments?" Pointing toward each team of men, he continued, "Accident sight. Clinic and Dr. Winter. Accident reports." Pointing to Matthew and Luke, he directed, "You two, I want plenty of footage around town. And lots of sound bites from the people." Jerking a thumb toward the West, he explained, "One of that socialist *Mountain People's Co-op* next door. One of that..." Making quotation marks with his fingers, he said, "*Medicine Shield Book Store* across the street. And, of course, that *Nature's Own Rock Shop*. Paul, you stay here and coordinate communications. I want everybody back here at 6:00. And the car comes to me. Understood?"

In teams, the men organized gear and left the building, much dismayed as small pods of people broke off from the group outside to follow them.

"Reverend Marks?" Paul complained.

"Yes," Marks turned away from the window.

"We have no phones, Reverend. The lines are dead. All of them. And the cell phones don't get reception up here. No phones. No modems."

"Three days in the wilderness, then," Marks pronounced. "We must be strong."

Center State Complex

"Monuments to arrogance." Arthur Tabbot nodded toward the centuries-old buildings of Capital City as he and an LRA confidant zoomed toward Center State Complex. "I have to admit that I feel a bit smug today, myself. After all," he boasted, "we did shut Fells down, at least temporarily. We bought a lot of time and confused the issue surrounding Morrison. And..." he chuckled. "We have his matrix tower. My guess is, we won't be arriving unnoticed."

The rear view screen of Tabbot's EcoSkiff suddenly filled with the menace of a jet black Stinger. "Right on time," the councilman joked. "Well, this could be colorful."

Just as the Stinger closed on them, Tabbot cheered the arrival of two Council escorts, one on either side of the skiff. At that, the Stinger dropped below them and disappeared into other airborne traffic.

Easing the skiff into his reserved slip, Tabbot and friend deplaned and wound their way through a corridor of uniformed honor guards to the marble steps of the Democracy Forum. Just as they reached the top, an imposing figure tore away from the crowd and loomed above Tabbot, hissing under his breath, "How dare you?"

"Ah, Imperator Fells," Tabbot replied. "It takes no daring whatsoever to obey the law. Don't tell me I embarrassed you."

Fells glared and seethed unable to rejoin.

"Besides," Tabbot insinuated, "my most dastardly doings pale when compared to your deeds du jour."

"You'll pay for this, Tabbot," Fells spat. "Count on it."

"By the way, Director. I've filed a Cease and Desist for the audit on Alpha II. Looks like a lot of your minions will have time on their hands. Considered yourself served." Tabbot handed the director an official Council holodisc. "See you in court." Tabbot turned and entered the Forum.

Walking down the polished corridors of intergalactic democracy, Tabbot caught sight of Fells, who was venting his fury on Governor Durbin Coleman. The cocky little leader of the free worlds straightened his shoulders and puffed out his chest in attempt to spare his polished dignity. "What is it, Fells?" he snapped.

"What the hell happened to my ops center?" Fells demanded, making no attempt to lower his voice.

"Imperator," Coleman simpered, "just because we are political allies, you cannot expect me to turn a blind eye to your flagrant violation of Council Directives — especially when it becomes so very public."

"Perhaps it's time to re-negotiate our friendship, Governor," Fells threatened.

"Perhaps it's time to be more circumspect, Imperator," the governor whispered.

Shoving the little man away from him, Fells whipped around and marched down the hallway. Coleman brushed himself off. And Arthur Tabbot smirked at the progress of the morning.

Councilman Tabbot looked around the High Court of Justice: polished mahogany walls framed in federal blue; blue carpet; blue upholstery; massive judicial bench. He shook his head and smiled. Only the finely detailed mural of Themis, blindfolded and impartial, broke the ancient patriarchal ambiance of the place.

"Another five minutes and we begin without him." Judge Mildred Hawthorne roused him from his musings.

Just then, the heavy mahogany doors crashed open, admitting the stalking Fells and a bevy of chattering advisors. Fells' scowl deepened at the sight of the last remaining liberal judge in Capital City.

"Order, order." She pounded the gavel. "Imperator Fells, if you cannot be on time could you at least make a civil entrance?"

"Your Honoress, I beg your pardon." Fells bowed slightly, glowering at Tabbot beneath the gesture. Then he and his entourage noisily took their seats.

"As I understand it, the case before us is a Cease and Desist to the military audit of a civilian facility. Begging the court's indulgence… This seems like a no-brainer to me," the judge remarked.

Flying to his feet, Fells roared, "I object! Your Honoress, it seems you are pre-disposed to favor the petitioner."

"On the contrary, Imperator Fells," the judge admonished. "I am predisposed to the letter of the law and to human rights. Please present your case, Councilman Tabbot."

"Your Honoress," Tabbot began. "As you have noted, this case is simple. Imperator Fells sent an ICom monitor to audit a civilian facility. Our Constitution clearly prohibits such blatant violations. I see no reason to even discuss this further. I rest my case."

"Imperator Fells, can you offer any compelling reason why I should allow this farce to continue?" She folded her arms on the bench and stared down at the belligerent man.

A flurry of activity snaked its way down the table of advisors ending when the one nearest Fells smugly deposited a holodisc in the upturned palm of his expectant hand. "Your Honoress, if you please, Alpha II is due to be audited now." Smiling like a cat, the director approached the bench and activated a holographic document. "A sub-contract between the ICom and the Inner Circle for routine auditing services," Fells pronounced.

Tabbot stormed to the bench, incredulous, until he saw the official seal of Governor Durbin Coleman in the bottom right-hand corner.

"You've got to be kidding me." Looking down at Tabbot, Judge Hawthorne apologized, "I'm sorry, Councilman Tabbot. Until this contract is set aside by the Constitutional Court, I am legally bound to honor it — my own suspicions notwithstanding. However..." She glared at Imperator Fells. "This farce will not be conducted under your authority. Monitor Williams will report to me. And there will be no violation of personal liberties. This will be a standard civilian audit, no voice analyzers will be used. And none of the toys the ICom holds so dear will be permitted."

Fells sputtered in fury, "This will impede my investigation." Raking his hands through his hair, he yelled, "I had physical proof to secure the necessary warrant, but he stole it from me." Fells jabbed a finger at Councilman Tabbot who turned calmly.

"And from where was this supposed evidence stolen?" Tabbot challenged.

Slamming her gavel down on the bench, the judge pronounced, "Enough. Gentlemen... This is my ruling. If you don't like it Imperator Fells, appeal it and I'll see you back here in a year. Providing, of course, that your contract holds up." She hammered her gavel down again. "Court dismissed."

Stifling his smile, Arthur Tabbot strolled the corridors of the Forum nodding to well-wishers and wondering if his good fortune of the day was in any way connected to the actions of a biomech 200 years in the past.

Nederland

Marshal Burrows slammed the door to his tiny office and stomped inside. "Dammit it, Alan! We were supposed to keep this whole thing with Grueter under wraps. How the hell did Marks find out about it anyway?"

The deputy hung his head. "I guess it was the update."

"Are you telling me that you sent *The Investigator* an update?"

"They requested it, Marshal. What was I suppose to do? You said yourself this isn't an official investigation."

"I know, Alan, and it isn't. I'm just trying to keep it from becoming a full-fledged circus." Burrows shook his head. "No matter, Alan. Go home and get into uniform, the whole crew will be here in just a few minutes."

"Okay, Marshal. I'm sorry. I had no idea he would get my update so quick."

"Well, it will all be over soon enough."

Jeremiah Marks glided through door of the Marshal's Office, Matthew and Luke in tow. Brushing a hand along the rustic walls, then quickly wiping it off on his jeans, he demanded, "Where is this witness?"

"Let's get something straight right now, Reverend. This is my investigation. You are here only as a courtesy. And if Mr. Grueter chooses not to talk to you, then you will leave. Understood?"

"Of course, Marshal. But I have a feeling he will want to talk to us."

"Hey, hey! What do you think you're doing?" Burrows glared at Matthew and Luke as they pushed his desk against the wall to accommodate the cameras and sound equipment.

"Marshal, they are merely preparing to record the interview."

"Absolutely not," Burrows insisted. "You will not violate Mr. Grueter's right to privacy. And I mean it." He glared at the two Marks henchmen.

Deputy Burgess jogged up the grass to the Marshal's Office and intercepted Carl Grueter who was having serious second thoughts about the interview.

"What's all that equipment for?" the shy man asked, bewildered.

"Don't you worry about that, Mr. Grueter. It's just Reverend Jeremiah Marks and his team investigating the John Worthington case."

"I don't understand," Carl replied.

Taking the hesitant witness by the elbow, Burgess escorted him through the door and introduced him to Marshal Burrows, Reverend Marks, Matthew, and Luke.

"You just say the word, Carl," Burrows assured, "and these men are out of here."

"Don't be hasty, Mr. Grueter," Marks simpered. "*The Investigator* and God's Fortress are prepared to offer you $5,000 for this interview on tape."

The deputy's head snapped to attention, but before he could open his mouth, he saw the marshal shake his head in an emphatic "No!"

Carl plopped into a nearby chair. "Well, I could use $5,000. But I don't know as I want my face spread all over some tabloid or TV show."

"It's your call, Mr. Grueter." Marks steepled his fingers and waited.

"Well, heck. I've lived with this so long that I guess it doesn't matter. When can I get my money?"

"I can write you a check today." Marks smiled.

Burgess shook his head sadly, but held his peace.

"Well, okay. But I'm not very comfortable talking about this," Carl Grueter explained softly.

"I appreciate your feelings, Carl," Burrows replied. "But this whole case is strange and I would really appreciate any information you can give me. How about a cup of coffee?"

"Sure. Thanks. Well, here goes."

Cameras rolling, Carl Grueter began his tale:

"Well, it was back in 1989. I was just coming back from Denver, nursing the old Subaru up Coal Creek Canyon. I remember because she was chugging pretty bad. Wasn't sure I'd get her up over Wondervu. Anyway, when I get to the top of my driveway, I see this Blazer sitting in the middle of the road at the bottom of the switchback. It's pretty beat up like it's been in one hell of a wreck. So I jump out and head down to see if anybody's hurt. Then I see this guy in a white lab coat pulling a body from the driver's seat. I figure maybe he's a paramedic or something and I'm thinking that it's a good thing he's there cause I don't know nothing about that sort of thing." Carl looked up at the bright lights shining directly at him, and shielded his eyes. "Do we have to have those lights like that?"

"Yeah, we do," the cameraman answered.

Carl continued, "Anyway I start down the switchback but before I can take two steps down the bank, I hear this crackle or sizzle or something like I've never heard before. And the white-coated guy and the body just go POOF! Just like that. POOF and they're gone."

Raising a neatly combed eyebrow, Marks repeated "POOF?"

"Yeah. Just like I said. They disappeared just like that."

"Then what happened?" Burrows asked.

"Well, you know, Marshal, once you start down an incline like that, it's best to keep on going. So, I did. When I get to the Blazer, there's all kinds of blood all over the inside. That Blazer was sure banged up. But there was nobody there."

"So, what did you do?" Marks interrupted, raising a scowl from the marshal.

"I'm just getting back my wind to climb back up and call 911 when I hear that crackling sound again. And all of a sudden, three soldiers just pop out of nowhere right in front of me."

"I don't understand, Carl. What do you mean pop out?" Burrows pressed.

"Like they weren't there, and then they were. Like the opposite of what happened to the white-coated guy. You know, like on Star Trek."

"What happened next?"

"Well, one of them's throwin' up and saying *I hate this time bullshit*, whatever that means."

Burgess barely suppressed a gasp, instead elbowing the marshal with an I-told-you-so look on his face.

"Then what happened?" Burrows prodded.

"Well, I don't mind saying I was scared. One of them starts questioning me like I know what the hell's going on. He has this 3D picture thing and asks me if I saw the guy it showed. Well, I say maybe it's the guy who just disappeared but I'm not sure. The other two guys are ransacking the Blazer. I figure they didn't find what they're looking for because they're doing a lot of swearing. Then the leader guy tells me to stand back — which I gladly do. Then POOF! They're all gone."

The men in the Marshal's Office looked at each other, speechless. Carl Grueter shrugged. Finally, Burrows broke the silence.

"And you never told anyone else this story until now?"

"Nope," Carl answered. "Didn't want people thinkin' I was nuts."

"So..." Marks solicited after Carl Grueter left. "What are we going to do now?"

"Reverend, there's nothing we can do. I have no evidence of a crime. There have been no complaints filed," Burrows explained patiently.

"Well, maybe there's nothing you can do, but I'll investigate this on my own if I have to." Marks glared at the marshal. "You have to admit, there's something strange going on here."

"But you have no authority. *I* have no authority," Burrows argued.

"That's where you're wrong, Marshal Burrows. I have God's authority. And I'm not afraid to use it." With that, the reverend stomped out of the office and down the street to the Teen Center, leaving Matthew and Luke to catch up.

Wildwood

"Ta Da!" REL sang with a flourish, gesturing to the kitchen as Barry, Dot, and Fletcher carried in the supplies from their shopping trip to Amber. The huge trestle table sat bathed in candlelight, bedecked with wildflowers and a scrumptious meal. "Valerie and I just wanted to show you how much you all mean to us," he said shyly. "So, we made dinner."

John shooed them to the table, playfully teasing Dot as she snagged a mushroom from the top of a casserole.

"Actually, I have a private agenda for dinner," REL advised, holding a chair, first for Valerie, then for Dot. Seating himself, he continued. "I know you are all curious about how I intend to salvage my mission. Well, I can tell you now. I've been thinking about it ever since Washington D.C. and I realize that it all boils down to a question of love and fear." His eyes swept from one beloved face to the next until he had made eye contact with everyone at the table. "And God," he concluded.

Compliments and mmmmm's and aaahhh's interrupted the conversation as the family sampled dinner. Then the bio-mech continued, "You understand that the dominant paradigm views God as a distant, temperamental entity, who lives aloof and judgmental. But I have discovered that Spirit, in fact is immanent in everything — down to and including the quantum level. Do you know that even with the technology existent in my time, the year 2191, scientists still cannot determine the exact point at which a particle becomes a wave? Or why? That's because scientists believe they are observing *things*. Inanimate things. They don't realize that they're watching Creation at work. Or that there is no such thing as an inanimate object."

Fletcher set his fork on his plate and challenged, "So, you're telling me that... say... a rock is alive?"

REL patted his breast pocket, the one cradling his amethyst. "What I'm saying is that we live in an intelligent universe which is, itself, alive and responsive to our every thought. Like the wave and the particle, there is no discernible point at which God becomes us and we become God. This intimate relationship with Source gives each of us the power to create the life we want to live. We need only ask, in full understanding of who we are, and Our Creator, indeed, provides. The only reason people experience drama and chaos in their lives is that they are caught up in the dominant paradigm — the polarity of fear and love. Fear prevents an intimate relationship with Source, so people react and respond to seemingly random and traumatic events, never knowing that they are the co-creators of those experiences. I'll give you an example. Dot, if you pray and say 'Dear God, I am so afraid' what do you think happens?"

Dot thought a moment and then shrugged. "I don't know, John. I guess God helps me not be so afraid."

REL smiled and nodded. "That's what most people believe. In truth, God replies, 'So you are.' And you get more of the fear you affirmed in your prayer."

"Ooh," Dot grimaced. "So, how should I pray, then?"

"If you say, 'Dear God, I am so blessed,' God will respond, 'So you are.' You see, God — for lack of a better analogy — is much like a computer. God takes your words very literally and responds to your beliefs. Contrary to popular myth, God is *not* judgmental — does not respond on whims or jealousies, but directly to what you believe about life. The reason you get what you believe rather that what you ask for is to help you understand who you are. That understanding makes you privy to the mind of God."

Barry looked thoughtfully at John for a moment, then quietly said, "It makes sense to me, REL. But I don't understand what this has to do with your mission."

Gently chuckling, REL explained, "That's simple, Barry. My original mission was to change the dominant paradigm by disseminating the secrets from the TechniCom. I have decided to change the dominant paradigm by teaching the power of love."

"As I recall..." Fletcher argued, "The last guy who tried that got nailed to a cross. What makes you think that you'll fare any better?"

"For one thing, Mr. Fletcher, I'll have direct access to people everywhere."

"I'm listening."

"Two thousand years ago, before word reached the masses, Christ's message had already been politicized and edited for content. The last thing The Powers That Be wanted was for the people to believe in their own divinity. So they deleted much of that message and ultimately killed the messenger. But I have an advantage."

"You have an advantage over the Son of God?" Fletcher barbed.

"Yes, Mr. Fletcher. I have the internet. My message will go directly to the people."

"What are you going to do? Have your own chat room?" Dot wondered aloud.

"There will be many chat rooms." REL smiled. "I have in mind a wondrous home page with links to all imaginable love-oriented spiritual information. Rather than arranging the links by subject, dictionary-style, I will arrange whole pathways that are guided by affinity."

"Wow. You lost me there." Barry wrinkled his brow.

"Barry, say you are a policeman, for example, and you log on to the internet. The more interested you are in spiritual development the more likely you are to arrive at our home page."

"How is that possible?" Valerie asked.

"Not by programming, but by a calling to the heart. There is a sympathetic resonance that can be forged with the human heart by the conscious use of harmonics and symbols and words. And it only responds when invited. Just like God."

"Yes, but how does it work? Physically, I mean?" Fletcher asked.

"Well, the internet is just a physical extension of thought. And it works in the same way. Certain frequencies of thought will magnetize certain search results, over and above what any software explains. Search results for a head-centered person will vary from those of a heart-centered person because the difference in their frequencies will lead them to different places — as is true in life."

"Even if that is true, not that I'm convinced, mind you. How will your home page help people?" the big man pressed.

"My program will guide them to their own discovery of their own heart connection, then to love, and finally to God. I'll draw you a mental blueprint. Everybody close your eyes and imagine a glassy sphere, dark blue like a midnight sky. Lightly, it floats in infinite space, satiny and warm with possibilities. Now..." he breathed, teasing their visions. "Imagine countless filaments of light, stringing and twining and girdling the sphere. Picture grids on a globe, manyfold and brilliant. Now watch them grow pliant, undulating as the sphere constantly rotates. Shifting. Intersecting. And moving on again. Do you see?" He whispered, pausing till each silently nodded. "Now, let me tell you what you are seeing. Each lighted walkway, each filament of experience leads you to your God-Self. Each intent of the heart magnetizes a new experience, each one leads to God. See, my beloved friends, no matter where you go, you end up where you need to be."

Alpha II

Timball guzzled his second brandy. Finally freed from his biosuit, he slumped in his office clothes, shaking his head in despair. "I've heard they torture you, Phil. You know, the cross counselors."

"Stop it, Dan. That's just an old wive's tale. Besides, Williams has a long way to go to prove anything."

A bright electronic voice made Timball jump. "Secured message, Alpha Com. Will you take it Dr. Morrison?"

Brow furrowed, the doctor affirmed.

"Phil..." The smiling face of Arthur Tabbot invaded the early morning gloom. "Sorry for the hour but I thought you'd like to know. Oh, hello, Dan."

Timball nodded and smiled bleakly.

"Arthur, no matter the hour. As you can see we're wide awake. What's up?" Morrison asked.

"Well, I've had quite the day. I spent it waltzing with Fells. The result is that the imperator has been told to back off and you no longer have a monitor on your station."

Timball sat bolt upright and heaved a huge sigh of relief, "Oh, thank God!"

"Well almost, Dan. Phil, our LRA friend, Judge Mildred Hawthorne, couldn't order the Cease and Desist, but she did something that might be even better. Williams now has the status of any civilian auditor and reports directly to her. He can do nothing without her personal approval."

Laughing, Morrison reached to Timball and slapped the director on the knee.

"And that's not all, gentlemen. Fells is completely out of it. He has no authority over Williams. Now that we've dismantled his ops center he's flying blind, and man is he pissed."

"What ops center?" Timball asked.

"Tell you about it later," Morrison volunteered. "So the upshot is that you've had a pretty good day, huh, Arthur?"

"I'd say so," Tabbot agreed. "I've been thinking this whole upturn in LRA good fortune might be more than just really good luck."

"You mean REL?" Timball asked.

"All I can tell you is that I have reason to believe that everything is proceeding in very close proximity to our original plan." Morrison grinned momentarily then took on a more serious air. "But, Arthur, don't count Fells out of anything. He's desperate. No doubt he's more dangerous than ever before."

Monitor Williams stared dumbly at the communiqué. After fifteen years in the ICom, he was suddenly, unexpectedly, a civilian. At least for now. Not quite sure how to feel, he pressed the connect code for Kyle Zephyrs' transport.

"Garner…" The youthful face split in a grin, then sobered. "Is something wrong? You look awful."

"Kyle… no… at least… Ah, hell. I don't know." The monitor shook his head. "Fells has been busted. At least for the moment, I am under civilian authority. According to the judgment, Fells isn't even supposed to contact me."

Lt. Zephyrs was quiet for a moment. "Yeah. I heard something was up. Especially after the raid on Wright-Patterson. So how does it feel to be a civilian, Garner?"

"That's just it. I'm not sure how I feel. I've dedicated my entire life to the ICom. But lately, everything's gotten so ruthless. I'm not sure our tactics are any better than the people we're supposed to prosecute. Take Morrison, for example."

"Yeah. He's a smart one. What's he like?"

"The truth is, I like him. He's done a lot of good things, on a global scale. And he's a really nice guy. I don't trust him for a second. But he's nice. And it seems that he's behind things I would like to believe in, but don't think will ever happen. You know what I mean?"

"He's a liberal idealist," Kyle summed it up.

"Yeah. Well, maybe this will give me the chance to re-evaluate my career path and reconsider my politics," Williams sighed. "Hey, what are you going to do, Kyle?"

"Oh, I have a grunt assignment at Center State Complex. No big deal."

"Well, keep in touch. Okay?"

"You bet, Garner. Anytime you wanna talk, just holler."

The monitor disconnected and drummed his fingers on his desk. *Re-evaluate, indeed.*

211

Nederland

"Mmmmm. Thelma this rhubarb pie is wonderful." Jim Burrows licked his lips, considering a second piece. "Maybe I should give up law enforcement and we could open Thelma's Pie Palace," he only half-kidded.

"No way, Jim, you'd eat all the profit," Thelma laughed. "Boy, Marks really had this town going, didn't he? Even Dr. Winter was pissed by the time he and his apostles finally left."

"My curiosity really stirred up a hornet's nest, didn't it? And it's far from over."

"What do you mean, Jim?"

"Marks informed me just before he left town that he's not giving this up. He's gonna follow Worthington to, in his words, 'the ends of the Earth to run the demon to ground.' He's a lunatic, Thelma. And I'm afraid he could be dangerous."

"Oh, Jim… He touts himself as a man of God, or at least his interpretation thereof. But with his high profile, I doubt he'd do more than run over women with his car," she laughed.

"Yeah. Maybe. But he's got hundreds of thousands of followers and I'm pretty sure that at least one of 'em's crazy enough to hurt somebody. And since Barry and Valerie are with Worthington, I feel responsible for any danger they may be in."

"So Jim, what are you going to do?" Thelma asked.

"I guess I need to stay on the case. At least find out where they are. And I suppose I'll need to talk to Valerie or Barry to warn them about Marks." Burrows shook his head. "At least the circus left Nederland."

"Hello," Burgess garbled into the phone through a mouthful of pie that he was eating straight from the pie pan.

"Deputy Burgess?" a timid female voice asked.

"Yeah. Who's calling?" He propped his fork in the pie pan, balanced it on his desk and reached for a pen and note pad.

"This is Cindy Vinwire. You know, from Data Pioneer in Phoenix."

"Oh, yeah. Hi Cindy. The marshal's left for the day. Can I help you?"

"Actually, I called to talk to you."

Burgess blushed, unnerved at the thought of a woman calling him. "What do you need?" he blurted.

"So... How's the Worthington investigation going? Have you found them yet?"

"Well, not so far. We've been pretty busy the last three days. Reverend Jeremiah Marks and his investigation team have been here."

"Reverend Marks?" The adoration in her voice was unmistakable. "Did he find anything?"

"If you ask me, the guy's really out there on the edge, Cindy, with all that demon stuff. Besides, according to an interview we did yesterday, it looks like time travel's involved."

"Time travel?" Cindy scribbled hasty notes in her notebook. "That's amazing. What did the reverend say about that?"

"He said he's going to keep after them until he exposes Worthington for what he is."

"A demon, huh?" Cindy affirmed.

"Well, you're entitled to your own opinion about that. I just think we're dealing with an advanced civilization. That's all, Cindy." Burgess scowled, uncertain how to cultivate this strange alliance to his investigative advantage. "So you really like Reverend Marks?" he baited.

"Yeah, he makes so much sense. And I've got his private e-mail addy. Write him every day. Maybe he'll even answer. I think I can help him with Worthington, you know."

"Maybe you could help me, too. You know, with the case. If I give you my home phone number, would you call me sometime?" he asked, weighing the next question.

"Sure."

"And, maybe you could give me yours, too?"

"Sure. Why not?"

After exchanging numbers, Burgess hung up the phone, determined to redeem his earlier miscalculations with *The Investigator*. Smiling at his own cunning, he once again attacked Thelma's pie.

Burrows strolled through the door of the Marshal's Office, surprised to find the lights still on and Burgess seated at his desk. "Hey, you're here late. Anything going on?"

At first, Burgess thought not to mention Cindy's phone call, but his sullied credibility prompted the truth. "You know that Data Pioneer girl? That Cindy? Well, she called."

"I really hope she doesn't want me to call her back." Burrows moaned.

"Actually, Marshal, she called for me." Burgess blushed again.

Burrows pried, "Well... Was it personal?"

"Nope. I think she's fishing. You know for the lowdown on the Worthington case?" Burgess explained.

"So..." Burrows glared. "Did you give her one of your famous updates?"

"Nope. In fact, Marshal, I think we can use her." The deputy grinned at his plan.

"How so, Deputy?" Burrows asked with an eyebrow raised.

"See, she has this crush on Reverend Marks, e-mails him every day. The way I see it, if I keep in touch with her, we can keep tabs on Marks." Burgess nodded emphatically, certain of his strategy.

"Good idea, Alan, but..." Burrows warned, "...just don't get loose-lipped with her. Okay?"

"Sure thing, Marshal. I've learned my lesson. Besides, all that demon stuff really gives me the creeps. Maybe Cindy can help us warn Valerie and Barry," he boasted. Waving the half-finished pastry at the marshal, he offered, "Hey, want some pie?"

Looking down at his straining belt, Burrows declined, patted his deputy on the back and headed home in hopes of a good night's sleep.

God's Fortress

Reverend Marks preened his fingernails as he watched the rough video on Luke's computer screen. "There!" he pointed with his emery board. "Now, can you add a nuclear halo to that sign?"

"Sure thing, Reverend." Luke selected the *Mountain Wiccan* sign with his cursor, clicked on *effects* and framed it in a faint bile green nimbus.

"Perfect," Marks gloated. "Now, let's go to the view of the town. That valley is entirely too green. What can you do about that?"

In moments, Luke's computer wizardry transformed the pristine valley into a dying panorama of brittle brown trees and murky gray lake. He crowned the whole vista with a brownish red smog.

"Son, you do know what I like." Marks smiled at his progress. "What can you do with the marshal? I mean, that won't invite a libel suite."

"Well," Luke said, adding just the hint of jowls. Then he washed out Burrows' complexion and concluded with strokes of shadow just beneath bloodshot, yellowed eyes. "Is that too much?"

215

"Not at all." Marks clapped with glee. "Not at all. Let's move on to the town, itself. What can you do with the rock shop and co-op and book store?"

Deftly, Luke recast the once-inviting signs and buildings into lurid, garish caricatures. "Next?" he asked, mouse poised for more deprecating artistry.

"Okay, the Grueter guy. Clean him up a bit. Give him some credibility."

After adding a little extra blue to Carl's eyes, tucking his chin, and clipping away stragglers of hair, Luke altered sound bites here and there and rearranged them to subtly enhance the story. "Aren't you afraid this guy will sue? He wasn't too thrilled to be the center of attention."

"You forget, I got a signed release before he got his check. Now for Deputy Burgess."

"He doesn't need much to look a little out of touch, Reverend."

"That's just it, Luke. We want him to look better. I might be able to use him."

With a dexterous mouse, Luke smoothed the deputy's hair, whitened his teeth, and added hints of muscles to his lanky frame. "Well?"

"Very nice, Luke. You are a true master. How soon till it's ready?" Marks grinned in anticipation.

"Give me a day to edit everything and add a little background music. I'll have a digitized master day after tomorrow."

"Excellent!" Marks sibilated. "I want to have them ready to sell when we do the revival in Atlanta." Humming a gospel tune, Marks patted Luke on the back. "Oh, and on one copy, which I would like A.S.A.P., please do that reward thing we talked about." With that, Marks headed for his office.

Booting his computer, the reverend logged on and found another message from Cindy:

Dear Reverend Marks,

I guess you don't have time to answer everybody. But I think I can help you with that John Worthington investigation. For one thing, I'm an amateur detective, myself. I almost got my own case on Public Enemy. *Also, John Worthington used to work here, until he disappeared. And I still might be talking to Mr. Fletcher, the other guy he's with. I also called Deputy Alan Burgess, the cop who was here a while back. I have his home phone number, too. If you want me to help you, I would love to. I want to stop these demons before they bring the Devil to earth.*

God Bless You,

Cindy Vinwire

"Well, Cindy, I think I can answer your prayer." Clumsily stabbing the keys, Marks answered her and planted another seed in his grim plot of salvation.

Wildwood

Sensing the minute change in air pressure and humidity, REL squeezed Valerie's hand. "It's going to rain soon, let's find some shelter."

"It's not supposed to, but I can smell it, too." She laughed as they ran to the overhang of a huge rock outcropping.

Concentrating his olfactory sensors, REL drew a deep breath to see if he, too, could smell the oncoming rain. The sweetness of the scent surprised him. Rich earth, green leaves, flowers, water — a dizzying cascade of living aromas swept through him. "Mmmmm," he sighed, tears of joy springing to his eyes. "Let's just sit and enjoy this," he said, drawing her down to a fallen log beneath the rocky canopy.

No sooner had the couple snuggled into the shelter when a fragrant downpour burst from the churning skies. Lighting arced across the firmament and thunder rumbled exuberant reveille above the dancing trees. They sat in silence, watching huge drops splash ripples on the surface of the lake. A resident family of ducks glided in front of them, quacking and jabbering in the cool of the storm. Adjusting his body's thermostat to compensate for the dropping temperature, REL wrapped a warm arm around Valerie's shoulder and hugged her nearer.

Nestling into his embrace, Valerie sighed, "Isn't it magnificent, REL?"

"Oh, Valerie, it is..." Even with his prodigious vocabulary, he struggled. "Numinous."

"Numinous?" Valerie repeated. "What a beautiful word... But I don't know what it means."

"See that fern over there?" He pointed to a huge fern whose soft, emerald fronds sparkled with jewel-like beads of rain. "Can you see the face of God?"

Valerie leaned forward just until rain misted her face and gazed at the green presence before her.

"See how filled it is with Spirit? It is alive beyond its roots and foliage — one perfectly unique expression of God. It is numinous."

"I've read about plant spirits and how they can heal..." Her voice trailed off as she mentally reached out to the fern.

"We breathe in more than their scent, Valerie. We inhale their quintessence and literally exchange molecules with each and every living thing. We dance through a living medium every moment of our lives. You know," he mused. "I marvel when I hear people describe something as 'godforsaken,' for there is no such place as where God is not." Reaching into his pocket, REL gently withdrew his amethyst. "Even here, in the most solid of creations, intelligence resounds. Alive." He placed it into the cup of her hand and softly folded her fingers around it. "Close your eyes," he whispered. "And tell me what you feel."

Breathing quietly for a moment, she slowly opened her eyes. "I've felt amethysts before, but this one carries your energy, too."

REL laughed, "See, we've exchanged molecules, that crystal and I."

Just then, a brilliant spear of lightning split the sky and booming thunder shook the earth where they sat. Valerie flinched in spite of herself and REL chuckled, nuzzling her damp hair. "Fear not, My Lady," he said kissing her hand. "Love surrounds us." He gestured to the rain-drenched forest around them.

"REL, remember when you told us about the dominant paradigm?" Valerie asked.

"Sure." He grinned. "I remember everything."

"If people really understood that we are surrounded by love, it would have to change the paradigm, don't you think?" Valerie turned and looked into his eyes.

Nodding, he said softly, "You're right. Will you help me tell them?" Cuddling back against the rock, the lovers settled in to wait out the storm.

Sheets of water sliding from the cabin roof and billowing walls of mist hid the lake from Gary Fletcher. An occasional flare of lightning hinted at the forest beyond. He shook his head. "I guess we can expect a couple of drowned rats to come straggling back any minute, now."

"Don't count on it, Gary," Dot quipped. "If I know John, he'll find a way to savor every drop that falls."

"No doubt," Fletcher agreed. "I wish I had his enthusiasm for life."

"Well, if he has his way, it's only a matter of time before you share it," Dot answered. "Before we all share it." She smiled, thinking about her friend. "Gary, so what are your plans for after this... um... fishing trip?"

Glancing ruefully at the two untouched fly rods, Fletcher thought long moments before responding. "For two cents, I'd stay right here. John's had at least that much influence on me."

"Hey, Barry, what are you going to do?" Dot called over to the hearth where Barry stood, back to the fire.

"I'm going to go with the flow. You know, before all this happened, I wasn't sure what I wanted to do with my life. John's given me a lot to think about." Barry grabbed his cup of cocoa and wandered over to Dot. "What are you going to do?"

Shaking her head, Dot said, "I haven't the foggiest. I'm not even sure what my choices are right now. I really don't have much of a life, to tell you the truth."

The three stood lost in thought, watching the rain, listening to it softly patter and slow. Sheets of water gave way to a gentle drizzle. Finally, a finger of blue sky etched its way above the lake. Then the creaking of the back door drew everyone's notice to the kitchen.

"Hey, swamp rats..." Fletcher swallowed his words when the nearly dry pair entered the cabin.

"Boy, did you guys miss a great storm." John and Valerie beamed as they removed their muddy shoes.

Elbowing the big man, Dot laughed, "See, I told you so."

"We've been talking about plans," Fletcher pronounced ominously. "I mean, what we're going to do after our vacation."

"Uh, oh," Dot mumbled. "Better put on some coffee."

As the coffee perked and filled the cabin with its mellow aroma, Valerie and REL moved to the fire to warm their chilly hands near the blaze. Barry settled into a comfy chair and Fletcher paced, pensive and silent.

"Want to hear my dearest wish?" John began quietly. When everyone nodded, he continued, "My dearest wish is that

220

we could all stay right here, together, to launch my new web page, and hopefully a new path for humanity."

"But that takes equipment and people..." Fletcher argued. "And money, John. That takes money."

"I have $23,000.00 for college," Barry volunteered. "And a great laptop."

"Your college money," Dot gasped. "You'd use that?"

"Dot, that money's for my education. This could be the best education there is."

"I've got a computer." Dot winked at REL. "A few hundred bucks in savings and a paid-off car that my ex has been badgering me to sell him."

"Wow, I don't have much," Valerie murmured. "I mean, I have a nice SUV and a bunch of books. Other than that, I don't have much else to offer."

"Valerie, are you kidding? You're a healer and the wisest woman I know." With a wink, REL concluded, *"Besides,* you have a keen understanding of numinousness."

Fletcher stared in frank amazement. "Dot? Valerie? Barry? You're willing to give up everything you own for this dubious spiritual revolution? Besides, even if I anteed up my 401K, savings, checking... everything, I couldn't come up with more than about $65,000. Even with everything you've all offered, we couldn't run something like this for more than six months. What could we possibly accomplish in six months?" Fletcher challenged.

"But Mr. Fletcher, the Universe will provide for this venture, if this is what we choose," REL assured.

"That's very nice, John, but I haven't seen any cosmic ATM's around here," Fletcher countered.

"Well, let's take inventory. With my Blazer, we have three vehicles, one computer and two laptops. Between Valerie and me, we have the makings of a pretty good library. And as near as I can calculate, with our furnishings and cash, we have about $409,000 in assets."

"Jeez, John, I'm glad you're not my accountant. Where did you get that figure?" Fletcher questioned. "There's not more than $89,000 in cash and three cars. What are they worth? Forty thousand. Tops. That's only $129,000."

"But you did not count the $280,000 that Dr. Morrison gave me. It's in my bank back in Phoenix."

Four pairs of eyes snapped to his face accompanied by a unified, audible gasp.

"So, do you want to do this with me?" he asked hopefully. "Will you be my partners in this?"

Alpha II

"How do you people stand it up here?" Mildred Hawthorne steadied herself as she stepped from the space dock into the lighted reception bay.

"Judge Hawthorne…" Timball said, extending his hand. "Welcome to Alpha II."

"Thanks," she mumbled, walking right on past the director to the closest bench. She plopped down holding her head in her hands. After a moment she looked up at the concerned man in front of her. "Sorry, Director, but space travel just does not agree with me. I'm afraid I was meant to be earthbound."

"Well I, for one, appreciate your sacrifice." Timball reached to help her as she struggled unsteadily to her feet.

The judge nodded then took the director's arm. Timball guided her down Central Expressway to the main conference area. They arrived in front of a door that whooshed open at his approach. "Please help yourself to coffee or refreshments, Judge Hawthorne."

Williams stood stiffly, started to salute, then dropped his arm.

Morrison rose. "Mildred..." He nodded, smiling. "How good to see you."

"Phillip," the judge acknowledged. "Space life seems to be treating you very well. You look younger than when I saw you last."

Morrison laughed. "Still myopic I see. Have you met Garner Williams before?"

Reaching out to the former monitor the judge took his hand in both of hers. "You have an impressive career record, Mr. Williams."

"Thank you Judge Hawthorne. Please call me Garner."

"Very well, Garner. Now gentlemen please sit down." The judge gestured toward the conference table. Seating herself and clasping her hands in front of her, she continued, "I braved the perils of space flight for one reason and one reason only. What we do here and how we conduct ourselves can either make or break a tense political situation. It's no secret that the political tides are going to turn in this Council session. Our calling is to serve humanity over and above any political party." Clearing her throat, she continued, "Now then, let me be clear on this. Garner, this is not a witch hunt. And let me be clear with you two as well." She nodded to Timball and then to Morrison. "If there is any impropriety, our long-standing acquaintance will not protect you. This is literally bigger than any of us."

"Thank you, Mildred." Morrison smiled. "I wouldn't ask anything more from anyone."

"Dan, Phil, may I have a few moments with Garner? Do you mind?" Judge Hawthorne asked.

"No problem, Mildred. Phil, join me across the hall." Timball grabbed the doctor's sleeve.

223

"When you two are finished, we'll have time for lunch before your transport takes you back," Morrison offered.

"Thanks, Phil, but I couldn't eat a thing. I think I'll stick to tea. Gentlemen…" She motioned toward the door then turned to Garner after they had gone. "Now, do you understand what I'm saying? There will be no ICom strong arm tactics used in this audit."

"May I speak freely, Judge Hawthorne?"

"Of course, I wouldn't have it any other way."

"Ma'am, the truth is that I'm not that unhappy with this turn of events. It was becoming painfully evident to me that Imperator Fells has a personal agenda."

Raising an eyebrow, the judge offered, "Would you care to talk about this, Garner?"

"Thank you, Judge Hawthorne, but it's ICom business and I can't discuss it."

"Fair enough. We'll leave it alone."

"I want you to know that I have come to respect both Dan Timball and Dr. Morrison. Despite our political differences, I have no grudge against them. Any suspicions I do have, I'll chalk up to ICom paranoia. I'll start this audit over with a clean slate."

"Garner, I appreciate your candor. I think we'll work well together. Please feel free to contact me with any questions or problems. And if Imperator Fells violates the judicial order and tries to pressure you in any way, I must know about it immediately."

Across the hall, Timball propped himself wearily on the edge of a conference table. "We will get caught, you know, Phil. All this judgment will do is buy us a little time and spare us Fells' brutality."

"Always looking on the bright side, aren't you, Dan? We can pray that REL's actions minimize the damage. And I still have a few small tricks left up my sleeve."

"Don't you find it at all odd that Williams hasn't even hinted at his suspicions that we poisoned him?" Timball mumbled gravely. "Maybe he's going to spring it on us at the most inopportune time."

Exasperated at his friend's pessimism, Morrison chided, "Dan! Can't you just accept this good turn of events and enjoy it as long as it lasts?"

"Yeah. As long as it lasts..."

Nederland

Late Autumn sun filtered through the overhanging trees and coated Thelma's deck with the sweetness of the changing season. Geese called overhead, and resident birds sang atwitter among the sheltering pines. "Mimosa?" Thelma offered.

"I'd love one." Dr. Winter smiled.

"Me, too." Alan Burgess nodded his head.

"Need some help?" Marshal Burrows offered.

"Sure, you can bring out the croissants. Made 'em myself." Thelma glowed in the midmorning brightness.

Settling down at the picnic table with its perfect view of Barker Reservoir, the four savored refreshments a moment before Marshal Burrows spoke.

"Dr. Winter, I'm concerned about Valerie..." he began. "...and Barry. It was bad enough when they disappeared. I'm still not convinced that this Worthington fellow is on the up and up. But since Reverend Marks got himself involved in this debacle, I'm even more concerned with her safety."

"He's a scary one, isn't he?" Dr. Winter brushed croissant crumbs from his shirt. "Fanatics like that make me nervous. And he's absolutely certain that Worthington is some kind of supernatural — and evil — entity. Nothing I could say to him about my examination of the man would make him change his mind."

"Just for the sake of argument and to put my mind at ease, there was nothing odd about Worthington?" Burrows asked, needing one last reassurance.

"Marshal, as far as I could tell from my examination, he was a perfectly healthy, albeit somewhat traumatized, *human being*," Dr. Winter emphasized. "Besides," he continued. "Valerie seems positively smitten with him. And that can't be all bad."

Burrows stared at the doctor. "You've heard from her?"

"She called me last night. She and Barry are coming back here to close up their respective abodes. From what she told me, Worthington, a couple of people from Phoenix and she and Barry are going to launch some kind of internet business in service of humanity or something. I didn't really understand that part."

"When are they going to be here?" Burrows asked. "I want to talk to her."

"Look Jim, I probably shouldn't even have told you. She thinks you have some kind of vendetta against Worthington or something. All she wants is to get her stuff and start a new life. I'm really going to miss her. But I'm happy for her, too. She's an extraordinary young woman."

"Okay, I won't press the matter. If you don't want me to talk to her, I guess that's okay. But I would like to know how to get in touch with her. If Marks goes off on some demon-hunt, I would like to be able to warn her."

"Do you really think Marks is that dangerous?" Dr. Winter asked.

"I do," Burgess interrupted. "I used to think he was the foremost expert on UFOs. But after meeting him, I just think he's a kook with a lot of information."

Burrows looked at Burgess in frank amazement.

"Well, from my experience with the guy," Thelma added. "I'd have to say that Valerie is in much more danger from him or one of his minions than from John Worthington. Besides, Valerie has excellent intuition. If she's sold on Worthington, he must be something special. Yeah, Marks is the one to watch. For sure."

"The truth is, Valerie wouldn't tell me where she's going. I think I lost a little of her trust when I told you about Worthington's job in Phoenix." Dr. Winter thought a moment. "I'll tell you what. I'll let her know that you're not after Worthington and tell her your concerns about Marks. If she wants to talk to you, I'm sure she'll be in touch."

"So, how are you going to keep tabs on Marks?" Thelma wondered aloud.

"That's easy," Burgess blurted through his second croissant. "You know that Cindy girl from Data Pioneer? Well..." He polished his fingernails on his shirt pocket and glanced at the marshal. "I think she likes me." He grinned. "Not that there's any future there, you know. But she is real keen on Marks. E-mails him every day. I think I can get her to keep me informed of his plans," he assured.

"Alan, all I ask is that the information exchange be one way. And no more *Investigator* updates. Okay?" Burrows pressed.

"Sure thing, Marshal. Consider it done." Burgess nodded.

"Well then..." Dr. Winter smiled. "I guess that's all we can do. Valerie will be here next weekend. I'll pass along your concerns."

Puppets & Prophets

Wildwood

The fire crackled in the great hearth at Wildwood. Outside, chilled stars flickered in the waning Autumn night. John's family, for such he thought them to be, gathered around the fireside for a quiet chat. In the center of a rainbow-colored woven rug REL stood, as if on stage. Valerie and Dot shared one of the massive leather couches that framed the hearth, Barry and Mr. Fletcher the other.

"Well, we're all heading out tomorrow to close an old chapter of our lives in preparation for a new one." John smiled at them, warm more from the love in his heart than from the flickering blaze behind him. "And there's something I would like to share with you before we go."

No one could answer, captivated as they were by the man who had already profoundly changed their lives.

"Everyone," REL went on, "place your hands like this." He placed his hands, one over top of the other, on the center of his breastbone. "Our hearts are not merely organs for pumping blood through our bodies. Our hearts are our literal connection with Spirit." John moved closer to Dot and Valerie, kneeling down before them. "We are all part of a loving, nurturing universe, yet many of us are afraid to accept that simple fact. Instead we live in fear that every step we take is a misstep and every decision we make could lead to disaster."

Dot smiled. "I know what you mean, John. Like packing up all my stuff. It's weird. I don't have anything back in Phoenix beyond a few shattered dreams and yet I feel a tremendous reluctance to leave there."

"I understand exactly what you mean." REL nodded keeping both hands firmly in place over his heart. "God has given us free will to choose between the universal expressions of love and fear and we have all largely chosen fear."

"Like in the garden of Eden," Fletcher suggested.

"Exactly," REL agreed standing and turning to face the big man. "It's a terrific metaphor. We are offered a choice of having the very best of everything or the very worst. We choose the worst because we've forgotten how to let our hearts guide us. It's really amazing isn't it?" REL turned toward Barry. "Barry, do you ever think of your heart?"

"Only when I hear about heart attacks and such."

"Are you having a tough time even now holding your hands over your heart?"

"Yeah. I feel like my heart is vulnerable. You know to heart attack, disease, all of the things we hear on TV." Barry pulled his hands away then put them back to his breastbone.

"Fear instead of love. Why would we ever make such a choice?" REL asked staring up at the polished branches of the cabin's support structure. "Barry, let me tell you that our hearts are really very powerful organs that get their strength from realms beyond the physical. Don't think of your heart as weak and vulnerable. It is far from it. Once you have fully connected with it you will begin to see how truly magnificent your heart is." REL gracefully guided his body to the floor and sat upright in the center of the rug with his legs crossed. "Now then, your heart is *the* center of intelligence for your body. Your heart literally tells your brain what chemicals to make. Science is only just beginning to comprehend this fact, but you will know it without science. You will feel it. Not only that, your heart is your literal interface with Spirit. Ready? Everyone close your eyes." REL closed his. "Now breathe several circular breaths in through your nose and out through your heart in one continuous breath. Let your breath relax and cleanse you." REL waited until he had heard everyone breathe several times. "Think of a place that soothes you. Some place like Wildwood. Imagine yourself in this place fully immersed in its peace and serenity then breathe that image into your heart." After several more breaths, he continued, "Now talk to your heart. Ask it how it can help you to become more loving, to always chose love over fear." After a moment he added, "Now open your eyes. What we have just done is the first step in connecting with our hearts. We aren't finished after just one attempt. Even if we felt a profound connection we must do it over and over and over so that love becomes our natural response to every situation. It *will* happen. And when we are very good at that, I will teach you how to reach out with your heart to touch another. Now close your eyes one more time and breathe through your hearts. I am going to send you all my love." REL closed his eyes, imagining the connection between his own heart and each member of his family. Then, he imagined his own link to a flowing pathway of energy that entered through the top of his head. The current flowed out through his heart and into each of the others, jumping from heart to heart to heart. He held the image for a full 60 seconds then opened his eyes.

The results were apparent. Valerie blushed and smiled. Dot laughed. "I felt that, John."

Fletcher leaned forward. "I did, too, John. It felt like a very warm hug."

Barry nodded. "Yeah, like when I was little and my mom used to sweep me up into her arms."

"Then you all have a beginning understanding of what our mission is about." REL beamed. "We must transmit over the internet, to millions of people, all of the most wondrous aspects of our physical and spiritual existence and we must do so through our hearts at the exact frequency of love."

Nederland

Valerie hugged Dr. Winter good-by and headed for the Marshal's Office. Dismayed at the note on the door, she headed to Town Hall. "Hi, Thelma. Is Marshal Burrows gone for the afternoon?" she asked.

"Yeah, you just missed him, Valerie. Do you have a minute?"

"Sure, Thelma. Want to go get coffee? I have to wait for Barry to get back. He has my Rodeo."

"I hear you're leaving Nederland, Valerie," Thelma began as the women opened the door to Whistler's.

Scooting over the bench by a sunny window, Valerie smiled. "That's right. Barry and I both are heading out. I'm gonna miss good old Ned, though."

"Coffee for me," Thelma told the waiter. "Valerie?"

"My usual, but I'm taking my cup with me this time." She smiled and turned to Thelma. "I've met the most amazing man, Thelma. I can hardly believe it myself. You know, all these years, Dr. Winter has hinted that I needed to get a life. And all of a sudden I've got one and it's everything I ever dreamed." Valerie glowed as she spoke.

Thelma reached over and placed a gentle hand on the young woman's arm. "Tell me all about him."

"I'm sure Marshal Burrows has mentioned John Worthington. For a while, it seemed like he was chasing us, you know."

"Well..." Thelma hedged. "I have heard a couple of things."

"Let me guess, Thelma," Valerie laughed. "You've heard about mother ships and conspiracies and organized crime. But none of it is true. John is the most wondrous person I've ever met."

"Really? How so?"

"He is so loving. To everyone. He's the most spiritual person I've ever known."

"Whew, that's saying a lot, Valerie. What religion does he teach?"

"That's just it," Valerie explained. "He's not religious. He's just loving. And brilliant. To talk with him, you would think he had read everything ever written about spirituality and philosophy. And he lives what he believes. He's amazing."

Thelma looked at the young woman across from her. She exuded joy and serenity. "I'm so happy for you, Valerie. I'll make sure Jim stays mellow about this."

"Thanks. But you know what? I'm too blessed to be worried." Valerie grinned.

"So, are you leaving a forwarding address?"

"Not just yet. But I promise I'll write. What's your P.O. Box?"

Thelma wrote her number on a convenient napkin just as the red Rodeo rolled up to the cafe. "Uh, oh. Gotta go." Valerie gave Thelma a quick hug, grabbed her mug of tea and hurried out the door.

Phoenix

You have mail. The electronic voice made Cindy's heart skip. It could only mean one thing, Reverend Marks had written again. She quickly typed in her password and waited for the server. Trembling with excitement, she clicked on the little envelope icon and held her breath while the message unfolded down her screen.

My Dearest Miss Vinwire,

Thank you ever so much for your devoted messages. It is faithful people like you who make God's work such a pleasure.

Regarding the Worthington Investigation: There may be an opportunity for you to further the cause of righteousness. You may not know this, but I have been in the field investigating the episode. And I have gathered considerable, compelling evidence. However, no one seems to know where Worthington and his hostages can be found.

That's why I am calling you into the Lord's Service.

Please pay very close attention to any information regarding any of them. If you find something suspicious, please contact me immediately. Also, I encourage you to take advantage of your contact in Nederland. Above all, if you find them, I must know A.S.A.P.

Please send me your physical address. I would like to send you a copy of our Nederland video, First Contact: Demons in the Mountains, *and a first run edition of* The Investigator. *Thank you for your faithfulness. May God bless you.*

Yours in the Lord,

Rev. Jeremiah Marks

"Uuuuh!" Cindy inhaled sharply. Prying her notebook from her back pocket, she flipped to a fresh page, dated the top and exultantly wrote: Official Investigation of John R. Worthington.

Moments later, Cindy pressed *send*, and answered Reverend Marks' call to service. Just then, the reflection of a large yellow rental truck pulled her from her fantasy. She gasped as John Worthington, Dot, and Mr. Fletcher tumbled out the doors. The trio headed to the back of the truck, grabbed a half dozen new, unassembled packing boxes, and walked across the parking lot to the office. Quickly, Cindy flipped her tablet to an unmarked page, then exited from her e-mail. Composing herself, she conjured a smile and greeted her suspects. "Hi guys," she laughed nervously. "Nice of you to drop by. I've got a ton of messages for all of you."

"Hi, Cindy." John smiled genuinely.

Gary Fletcher shook his head and advised, "You can save my messages for the next guy. Except for the ones from my ex-wife. You can shred those."

"Why? What's going on?" Cindy's fingers twitched, eager to record every detail.

"Let's just say, we've found a higher calling. We are outta here." Dot scowled, eager to bid Cindy a final farewell.

"I don't understand," Cindy said, following them down the hall.

Fletcher turned and explained. "We quit, Cindy. We are done here and have new employment plans. I'm sure corporate hasn't passed down the word, yet. But our replacements should arrive tomorrow."

The big man strode into his former office, popped open a large box and began pulling pictures and certificates from the walls.

"Just like that?" Cindy badgered. "So... where are you headed?"

"Are there any newspapers in the lobby?" Fletcher dodged. "I forgot to bring any."

Returning with a stack, Cindy persisted. "So, what are you gonna be doing?"

"Hey Cindy, would you see if anybody else needs help? Oh, and if we get any calls, we're not here."

Undaunted, Cindy headed toward Dot, but stopped in her tracks at Dot's icy demeanor. Gulping, she made her way to Worthington's office, fingering her WARS pin as she walked.

"Gee, John…" she began, "you weren't with us very long. I'm sorry we didn't get to know each other better. Maybe we could keep in touch?" she suggested timidly.

"Oh, great idea. Do you have an e-mail address?" He grinned a disarming grin.

Girding her resolve, she grabbed a slip of paper from his disordered desk, jotted down her addy and handed it to him.

"Great. When I get my e-mail up and running, I'll send you my address."

"So… what are you guys gonna do?" Cindy prodded.

"Oh, we're working to initiate a paradigmatic shift," he explained.

Paradigmatic, paradigmatic, she repeated to herself. She opened her mouth to press further, but a ringing phone demanded her attention. A long distance, dictated letter from a salesman bound her to her desk. She watched helplessly as the trio carried box after box out the door. Finally, in desperation, Cindy punched *hold* and left the man dangling. "Bye, John," she called as he passed her desk, waving.

"Bye, Cindy. I'll e-mail you as soon as I launch my home page. Take care." He smiled and disappeared out the door.

When the door whispered shut, Cindy looked at the display on her phone. The *hold* light no longer blinked. Relieved, she quickly logged on and reported to Marks.

"I'll drive," Fletcher boomed. "At least for a few hours."

Piling into the rental truck, REL and his friends settled in for the grueling drive home, worldlies packed in the truck and the white Blazer in tow. Miles flashed by, eating up the barren terrain. Dark descended and Fletcher yawned. "Let's stop for something to eat, and then you can drive, John."

"My pleasure," John responded, pointing to a Denny's sign. "I can drive all night."

"No doubt you can do it, John." Dot squirmed. "But, I'm not sure I can ride all night." Turning to Fletcher, Dot jabbed him in the ribs. "Gary, is this little cost-saving idea yours?" she complained. "I would have sprung for a moving company."

"Come on, Dot. This will be fun. I've never been any of these places before." John grinned.

"Maybe it would be fun in a car," Dot retorted, "not in a friggin' truck."

Hours later, REL looked in the rearview mirror, the silence of the midnight road was peaceful and soothing. He glanced over at his sleeping friends and smiled at the grimace on Dot's face. Turning his attention back to the road and surrounding countryside, he memorized every vista, every change in terrain. *How wonderful,* he thought, *to see so many states.* Eagerly anticipating the color of daytime, it occurred to him that Dot and Fletcher might question his ability to stay awake the whole trip. Basking in his well-being and the joy of his journey, he mused. *Maybe I'll just tell them why I can do it.*

Bludgeoned by his program at the mere suggestion, REL struggled to keep the truck straight on the road. Every alarm in every single circuit screamed at him, pushing him perilously close to peak load. Dumfounded and furious at the limitation, REL probed for the logic of it. He breathed deeply to steady himself, then sought directly for the source of this peremptory command. He reluctantly found solace in Morrison's reasoning. The doctor was right. Should Earth 1999 discover his true nature, his mission would surely fail. He would undoubtedly be hunted down and dismantled. His structure would be back-engineered, resulting in radical and unpredictable distortions in the timeline. He could not, he must not imperil the present or the future.

But neither could he allow this limitation to endure.

"Hey..." Cindy's voice jangled Alan's sleepy calm. "Sorry I'm calling so late. But I had to go to prayer meeting."

"S' okay," Burgess slurred. "What's up?"

"Guess what? Worthington and his boss and his boss' assistant came back today. Cleared out their offices and left town in a moving van. So, whadda ya think of that? Good thing I found Jesus, or I might be traipsing off behind them."

Burgess perked up to carefully measure every word. The marshal's promised wrath loomed heavy before him. "So... Cindy, are you thinking mind control?" he asked.

"Yup," she replied. "And you know what else? They're planning some para... para-something-or-other kinda shift. I couldn't write it down when he said it, and I forgot."

"Paradoxical?" he questioned.

"I... uh... think so," she said, uncertain. "And they're using the internet to do it, Alan."

"Wow," Burgess blurted. "Did they say where they're going?"

"Nope, but John's gonna send me his e-mail addy as soon as he gets one and then I'll get his physical address. And guess what else? Reverend Marks called me to the Lord's Service. He wants me to join the investigation. He's even sending me a copy of the video he made in Nederland."

"Hey, will you dupe it and send me a copy?" Burgess asked.

"You bet," Cindy assured. "This is really cool, huh? Scary, cause of the demons and stuff, but cool."

"Yeah. Cool," Burgess responded half-heartedly, engrossed by the thought of a paradox shift. "Well, I'm going to let you go now," he interrupted. "Thanks for calling me. Keep in touch, okay?"

"Sure thing, Alan. And God bless you," she offered timidly.

"Yeah. You, too," he stammered. "Good-night."

Next morning, over coffee, Burrows groaned, "What now?"

"Cindy said something about a paradox shift, Marshal. She wasn't real clear." Burgess ripped a huge bite from his jelly-smothered bagel and chewed with gusto.

"Naturally," Burrows grinned indulgently. "God, you're a mess, Alan. You've got jelly all over your face." Handing the deputy a wad of napkins, he continued. "What's a paradox shift, anyway."

"That's just it, Marshal. In all my reading, I've never come across it," he mumbled, wiping a gob of jelly from his cheek. "Paradox usually refers to time travel — as in if you meet yourself in another time — that's a paradox. I'm not even sure if Cindy got it right. But it's something to think about, isn't it? By the way…" He stopped to eye another bite. "You'll be happy to know that I didn't tell her one, single thing."

Wildwood

REL beamed. The bright red Rodeo shone like a welcome at the end of the drive. "Valerie and Barry beat us home," he chuckled, anxious to see Valerie.

"Jeez. Imagine that," Dot groused. "They even drove a thousand more miles than we did." Rubbing her backside, she emphasized, "Maybe it's because they drove a Rodeo, not a buckboard."

Valerie burst through the front door. "What took you so long?" she joked.

Dot groaned, crawling stiffly from the truck. "Good, you're not crippled, you can unload this abomination."

John jumped from the cab, and bounced over to embrace Valerie. "I missed you so much," he murmured into her ear. Taking her hand and turning her back to the truck he called, "Let's go unpack."

"Are you nuts?" Fletcher rejoined. "We've been on the road since 3:30 this morning! That stuff can wait until tomorrow."

"Or whenever we hire some help," Dot moaned, limping to the cabin.

"Okay, if you're sure," John relented. "But Valerie, come and see what we have." He drew her around to the back of the truck and unlocked the rolling door. Valerie gasped when she saw the dozens of boxes of new computer equipment. "We decided to do a little shopping. We have *everything* we need, Valerie. We have Macs, PCs... even a couple of UNIX boxes. And software!! We got the best stuff. Oh, Valerie, this is going to be so much fun," he bubbled.

Next morning, Dot shuffled down to the kitchen in slippers and bathrobe seeking desperately needed coffee and aspirin for her aching back. Instead, she found Gary Fletcher, staring in astonishment toward the great room.

"Mr. Fletcher, all your stuff is over in that corner. And, good morning, Dot! Your stuff's over there." REL pointed to the other end of the room. "And, you've *got* to see this." He grabbed Dot's hand and drew her gently toward the largest bedroom on the ground floor, then gently pushed her inside, guiding Fletcher to follow.

Barry picked up the remaining styrofoam packing material, then stood back to give full view to the room. "Ta Da!" he sang.

Valerie leaned against the window frame surveying the room that was wired and filled with a maze of computer equipment — all machines on and humming. "Fresh coffee's in the kitchen." She grinned at the dumfounded Dot. Behind the wide-eyed woman, Fletcher stood shaking his head in disbelief.

"Today, we start programming," John announced cheerfully.

Fletcher looked longingly at the still-untouched fly rods that leaned forlornly against the front door jamb. "Oh well..." he sighed.

Nederland

"Great, Jim. I'll make popcorn. Are you sure you won't tell me the name of the movie?" Thelma prodded.

"Nope. It's a surprise. See you soon." Burrows hung up the phone and hollered to Burgess, "Come on. Let's get this over with."

Burrows stood at Thelma's door, Alan behind him, stifling a mischievous grin. "Come in, you two. Whose canary did you swallow, Deputy?" She laughed.

Jim pulled the blinds while Thelma set out bowls and salt and napkins. Burgess poured beer for them and popped the tape into the VCR.

"So what's this mysterious movie?" Thelma badgered as she settled on the couch next to the marshal.

Without answering, Burrows aimed the remote at the VCR to show her.

Rasping metal music blared, prompting the marshal to hurriedly turn down the volume. Across the television screen, toxic clouds boiled, lightening blasted and thunder bellowed. *First Contact: Demons in the Mountains.* The words bled down the screen, pooling, then morphing into Barker Reservoir. The vista panned across the bloodied water to close upon the town, tawdry and huddled beneath the roiling clouds.

Thelma hooted at the television. "Is this for real?"

The music dimmed and died as Nederland dissolved into golden text. *God's Fortress Investigates* floated atop a celestial vision of blue sky and pristine clouds. A slide guitar whined hymnal riffs as Reverend Jeremiah Marks sharpened into view, standing next to the Mountain Wiccans Adopt-A-Highway sign.

Thelma held her sides, tears streaming down her face. "Much more of this and I'll pee my pants. Oh God..."

"Ssshh, Thelma," Burrows hushed her with his stony face. "This isn't a comedy."

Burgess sat wordless, his attention glued to the screen.

Thelma's laughter turned to a gasp at the first view of the marshal. The camera slowly panned from the dirt path, up his scuffed shoes to his plumped-out frame. From there, the view shifted to his jowly, pasty face and dark-circled eyes, then up over his head to the Nederland Marshal's Office sign. At which point, a grainy Burrows voice said, "A lot of people believe that alien contact is an honor."

"I said no such thing," Burrows protested.

"Now wait a minute, Marshal. You said something like that when we were at God's Fortress. Remember, we talked about *X-Files* and Thelma's theories."

Appalled, Burrows spat, "He *taped* our conversation?"

Stunned by the deplorable manipulation of the facts, the trio watched the rest of the film in silence.

At the tail end of the credits, like an afterthought, a strange, poorly scripted message flashed on the screen: *God's Fortress offers a reward of $50,000 for information leading to the exorcism of this demon. Contact (800) 555-7777 with leads.*

Burrows burst from the couch. "He can't do that. My God, he'll have every nut in the country out gunning for Worthington. That's practically a public murder contract."

"No," Burgess said quietly. "Marks made this copy just for Cindy. The others aren't even out yet. According to her."

Burrows sat back down. "He's setting her up."

"For what?" Thelma asked.

"I don't know, but I don't like it one bit." Burrows scowled.

Phoenix

Hugging her arms tightly around her chest in attempt to still her thudding heart, Cindy Vinwire walked unsteadily toward her front door. Three feet before she reached it, she stopped and squinted to check the deadbolt. Then she tiptoed to the small peephole. Drawing a quick breath, she peered out into the hall of her apartment building, glancing first to the right and then to the left, toward the stairs. *It was just the wind*, she reassured herself. *It was nothing*. Clutching the remote to her VCR, she returned to the couch. Only this time, she left the lights on.

Compelled to watch it again, Cindy rewound *First Contact: Demons in the Mountains*. Tucking her new Bible to one side and a decoupaged picture of Jesus to the other, she clasped her small gold-plated cross between her sweaty palms and stared at the screen. Drawing a brave breath, she pushed *play*. As the camera panned across the eerie lake to the evil little town, she closed her eyes, and when she saw Alan Burgess she almost cried for him, trapped as he was in Nederland.

Pausing the video, she heaved a ragged sigh, picked up the phone and dialed Alan's number.

"Hello?" his voice echoed through the phone.

"Hey, Alan. Are you okay?" Cindy stammered.

"Yeah. Just got home a few minutes ago. Are you okay? You sound funny."

"Oh, I'm just a little spooked." She laughed nervously. "Did you get my package?"

"Yep," Burgess replied, unsure of how to respond to the picture of Jesus and the glamour shot of the young woman. "Thanks. So, what's got you spooked, Cindy?"

"Oh... I've been watching you in the video. And I'm afraid for you, Alan."

"Why?" he asked.

"The place you live. It looks so awful." She glanced again at the frozen image on her TV.

"I love it here, Cindy. It's nothing like what Reverend Marks makes it out to be. The people here are really nice. And the mountains are wonderful. You should come for a visit, sometime."

Shuddering at the thought, she asked, "Alan... You know a lot about guns, don't you?"

"Oh yeah. I know a lot about guns. Why?"

"I've kind of been thinking about getting one. Thought I'd ask your advice."

"Wow, Cindy. This demon thing has you really scared, huh?"

"Don't you understand, Alan? Armageddon is right around the corner. And the demons are already here. Here! Recruiting their armies. And here I am, all alone in this world. Just me against an army of evil." She choked, walling herself against the impending torrent of tears.

"Cindy..." he tried to calm her.

"You of all people know about it, Alan! For cryin' out loud, you see demons every day. Robbers and rapists and murderers. That's what they are. And even regular people. Nice people like John Worthington can even turn out to be evil. No. I have to know how to protect myself."

"But, Cindy..." he spoke softly. "You..." he paused. "You say you believe in Jesus. You even sent me his picture. Isn't he supposed to protect you?" Burgess swallowed hard.

244

"Alan, he's just for saving our souls. He can't stop a bullet for me." Cindy wept uncontrollably now.

"But people, lots of people carry pictures of him in their cars to keep them safe from accidents. Isn't it sort of the same thing?" Alan reasoned, heart aching for the girl.

"Oh, you just don't understand. I'm a sinner, Alan. I don't deserve that. I have to take care of myself. I'm getting a gun, Alan. Won't you help me?" she begged in despair.

Doing his best for her, he suggested, "Why don't you join a gun club, Cindy? Maybe one where they have programs for women. First, learn how to shoot a gun. Then learn which is best for you before you buy one. That's really the smartest thing to do." Stretching every social grace he possessed, he offered gently, "Cindy... Really, it will be okay. Even though I'm a cop, I still see far more nice things in this world than bad ones. I promise."

"Thank you, Alan," she sniffed, calming a little.

"And if you want, I can use my police contacts down there to find a good club and maybe an instructor." He paused. "Are you all right?"

"You would do that for me, Alan?" she whimpered.

"Sure, Cindy. I'll find out and I'll call you. Take care of yourself."

As he hung up the phone, Alan Burgess leaned forward in his chair, hand clamped over his mouth to stifle his sadness for her. "Poor Cindy." The pixieish blond smiled timidly up at him from the glamour shot. "Poor girl." He shook his head.

Wildwood

"Everybody ready?" John grinned. Poising his hands like an orchestra maestro, he drew them down with a flourish and struck *enter*. Instantly, images loaded across his high res, 21 inch monitor, officially launching the *Second Messenger* home page.

"Oh my," Valerie marveled as the etheric vista unfolded. Golden light chased a hurrying aerial view of lovely planet Earth. Oceans and clouds, cities and landscapes spun away below, blushing — inviting the viewer to enter. The retreating horizon summoned the eyes, then drew them up and away to the Heavens and beyond.

"My God, John, I've never seen a page like this before. You'll win web awards for this. It's fabulous." Dot gazed in wonder.

Elbowing John, Barry grinned. "Turned out great, didn't it?" The young man beamed at his contribution. "Did you ever come up with the dedication?"

Nodding, John loaded the next page. A be-ribboned scroll spun out from one corner, growing larger until it filled the center of the screen. With a click, REL untied the bow, unfurling a universe captured within the parchment. A tiny, tailed comet shot across the darkness as miniature galaxies spun and tumbled within the three dimensional space.

"REL," Valerie gasped. "It looks like the real thing."

Just then, luminous stars drifted to the fore, each exploding in a shower of words that read:

Second Messenger is dedicated to universal love – may it become the new dominant paradigm for humankind.

"Now then," REL announced. "Each one of us will have a job to do here, but I want it to be fun. If it doesn't feel like joy then we need to rethink. Understood?"

Everyone nodded.

"How exciting!" Dot wriggled into a chair in front of her chosen computer. "I'm ready. Just bring me coffee and tell me what to do."

REL laughed. "Every day we need to answer e-mail."

"And the chat rooms will need continuous attention," Barry explained. "We will want to be able to jump in at any time to keep conversations stimulating and uplifting."

"And, Gary..." REL grimaced. "I hope this isn't too terrible. I was thinking you could handle our money. You know, set us up as a non-profit entity. Keep track of income and expenses and make sure everyone gets a regular salary and whatever they need to do their jobs."

"John... Surely you jest." Gary scowled. "Of course I'll do that." He cracked a huge smile. "And I'll love it."

REL sighed in relief.

"And, Valerie one of the chat rooms is dedicated to vitality. It's yours to take in any direction you choose." REL smiled.

Valerie laughed, "Great!"

"Come closer." REL gathered everyone together in a tight circle. "I want this to be the best experience of your life."

Phoenix

Pop! Pop! Pop! Cindy awkwardly squeezed off the rounds, small hands barely controlling the recoil of the long barreled .38. Nonetheless, she smiled grimly when the target rolled to her and revealed one hit in the outside ring. Slipping the ear protectors to the back of her neck, she turned to her instructor.

"Let's try the snub tomorrow, Cindy. You're doing good, though. Can I buy you a cup of coffee?" The older man gestured toward the snack bar and nearby picnic table.

"Thanks. I've only got a minute, though. Got to get to work." Cindy slung her backpack to the table, plopped down on the bench, folded her arms and waited for the man.

"Deputy Burgess asked me to look after you, Cindy," the fatherly, graying retired policeman told her.

"So, do you know Alan?" she asked.

"Not, really. Professional courtesy. I know Jim Burrows, though. So why did you decide to take up shooting?"

"Oh, you know... I live alone in a rough neighborhood. The usual." She sipped her coffee. "It would be nice to sleep at night. Oops, gotta run." Cindy confirmed tomorrow's lesson and hurried to her car.

Raking her fingers through her short, blond hair, Cindy sat at the Data Pioneer reception desk, tapping her foot as the server loaded her e-mail. "Well, I'll be damned..." Catching her curse with a hand to her lips, she double-clicked on the message from John Worthington.

She copied down John's URL and e-mail addy, saved his message then opened a new one for Reverend Marks. Proudly, she reported the *Second Messenger* home page URL and included John's e-mail address. She made short mention of her shooting class and closed with, "I can't wait for the Atlanta Revival. Maybe I'll see you there. Yours in the Lord, Cindy Vinwire."

God's Fortress

Reverend Marks stood patiently, one arm to his side, the other raised to accommodate the tape measure. "You can assure me that this suit will be done before the 10th?" he droned at the kneeling tailor.

"Absolutely, Reverend. The silk arrived yesterday."

Scrutinizing his new hair style in the full-length mirror, Marks hardly noticed when the tailor left. Checking his watch, he smiled a toothsome grin and headed for his computer. Once on-line he reread his personal schedule for the four-day Atlanta Revival. "Ah, Miss Vinwire," he whispered, clicking to open her message, then clapped his hands in delight at the sight of John

Worthington's internet info. "Well done, Dear. Well done. You can count on seeing me in Atlanta." He made a note to himself, replied to her message then headed to the Second Messenger home page.

The reverend scowled as the page unfolded. He fumed at the demon technology that outshone anything else he had seen on the net. Even his own God's Fortress site paled in comparison to this. He penned a quick note to Matthew, his in-house internet whiz, to take a look and design something to rival it.

His stomach lurched ever so slightly as the page panorama sped into outer space. He sneered at the dedication and went directly to the visitor's roster of chatters. Selecting the topic of ascension, he stabbed in SkyPilot and clicked to enter the chat.

Wildwood

"Hey, John," Dot called from her computer. "Remember that SkyPilot guy that buzzed through the Spirit Forum chat room? Well, he just dropped in here."

John grabbed Valerie's hand and drew her with him to the computer room.

"And here's 2nd Sight! This ought to be good. Do you think she'll really remember his energy?"

"I don't know about her, but I sure will," John assured, logging in from his own computer. Grinning, he typed:

REL:	{{{{2nd Sight}}}} I've missed you! How nice to see you again.
2nd Sight:	{{{{REL}}}} Wow. I just found this place. It's GREAT! How long have you been coming here?
REL:	Actually... This is my web site.

2nd Sight:	Oh, you're blushing. I can feel it from here! :o} This is fabulous! I need not ask how your search for God is coming.
elemental:	Greetings! May I join you?

John stood up and looked over his computer at Valerie, who had just logged in. "Nice nick, elemental." He smiled at her, delighted just to share the same room.

"Wait for me!" Dot laughed and logged in as sandrose. "WooooHooooo!" she laughed again. "Let's have us a chat."

REL:	{{{{elemental}}}} & {{{{sandrose}}}} // 2nd Sight, these are two of my very best friends. :=) // SkyPilot, do you want to join us? Let's talk about ascension and the heart connection.
SkyPilot:	I did not come to chat. I wish only to observe.
REL:	Suit yourself. You are welcome here.
2nd Sight:	The heart is the doorway to God.
REL:	You're right about that, 2nd Sight. It begins when you discover the source of intelligence residing there.
elemental:	2nd Sight, have you visited the heart section? There are some great heart connecting exercises there you are welcome to pass on to anyone who can use them.
REL:	Of course, 2nd Sight, I already know that you know how to channel energy through your heart. I felt it before. *s* And my hit is that you came to the ascension chat to offer your wisdom.
2nd Sight:	We are all students and teachers. I came to exchange ideas and energy, too. I'm interested in your insights, REL, {{All}}.

REL: I have found that by channeling every-
                thing through my heart, consciously, it
                makes all the difference in my experi-
                ences. For one thing, you cannot be
                afraid when you come from your heart.

elemental: I know! It's like your heart disallows
                that vibration so fear can't color your
                beliefs.

REL: You know, there is a reason for that.
                See, fear has its own signature frequen-
                cy of vibration. In order to exist at all,
                fear literally must drag energy down to
                affect it. It cannot be so within the
                realms of the heart. Anything passing
                through the heart must rise to meet its
                vibration, so to speak.

sandrose: That sounds pretty scientific, REL.

REL: It's my version of quantum physics. But
                the important thing is that mystics and
                holy people have known this since the
                beginning of humankind. THIS was
                what Christ came to tell us. His mes-
                sage was love. And love is the language
                of the heart. Beautiful circle, aye? It all
                leads back to God.

In righteous fury, Marks jabbed out a seething message
to the group.

SkyPilot: Listen to yourselves! You talk about
                channeling and mystics and vibrations
                in the same breath with which you
                claim to understand Christ. How dare
                you? You flirt with an evil you cannot
                possibly even comprehend!!!!!

elemental:	SkyPilot — we each find our own truths as they work for us.
2nd Sight:	Why are you so angry, SkyPilot? Your energy exudes beyond your computer.
SkyPilot:	Don't you hex me, 2nd Sight!
2nd Sight:	Hex you? ***ROTFL*** SkyPilot, lighten up. Just because you believe in evil doesn't mean that we do. Nor does it mean that we practice it. Be at peace.
REL:	I, too, would ask what you are so angry about. Is your own faith not strong enough to tolerate ours?
SkyPilot:	How dare you? I am a man of God! I have no more time for you now. But I warn you!!! I will be watching every-thing you do! ***POOF***

Transcendent Burlesque

Atlanta, Georgia

"Now, Roberts, make sure you find her. Her name is Cindy Vinwire. Alert the check-in tables to page you as soon as she arrives. Then find her and casually steer her in my direction. Nothing obvious. Understand?" Reverend Marks stood in the make-up room of his big tent, barking orders over his cell phone. Preening before his first appearance in Atlanta, he smiled at the reflection he saw in the mirror. Today's sermon would rock them. He knew it. Calling Matthew and Luke to him, he reminded one last time, "Lots of footage. Lots of sound bites. I want close-ups of me and of people in the crowd. You know what to look for. We're going to sell the Atlanta tape in Boston."

"Consider it done, Reverend," Luke assured. "We have 20 cameramen stationed around the stage and all through the crowd. We've got you covered."

"You're up, Reverend," the stage manager called through the tent flap.

Even from backstage the roar of the crowd was thunderous. Reverend Marks straightened his jewelry and his tie, then flanked by shiny-robed gospel singers, he marched out from behind the curtain.

"Praise God!" Marks shouted.

253

The crowd returned an ear splitting, "Praise God!" Then the congregation screamed wildly, hushing only when the six gospel singers burst into a chorus of hallelujahs.

"Brothers and Sisters! I have been to the habitat of demons," Marks declared.

A unified shudder swept through the congregation.

"Three days in the wilderness did we spend, blazing a path for God. I tell you there were idolaters, witches..." Making fingertip quotation marks, he sneered, "New Agers, and every other kind of sinner. But most frightening of all Brothers and Sisters... There was the stench of demons!" Marks paused while the gospel singers provided eerie accompaniment. "Brothers and Sisters the legions of evil are arriving on our planet in hordes. Are you ready. Have you repented?"

The full choir surged onto the stage wrapping around the reverend like a swarm of bees. Their song of repentance started the audience swaying and shouting "amens." When the audience quieted, Marks waved a clearing around himself and retook the microphone. "Witness the power of God. There is a man from Mobile whose body and mind have been corrupted by demons. He is begging now for salvation."

From the back of the tent, a wheel chair rolled down the long red aisle. A whimpering, doleful man slumped, barely able to lift his head. As he approached the stage he rolled his eyes to meet Reverend Marks.

Six men lifted the man to the stage where the reverend reached out to him, pulling him to his feet. "Feel the power of God. Demons, release this man, now!" Marks dropped his arm and the man fell back into a bevy of waiting evangelicals. Finally, the man rose to his feet and smiled.

"Praise God," Marks cried. "Praise God."

Hours later the reverend bowed and strolled through the writhing crowd. From all sides, hands reached out to him, content to merely brush the shiny fabric of his suit. As he stepped outside the main tent, a young woman bounced headlong into him. "Ugh!" he belched as her weight drove him back. With the help of his disciples he kept his footing.

"Oh, Reverend Marks!" The young lady's crimson face announced her embarrassment. "I'm so sorry, sir."

Marks saw the thumbs-up from Roberts. "It's quite all right my dear. Accidents certainly do happen. Here, let me make sure you are all right." He held her by the shoulders and drew her upright.

"Cindy Vinwire," he read the white and gold paper name tag. "Why, I can't believe it's you! How delighted I am to actually make your acquaintance."

"Oh. Oh no, Reverend Marks," she stuttered. "It's me who is delighted. It really is."

"Well, Miss Vinwire…"

"Oh, please Reverend Marks, call me Cindy," the young blonde interrupted and curtsied slightly.

"Very well, Cindy. Would you care to join me in my limo? I'll drop you at your hotel and we can talk."

Alpha II

The lights flickered and Williams cursed himself for not saving his last few minutes of work. Irritated, he called Timball, "What the hell is going on here, Director? This is the third time this morning," Williams complained.

"I know Mr. Williams. We are experiencing an unusual amount of solar flare activity. It is the season for it you know," the director explained. "Just work slowly and archive often."

"I seem to recall reading somewhere that these newer facilities were immune to solar flares. Some kind of shielding technology," Williams argued.

Timball shrugged. "Maybe true, but this is not one of the newer facilities. It's fifteen years old already. Sorry for the hassle. I'll do what I can," he promised and disconnected.

Timball grumbled to Morrison who was working intently on the director's main computer. "First we poison him. Now we're trying to drive him insane. Is that the plan?"

"There. I think I have this programmed now so that the outages will only affect the First Station but will get logged as a total station failure." The doctor gently brushed the spinning icon. "We have to use every opportunity we're given to buy time and cover our tracks, Dan. Hang in there."

Williams passed an angry hand over his short-cropped hair. Nothing about this assignment added up. A prompt from his com spared him further frustration. "Williams, here," he answered patiently.

The looming face of Imperator Fells filled his view. "Williams, I have to make this quick. Damned liberal judge has me barred."

Williams stuttered, "Im... Imperator, I'm not supposed to talk to you."

"Then just listen, you fool!" Fells raged. "Look, Morrison and Tabbot are in cahoots. They've launched some kind of illegal technology to destroy me *and* the ICom. You've got to expose them."

"Imperator Fells, so far I've found absolutely nothing that even hints at any alleged conspiracy. Nothing," Williams reasoned.

"Don't be an idiot, Williams. You got sick the moment you stepped foot on Alpha II. Do you think that was just a coincidence?" Fells snapped.

"But there's no proof. No proof at all."

"Who knows what they'll try next to stop you. One of my tecchies has designed a program for you. It will help identify irregularities you may overlook. I can't upload it from here without getting caught, so I sent Kyle Zephyrs to deliver it. Use it, Williams. And get Morrison." Fells glowered. "Do you understand?"

Williams nodded then signed off. "Oh, shit!" he wailed. Just then the lights in the First Station flickered and went out altogether, bathing him in darkness.

Kyle Zephyrs strode down Central Expressway heading for the First Station and marveling at the homey feel of the space-borne hulk. *An amazing accomplishment*, he mused to himself. Following the wall-mounted map, the young man guided himself to Williams' suite and signaled at the door for entry. "Hey Garner…" Zephyrs laughed. "Sitting in the dark for any particular reason?" he asked as he stepped into the dim First Station.

"Well, in case you haven't noticed, the whole station is dark, except for the emergency lights in the hallways," Williams explained. "Solar flares."

"Uh, I don't know where you got that idea. This place is as bright as a Christmas Tree."

Williams' face reddened like a climbing thermometer. Grabbing the younger man's elbow, he stormed down the hallway and straight to the director. Shaking with anger, he drew a deep breath in preparation for his tirade. He rounded the corner nearest Timball's office and ran smack into the man. "We're going to have a talk," he growled, resisting the powerful urge to grab the director by his collar. "Now!" he barked and turned Timball back the way he had just come.

Like a man held at gunpoint, the director shuffled back to his quarters, protesting loudly as they approached his door. "What's this about Mr. Williams," he enunciated as the door whooshed open to reveal Doctor Morrison, leaning back against the station's master computer.

"Mr. Williams! What a surprise," Morrison humored.

"Good. You're here, too." Williams brusquely motioned Zephyrs to take a seat, then began his accusations. "Look…" He barely kept his voice civil. "I do not dislike you two. Whatever you may think. I came here with a job to do and have tried to do it. I wasn't heavy-handed, even when I had the authority. And yet…" He began to pace. "I'm pretty sure you poisoned me and put me through hell for weeks. I lost my commission with the ICom. And now, I can't even get dependable electricity. What the hell's going on here!" He glared at the men, defying them to explain.

Timball gasped for breath. Morrison sighed and began very quietly. Only his reddened face betrayed any emotion. "Mr. Williams, let's explore a hypothetical situation. Okay?"

"Hypothetical?" Williams snorted.

"Purely," Morrison replied. "Let's just say that a soldier, who worked for the likes of Fells, was assigned to this station with specific instructions to destroy a mad scientist. And let's say that this personal vendetta carried ramifications the soldier could not possibly imagine. Suppose, based on the aforementioned, the mad scientist blurred the lines of decency. No real harm done to anyone. Assume, then, that the scientist discovered — much to his surprise — that the soldier was a gentleman." Morrison looked directly into Williams' eyes and continued sincerely, "Given your years of experience, Mister Williams, would you think it possible for the soldier and the scientist to reach a gentleman's agreement to respect each other and be allowed to do their jobs?"

Thunderstruck at the doctor's humility, Williams plopped down in the nearest chair and just stared at the man. Finally, he breathed, "Yes. Hypothetically, I think that could happen. But there would have to be no more games. Ever." He looked Morrison in the eyes.

Extending his hand, Dr. Morrison looked Williams in the eyes. "Here's to hypothetical agreements," he said. With a firm shake, he quietly added, "And honorable men."

Kyle Zephyrs remained silent all the way back to the First Station. Finally ensconced in his friend's rooms, he asked, "Did I miss something here? Didn't Morrison just confess to something then solicit your complicity?"

"That's not what I heard, Kyle. Morrison never admitted to anything. As for the complicity... We just agreed to be gentlemen. That's fair, don't you think?"

"I'm not sure Fells would agree, Garner." Pulling a tiny disc from his shirt pocket, Kyle flipped the program to Williams.

"I won't use this, Kyle. No matter what Fells demands. I've given my word twice to act with my highest integrity. Fells may scare the crap out of me, but compromising my own ethics scares me more."

"Are you out of your mind, Phil? You just *mea culpa'ed* to the toughest monitor the Icom ever produced!! What ever possessed you to do such a thing?" Timball ranted.

"It was the decent thing to do, Dan. Williams was right about that. I've felt guilty about our actions all along. I allowed my own desperation to drive me to things I'm not proud of. Besides..." The doctor winked. "Wouldn't you say that I'm a pretty good judge of people?"

Timball begrudged his agreement, but nodded his head anyway.

"I think Williams makes a much better ally than enemy," Morrison pronounced as if the task were a *fait accompli.*

Nederland

Alan Burgess fluffed the red flannel pillow and settled down once more to try to sleep. His mind had just ceased its chatter when the phone rang. With a groan, he fumbled to reach it and mumbled, "Hello?"

"Alan?" Cindy questioned quietly. "Oh... I woke you up, didn't I? Sorry."

"It's okay. What's up?" Alan squeezed his eyes closed then popped them open.

"I got you something," Cindy teased. "Something really cool."

"What?" Alan perked up.

"Well..." She tried to stall for effect, but could not. "It's a first run plate from *The Investigator's* Nederland Issue. I got it framed for you."

"Cindy. That must have been expensive. You shouldn't have. I mean, it is really cool. But you can't afford stuff like that." Burgess frowned at her apparent attachment to him.

"Sure I can. I just came into a tidy sum of money, Alan. Got me a new computer for my apartment, got a few new clothes. Oh, and I bought me a gun. Cutest little snub-nosed .38," she gushed.

"So... Did you get a raise or rob a bank?" Alan pried.

"Oh you! Neither. I'm doin' a special assignment for Reverend Marks," Cindy announced.

"What kind of assignment, Cindy? What's this all about?"

"Well, it's between me and God, Alan, or I'd tell you. I'm just so excited, I wanted to call. I express-mailed the plate this afternoon so you'll have it tomorrow morning. I'm gonna let you go now, Alan. Take care," Cindy said.

"Yeah. You too, Cindy. And thank you. I really appreciate it. Good night." Burgess hung up the phone and settled in for a sleepless night.

Alan sprinted across the Post Office parking lot toward Whistler's, express mail package in hand. Bursting through the door of the cafe, he made his way to the table where Thelma and Marshal Burrows sat sipping their mid-morning coffee. "Well, here it is!" the deputy announced, nervously pulling at the stubborn flap.

"Let's see this thing, Alan," Burrows prodded. "I still don't understand why she would do this for you unless she needs something in return."

"That's not nice, Jim. She might be as mad as a hatter, but she still has a heart. I think it was very kind of her to think of Alan," Thelma said, restraining a helpful hand from meddling in the deputy's clumsiness.

"Yeah. She may be crazy, but now she has money." Burgess laughed as he wrestled the padded object from the box. With more bumbling, he finally snapped the thin foam free, exposing the full face of the printing plate.

Thelma hooted and pointed at the garish display. "I should have expected as much," she guffawed. There on the pine table, shimmering in the morning sunlight, an artistic rendition portrayed the forested bowl of Nederland. An enormous gray alien cradled the town in crooked fingers and glared down at it with bestial eyes.

"This is going to be so embarrassing for Nederland," Burrows moaned. "God, I don't even want to know what that articles says."

"Oh Jim, stop whining. Anyone with half an IQ point will laugh their butts off at this," Thelma scolded.

"You're right, Thelma. It's Marks who should be embarrassed. Hey, Alan, where did Cindy get all her money?" Burrows changed the subject.

"Well, that's kind of mysterious, Marshal. She says she's doing some special assignment for Reverend Marks. But she won't tell me what," he whispered, "Says it's between her and God. To be honest, I don't like the sounds of it."

"No shit, Alan. All I can think of is that reward at the end of the video," Burrows said, "I hope this isn't some kind of pre-payment."

"Well, I'm gonna keep in touch with her, just in case. But there's one other thing…" The deputy paused for a moment. "Now she's got a gun."

Wildwood

Barry yanked the front door open and called to all inside. "Hey, you guys! You've got to see this. Hurry up!" Then he bounded away, leaving the others to trail behind. John was first out the door. Looking up, he was amazed to see a stream of people walking up the grassy lane to Wildwood. Young parents cradling babies and shepherding children walked quietly together. A white-haired woman, tall and gaunt, strode through the trees, swinging a long walking stick. A small band of teenagers joked and looked up self-consciously at the people on the porch.

"Who are these people?" Gary Fletcher asked, wide-eyed.

"I think they're here to see me." John gladdened, then opened his heart to greet them.

From the porch of the cabin, Valerie, Dot, and Gary watched as John extended open arms to the first visitor and was immediately enfolded by the crowd.

Nudging Dot, Valerie gasped, "Whew, talk about unexpected company. We better make a lot of coffee."

"Or something," Dot responded. Grabbing Fletcher by the arm, she said. "Come on, Gary. Organize. Organize." She shooed him along. "Barry?"

"Are you kidding? I'm getting the video camera."

Gary Fletcher stood, jaws agape, as John guided his visitors smoothly down to a sloping green meadow adjacent to the lake, less than a hundred yards from the cabin. Unbelievably, the crowd unfolded, spreading blankets and opening backpacks and picnic baskets. By the time that Fletcher, Dot, and Valerie arrived with lemonade, coffee, and yesterday's oatmeal cookies, a banquet had already materialized. Complete strangers shared sandwiches, fruit, cheese — whatever they carried — as they sat in a semi-circle around REL. He sat on the ground, pretending to gobble a cookie proffered by the small girl perched on his knee.

Barry zoomed in on REL's face just as the sun finally burned through the morning cloud cover and sent one shaft of light that singled him out. "Wow!" Barry looked up at Valerie. "Did you see that?"

Just then, REL set the girl in her mother's lap and sprang lightly to his feet. "Welcome, everyone. Before we do anything else, I would like us to all get connected. So..." He walked the entire semi-circle, looking down into the faces. "Let's start by breathing in through our noses and out through our hearts, just like we do it at the *Second Messenger* site."

"That's who they are!" Dot whispered to Fletcher. "These are some of the chat room regulars. They must have pm'd each other to arrange coming here. Wow!" she said, scanning the crowd. "I'll bet I can pick them out. That's got to be 2nd Sight." She nodded her head at the white-haired woman. "We all know these people. How very cool!" She nudged Gary.

After a few moments of breathing gently with the crowd, REL opened his eyes as one single tear slid down his cheek. "How lovely," he whispered. Nonetheless, everyone heard him.

"I am deeply honored that you came here to see me. Shall we talk about judgment and the paradigm shift?"

A murmur of assent moved through the crowd.

"Let's begin with the consensus that everything, every single thing and every single being is an expression of God. Beloved and unique and holy." He looked each in their eyes and saw that they agreed. "Now, most of us have given a lot of thought to judgment, but let's briefly touch on how it undermines our ability to come from love. First of all, judgment disavows God."

A small murmur rippled through the crowd.

"It's true. Every time you judge another, you essentially say that the person you judge is somehow not worthy of God's love. Judgment is just another form of separation."

People nodded their heads in understanding.

"On the other hand, judgment, if you allow it to, will show you your fears. Look at what you judge about someone else and see if it doesn't reflect a fear you hold about yourself." REL nodded, smiling.

"So, what do we do to stop this rather stubborn habit of humanity? Well, the more you come from your heart, the less you will judge and the less you will fear. When you're feeling an oncoming attack of judgment, take a minute to breathe through your heart. The more you do that, the easier it will become to allow others to be who and what they are."

A timid hand slowly raised, pulling a tattooed teenager to his feet. "But what about really creepy people? You know like mass murderers?"

"Well, when I see someone who seems to be truly reprehensible or does something really deplorable, I thank them for showing me an aspect of life I would prefer not to experience myself. Remember, everyone and everything is a sacred expression of God. Sometimes, the most heroic souls masquerade as the most horrific people to show us a physical manifestation of our most fearful beliefs. Mentally send those people your *unconditional* love and thank them for their valor."

Barry nudged Valerie, who sat mesmerized by REL. "I'll have this up on the net in three hours." He pointed to the video camera.

"Then I guess we better be prepared for even bigger crowds, Barry. This is amazing."

"You know..." REL continued. "It is sad that this knowledge is lost on our leadership. Very few of the people in positions of real authority understand the power of love because their entire framework is built upon fear." Leaning back against a huge rock, he continued, "If they could embrace the vibration of love, they could easily shift para-digms." REL winked, "But, we don't need to wait for them to 'get it.' We can suspend our own judgment of others and in so doing, we can tap into the power of Universal Love and lead our leaders to a new way of being in the world."

REL closed his eyes and took a deep breath. Summoning all of his love for the people in the crowd, he channeled his energy through his heart and blasted them with joy and love and peace. Though no one said a word, his gift registered on the faces of those who surrounded him.

Within moments, the people were on their feet, min-gling and touching his hands. And as they approached, he called to them by their chat room nicknames as he recognized them by their energy alone.

At last, all but one couple had greeted him. Standing apart from the rest of the crowd, the middle-aged husband and wife sipped lemonade and gazed at the lake. REL walked over to them, smiling.

"I remember you," he said to the man. "You almost gave us a ticket back in Washington D.C. weeks ago."

"I thought you looked familiar," former officer Craig Landwehr laughed. "That was my last day as a cop. I guess I was feeling charitable. Whew! I'm glad I didn't bust you. It would be pretty embarrassing right now. This is my wife, Jenny."

REL extended a warm hand. "Glad to meet you Jenny. May I ask what brought you here? These other people are friends from my chat room."

"Oh, Esther..." Craig pointed at the white-haired lady. "She's a regular at our shop in Amber. She told us about you and invited us to come."

"Well, seems I have a lot to thank her for. Glad you are here." REL smiled and excused himself then walked over to Esther.

"2nd Sight!" REL greeted the white-haired lady with open arms. "I'm so glad you are here. I have much to thank you for."

"Oh REL, it's my pleasure," Esther laughed. "You've given me a lot to think about."

"Well, 2nd Sight," he said fondly. "You put me on the road to my heart and helped me to remember who I am... who we all are."

After the crowd dispersed, Gary Fletcher slipped into a funk. As the evening wore on, he grew grumpier and grumpier, finally withdrawing from the family. By 8 o'clock, he was in bed with a fever of 103°.

Valerie worked gently, three colored bottles of herbs at her elbow and a small mortar and pestle before her. "These will fix him. Well..." she corrected. "These will help him physically."

"What's wrong with him, Valerie?" REL watched in fascination as she took a pinch of herbs from one of the bottles, smelled its sweet aroma, breathed softly on it and dropped it into the small marble vessel. "What made him sick?"

"You mean officially or really?" she said, pinching a measure of herbs from a second bottle.

"Really, Valerie. What's really wrong with him?" REL asked, lifting the third bottle and smelling its contents.

"All the changes in his life, REL. You know, meeting you, changing careers, moving here. Sometimes your body shuts down so your mind can catch up." Valerie added the third herb, stirred the mixture with her finger, then transferred it to a bamboo strainer, placed it in a cup and poured on boiling water.

"I made him sick?" REL asked, concerned.

"Of course not. This is really a healing process, not an illness. He's purging a lot of fear, right now. He'll be fine and more at peace with himself in no time. Until then, I can help him feel better."

Removing the strainer and adding a spoonful of honey to the tea, Valerie set the cup on a tray beside a bouquet of wildflowers. She grabbed a small bottle of aspirin and led REL to Fletcher's room.

"A little warm in there, are we?" she asked teasingly, then kissed the big man softly on the forehead. "You're gonna be fine in no time, Gary. Visualize yourself floating on the lake in the moonlight and feel the breeze cooling your skin. Imagine the cool water lapping up to refresh you. It will help you get better faster. Really." Pointing to her brew and handing him two aspirin, she said, "These will boost your immune system and soothe your aching head."

"Thanks, Valerie. I don't know what's gotten in to me, I hardly ever get sick," Fletcher sighed.

"Well, no matter. This won't last long. Just relax and don't think. Come on, REL, let's let him sleep." She slipped her arm through his and led him from the room.

Later, Valerie called to the balcony, "Are you coming to bed, REL?"

He walked back into their room and stood watching her brush her hair. Finally, he stepped up behind her. Nuzzling her neck, he whispered, "I think not. I have something to figure out. Sweet dreams, Sweet Valerie." He turned her in his arms and kissed her then tucked her into bed and left to visit Gary Fletcher.

REL hesitated outside of Gary's room, then knocked softly on the door. It creaked open at his touch. Peeking into the room, he found the bed empty, then saw the big man out on the balcony silhouetted by the moonlight.

"Mr. Fletcher…" REL called in a whisper, "would you care for some company?"

"Sure, John, come on out." Fletcher eased his aching body down onto a large chaise.

"How are you feeling?" REL leaned against the rail, admiring the silver-cast lake.

"Much better. Valerie brews a mean cup of tea," Fletcher chuckled. "She'd have my hide if she saw this, though." He produced a huge cigar from his voluminous robe pocket.

"So…" REL began. "I've been thinking."

"Uh, oh." Fletcher rolled his eyes. Producing a lighter from another pocket, he stuck the cigar in his mouth, savored it a moment, then struck a sizable flame. Puffing thoughtfully until the end of the cigar glowed in the dark, he asked, "So, what have you been thinking, John?"

"I have a problem that I think you can help me solve. And in the process, I think I can help you solve your problem," REL ventured, sitting on the arm of a large wooden chair.

"What's my problem?" Fletcher tipped his head and stared at John.

"It's a lot like mine, actually. We are both afraid. You are afraid you made a mistake when you quit your job — ended your career — to work with us. Just at the time society deems it most important for men to be at the top of their game, you walked away."

"Boy, you don't pull any punches, do you?" Fletcher sucked on his cigar.

"It's true isn't it, Gary? According to Valerie, it's probably what made you sick."

"And?" Gary asked around the bulk of the cigar.

"Well, logic suggests that a better understanding of God will free you up so you can enjoy your life."

"Logic, huh? What about the heart stuff?" Gary raised an eyebrow.

"Well, the heart is our final destination, naturally. But if you need a rational explanation to help you get there, I can give you one. You see, pure, mathematical logic led *me* to *my* heart. Maybe, when you hear what I have to say, you won't have to make such a huge leap of faith to make your connection with God."

Gary shrugged and gestured for REL to continue.

"Let me briefly explain the science. You already know, for example, that fear vibrates at a certain frequency. Love at another and so on. Your heart also carries its own signature vibration, so that in very real terms, your entire body is a sender and receiver of frequencies."

"So, I just sort of vibrate my way through life? Is that what you're saying?" Fletcher frowned.

"Essentially, yes. Frequencies also have magnetic properties, they attract what resonates with them. So, if you are afraid, you magnetize fearful experiences. If you are loving, you attract love. It's as simple as that," REL nodded emphatically.

"Oh no," Gary whispered. "So, to get over this fear that's making me sick, I have to change my... vibration? You mean I'm not going to feel better until I figure it out?" he groaned.

"It's a lot easier than that," REL laughed gently. "Every time you feel a fearful thought, breathe it through your heart. You'll be amazed at the transformation. Trust me."

Gary thought for long moments, his dying cigar propped in the corner of his mouth. "And when I get my vibration raised," he asked sheepishly. "Then it will be easier for me to connect with God? That *has* been kind of hard for me," he confided.

Kneeling down to look Gary in the eyes, REL said, "That's what I promised, Gary. Just stay with me and remember to breathe through your heart." Reaching into his front pants pocket, REL withdrew a small key ring. Prying open the ring, he removed an ornate silver cylinder. He held it up to the light while he unscrewed the lid and removed the slip of rolled pink paper. Unfurling it with a flourish, he read: *The journey to enlightenment begins in the heart.* Reassembling the scroll in its holder, REL handed it to Gary. "Here, keep this as a reminder. It has helped me a lot."

Studying the small gift in the palm of his hand, Gary said, "I'm very touched by this. And I do feel better. Thank you, John." With a sly grin around his cigar, Fletcher watched as John scooted into the chair facing him and asked, "So, what's *your* problem and where's my rational explanation?"

"It just so happens that I have my own leap of faith to make so I can provide your evidence. I'm also afraid that you won't listen to me — that you'll get caught up in disbelief and tune me out, rather than understand."

Both hands extended, Fletcher quipped, "Give me some credit, John. Let's hear it."

"Okay. I need you to promise me that you'll never tell another living soul. Can you handle all this?"

Fletcher nodded, more than curious, now.

"There's one last thing," REL continued, "I'm about to commit one whopper of a program violation. I think I can handle it, but there are possible side effects."

"Program violation? Side effects? Come on, John. Get on with it." Fletcher beckoned, darkened cigar wafting stale smoke through the night.

"Gary, telling you is the only way I can shatter my program's hold over me." Wincing at Gary's growing impatience, REL hurried, "I have to be careful how I say this. So, I'll do the details first, then brace myself for the finale."

"Oookay, John. Whatever." Fletcher re-lit the cigar and slumped back into the chaise.

"Is there a computer on Earth more powerful than the TechniCom?"

"Well, if there is, I don't know about it. Why?"

"Imagine this, Gary... Imagine a computer that makes the TechniCom look like an abacus."

"Wow. You have those where you came from?" Gary marveled.

"Yes, just one. It's the marriage of technology and biology, a science that will be perfected within the next two hundred years. Dr. Morrison..."

"The guy who sent you here?" Gary interrupted.

"Yes. Dr. Morrison is Einstein and Tesla and Schweitzer all in one man. He not only created the matrix tube and time mapper that led me here, he also created this computer. And, he did it all by himself.

"Now, I want you to think about all the things I've done since I've been here. From memorizing every Data Pioneer spec in minutes to fixing the TechniCom in less than half an hour. Even the *Second Messenger* site is indicative of advanced technology and ability." REL looked at Fletcher, hoping for a glimmer of realization. Instead, he drew a blank

271

stare. He inhaled slowly, steadily through his heart, consciously maintaining the connection in hopes it would somehow cushion the blow from his program. "You see, Gary... That computer is so sophisticated that it quantified harmonics and vibrations and unimaginable data to prove beyond logic or question that God abides in everything. Gary..." He squeezed his eyes shut. "I am that computer. *I am* evidence of God." He breathed the words out through his heart and waited. A tiny shudder rippled through his structure. Instantly, he knew it to be his program relinquishing its grip once and for all. "That wasn't so bad," John sighed and opened his eyes to Gary Fletcher's frozen glare. "How are you doing, Gary?" he asked hopefully.

"Tell me there's a punch line here, John."

"No, I'm telling you the truth and the implications are fantastic. Like I said, I've been able to prove to myself, unequivocally, that God exists. I traced the connection through my heart. Gary, God isn't abstract theory, God is concrete, computer-validated fact."

"*You* are a computer," Fletcher mouthed then took a long drag of his dwindling cigar.

"The correct term is..." Flinching, REL continued, "biological mechanical biped. Biomech for short. "

"And just how is this supposed to make me feel better about anything, John?" Fletcher buried his head in his hands.

"Gary, I told you this to shatter my last limitations. Accept the truth of my conclusions and shatter your own." REL patted Gary on the back and silently returned to his room.

Gary Fletcher capitulated to the hours of tossing and turning. His fever, his headache, his conversation with John all conspired to chase him from one nightmare to the next, hounding him sleepless through the night. Rising quietly, he dressed and tip-toed to the kitchen in the half-light of the impending dawn. With all the stealth he could muster, the big man made a thermos of coffee, stuffed two muffins into a baggie then into his jacket pocket and slipped out the kitchen door. He paused only briefly while grabbing a flashlight to consider taking his virgin fly rod.

No.

He headed down the forest path alone. Naked of distractions.

Forehead finally cooling in the morning chill, Fletcher slackened his pace and relaxed into the sunrise. He spotted a fallen tree snugged up against the trunk of a massive oak and made himself comfortable, poured a cup of coffee and stared as pink and golden fire flared across the lake.

There he sat, inert, as a hundred people filtered through the morning trees across the lake from him and filled the grassy meadow. There he sat, inert, when REL stood up to speak to them. He bestirred himself only enough to listen.

"My beloved friends..." The words penetrated Fletcher as if REL stood beside him rather than across the lake. "Today, we look for God." And although Fletcher could not see his face, he knew without question that REL smiled as he spoke.

"In my travels and my studies," the biomech continued, "I have heard of many places to find God. Some find Spirit in sunsets and redwoods. Others, in crystals or a lover's eyes. Some see Creation in a newborn child. A lot of people see God as throwing lighting bolts from Heaven. There are as many places to find Our Maker as there are people seeking."

"Where do you see God, REL?" a young man in a rainbow shirt asked.

"Everywhere," REL answered simply. "You see, God *IS* everything. The reason so many fail to find Source anywhere, especially within, is because they look for something different than what God *IS*. Many expect thunder and displays of frightening grandeur. I would ask you to consider, also, that the true magnificence of God lies in the subtle. A snowflake is spectacular because it is literally — in all of creation — the only one of its kind. The same is true of you and of me. That is Spirit's brilliance, along with mighty canyons and impossible mountains and every other glory of reality. What I am saying is not to overlook God smiling back at you in the mirror each morning. Do not fail to notice The Divine in the dew drops in your garden or in the luscious flavor of a fresh peach. Form a personal relationship with God by recognizing that God *IS* indeed *everything*. Including you."

"Supposing we accept this... perspective," Craig Landwehr asked. "How can knowing this make any real difference in our lives?"

"Good question. You must understand that when we live in fear and separation, not knowing that we are literally pieces of God, we are much like a twig in a stream swept helplessly out to sea..." Although REL spoke softly, a curious resonance carried his every word across the water to Fletcher. "We find ourselves battered and bruised by a tidal flood with its own agenda. But by accepting our relationship to the tides, we grasp our own source of power. Acknowledging that we are each a unique expression of God allows us to alter the breadth, the depth — even the color of our mythical ocean."

One hundred people sat transfixed, eyes fast on their charismatic teacher. Gary Fletcher sat alone, timidly breathing through his heart, his own eyes moist with hope.

"I don't expect you to believe that accepting this today will automatically endow you with the power to wield spectacular magic like Merlin. Understanding how creation works and your role in it *will* allow you to wield subtle magic, though. You see, thoughts carry electromagnetic energy. And scientists will soon discover that even subtle electromagnetic energy, like a thought, affects matter. So, imagine each consciously directed thought as a ripple in our ocean. We have all seen how one ripple touches the whole of a body of water. So, too, do our thoughts touch the whole of humanity. Never underestimate the power of conscious intent. When you take responsibility for your own thoughts and understand how they create your experience, you will, quite literally, dwell within the mind of God. And acting from within the mind of God, you can make miracles."

Brushing a stubborn tear from his face, Gary Fletcher headed back toward the cabin. Slowing as he reached the porch, he turned instead and walked to the meadow where REL stood surrounded by well-wishers. Patiently waiting his turn, Fletcher stood silent until he reached his friend. He clamped a huge hand on REL's shoulder, and whispered through tear-beaded eyelashes, "Do you know what *namaste* means? It means *the god in me honors the god in you.* Namaste, REL."

Nederland

The sound startled her. Thelma looked up from a report to the back of the Town Hall. There crept Marshal Burrows and Deputy Burgess.

"Thelma, you gotta hide us," Burgess blurted. "At least until the news trucks and reporters leave."

Straining for a better look at First Street, Thelma gasped at the three news station satellite trucks that clogged the parking lot. Looking at Alan and *The Investigator* he held in his clasped hand, she groaned, "Oh, no."

"Thelma," Burrows sputtered. "It's way, way worse than we ever imagined."

Motioning with her fingers, she prodded, "Come on, Alan. Let's see."

"I'm not movin' till you lock the door," Burgess stubbornly refused.

Thelma managed to lock the door and turn the *out to lunch* sign over just as the first wave of reporters struck. Smiling and shaking her head, she pulled the shade and returned to her desk. "There. Now, let's see this thing."

"They've really got me playing the heavy, Thelma. I'm supposedly protecting the demon's identity." Burrows rolled his eyes. "Marks has me cornered there, because when those vultures out front finally get to me, I'm bound by law to say nothing about him."

"Jeez, Jim, they've even named names. Can they do that?" Thelma asked.

"No doubt his bevy of lawyers has that one covered. Notice the only name he doesn't mention is Worthington's," Burrows muttered.

"Why Alan, Marks has some nice things to say about you."

"Yeah, I know. It makes me nervous, too," Burgess said shyly.

"Well at least they didn't trash you like they did the rest of the town, Alan. Did you see that quote from Dr. Winter? They made him sound like an idiot. God bless freedom of the press… I guess," Burrows mumbled.

"Speaking of Worthington, you're never going to believe this…" Thelma handed the magazine back to Alan. "You know my friend Craig?"

Burrows nodded.

"Well, he goes to see Worthington every Saturday. He sees Valerie and Barry all the time, too. I guess a couple of hundred people meet every week to discuss spiritual things. With all the crowds that keep coming, they've had to move to a hall in Amber for the winter."

"So, what does Craig think of Worthington?" Burrows asked.

"Says he's wonderful, Jim." Thelma looked him in the eyes. "And from what Craig tells me about Worthington's message, I suspect I would agree."

Wildwood

Steadying the bags of groceries on the kitchen counter, Barry carefully extracted the magazine and called to Valerie, "Oh Valerie, are you prepared for your fifteen minutes of fame? According to this, we were brainwashed and are now pillars of a demonic cult."

"Let me see that," Valerie eased the magazine from Barry's grip, first holding it out to examine the cover then diving into the feature story. "Oh, my God!" she gasped. "Listen to this sidebar. It's called *Demons on the Internet*. This Marks guy is a nut!"

As everyone crowded around, Barry handed out three additional copies and cleared his throat, "There is one other interesting piece of mail here." He handed an envelope to John.

Rubbing his fingers over the raised, varnished logo of the Philadelphia television station, REL briefly pondered his growing fame. "Remember," he advised the others who huddled over their individual copies of *The Investigator*. "We can't let all this glamour go to our heads," he laughed. At that, REL ripped the envelope and pulled out the letter. "Interesting." He handed the letter to Fletcher.

"Oh, no," Fletcher exclaimed protectively. "This stuff is bad enough without encouraging it." Waving the letter at REL's grin, Fletcher reiterated, "Absolutely not."

"Absolutely not, what?" Dot asked

"John's been invited to be on some talk show," Fletcher grumbled. "But he's not going to do it."

Shaking a gentle finger, REL admonished, "No fear, Gary. Remember?"

Barry whistled a low whistle and passed the letter to Dot. "This isn't just any talk show. This is Harry Parmakian. He's huge." Then laughing out loud, he announced, "And his special guest is Jeremiah Marks."

"You mean this Jeremiah Marks?" Dot said, stabbing *The Investigator* article with her index finger.

John observed the discussion for a moment then ended the debate with his recent discovery. "Dot, Jeremiah Marks is SkyPilot. I recognize his energy. He preaches to millions of people every week from his soapbox of fear. I need to counter the damage he spreads. I need to do this talk show."

Alpha II

"Good morning, Garner." Judge Hawthorne smiled into the com. "Don't tell me that Fells rousted you again. You look pretty grim."

"No, it's not that, Judge Hawthorne. I need to ask for a warrant to search Dr. Morrison's personal financial accounts," Williams sighed.

"I don't like the sounds of that. What's going on?" The judge's heart sank.

"That's just it. There's nothing conclusive. I've just found little snippets of clues that lead nowhere. But something is definitely amiss. I've hit a brick wall unless his personal files reveal something. I hate doing this, Judge Hawthorne. I've come to genuinely like the man. And his accomplishments boggle my mind. But something's definitely wrong here."

Reluctantly, Judge Hawthorne acquiesced, "I'll have the hard copy delivered on the next shuttle. Until then, this electronic order will suffice. Thanks for your candor, Garner. This is difficult for all of us." Nodding, she broke the connection and punched up Arthur Tabbot's personal number.

"Hello, Mildred. To what do I owe this honor?" Tabbot's smile faded when he saw the look on her face.

"Bad news, I'm afraid. Garner Williams just requested a search of Phil's personal financial records." Judge Hawthorne shook her head. "I'm looking at some pretty suspicious evidence here, Arthur. According to waste management records, Alpha II discards twice what it takes in."

"So what does this have to do with Morrison's personal finances?" Tabbot asked.

"Apparently, Williams suspects that Phil is laundering Alpha II credits through his personal accounts. I hope he's wrong, Arthur. There's nothing we can do to protect him if Williams finds something like that."

"I know, Mildred. And Phil knows it, too. He took the risk quite consciously. We'll just have to let it play out as it will. Keep the good thought for him. So much is riding on his project."

Arthur Tabbot poured himself a cognac and keyed in Morrison's com number. "Shit," he cursed. "I thought we had it made." Looking into the holographic face of his friend, he murmured. "Phil... Better sit down."

"How very cheerful of you, Arthur," the doctor quipped. "Let me guess, Mildred just called you to warn of increased scrutiny? It's okay. I expected as much, you know."

"Will Williams find anything in your personal accounts, Phil?" Tabbot worried.

"Hhhmmm. Probably not much, but it may lead him to something worse. Depends on how good he is. And I think he's real good. I just hope it takes long enough for me to properly prepare Dan. He's not doing too well, you know." Morrison pondered a moment. "Arthur, when this all falls apart, will you keep an eye out for Dan? He'll need you."

"Sure, Phil. Don't worry about him. Worry about yourself. This is going to get nasty before it gets better."

"Ah, but I have a plan, Arthur."

"Of course you do, Phil. You always do." Tabbot smiled.

Double Refraction

Philadelphia, Pennsylvania

In a downtown Philadelphia studio, John sat just off stage, waiting for his introduction. Center set, popular and controversial talk-show host, Harry Parmakian, sat calmly in a director's chair. The host's herringbone jacket and preppie sweater, coupled with his short-cropped hair and freckled forehead, gave him a rather boyish look that disguised the sting of his acid wit. Parmakian lounged with his head tilted back and his eyes closed, calm facade refuting everything REL had recently learned about the man.

Momentarily assailed by the collage of frenetic energy swirling about the studio, John took a moment to breathe through his heart. Calmed, he brushed off his jeans and straightened the cuffs of his white cotton sweater. Inwardly smiling, he looked forward to the challenge. Refocusing his awareness to his surroundings, REL suspected that it was the wild Parmakian audience that earned this show its ratings.

On the producer's cue, Parmakian opened his eyes and stared directly into the camera. "Welcome Philadelphia. I'm Harry Parmakian and this is *Our View*."

The cameraman panned the Parmakian crowd of five hundred, treating the television audience to a raucous kaleidoscope of floating Frisbees and bouncing beach balls, punctuated by the cacophony of official Parmakian cow-bells. Every Thursday evening, millions of viewers from New York to Cleveland gathered before their TVs to watch this spectacle. National advertisers clamored for air time and network media took increasing notice.

On this night, a large contingent of *Messengers*, as they called themselves, sat laughing in joy at the studio antics. REL's young, tattooed friend stood in the midst of the group, returning errant Frisbees and fending off beach balls. The audience hooted as Harry began to speak.

"You all know our first guest, author, noted Armageddon scholar, UFOlogist and founder of World Alliance for Religion in Society... Now, hold on Philly!" He hushed the crowd. "I know you know his name but I still have to say it. Welcome, Reverend Jeremiah Marks!"

Marks glided across the stage, stroking the small gold cross that tacked his tie to his starched white shirt. Just beneath one sleeve of his dark silk suit, the glint of a Rolex shot a spear of light into the crowd. He bowed a low bow then swooped into the chair slightly behind and to the right of Harry Parmakian. A roar of cheers swelled across the stage, finally silenced by electronic prompts.

"And tonight, for the first time, let me introduce... Wait a minute," Parmakian said, looking over his left shoulder to John, who stood patiently in the wings. "Just how do I introduce you? You sort of came out of nowhere and we don't know much about you." Turning back to the audience, he wrinkled his face and jerked a thumb toward REL. "Except that he somehow managed to attract a lot of followers over the internet."

Nearly one hundred *Messengers* cheered for themselves and for REL.

"Here's what his own people say about him. And I quote," waving a one-page press release above his head,

Parmakian continued. "REL... That's Remote Emissary of Life," Parmakian grimaced. "Anyway, REL teaches that no matter the question, the answer is love. He came to lead us to a paradigmatic shift, to replace structures of fear with the freedom of love.'" Whipping back to confront REL, he jeered, "Free love? Aren't we past that already?"

The audience erupted, cow bells clanking.

Parmakian waited a moment then beckoned to REL. "Ladies and Gentlemen, meet John R. Worthington, Remote Emissary of Life."

John stepped around the curtain, bowed shyly then walked to Parmakian, both hands extended in greeting. "Thank you, Harry," he said sincerely. REL then walked behind Parmakian and offered his hand to Marks, who did not rise from his chair. Instead, the reverend scrutinized Worthington from head to foot and finally presented a disdainful hand. The touch of it jolted REL with fear so entrenched, he longed to brush its residue off on his jeans, but did not.

He had barely reached his chair when Marks intoned, "Love??!!" Bejeweled hands outstretched, he leaned forward in his chair. His slick demeanor conveyed a honeyed-invitation. "Sounds like a re-hash of the sixties. Is that the best you can do?"

"Love is the best thing there is, Reverend. Love is the power of God. How can you top that?" REL beamed.

"You must first be worthy of that love, Mr. Worthington," Marks sneered.

"We are not only worthy of God's love, we are walking manifestations of it," REL answered.

Harry Parmakian, stifling a stage laugh interrupted, "Boy, you are really over the edge, aren't you *REL*?"

"You must repent to be worthy of God's love," Marks scorned.

"Repent of what, Reverend? ...Of being perfect reflections of God?" REL spoke gently, earnestly.

"Perfect?" The reverend glared. "Surely even you know that we are all sinners."

"I fear you underestimate the God you so loudly claim to serve. How can you believe a perfect being would create an Earth full of sinners, Reverend Marks? Was it a colossal miscalculation or divine sadism? Either way, the concept that we are sinners belies the perfection of God."

"The Bible says that we are all sinners," Marks snapped.

"What if I told you that sin comes from the Latin word for *separation*? Ergo, the belief that you are a sinner is the belief that you are separate from God." REL breathed through his heart as he spoke, consciously directing the flow of his energy toward Marks. "It is precisely the belief that you are *apart from* God rather than *a part of* God that begets ungodly actions. Don't you see, Reverend Marks? Only the soul who believes itself to be a sinner can steal or kill. The soul who knows itself to be holy is incapable of such actions."

"I take it, then, that you don't subscribe to the Ten Commandments, Mr. Worthington?" Parmakian baited.

"Well, I interpret them a little differently than most..." REL began.

"Of course you do!" Marks hissed.

"May I explain?" REL rejoined. "I see them as indicators of your harmony with God. For example, when you truly accept your relationship to Spirit, it would never occur to you to commit murder because you would understand that perfect abundance is your birthright. Once you feel that undeniable Divine Love, these cease to be commandments and become a way of life."

"Is that so?" The reverend leered with a reddened face. "Then how do you explain this?" Reaching into his suit pocket,

Marks withdrew a quartz crystal suspended from a dull silver chain. Dangling it gingerly before the camera as if it might scald him, he rasped, "I'm told you worship these. Does that not violate the very First Commandment? Hhhmmmm?!" Throwing the crystal to the floor, he kicked it across the stage so it landed at REL's feet.

Reaching to retrieve the stone, REL cradled it gently then turned to Marks. "Again, I fear it is a matter of perspective. When I look at the world, I do not see dead matter populated by soulless animals and sin-riddled humans. I see, in everything, the brilliant face of God. I do not worship these crystals, Reverend Marks. Instead, I see in them the omnipresence of God, as is described in the Bible you so often quote."

"Well, Mr. Worthington, it seems like you have an answer for everything. Let's see how well you do after we return from station break. We're going to take questions from the audience." Parmakian pantomimed a drop kick to signal the break, then turned to John with amusement in his eyes.

During the commercial break, stage hands scurried to re-fill the water pitchers and make-up artists rushed to powder beaded sweat on chin and brow. They noted that Worthington needed no touch-up. He remained calm and cool, even joking with the crew.

As he relaxed awaiting the next segment, REL scanned the audience for friendly faces. Gary Fletcher gave him a thumbs-up and Valerie blew him a kiss. Dot and Barry waved, as did many of the assembled *Messengers*. Eyes wandering over the rest of the crowd, he was surprised to find Cindy Vinwire, sitting all alone, chewing her fingernails. The moment their eyes met, she looked anxiously away. Following her gaze, REL traced her attention to Jeremiah Marks. Deeply curious, he felt a palpable exchange of energy between the two. *Fear*. Like incubus and succubus, they fed each other's fear. Chagrined, REL turned his attention to the bustling Harry Parmakian, who flashed a sardonic grin, patted Marks on the shoulder and settled into his director's chair. "This should be fun," he tossed the words over his shoulder at REL, with nary a glance in his direction.

"Welcome back, Philadelphia. We're having a rather spirited… get it… spirited?" He made quotation marks with his fingers. "A spirited debate between respected Biblical scholar, the Reverend Jeremiah Marks and Rage of the New Age, John R. Worthington. Remote Emissary of Life, for short, who was just telling us that he sees God in crystals and why the Ten Commandments are more like suggestions."

John stretched his legs out in front of him and crossed his ankles. Looking up, he caught a grimace of frustration on Gary Fletcher's face. Grinning at the big man, REL winked and sent three breaths from his heart. Feeling the reverend's icy stare, John turned to him and repeated the gesture.

"Okay, Philly. Who's going to ask the first question? Please address it to the person you want to answer, but as always, our other guest gets to comment, too. On your feet, Philly."

A young man in a large cowboy hat stood timidly eyeing the microphone held to his mouth by a young woman in a studio blazer. "Yeah. Mr. Worthington," he mumbled. "Where did you learn all the stuff that you teach. I mean, did you read it or make it up or what?"

"All of the above," John laughed. "I've studied hundreds and hundreds of books, all the major religions as well as dozens of lesser-known ones. I've compared those teachings to the most advanced quantum physics theories as well as meteorological, geophysical and astrological events. Hundreds of thousands of human hours of quantification and analysis have verified my teachings. But most important of all, my heart tells me these things are so."

"Then, the gospel plays no part in your teachings?" Marks sputtered, anxious to speak. "*My* authority is the gospel. The Word of God. Nothing more and most certainly nothing less! What Mr. Worthington preaches is heresy, Ladies and Gentlemen. Don't you see it?"

John tipped his head toward Marks and asked, "Reverend, did you not know that *heresy* derives from the Greek word for choice? You claim to teach the doctrine of free will and yet you condemn, sometimes even to death, those who exercise choice. I don't understand."

Before Marks could gather his thoughts to answer, Parmakian interrupted. "REL," he mocked, "the audience gets to ask the questions here. You, the young lady in the denim jacket." He pointed to a small blond standing before a mounted mike.

Clearing her throat, Cindy Vinwire spoke softly. "Hi, John...... Um... I wanted to ask you what you think of demons?"

Marks drew a sharp intake of breath and glared at the girl. John recognized the fear in her eyes and answered gently, "I personally don't believe such things exist, Cindy. All the stories are metaphors and allegories about the damaging consequences of fearful beliefs and how they can tear us apart. I prefer to believe in love, Cindy. Not demons."

Leaping to his feet, Marks pointed at REL and blasted, "You heard it yourselves! He disputes the Word of God. He twists the scriptures to fit his own agenda. Who does that remind you of, Ladies and Gentlemen? The Antichrist, that's who!" Pacing now, sweating in evangelical frenzy, Marks raised his hands "I've been to your web page, Mr. Worthington. I've seen what you write about meditation and metaphysics — euphemisms for pagan rites. You can't deny it!"

"Now, now... Reverend Marks, let's not insult our guest. But, let's have him answer. REL are you a pagan?"

Shaking his head, REL responded softly. "It is not I who twist the meaning of words. Look to yourselves. You toss the word *pagan* as an epithet when it simply designates someone who uses sources other than the Bible as spiritual reference. Two-thirds of the world's population claim a religion other than Christianity, Reverend Marks. Do you truly believe that God repudiates two-thirds of the people alive today all for the sake of an egoistic religious designation?"

Harry intervened and pressed, "So you *are* a pagan, REL?"

"I am a child of God, as are you. Don't you see that by naming me one thing and yourself another, you create an artificial division between us? Why?" REL quizzed. "How does that serve God?"

"To distinguish between good and evil, Mr. Worthington," Marks scowled.

"Judge not..." REL quoted. "Why do you disregard that most pivotal teaching of the man whose name you use?"

"Hold on. The questions are supposed to come from our audience. How about the lady in the red suit?" Parmakian directed.

"Reverend Marks, is Mr. Worthington the demon on the internet and the subject of your investigation?" The woman glared at REL.

"Of course, you must draw your own conclusions, Ma'am. But, let's just take a look at the facts that are a matter of public record. First, Mr. Worthington can be placed in Nederland, Colorado at the time of the incident. Second, he has a web page with thousands of followers." Marks paused and the camera panned to the audience.

There sat Gary Fletcher, rage growing with each spoken word. "Valerie!" he whispered hoarsely, "What if they expose him? God, what if the Feds get involved?"

"Gary," Dot interrupted. "They have nothing but para-noia to go on. They have no evidence that can expose him."

"But what if their investigation uncovers who he really is?" Barry drew them into a huddle.

"Wait," Valerie cautioned. "REL knew perfectly well that this could happen. We talked about it. He isn't concerned at all and we shouldn't be, either."

"Three." Marks continued, holding up three fingers. "He drives a white four-door Blazer just like the one in the Nederland accident. But, as I said, you must draw your own conclusions."

Harry Parmakian stood and turned to REL. "Well, I'm speechless. But it's your turn to talk anyway."

REL straightened in his chair, his eyes riveted on his friends in the audience. He smiled to reassure them and then answered softly, "Why must you always look for something to fear, Reverend? Wouldn't it be better for you and your followers to look for love instead?"

"Maybe you haven't been paying attention, tucked away from reality as you are up there in your little compound. But, the world is rife with drugs and murder and perversion. Where's the love in that?" On cue, the camera zoomed in on Marks' face to catch an exaggerated grimace.

Parmakian was on his feet in no time. His extravagant gestures fueled the frenzy. "I'd like to hear the answer to that. But first, we must take another station break."

Marks sat like a cat, content with himself.

REL turned his attention to his friends.

Gary Fletcher shook his head. "I told you this whole thing would be staged to make John look like a fool," the big man complained.

"Come on, Gary. He's doing just fine. Before this show is over, he'll look like a prince," Valerie assured.

"She's right," Craig Landwehr added. "He's the only sincere one up there. And that comes across."

Backstage, Marks collared Harry Parmakian. "I tell you, I want to go first. I have momentum in my favor. I want to expose him before he says another word." Marks' eyes gleamed beneath the colored stage lights.

"Whatever you say, Reverend." Parmakian extricated the reverend's hands from his lapels, brushed himself off and returned to his director's chair.

Without introduction, Marks strode to center stage and stopped only a step away from blocking Parmakian's camera angle. "Most of you know me as an expert on Armageddon. That's a subject we haven't directly addressed today. Or so it may seem. But I tell you that the speculation, the suspicions, the evidence of wayward ministries all have direct bearing on the End Times Prophecies." Gesturing toward REL, the reverend continued. "And this man. His teachings, his own words reveal him to be not a servant of God — as he would have you believe — but a messenger of a more sinister force. He uses God's own words to lure you to a darker master. Listen up, *Messengers*," Marks threatened. "You should be aware of our on-going investigation into events surrounding this man. Think well whether you want to get caught up in the midst of it."

From the audience, Fletcher blurted, "Lawsuit!" Followed immediately by a collective "Ssshhhh!" from the group.

REL smiled at the *Messengers* and gave a shielded thumbs-up. "Is it my turn?" he asked Parmakian.

Looking over his shoulder toward Marks, Parmakian cued, "You still have twenty seconds, Reverend. Anything else you want to add?"

"Yes. You can get all the information on today's topic and more at my web site." The address flashed on the screen.

"You can order *The Investigator* and the Nederland video from there, too." Bowing, the reverend returned to his seat and smiled smugly at REL.

"You are a merchant of fear, Reverend Marks," REL chuckled. "I've read *The Investigator* from cover to cover. I've watched several of your Sunday morning broadcasts. And I've yet to hear a message of love from you. Even in this discourse, your only mention of love was derisive. By what reasoning do you claim to be a follower of Christ when love was the message he brought and the very mention of the word evokes your wrath?"

Marks lurched forward to object, but REL held up a commanding hand and kept him in his chair.

"Reverend Marks, don't you see that God is pure love? That we are products and conveyors of that love? God's love permeates absolutely everything, so we are constantly immersed in it. And whenever we choose love instead of fear, we tap into the magnificent wellspring of All That Is.

"On the other hand, when you choose fear, God, in infinite benevolence, honors your choice by giving you what you ask for."

Parmakian waved frantically to the director to cut for a break. Mesmerized, the man missed Harry's cue. The furious host turned back to his guest, rising to interrupt.

But REL continued, "Don't you see, Harry, Reverend? We are — each one — an emissary of God, a joyous expression of Divine Love. It is the choices we make about the quality and integrity of our lives, not mindless lip service, that glorify our Creator. We venerate God most profoundly when we choose love."

The cameraman focused on Reverend Marks, who sat stiffly in his chair, fingers knotted around the arm rest, face pale and beaded with sweat.

"Don't you see what an honor this is, Reverend? To be human? Not filth, needing to be cleansed. Not sinners, needing blood sacrifice for redemption. Not grovelers at the feet of an egoistic deity. We are eternally joined to God through our hearts. All that remains is our choice of how to experience that." Smiling broadly to the non-*Messenger* audience, then gazing a long moment at Cindy, REL concluded, "I also invite you to visit the *Second Messenger* web site. In fact, I urge you to visit the Reverend's, too. Then ask yourself which is love and which is fear and which is the expression of God you choose to invite into your lives."

Because of the missed cue, the near-hysterical director had no choice but to cut to the credits. Between the rolling lines of acknowledgment, viewers caught glimpses of a dumfounded audience — cow-bells, silent.

Somehow, to those same viewers, the image that lingered the longest was that of two loving blue eyes.

"He made me look like an ass!" Marks raged at Harry Parmakian. "And I blame you."

"What are you talking about, Reverend? You asked to go first in the final segment. In fact, you insisted upon it," Parmakian defended angrily.

"You should have stopped him. You saw how he manipulated your own director. You should have done something. He played you for a fool!" The reverend shook his finger.

Jeremiah Marks stormed away from the talk show host and stomped down the hall to his dressing room. There, he found Cindy Vinwire, pacing back and forth in front of his door, hugging her arms around herself to still her shivering.

"Reverend Marks..." She was breathless. "I'm so glad to see you."

"Nice to see you, too, Cindy." Marks stifled his urge to send her away. "How was your flight out? Did they get you a good seat?" Marks opened the dressing room door and gestured her inside.

"It was fine, Reverend. Thank you for making the arrangements. And I'm sorry I forgot the question I was supposed to ask. I was just so nervous. And he was looking right at me." Cindy slumped to the chair in front of the vanity, her back to the mirror.

"Never mind, Cindy. We both underestimated him. I promise you, it won't happen a second time." Marks loosened his tie, hoping for respite from his throbbing head.

"Reverend?" Cindy asked meekly. "Do you really think John Worthington is the Antichrist?"

Carefully choosing his words, the reverend hesitated before answering. Turning to her, taking her frozen fingers in his hands, he replied, "You've seen me use the power of God to heal. I have made the broken whole. But even my powers pale beside the evil of this man. He tied your tongue, Cindy. He assailed your mind." Staring into her eyes, unblinking, he prodded, "Alone, we are at his mercy. Aligned in Christ, we have a chance."

"What can I do, Reverend?" she whispered, wide-eyed.

"Go home, Cindy. And pray for a sign. Be vigilant and watch for a sign. Do you have enough money?" Marks cajoled.

"I'm fine, Reverend Marks. I'm not sleeping real good. But other than that, I'm fine," Cindy sighed.

"I have something for you." Marks reached into his briefcase and withdrew a present wrapped in iridescent white paper and crowned with a gold foil bow and cross.

Shocked, Cindy eagerly tore off the paper to find the words *Armageddon Alert* smeared in silver letters across the glossy blood-red cover of the book. Looking up, she said, "You wrote this?"

"Look inside." Marks smiled.

On the inside flap of the front cover Cindy read: *To Cindy Vinwire, God's Own Sentinel, Yours in the Lord, Reverend Jeremiah Marks.* "You autographed it for me? Thank you."

"Open it to the center," Marks directed.

Obeying the reverend, Cindy flipped the book open and found a small gold bookmark shaped like a cross. "Oh, Reverend, this is so sweet. I'll read it every night."

"The End Times are here, Cindy," Marks intoned sternly. "The Antichrist is here. Prepare yourself, Sentinel."

Setbacks & Chicaneries

Alpha II

Garner Williams pulled gently on the end of his newly grown mustache, the only tangible evidence of his months as a civilian. Staring at the columns of perfectly ordered finances, he shook his head in frustration.

Nothing.

Keying in Mildred Hawthorne's personal com number, he sighed as he waited for her to answer.

"Garner. Good morning." The judge took a sip of her coffee. "Anything new to report?"

"The only thing I can tell you is that whatever Morrison is doing, it clearly isn't for personal gain. He's squeaky clean, Judge Hawthorne." Williams shook his head. "Do you have any idea how much money he gives to different charities? It staggers the imagination. And every cent, every credit is traceable to a legitimate source. The only thing I can't explain is the odd discrepancy in the station's waste management budget. It's so blatant, it's probably just a mistake."

"What does Dan Timball say about this?" Mildred asked.

"I haven't asked him. I've just completed running the numbers. Garbage. I can't believe I'm going to interrogate anyone about garbage. Judge Hawthorne, how long have you known Dr. Morrison?"

"Oh my, Garner. At least 30 years. Maybe more. But, I'm committed to being objective here. You needn't worry about that. If I feel compromised, I will recuse myself."

"That's not why I asked, Judge. The truth is, the more I learn about Dr. Morrison, the more I admire him. I didn't expect to. He's really a nice man, very kind and — I know this sounds odd for me to say — very ethical."

"Well, Garner. I happen to agree with you about Phil. But the law is the law. If he's done something wrong, I will do my job. I'm sure you'll do yours, too."

"I called to request a physical search of his quarters, Judge Hawthorne. I have nowhere else to go with this."

"Absolutely not, Garner. You haven't even talked to Director Timball, yet. I will not invade the man's privacy for a fishing expedition. Nor will any judge on the bench. Sorry."

Williams glimpsed the back of Timball's head as the director disappeared through the door of the cafeteria kitchen. "Director! Director!" he called as he hurried to catch up. Racing through the door himself, he caught another glimpse of Timball as he rounded the corner by the huge commercial dishwasher. "Director Timball!" he barked, drawing stares from the kitchen employees.

A burley female cook looked up at Williams, then intercepted the fleeing Timball. Pointing him toward Williams she explained, "There. He's trying to get your attention."

Squirming away from the woman, Timball muttered "thanks" and stood his ground until Williams came to him.

Extending his hand to the director, Williams laughed. "You're a hard man to catch up to. It seems that no matter where I am, you're on some other level of the station."

Timball looked at his shoes and shrugged. "I've been pretty busy, lately. You know, this station never sleeps."

"No doubt. The reason that I wanted to talk to you is to set up a meeting to discuss some irregularities in the station's accounts. When would be good for you, Director Timball?"

"Oh gosh..." Timball drew a deep breath. "Tomorrow morning, maybe? Uh, say 0800? Today's kind of..." Timball trailed off.

"Sure. That's perfect. My quarters at 0800, then." Williams smiled and walked away.

As soon as he had disappeared around the corner, Timball slumped against the dishwasher, heart racing. Composing himself, the shaky director headed to Level 14. He stood long moments waiting for Morrison to answer his door. When the doctor finally appeared, he was holding a medbar assembly that resembled a human elbow.

"I think I may have done it," Morrison gloated. "Hi Dan. What's up?"

"What's up??!! Garner Williams wants to interrogate me tomorrow morning, and here you are, playing with robot parts that you should have destroyed. Don't you get it Phil? We're under the gun here. Get rid of the evidence!" Timball slumped to Morrison's couch, gasping to catch his breath. "I hope to hell you've erased all your tracks on the research web. Have you?" he croaked hoarsely.

"As much as I can. Not everything can be covered up, unfortunately." Setting his project on a nearby shelf, Morrison poured two glasses of crystalline. "Here, Dan. Calm down," Morrison pressed the hesitant director to accept the liqueur.

Groaning, Timball struggled to take a deep breath and sipped the crystalline. Finally, he muttered, "At 0800, I have to meet with Williams in his quarters. It's over. We're done. You know, there for a day or so, I allowed myself to believe it was all working out. I thought we might even get away with it. I should have known. I should never have gone along with this."

"Jeez, Dan, I'm sorry you feel that way. Although I would like to, I won't ask you to trust me even one more time. I will say this, however, I have not given up by any stretch. I'm sorry if you have." Placing a steadying hand on Timball's shoulder, Morrison whispered, "You know, Dan, whatever happens, you're still my best friend."

Assembling the data for tomorrow morning's meeting, Williams frowned when the face of Imperator Fells burst into his quarters. No com alert warned him of the transmission.

"Like the new program?" Fells glowered. "Now fill me in, Williams. I don't have much time."

"Imperator Fells, not only will I not speak with you, I am obliged to report this illegal contact to Judge Hawthorne," Williams clipped. Manually shutting down the com, Williams grimaced as Fells' face dissolved into a shimmer of holographic anger.

Fells, frothing in rage, stabbed Governor Coleman's private number into his com.

"Not now, Fells," Coleman simpered. "I have guests."

"Don't cut me off," Fells warned. "I need to get rid of Hawthorne. She blocks me at every turn. Hell, she's got Williams eating out of her hand. Initiate a recall."

"Are you mad?" Coleman shrilled. "Even if I could, it would take months. How can that possibly help you?"

"Then get me an order to search Morrison's quarters," Fells demanded.

"On what grounds? I have a constituency to answer to, Imperator Fells," Coleman sulked.

"You have me to answer to as well," Fells hissed. "And I always collect what's owed to me. Do something!" Fells screamed and disappeared.

An alert from the com drew Williams' ire. "Not again!" he muttered to himself. Punching *answer* with an angry finger, his mood brightened at the face of Kyle Zephyrs. "Kyle. I'm so glad it's you and not Fells."

"Thanks, I think." Zephyrs grinned. "What's up? I haven't heard from you in days."

"I've been up to my armpits in this audit, Kyle. And I'm going nowhere fast. I'm almost relieved to be at a dead end."

"So, you've got nothing on him?" Kyle questioned. "After all of the drama and all of this time?"

"I'll tell you how bad it is. The only evidence I can find is too much garbage," Williams laughed wryly.

Laughing, himself, Zephyrs responded. "Garbage. Really? You know, back in '88, that would have been a big deal."

Suddenly somber, Williams asked, "A big deal? Why?"

"Don't you remember? Back in '88? The outer orbit garbage strike? Every station had garbage scows tethered around them for months... Hey, Garner. What are you doing?"

Punching up the spreadsheet of suspicious accounts payable, Garner Williams groaned. The largest entry read: Waste Management Services - 6/18/2188.

Phoenix

Shadows slithered up the walls and curious noises troubled the darkness of the night. Cindy pulled the covers up to her chin. Shoving her arm over her head and under her pillow, she fumbled to find her pistol. Reassured by its presence, she fiddled with the small book light and turned to Chapter Five: *The Lake of Fire.*

A screeching alley cat made her jump. Grabbing the gun, she tumbled out of bed and skittered to check the deadbolts on her front door. Rushing through the kitchen, she checked the window locks. Weighing the choice only a second, she left the hall light burning and scrambled back to bed. Tucking the pistol back under her pillow, she found her page in Reverend Marks' book and read until midnight. Trembling.

Shivering so badly that her teeth chattered, Cindy finally succumbed to her terror and called Alan Burgess.

"Hi Alan," she said sheepishly. "I guess I woke you, didn't I?"

"That's okay. You sound like you're crying, Cindy. What's up?" Burgess struggled to sit up in bed and shook his head when he saw the time.

"I'm so scared, Alan. Everything's falling apart. There's crime and violence everywhere you look. Is it getting bad in Nederland?" she sniveled.

"Here? Are you kidding? The worst problem we have in town is bickering politicians. Cindy, where are you getting these ideas?"

"These are the End Times, Alan."

"The End Times?"

"You know, Armageddon," Cindy proclaimed.

"Look Cindy, that's just somebody's opinion. People have looked for the end of the world for two thousand years that we know of."

"I've got proof, Alan" Cindy fingered the gold bookmark sticking out of *Armageddon Alert*.

"You know, Cindy, before you get yourself all worked up over this, you really should talk to someone," Alan suggested.

"You mean, like a shrink? Alan, sentinels of God are always accused of being crazy. But you'll see. I'm right... Reverend Marks is right about this," Cindy sniffed.

"Okay, Cindy. Whatever you say. Just be careful and take care of yourself." Burgess disconnected and grabbed his copy of *The Investigator*. Snapping it open to the Nederland story, he re-read the twisted words of Reverend Jeremiah Marks.

Wildwood

"Well, that's that," Barry announced, dragging in a large bag of mail. "From now on, we have to go the Amber Post Office to pick it up. Poor old Pete doesn't have enough room in his mail truck to carry this much out to us."

Fletcher laughed. "And I was afraid that Parmakian's show would be bad for your reputation, REL. As of yesterday's donations — all unsolicited — people have contributed almost twenty thousand dollars to our work."

"Gary, I've been thinking about our publishing party." REL beamed. "I still can't believe I have a book coming out!"

"I can't wait until *REL's Guide To God* is on the shelves," Valerie bubbled. "Don't you have some brilliant plans for your publishing party, REL?"

"What do you think of this? Lots of our internet regulars have interesting talents, like Tarot and channeling. Some of them have been published, themselves, like 2nd Sight. What if we have a Metaphysical Fair during the day and a party that night? That way, we could mingle and visit and really celebrate. What do you think?" REL looked hopefully at his friends. "It would be fun, wouldn't it?"

"That's a great idea!" Barry enthused. "I'll get busy organizing it."

A low whistle interrupted the conversation. Everyone turned to look at Fletcher, who held a letter in his shaking hand.

"What?" Dot blurted.

"Our very first death threat," Fletcher muttered angrily. "Some nut from the talk show. Seems to think REL will bring on

301

Armageddon unless he's stopped. Ick!" The big man grimaced, tossing the letter into the wastepaper basket.

"Wait a minute," Barry retrieved the letter. "Shouldn't we call the cops or something?"

"No. I won't succumb to fear. Besides, I have this theory about the vibration of love. I think it acts like a shield of sorts. I don't feel like I'm in any danger," REL assured. "I think I'd like to read the letter, though, maybe I can send them love."

"Oh, hey, look at the time. The *Messengers* will be here soon," Valerie reminded. "Come on, Dot, Barry, Gary, let's get going."

"It will be nice to have them back here, even if we do have to build a big bonfire," Barry joked. "What is today's topic, REL?"

"Well, I thought the first day of Spring would be a good time to talk about the changing magnetics of Earth."

"Oooh, what about it?" Valerie asked as she slipped on her jacket.

"Well, the magnetics of Earth are fainter than they've been in two thousand years. As a result, the Schumann resonance has increased."

"Schumann resonance?" Gary asked.

"Yes, the Schumann resonance is a measurement of how fast the Earth vibrates. For ages, it has remained at roughly 7.25 MHz. Just recently, scientists measured it at 12.8 MHz and rising. The faster Earth vibrates, the faster our fears and beliefs manifest. Now is the perfect time to initiate the paradigmatic shift."

"It doesn't sound all that easy, REL," Dot complained.

"Just stay in your heart, Dot, and you'll stay on the path," REL said as he donned his own jacket and headed out to light the bonfire.

Alpha II

Timball perspired nervously. His blood pressure sky-rocketed. His empty stomach burned and heaved. Emaciated and exhausted, the director's eyes were sunken and rimmed with dark circles that resembled wounds on his tightly strung face. Slumping against the wall outside Garner Williams' quarters, he tried, in vain, to still his hammering heart before signaling his arrival.

Pacing on the other side of the door, Williams passed a hand over the door sensor and found himself face to face with the haggard director. "Come in, Director. I didn't know you were here, yet." Williams motioned Timball to take a seat across the table from him.

Wordlessly, the director slumped into the chair, his laboring heart strangling his voice.

"I know about the garbage strike," Williams pronounced without amenities.

"Maybe it's just a typo," Timball offered weakly.

"Don't, Director Timball. Don't make this harder than it is already," Williams admonished. "What did you use the money for?"

"I... I... I have nothing to do with that money," Timball pleaded.

"That's not true. You have everything to do with the money. You're in charge of the money, Director. There's no escaping that fact." Williams stood and paced. "I hate this, Director Timball. I really, really hate this. Won't you at least explain it to me so that I can understand why a man like Morrison would risk everything on garbage?!" Williams implored. "And why a man like you would go along with it?"

Timball buried his head in his hands and mumbled, "I can't... I can't tell you anything."

"Director Timball, either you tell me or you'll end up bearing the brunt of the criminal penalties involved in this," Williams counseled sternly.

"Phil would never let that happen," Timball blurted. "Oh, God."

Placing both hands on the table between himself and the director, Williams leaned eye to eye with the shaking man. "Look, Timball. It's obvious you didn't plan this. Hell, you probably don't even know half of what's going on. Let me help you."

"Help me? You came here to railroad me," Timball wailed.

"Look, I know we don't agree politically. But that doesn't mean that I'm out to get you. I swore to uphold the law, Director Timball. That's as personal as it gets. If you're the only one standing when the guilty verdict is read, it will be by your own choice. I say again, let me help you."

Timball sat with his head bowed, shuddering in silent misery. When he finally looked up, Williams gasped at the horrific price his investigation had etched in the director's ashen face.

"Will I go to prison?" Timball whispered.

"I don't know, Director. You have to tell me everything."

Two hours later, Williams wearily connected with Judge Mildred Hawthorne.

"Garner, two days in a row?" she quipped, regretting her flippancy the instant she saw his face. "You must have found something." She frowned.

"Dan Timball just left my quarters. He told me everything. And the minimum charge we can prove right now is embezzlement." Williams shook his head. "Can I have that order to search Morrison's quarters now?"

"No, Garner. Not yet. But I will issue an order for Phil to appear. And an order that he can't leave Alpha II until then," the judge told him. "How deeply is Dan involved in this?"

"I'm not sure, yet. But I'll tell you this, he looks like hell. Oh, Fells burst into my com last night. I refused to talk with him," Williams advised.

"Boy... You can bet that when he gets wind of Morrison's appearance, he'll show up with bells on," the judge ventured.

"I hope that's all he brings." Williams frowned. "He's losing it, too."

Doctor Morrison sat reading a digital book outside Timball's office when the decrepit director rounded the corner. Immediately pocketing the small volume, Morrison rushed to his friend to lend an arm.

Shrugging away from Morrison's offer Timball whined, "No. You won't want anything to do with me when I tell you what's happened."

"I have a pretty good idea, Dan. Mildred sent me an invitation to appear as I was sitting here waiting for you. Don't worry. I expected as much. You look like shit, let's get you inside and sitting down." Despite Timball's resistance, Morrison took his elbow and helped him into the office.

"Phil..." the stricken Timball began. "I tried. I'm just not strong like you. I told him everything. The whole damned thing is coming apart down around our heads."

"Dan," Morrison soothed, "Sometimes God has to shuffle the deck to deal you a winning hand. Have faith."

Center State Complex

Arthur Tabbot leaned back in his chair, a snifter of schnapps hung loosely in his hand. A signal from his com finally roused his reluctant attention. "What is it," he said without emotion.

"Arthur..." Mildred Hawthorne's face greeted him. "I thought you should know, I've issued an order for Phil to appear."

"I've heard, Mildred."

"I'm sorry. I had no choice. The evidence cannot be ignored," Mildred stressed.

"I know you did what you had to do." Pausing to sip, he continued, "Sometimes I wonder if it's worth the effort."

"Why Arthur, that doesn't sound like you," Mildred admonished.

"Two fine men are at risk for trying to save humanity from itself, Mildred. What does that tell you about the virtues of idealism?"

"My mother used to suggest to me that it was better to believe in the highest potential of humanity and realize, with your final breath that you were wrong than to believe otherwise and be right. Besides, Phil knew the all dangers and chose to take this risk for all of us. We must honor that, don't you think?" Mildred concluded.

God's Fortress

Whistling a new gospel tune, Reverend Marks peeked around the corner of Luke's cubicle. "Is this it?" he said as he received the slender flip phone from Luke's outstretched hand. "They make them smaller all the time."

"Sure do," Luke confirmed. "And more efficient. This one will get reception almost anywhere."

"So, you set up the account so Miss Vinwire will never get a bill?" Marks asked as he replaced the cell phone in its box and added an autographed copy of *Devils, Demons, and*

Doomsday to the pile. "Where's the check?" Marks frowned. "I submitted the check request two days ago."

"Uh…" Luke stood up and shrugged his shoulders. "Well, Faith… you know, down in accounting? Well, she did cut the check, but she wouldn't give it to me."

"Really?" Marks glared.

"Yeah, she's concerned about… uh… propriety."

Marks made no comment and continued to glower at his minion.

Luke gulped and reasoned, "You do send Cindy a lot of stuff, Reverend. There are rumors…"

Marks' eyes narrowed dangerously. "First of all, Luke," he hissed. "God has purified me of all those carnal urges. Perhaps if you prayed as diligently as I, he would unburden you, too. Secondly — Sister Vinwire is our most powerful weapon against the antichrist! God has seen fit to visit her with certain emotional challenges. So, I contribute what I can to keep her focused on the task at hand. Any more questions, Luke?" The reverend sneered.

"Uh, no." Luke gulped. "I tried to tell Faith…" He trailed off and fumbled to pack the phone and the book in the mailer.

Marks snatched the package from Luke's desk. "I'll see to the check myself. And while I'm at it, I'll counsel Miss Faith on the evils of gossip!" Marks grumbled and stormed off down the hall.

Nederland

Burgess waited for the static to clear. "Hello," he answered again.

"Oh, hi, Alan." Cindy's voice crackled, far away, distorted. "I'm at the range. I aced three targets already today."

"So, how are the nightmares, Cindy?" Alan pried.

"I get them every night, but I'm learning to read the signs. The end is closer than you think, Alan. Unless..." Static muffled her words. When the connection cleared she continued, "So, did you watch the *Our View* video I sent you?"

"Yeah. I was really surprised to see you. What were you doing there?"

"I was just keeping my eye on Worthington. I'm a sentinel, now. I log onto his web page every day, too," Cindy announced.

"How can you be traveling all over the place and surfing the net all the time? What about your job?"

"That is my job. I'm a sentinel, I work for the Lord, now."

"But what about money?" Alan pressed.

"God gives me money, Alan. More than I've ever had before. And Reverend Marks always sends me nice things. Like my cell phone. Uh, oh, I'm up next. Bye, Alan."

Fumbling with the receiver, Alan let it drop to the floor. Hand over hand he pulled the cord until he could reach the receiver to hang it up.

"Alan, were you talking about reward money?" Burrows probed.

"I don't know. She calls it money from God. Jeez, Marshal, she's quit her job, she's stalking Worthington, she's surfing the net and Marks is footing the bill."

"So what is she doing for Marks?"

"The truth is, she's so out of touch with reality that I'm not sure where her job description ends and her fantasies begin. She's having nightmares and seeing demons. And, Marshal she's reading signs into everything. She's convinced that the end of the world is here now! She's one hurting unit, Marshal." Burgess shook his head sadly.

"Do you think she could be dangerous?" Burrows asked.

"Well, let's look at the facts, Marshal." He started counting on his fingers. "She has money. She has a target. She has time. She owns a gun that she knows how to use. And she's crazy. What do you think?"

Burgess reached into his bottom desk drawer to retrieve Cindy's video. Just then, Thelma stepped into the little office.

"Good morning, GentleOfficers," she bubbled. "Here's something interesting, Jim." She handed a sage green envelope to the marshal.

"Oh, it's from Craig Landwehr. An invitation..." Looking up, he asked, "For John Worthington?"

"Worthington?" Burgess blurted. "Boy, were we wrong about him, Marshal. Cindy sent me this video of him on some talk show... He's really amazing. I doubt he has a dishonest bone in his body. After hearing what he had to say, I'd love to go to one of his speeches." Alan held up the video, "Do you wanna borrow it?"

Burrows and Thelma stared at the deputy.

"Well, I'm invited to a publishing party for his new book. He'll be speaking then. You want to go, Jim?" Thelma asked.

"You mean all the way to New York?" Burrows wrinkled his brow.

"Oh, come on, Jim. I know you have the vacation time. We could drive back, visit Craig and Jenny and go to the party. I, personally, would love to meet this guy who has made so many waves. At least think about it."

"Wait till you watch the video, you'll want to go," Burgess assured. "If you do, can I come? Please?"

Alpha II

Morrison eyed the elevator light. With one final shove, he got the bulky supply pak through his door just before the tube reached his floor. He sighed in relief as it continued on to the skylock level. Safely inside his quarters, he divided up the load and carried it back to his newly fortified lab.

"Well, this is the last of it," he said to himself, wiping his brow.

Returning to his living room, he scanned once more for anything incriminating. Satisfied, he set his packed bag and briefcase next to the couch and poured himself a stiff shot of cognac. Just as he settled back, feet up on the coffee table, the door sensor chimed announcing Dan Timball.

"Come in, Dan. Come in." Morrison smiled.

Timball lurched, then doddered through the door, darksome and haunted. "Phil," he quavered, "Before you leave for the surface... I'm so sorry," he sobbed. "I'm so sorry for everything... for every decision I've made... everything I've ever done... I'm so sorry." He slumped to Morrison's couch and buried his head in his hands.

Rushing to his friend and placing a steadying hand on his back, Morrison murmured, "You are not to blame, Dan. In no way should you blame yourself. I chose this path. I've walked it all my life. You honored me by sharing it for a time. But now, you've got to take care of yourself."

The director's reddened eyes snapped up to meet Morrison's. "Why?" he groaned. "What is the point?"

"Dan, despite all outward appearances, I'm convinced REL is making a difference. I feel it!" Morrison clasped Timball's hand. "It's far too subtle to describe, but I feel energy shifting. I will find a way to hang on, Dan. Heal yourself and hang on, too." Staring into the director's shadowed eyes, Morrison pronounced,

"You look like hell, Dan. I'm going to help you back to your quarters and get a med tech to look in on you." Morrison took Timball's bony elbow and helped the shaking man to his feet.

Williams stepped back as the tube rose to reveal Dr. Morrison and the sagging Dan Timball. "Oh, my God! Is he okay?" Williams rushed to take the director's other arm.

"He's not well at all. Call a med tech, tell them it's the director," the doctor instructed. Morrison guided Timball to his bed, removed his shoes and eased him onto his back. Within minutes, an entire medical team converged on Timball's quarters, pushing Morrison and Williams out into the hall.

"Damn!" Morrison cursed. "I'll never forgive myself if anything happens to him."

"I'm sure he'll be fine, Dr. Morrison. I'll check on him myself." Williams paused, then spoke softly, "About tomorrow... It's nothing personal. Really. I wish I had never found that evidence."

"Mr. Williams, we made a gentleman's agreement to do our jobs. We did them. Everything unfolds as it must." Extending his hand, Morrison said, "No hard feelings. Thank you for looking out for Dan."

"My shuttle will be ready at 0700." Williams patted the doctor on the back. "I'm going to pilot you myself. After I check on the director, of course."

"Thanks. I'll welcome the company."

Second Messenger

Desperate Measures & Dastardly Deeds

Wildwood

At precisely 2:00 a.m. the lambent moon slipped into the frame of the window. REL felt its silvered caress across his shoulders as he posted a message to a group of *Messengers* online in London.

REL: The time is really right. The power of love is exponential in this new vibration. And when used consciously in a group, WoooooHoooooo! The pathway is simple: From God through your heart to you. From you through your heart to God. When you channel your experiences through this pathway, you automatically shed your doubts about your connection to God, to each other, to everything. This is the blessed journey. This is the stairway to Heaven on Earth. Oh, My Beloved Friends, this is so exciting. We chose to be here for this wondrous human experience. Shall we link our hearts for a sacred moment? For the next three minutes, let us breathe through our hearts. Let us direct our collective love energy to all of humankind. To the Earth. To All That Is. Let us channel the breath of God for the good of all.

A plunge in the ambient energy prompted REL to open his eyes.

SkyPilot: "The heart is deceitful above all things and beyond cure." Jeremiah 17:9 You are FOOLS to follow this man. He twists your souls. He makes you his tools to usher in Armageddon. Does he promise you power? Do not believe him. You will end up as slaves in the eternal lake of fire! Does he promise you godhood? All he can deliver is hell!!

LondonBard: Mellow out, SkyPilot. Do not disturb the peace here.

SkyPilot: THE PEACE YOU HEAR IS THE DEATH KNELL OF YOUR SOUL. WAKE UP!

REL deftly typed a private message to SkyPilot: *Reverend Marks, You are always welcome here, but you must respect my other guests. Be at peace.*

Seconds later, REL received a return post. *WHAT KIND OF DEMON TECHNOLOGY EXPOSES MY ANONYMITY? YOU ARE CURSED!!! YOU ARE THE ANTICHRIST!!! I WILL EXPOSE YOU!!!*

Marks stabbed out "POOF!" and logged out of the chat room. Logging back into the God's Fortress Network, he checked one, last time. Membership, contributions, sales — all down. "Worthington!" he cursed. Disgusted, he logged off the net and stomped to his suite.

"Cindy?" Marks smoothed. "Did I wake you?"

"No, Reverend, I was already awake from a nightmare," Cindy mumbled into the phone.

"Yes, I expect they're getting worse as his power grows. You need to pack for a party, Sentinel. Worthington's invited a few of his unholiest friends to celebrate the publication of his godless book. You will represent the Lord, Cindy."

"You want me to go to New York?" Cindy roused herself. "I can schedule a flight out tomorrow."

"Sentinel, you must be prepared to protect yourself from these fiends. Perhaps you should drive so you can take some defensive precautions, if you know what I mean," Marks baited. "Leave in the morning. Give yourself plenty of time to drive safely."

Nederland

Alan Burgess pulled the pillow tighter over his head. "Not again," he moaned and waited for the service to pick up the call. "Whatever it is, she can wait until morning." He turned over and fell back to sleep.

Toothbrush hanging from the side of his mouth, Alan punched in his code to retrieve last night's message. The deputy paled, spat foam into the basin and yanked on his uniform. Sprinting to Whistler's, he paused just inside the door to catch his breath. "Thelma, Marshal..." he blurted and rushed over to the corner table. "Cindy's gone," Burgess panted. "Left in the middle of the night to crash Worthington's party. I don't care what you two are doing, but I've got to go after her."

"I'll call Craig, book the flights, and we're out of here. Please don't argue about this, Jim. You know this is partly your doing," Thelma insisted, suspending further discussion.

Alpha II

"Dr. Morrison," Williams signaled from the hall. "I've come to escort you to the shuttle bay."

The door whooshed open. Dr. Morrison stood, bag and briefcase in hand. With a stiff nod of his head, he acknowledged Williams and started out the door.

"I'll try to make this as informal as possible, but there is protocol," Williams explained.

"I understand the protocol," Morrison mumbled mechanically. A tight, narrow smile flickered across his pale face. "Shall we?" Wordlessly, Morrison preceded Williams through the corridors of Alpha II. Head bowed, he avoided eye contact with those who wept for him.

Arthur Tabbot jostled through the swelling throng outside the High Court of Justice. The closer he drew to the steps, the denser and more stubborn the crowd became. Just as he despaired of getting through, the masses parted in front of him. "Councilman Tabbot, follow me." A young ICom officer sporting an escort band around one uniform sleeve reached out to guide him unhindered to the steps.

"Thank you," Tabbot leaned to read the man's name tag. "Lieutenant Zephyrs."

Judge Mildred Hawthorne banged her gavel the moment Fells made eye contact with Morrison. "Get settled in quickly. Either find a seat or leave. This is not a circus. Bailiff, help those people." She nodded to a crowd in one corner. Banging her gavel again, she proclaimed, "This court is now in session. This is not a trial. I want that understood. Dr. Phillip P. Morrison was ordered to appear to answer preliminary questions *only,*" she stressed. "Imperator Fells, you may sit with the inquiry panel, but you may not cross examine. This is not an ICom affair. Understood?"

The skeletal-faced Fells nodded, jaws clenched, eyes anchored on the judge.

Williams scrutinized Morrison, aghast that in less than twelve hours the man's resolve had crumbled so completely. The doctor did not speak once during the agonizing trip to the surface. And now, he sat absently staring, almost insubstantial amidst the clamor that surrounded him.

"Approach," Judge Hawthorne ordered. "Let's get these motions on the table." Looking up at the distracted doctor, the judge apologized, "Doctor Morrison, it appears that this day is reserved for the lawyers." She shook her head as the gleaming pile of discs accumulated on the bench. "And maybe half of tomorrow, too. Be patient. You'll get your opportunity to respond to the questions."

Morrison tipped his head and stared blankly at her. The judged frowned and continued.

At the lunch break, Arthur Tabbot elbowed his way through Morrison's escorts, seeking a personal moment. "Phil," he whispered across the table. "Are you okay?"

Morrison jerked at the sound of his name and turned to Tabbot. "Arthur…" He mouthed his friend's name without emotion. "Everything will be fine. The energy is shifting." And then he turned away, leaving the councilman puzzled and silent.

Motions and orders chewed well into the second day. As shadows waned through the courtroom windows, Judge Hawthorne pounded her gavel. "The court calls Doctor Phillip P. Morrison."

Staggering to his feet, the gaunt doctor shuffled across the expanse, stopping to steady himself on the rail before climbing into the witness box. He sat wheezing and dazed as the entire court stared at him.

"Dr. Morrison, are you all right?" Judge Hawthorne asked as she surveyed his ravaged face, the sunken eyes and yellowing complexion. "Dr. Morrison?" she prompted.

Dumbly, he turned to her. "Yes... Judge Hawthorne."

"Shall we continue?" She leaned to look in his eyes. They were huge, dilated and glazed.

"Yes, Judge Hawthorne. Please proceed," he pronounced dispassionately.

Checking the time and staring again at the doctor, the judge ordered, "We'll adjourn for the day and get a fresh start in the morning. Defense, I want to see you in my chambers. Court adjourned." She pounded the gavel.

"Get him some medical help," she instructed.

"We've tried. He won't have it. In fact, he refuses to even meet with us. When he's not in court, he's alone in his room," Defense Counsel complained. "We can't get him to eat anything, either."

"Is he competent?" the judge pressed.

"He seems to be. He's coherent, if a little slow. And he answers all the questions we put to him." Defense Counsel shrugged and shook his head.

"This is terrible," Mildred mumbled. "I guess we have no choice. We start at 9:00 a.m. Try to take him to dinner or something."

Enroute to New York State

Cindy rocked in the driver's seat. Her harrowed eyes darted from rear view mirror to side mirrors to the tunneled abyss ahead.

Hiss clack... hiss clack... hiss clack...

Demons paced her. Disguised as ghostly foliage encroaching the highway, they skittered and leered and whispered despair.

Hiss clack... hiss clack... hiss clack...

Fretting the visual circuit again — rear view, side, ahead — Cindy forced her brittle thoughts to attend the skeletal lines that split the undulating asphalt. Her sticky eyes refused to focus. Heaving a tattered sob, she peered on through the night until a distant sign threatened her resolve.

Rest Area 1 Mile.

Could she dare? A bathroom. A walk. A rest. She almost succumbed. But pinpricks of red in her rear view mirror and a yammering chill up her spine kept her faithful. Groping the seat beside her, she eased as she fondled her pistol and sadly sped by the exit. She fumbled through her purse for the gospel tape Reverend Marks had sent her. After three tries, she managed to get it to play. Screwing the lid from her thermos, she forswore the cup and drank coffee straight from the jug. Her headlights winked onward, fragile beams of futility against the cavern of the stygian landscape.

Hiss clack... hiss clack... hiss clack...

Denver International Airport

Staring at the lightening sky, Thelma sipped her coffee and joked, "Sorry about the hour, but there was nothing else available."

Burgess thoughtfully chewed his bagel. "I hope it's not too late for Cindy. Shouldn't we call the Amber police? Maybe they can head her off before she hurts anybody..." He paused. "Or herself," he whispered. Absently, he lifted the bagel to his lips, then looked at it in distaste and tossed it into a nearby garbage bin.

"I talked to Craig myself. He's got friends on the force and he's a veteran. They'll keep watch till we get there. Besides..." Burrows yawned, "...we'll be there hours ahead of her. Maybe even a day or so, if she stops for the night."

"She won't," Burgess argued grimly. "She doesn't sleep."

Center State Complex

Doctor Morrison shambled into the courtroom, an attorney at each elbow to steady his frail steps. Looking up from the bench, Judge Hawthorne swore the man had withered overnight. His shoulders sagged beneath his baggy suit. His eyes, lifeless and hollow, hinted at none of the man's legendary genius. Even his brilliant white hair clung to his head in dull, unkempt wisps. Arthur Tabbot took one look at his friend and ducked out the huge mahogany doors. Rushing to the nearest courthouse page, Tabbot directed, "Dispatch a med unit to Judge Hawthorne's High Court. I don't want them standing by, I want them here. Now!"

"Right away," the page nodded then raced up the marble hall.

Tabbot slipped back into the courtroom, winding his way back to his seat near Morrison.

Garner Williams, sitting with the inquiry panel, gazed aghast as the doctor slowly made his way up the center aisle then slumped wearily into his chair. A sharp elbow in his ribs spun Williams toward Imperator Fells.

"Look at the pathetic old bastard!" Fells gloated. "Nice work, Williams."

"You're mistaken if you think I'm proud of this," Williams snapped, turning away in disgust.

Banging her gavel for order, Judge Hawthorne declared, "This court is now in session. Defense, please approach."

Defense Counsel patted the doctor on the back and reported to the judge.

Leaning over the bench, Judge Hawthorne whispered, "He looks terrible. Did you try to get him medical help?"

"Same as before, he refused. We couldn't get him to eat, either, Judge."

"Is he lucid?" the judge asked, staring at Morrison.

"He seems mentally sound. Physically, he seems to be disintegrating," Defense advised.

Drumming her fingernails lightly on the bench, the judge took a deep breath then sighed, "I am bound by the letter of the law in this matter. Unless Dr. Morrison complains or asks for a recess, I can do nothing. Keep an eye on him, if he seems distressed, let me know." Addressing the courtroom, Judge Hawthorne looked at the haggard man, "Dr. Morrison, will you please take the stand?"

Morrison trudged to the witness box. Just as he reached it, he lurched then stumbled, grabbing the rail. Eyes wide and head flung backwards, he hung fast while his whole body shuddered.

Judge Hawthorne, Arthur Tabbot, and Garner Williams, jumped to their feet at once. But before they could move, Morrison's shudder flared into a convulsion that wrenched his hands loose and flung him to the floor. With a violent thud, he landed on his back, dead eyes staring at the inquiry panel.

Roaring to his feet, Imperator Fells screamed, "No!" Bounding over the table in front of Williams, Fells bent over the doctor. Knotting his fists in the man's collar, Fells screamed, "Tell me! Tell me how you plan to kill me!" and banged doctor's lifeless head on the floor.

Williams yanked the raging imperator to his feet and shoved him away. Judge Hawthorne knelt to take the doctor's pulse. Gasping, she looked up at the encircling crowd and whispered, "My God, he's dead."

Just then, the huge doors burst open as the med unit clamored into the room, gurney and equipment in tow. Hurrying through the parted crowd, the team reached Morrison and tried frantically to revive him.

The stone-faced Fells scanned the courtroom, alerting an ICom officer near the back. A nodding command sent the officer scurrying for the exit.

Looking into the stricken face of Arthur Tabbot, the med tech shook his head. "No response. Absolutely no response. I'm sorry." The tech covered Morrison's face, packed up his instruments and motioned the team to place the body on the gurney.

Tabbot turned to Judge Hawthorne, about to speak when the cadence of booted feet drew the attention of the entire court. A double column of ICom specials stormed through doors, weapons shouldered. Fells raced up the aisle to meet them, barking orders as the soldiers ringed the crowd. Six burley men followed Fells to the front. "Take it!" Fells demanded, pointing to the corpse.

"You will not!" Judge Hawthorne commanded.

"I *am* doing an autopsy." Fells bellowed.

"Bailiff!" Judge Hawthorne turned to see the man frozen, an ICom gun to his head and her courtroom encircled by soldiers with weapons raised.

Tabbot glowered at Fells. "This is an outrage!" he hissed. "This is despicable even for you!"

"You do know," Judge Hawthorne scolded, "this is not just abuse of authority, this is criminal, Imperator Fells."

Six ICom thugs shoved the med team out of the way, then wheeled the dead Morrison up the aisle and out of the court. Grabbing a bewildered Lieutenant Zephyrs from his post outside the courtroom doors Fells growled, "You're coming with me!"

Wildwood

Knocking softly on the kitchen door, Craig Landwehr smiled as Dot greeted him with a cup of coffee. "Did Jenny finally throw you out?" she chuckled.

Taking a sip, Craig spoke softly, "I wanted to tell you that Burrows called from Nederland to warn you. Supposedly some woman's stalking REL."

"Is he in danger?" Dot asked, alarmed.

"I'm not sure. In any case, I've got some friends watching the road in. We'll keep an eye on things. Just relax. It'll be okay." Handing his cup back to her he continued, "I just wanted to let you know that we'll be hanging around today."

"Thanks, Craig. I'll tell everyone to be sharp." Turning from the door, she narrowly missed running into John. "Good morning."

"Was that Craig?"

"You just missed him."

"Missed who?" Fletcher's deep voice rolled from the hallway into the kitchen.

"Craig Landwehr was just here," REL responded.

"How come?" Barry asked, reaching for the coffee.

Valerie entered the back door of the kitchen, rosy-cheeked from a morning walk. "Hey, I just ran into Craig. He says REL has his very own stalker."

Fletcher's head snapped up. "Is this person dangerous?"

"Craig's not too worried. He and his friends are keeping an eye on things. I think we should all pay attention, though," Dot advised.

"What do you think, REL?" Barry asked.

"I'm going to send love to whoever it is and enjoy my day with you." He winked. "No fear. Remember? Who's up for a picnic today?"

The Road to Wildwood

Marshal Burrows drove with his elbow stuck out the rolled-down window of the rental car. Thelma studied the map in her lap and Alan Burgess sat lost in his own thoughts, alone, in the back seat.

"We're getting close, Jim. Left hand turn after mile marker 171." Thelma admired the woods. "It sure is pretty, isn't it? I can see why Craig and Jenny moved here. There." Thelma pointed to the sheltered road.

Burrows flipped on his signal and slowed to make the turn. The minute they left the blacktop, the trio from Nederland found themselves immersed in the quiet of the forest. No one spoke as the car rolled on to Wildwood. Thelma kept an eye on the map and counted miles on the odometer.

From the back seat, Burgess piped up, "There's Cindy's car, Marshal. Stop."

Burrows stopped and turned to Burgess. "How do you know it's her car?"

"Well, she has a black Camaro. That one has Arizona plates and a WARS bumper sticker." Burgess unfastened his seat belt and stepped out onto the road. Looking around for signs of the girl, he sprinted over to her car. Retrieving a large photograph from the front seat, Burgess turned to the marshal.

"What do you think of this?" The deputy displayed the aerial view of Wildwood on the still-warm hood of Cindy's car. "Wow. Look here. There's a path that leads to the back entrance." Burgess traced the highlighted trail. "See. Here's where Craig is, at this turn-off clear on the other side. Here's where we are." Glancing inside the car, Burgess handed the map to the marshal and rushed to the driver's side. Holding up an empty box of shells, he said, "You and Thelma drive around, I'm going after her."

"Alan, you don't have a gun," Burrows cautioned.

"She won't shoot me, Marshal," Alan assured with confidence. Without another word, he grabbed his binoculars from the rental car and bounded down the narrow trail.

Moments later, the deputy stopped to scan the unfolding valley. Catching his breath, he heard branches crunching and snapping in the distance. Through his binoculars, he caught sight of Cindy stumbling through the trees one hundred yards ahead of him. He thought to call to her and decided not. Taking a deep breath, he sprinted a direct path toward her hoping her own noisy passage would muffle his approach.

Center State Complex: ICom Headquarters

Fells clamped his hand on the back of Zephyrs' neck and guided him to the morgue. Declining both mask and gown, Fells prodded the young officer across the grim floor to the autopsy in progress.

"Imperator Fells, Sir, I'm glad you're here. You need to see this." The ICom coroner beckoned them to take a closer look.

"See what?" Fells demanded, striding to the table. "What the hell?!"

"This is not a man, Director. This is some kind of android." The coroner wrinkled his brow. "This is real skin, but underneath, it's all circuits and flexors."

Eyes wide in shock, Fells whipped around to Zephyrs. "You were right about the android. My God," he gasped, "you could be right about the whole plot."

Zephyrs mutely nodded, dumfounded at his luck.

Whipping back to the coroner, Fells ordered, "Not a word about this!"

"Absolutely, Imperator Fells," the examiner agreed.

Hauling the young lieutenant beside him, Fells marched directly to his Stinger. "I've had it!" he barked. "I'll get to the bottom of this myself. With your help." He shoved Zephyrs toward the transport.

Alpha II

Hidden away in his secret lab, the allegedly dead Dr. Morrison stroked his grizzled chin. The past days of isolation and reflection had served him well, drawing him closer than ever to Spirit. At last at peace with any outcome, the doctor still checked each run of probabilities looking for signs of REL. News of his recent demise and of Fells' outrageous actions stabbed fear through his body that he found hard to dispel. Discovery imminent, he shook off his tension and made hasty preparations to leave. Whether or not he found REL, he was destined for Earth, c.e. 2000.

Garner Williams rushed out of the shuttle bay and directly for Director Timball's residence. The gaunt director answered his door in a robe and pajama bottoms, tears streaming down his face, "Arthur just told me, Mr. Williams." Timball heaved a ragged sigh and stumbled back into his living area.

"Are you going to be all right, Director Timball?" Williams whispered.

"They tell me I'll live," the stricken director murmured.

"I'll check in on you later, then." Williams reached out and patted Timball on the shoulder. "I'm sorry." He turned and retreated to his quarters.

Wildwood

Burrows skidded to a stop, his trailing cloud of dust billowing up to overtake the car. Craig Landwehr jumped from his perch atop the Wildwood gate, ready to challenge the intruders until he spotted Thelma in the front seat. Smiling broadly, he walked over to Thelma's window to greet her.

"Get in," Burrows barked before introductions. "We spotted the girl's car parked on the backside of the property," Burrows advised as Craig slid into the back seat. "My deputy went after her."

Turning to Craig, Thelma added, "Burgess is certain that she has a pistol."

Craig groaned, "What's this all about? Is she a nut or what?"

"Burgess thinks she's a religious fanatic who's one chorus short of a whole hymn, if you know what I mean. I think that Jeremiah Marks is pushing her buttons. What do you think of this?" Burrows asked, passing the aerial photograph back to his passenger. "We found it in her car."

Craig examined it closely. "Jeez, it's pretty recent. This striped tent has only been here a couple of days. And you know what else? There's a name and address on the back for a local photographer. I'll call him and see who commissioned this picture. Marks, huh?" Craig pondered. "He was pretty tweaked at REL on Parmakian's show. But a stalker? Maybe a hit woman…?" Drawing a sharp breath between his teeth, Craig let the thought trail off.

"Is that it?" Thelma pointed to the graceful cabin.

"Yep. Marshal, you can park right next to John's Blazer," Craig directed.

"Naturally, the infamous Blazer," Burrows whispered, killing the engine and setting the brake.

Whistling a ditty, Fletcher did not hear the car doors slam as Craig's party approached. Grabbing a large bottle of wine in one hand and draping a kitchen towel over his arm with the other, he headed to the back door. Multicolored lights, sparkling in the afternoon sun, caught his attention. There lay Valerie's odd pendant. Curious, he picked it up, squeezing it gently in response to the warmth it emitted. Suddenly, it came alive — the amplification-sleeve telescoped amid flashing lights and ceaseless chirping.

"Shit!" the big man groaned. Squeezing it harder to mute the sound, he carried the point with him to the picnic.

On the other side of the lake, Alan steadily closed the distance, careful not to give his position away. As Cindy neared the confluence where two tiny streams emptied into the lake, trees gave way to tall grasses and wildflowers. Alan hugged the forest as long as he could, until Cindy pulled away again. Surrendering stealth for speed, the deputy took a deep breath and sprinted across the boggy meadow. Before he knew it, he splashed into a hidden pool, drawing Cindy's immediate attention. Whipping around, pistol held before her in both hands, she aimed directly at his head.

"Stay away from me, Alan!" she screamed. "You can't stop me. No one can stop me!"

Raising both hands in the air, Alan edged forward. "Cindy. I just want to help you," he called up the slope that led into the woods. "Why don't you put the gun down?" He took another small step.

"Don't!" she screamed again, waving the gun. Then she turned like a rabbit and fled up the trail into the trees. Tripping over a shadowed tangle of roots, she fell heavily to the packed earth, somehow keeping the pistol aloft with one hand. Not even catching her breath, she rolled to her knees. Snapping her gun back to a two-handed grip, she aimed down the path as Alan approached at a dead run.

Topping the small rise on the fringe of the forest, Burgess stopped in his tracks at the sight of her. She knelt, jaws clenched and trembling hands pointing her small pistol right between his eyes. Her hollowed eyes were smudges against her chalky skin. Her matted blond hair clung to her head in tangles of dirt, sweat, and leaves.

Never taking his eyes from hers, Burgess walked steadily toward her, hands raised in surrender. "Cindy," he soothed. "Let me help you, please."

"You stay away from me, Alan Burgess!" she hissed.

"What is going on with you? What is this all about?" Alan pleaded.

"I've been telling you, Alan!" she sobbed. "I'm The Sentinel. I have to stop him."

"Who told you this, Cindy? How do you know?"

"The nightmares... the messages in the music... the signs... Alan, I've learned to read all the signs. Reverend Marks knows who I am." Her voice quivered.

Alan took half a step toward her. "What if you're wrong, Cindy? What if Marks has been using you?"

"No!" she shrilled, shaking her head violently. "He's the only one who really understood when I told him about the voices and the demons. He's the only one who knows how to make them stop."

Alan inched closer.

"That's it, Alan! Don't come any closer or I swear I'll pull the trigger."

Burgess stared into the silver barrel as Cindy pulled back on the hammer. Glancing from her face to her gun and then back to her face, the deputy slid a shoe forward in the dirt. Cindy shook her head lowering her aim to his heart, then squeezed the trigger sending Burgess stumbling backward against a tree, hands automatically flying to his chest.

"Lucky for you I always keep the first chamber empty." She spun to her feet and hands, launched into a sprint and disappeared into the timbers.

Alpha II

Doctor Morrison mopped sweat from his forehead as he ran one, last calculation. No sign of REL in any of the probabilities thus far, he had little to go on, now, but hope. Centering his search around the TechniCom, Morrison selected a probability at random knowing full-well the odds against finding his biomech.

Sickened at the thought of stepping into the tower, the doctor briefly debated simply standing his ground and facing Fells. *I won't give him the satisfaction*, Morrison mumbled to himself. Adrenaline-fueled tremors slowed his progress as he locked into his year 2000 target. He scolded himself for his fear and paused. *I will not cast my lot from a fear-riddled psyche*, he vowed. He closed his eyes and drew a deep, measured breath through his heart, making his connection to Spirit. Moments later, drifting through deep layers of his mind, he felt the touch of Universal Love that subdued his growing panic.

At that instant, the point scanner pierced his meditation with a joyous discordance. REL was signaling!

Wildwood

Fletcher jogged out the back door, slowing to a brisk walk as he reached the wooded path. Winding his way along the lip of the lake, he tried to mute the chirping point with his clutching fingers. Pausing to catch his breath before trudging the final incline to the meadow, Fletcher thought he heard strange voices in the woods. Listening for a moment and hearing nothing more, he strode to the picnic area, depositing the wine and towel on the convenient table rock. "Valerie, oh Valerie," He held his hand out to her. "I didn't mean to hurt it. I was just bringing it to you. You left it on the counter."

Valerie laughed. REL jumped from the blanket and met the big man. Gently, he lifted the point from Fletcher's persistent grip, and let it lie, undisturbed, in his open hand.

"Valerie," Fletcher apologized "I'm so sorry." He sat down beside her on the blanket. "I was just curious, that's all."

"It's okay," she comforted.

Just as Craig raised his hand to knock, laughter spilled through the trees. "Oh, I know where they are. Follow me." Craig led Thelma and Burrows around the side of the cabin to the path that led to the lake.

Alpha II

Fells' black Stinger swooped into the remaining slot, forcing a cargo transport to pull up to avoid a collision. "I said this is an emergency!" he screamed at the controller. Shoving past security with a flash of his ICom badge, Fells pressed Zephyrs against the wall in an isolated corridor. Nose to nose with the young lieutenant, Fells hissed, "Bring Timball to Morrison's quarters. I don't care what it takes, bring him!"

Kyle Zephyrs raced to the nearest elevator, punching in Garner Williams' com number as he ran. "Garner, meet me at Timball's quarters. Now!" Disconnecting, he bounded out of the tube as soon as the doors opened on Timball's floor. Rushing down the corridor, Zephyrs nodded to Williams, who hurried to meet him. "You're never going to believe this, Garner," Zephyrs panted as they reached Timball's door. "Morrison's not dead."

"Bullshit, Kyle. I was right there, I saw it." Williams studied Zephyrs' face. "What's going on?"

"Garner, you saw an android die. I just came from the autopsy. That was not Morrison. Fells is here to find him."

Timball stepped out into the hall, "I thought I heard voices." He frowned at the two men outside his door.

Pushing the bedraggled director back inside his quarters, Zephyrs warned, "Director Timball, you're in danger."

"What are you talking about?" Timball thrust Zephyrs' hands away.

"Fells is on the station looking for Morrison. He's nuts, Director. He ordered me to bring you to Morrison's quarters." Zephyrs stopped to catch his breath.

"But Fells stole his body," Timball sobbed.

"Fells stole an android, Director. I just witnessed the autopsy," Zephyrs assured. "What are we going to do about Fells? Where is Morrison, anyway?"

Timball gasped, "Of course! REL1! Even Phil's failures were brilliant. My God, we've got to get to his residence!"

Imperator Fells paced furiously around Morrison's spotless living quarters. *Nothing!* he snarled. And then he saw it. The subtle trail through the carpet nap appeared to end at the bookshelf. Kneeling to examine it closer, Fells discovered filaments bent under the bottom shelf of the bookcase. Enraged, he stood and shoved it, knocking dozens of books off onto the floor. Grunting, Fells assailed the shelf. But still, it would not budge.

Inside his sanctuary, Dr. Morrison shuddered at the ominous sounds of imminent discovery. He winced with regret at the thud of flying books and jerked each time the bookcase groaned. Grabbing his rucksack and murmuring a silent prayer of thanks for REL's signal, he stepped into the matrix tower as the scanner locked on. The harsh and ratcheting pull through time suspended further thoughts of Fells.

In fury, Fells tried to rake the remaining books from Morrison's shelves, but one refused to fall. Yanking it, he felt the bookcase move. He shrieked his triumph, then put his weight against the shelf and burst into Morrison's lab.

The hum of the matrix tower drew the imperator's attention. He slid behind the console, frantically trying to make sense of the controls. A familiar red sticker marked the emergency return. He slammed his fist down on the control panel and activated the sequence. Uncoiling to his feet, Fells unsheathed his sidearm and turned to face the tower.

Wildwood

Cindy Vinwire paced her own private demons. Stumbling up the forest path toward the laughter, she paused to brush the sweat and tears from her eyes. Footfalls behind her drove her on to the clearing and up the gentle slope. Scanning her surroundings, she caught sight of two men and a woman running toward her from the other side of the cabin. Glancing back up the slope, she spotted her quarry.

All eyes turned to Cindy, who marched purposefully for Worthington. Without a word, she closed to within ten yards of him, raised her pistol and squeezed the trigger. The very instant the shell exploded in the chamber, Alan Burgess launched himself to rip the gun from her hands and the air crackled and sizzled as molecules stretched to accommodate the time-traveling Morrison. The second the doctor materialized, he was flattened by the airborne deputy, now caught up in a momentum he did not understand. As the report rang through the startled trees, Alan Burgess disappeared into the sparkling air around him — pulled screaming, through time. With him on the trip to Alpha II, sped Cindy Vinwire's bullet intended for the Antichrist.

Alpha II

As telltale mist gathered in the matrix tower, a grim smile spread across the skeletal face of Imperator Fells. In seconds, Morrison would be his. A shadowy image flickered into shape within the purple luminescence prompting Fells' fingers to tremble in anticipation of his victory. A shock of surprise registered in his eyes as a silent thud knocked him to the floor and painted an oozing crimson stain across his chest.

Three frantic men rushed through the quiet corridors of Level 14. Even with Garner Williams supporting one arm and Kyle Zephyrs supporting the other, the director struggled to keep pace. Timball gasped in dismay when the trio entered the apartment to find the doctor's precious books strewn across the floor. Rounding the bookcase to the hidden lab, they saw a shadowy figure suspended in the matrix tower and Imperator Fells bleeding to death on the floor.

The young lieutenant quickly knelt beside Fells who looked up at him with glazing eyes. "You were right, Zephyrs…" he groaned and then died.

Wildwood

The crack of the gunshot echoed through the forest like denial. And for an instant, time held its breath. The clearing at Wildwood lay still in the flickering, late morning sun. Then Cindy's maddened howl sundered the silence and ushered chaos into the glen. REL responded first, diving to kneel beside the fallen doctor.

Craig tackled Cindy in a bear hug. She folded up like a rag doll, floppy and sobbing and unable to speak.

Valerie rushed to help REL as Dot, Barry, and Gary quickly checked for casualties.

And Marshal Jim Burrows stood, dumfounded, in the center of the clearing. Arms stretched to his sides and palms upturned, he slowly reeled a perfect three-sixty, disbelieving what he had seen. Finally, he whispered, "Where's Alan?" Raising his voice so all could hear, he repeated, "Where's Alan?"

Thelma rushed to his side, "Jim... Alan vanished."

"Remember what I said about the POOF, Marshal?" Barry interjected. "You just saw it for yourself."

"Dr. Morrison?" REL said gently, helping the white-haired man to his feet. "Are you okay?" Brushing the twigs and grass from the doctor's clothes, REL permitted a smile. "You're about the last person I expected to see at Wildwood." He hugged the wobbly man, held him away by the shoulders, then hugged him again.

In unspoken agreement, everyone edged nearer REL and Dr. Morrison. Even Cindy, still in Craig's iron grip moved shakily closer.

"Everybody... Everybody..." REL motioned with one hand, the other still on the doctor's shoulder. "I want you all to meet Dr. Phillip Morrison."

"Doesn't anybody care that Alan is missing?" Burrows pressed.

"I told you, Marshal, he disappeared," Barry replied. Tapping REL on the arm, he asked, "Where did he go, John?"

"I can only surmise that he stumbled into the time matrix and was transported back to Alpha II along with Cindy's gun," REL reasoned.

"Well, I'm calling the local police," Burrows bristled.

Fletcher intervened, "Haven't you done enough already?" He glared at the marshal. "Had you not opened this can of worms to begin with, your deputy would be safe at home in Colorado. And she..." he pointed at Cindy, "...would be answering phones at Data Pioneer."

Taken aback by the truth of it, Burrows stared at the faces in the small gathering.

"Please... Marshal, this isn't your fault," REL spoke gently. Then tipping his head to look Cindy in the eyes, he continued. "Cindy, it isn't your fault, either. In fact, we need to remember there are no victims. Each of us here co-created this experience for our own purpose. Including Deputy Burgess, who created his way to a space station in the future."

Gently nudging the marshal, Thelma chuckled, "Why Jim, isn't that just like Alan?"

Whipping around, Burrows gasped, "You mean this actually makes sense to you?"

"Of course it makes sense to me, Jim. This is how life works. We've been talking about it for eight years." Thelma touched his cheek and smiled at him.

Clearing his throat, Craig spoke, "What shall we do with her?" He pointed to Cindy. "She did try to shoot you."

As attention focused on her, Cindy moaned and feebly attempted to shake free.

Walking over to her, REL stopped short as she cringed away. Breathing from his heart, he murmured, "What is the kindest way to help her?"

Fletcher piped up, "Help her? She's been stalking you! She tried to kill you!"

"Gary, whatever mercy you deny her, you ultimately deny yourself." REL breathed peace to Cindy and turned back to the group. Morrison, fully revived, observed his creation in silence and wonder.

"Craig," Thelma began, "surely there's a reputable mental health clinic that can observe her and make a recommendation."

"No!" Cindy sobbed.

Craig gently turned the weeping woman to march her to his car. "We'll do what we can to help you, Miss." He patted her on the arm.

"Craig..." REL called. "Please bring Jenny and join us for dinner about six o'clock. I'll explain everything so you understand what's going on."

Alpha II

Looking up from the dead face of Imperator Fells, Lt. Zephyrs watched a lanky figure stumble from the tower. Deputy Alan Burgess felt the pistol slip from his stunned fingers as he lurched from the mist. A wave of nausea doubled him over at the waist. Zephyrs jumped to his feet to steady the wobbly stranger. "Trust me, I know how you feel. Here..." he guided Burgess to the nearest chair. "Keep your head low a minute. It will pass quickly."

Joining Zephyrs next to the prone imperator, Timball confirmed, "He's dead. Absolutely. God, half his heart's blown away."

"Then he had one after all," Williams mused. "What a mess!" Slumping to another chair, he looked at Timball. "Do you have any idea what just happened here?"

Patting Burgess on the back, Zephyrs offered, "I have a pretty good idea. Look," he said, enumerating with his fingers. "One: I just witnessed the autopsy of some kind of android that looked so much like Morrison it fooled a courtroom full of people. Two: We've got honest-to-God time travel. I've done it myself. And Three: We've got a lot of meddling around with people and events of two hundred years ago."

Raising his throbbing head, Alan mumbled, "You mean I was right about the time travel?"

Staring at the chaos around him, Timball turned back to Zephyrs. "Don't forget the secret lab, the dead imperator, and the missing Dr. Morrison. Oh God, and illegal technology. Before this goes one step further, I'm contacting Arthur Tabbot."

"And I'm contacting Judge Hawthorne," Williams said, shaking his head. "What in the hell did Imperator Fells get me into?"

Wildwood

"Really, Jim," Thelma took his hand. "What's the point?" They sat on a rock in the last of the afternoon's sunlight, still trying to make peace with the day's events.

"But I was right all along. Something fishy *is* going on," Burrows argued.

"You've said it yourself, though, Jim, it's not criminal."

"But... but..." the marshal sputtered.

"But nothing!" Thelma said sternly. "Your cynicism has brought you nothing but grief. Don't you think it's time to consider an alternative?"

"But what about Alan, Thelma? I can't just forget about him," Jim pressed.

"Of course not, Jim. But you need to hear John's explanation before you decide anything. Besides," she patted his hand, "if Alan did end up in the future, isn't that fitting?"

Allowing a brief grin, Burrows answered, "You're right about that. It's just that I feel responsible." He swallowed a lump in his throat. "And I'm gonna miss him."

"Well, that's that," Valerie pronounced, wiping her flour-coated hands on her apron.

Sliding plump loaves of dough into the oven, Dot sighed. "I don't know about you guys, but I would greatly appreciate a glass of wine right about now."

"Excellent idea." Barry twisted an ear of corn inside a shiny foil husk. "I'll pour. So... What you do suppose they're being so secretive about?" He dropped the last ear onto the stack of readied veggies and jerked his head toward Fletcher's private balcony.

Offering Dr. Morrison an enormous cigar, Fletcher winked conspiratorially. "I'm the only one who knows," the big man whispered and nodded his head.

"Oh?" Morrison smiled and looked at REL.

"He knows that I'm a biomech," REL stated matter-of-factly.

"You told him? How?" Morrison furrowed his brow.

"I had to, Dr. Morrison. I had to break the last shackle of my programming."

Morrison stared at the biomech. "Tell me more," he murmured.

"I don't mean to be rude," Gary interrupted, "but don't you think we need to decide what to tell Craig and Thelma and that marshal?"

"I'm going to tell them exactly what Dot and Barry and Valerie already know." REL grinned.

"Do you think they can handle it?" Gary protested. "Especially Burrows?"

"According to my calculations..." REL laughed, "that decision has the greatest odds of success. Besides, the work has to continue."

Tugging on REL's sleeve, Dr. Morrison asked, "What about the TechniCom? I could have sworn I felt an energy shift on Alpha II."

"I found a better way, Dr. Morrison. Come on, I'll show you. With that, REL gently guided Dr. Morrison to the computer room.

Alpha II

The moon deigned not to rise this night, lazing instead in the shadows as darkness shrouded the sky and haunted the dreams of men. Defying the seduction of self pity, Councilman Arthur Tabbot sat alone in his Capital City townhouse, a wraith of faded idealism. Too spent to further question his fate, he gazed numbly at the tunneled view of the overspread sky, the heaviness in his heart dwarfing even the ponderous government buildings that surrounded him. Grieving the loss of Morrison, the loss of hope, he could barely bring himself to answer his com. "Tabbot," he finally managed.

"Arthur, Dan Timball here." Without preamble, he announced, "Fells is dead."

"What?" Tabbot asked.

"He was accidentally shot — here, on Alpha II."

"What the hell was he doing on Alpha II?" the LRA Spokesman demanded.

Smiling broadly, Timball replied, "Trying to find Phil."

"Trying to find him? He stole Phil's body. I saw it with my own eyes." Tabbot cradled his head in his hands.

"Arthur, I have it on eyewitness authority that Fells bodynapped and autopsied a biomech. REL1," he added pointedly. "We believe that Phil managed to escape so he could find REL2. However, the situation is rather sticky."

Timball briefly filled in the details, watching hope return to Tabbot's eyes as he spoke. "So," the director concluded, "what do we do?"

"The first thing we do is arrange a secure conference communiqué with Judge Hawthorne, myself, and those of you on Alpha II. In fifteen minutes."

Still slightly pallid, but avidly sipping crystalline, Alan Burgess quietly gazed out Dr. Morrison's viewport. Mesmerized by the glowing Earth, he placed the heel of his hand against the plexishield as if cradling the tiny planet. "Careful what you ask for..." he murmured. Turning back to the room, he jumped at the two huge holographic faces suspended in the air.

Judge Hawthorne began, "On the matter of Morrison... Somehow that old wizard managed to courier a holodisc to me this afternoon. I'll cover the highlights with you. Morrison asks that his prematurely publicized death and his Order To Appear serve as the springboard for full disclosure of his entire project. He has covered absolutely every contingency. Except, of course, the death of Imperator Fells and the arrival of Mr. Burgess. He hopes to assist the paradigmatic shift of the Third Millennium from this end, too."

Arthur Tabbot explained, "You know, Phil always wanted to go public with this. He was convinced that his scheme offered enough hope to act as a magnet to the people. He believed a critical mass of consciousness could be achieved with media publicity alone."

"Well, it looks like he's going to get his wish. We can't cover up Fells' death," Timball whispered.

"I am confident that Imperator Fells' death will be ruled accidental. As for Mr. Burgess..." Mildred's eyes softened as she spoke to the nervous young man. "Our first ambassador from another time will create quite a sensation, I suspect. Yes..." She smiled. "It looks like Phil will get his publicity."

Second Messenger

The Medium of Miracles

Wildwood

The lake was a mirrored canvas for the artistry of Nature that surrounded it. The reflection of one ancient willow shimmered on the top of the water. "I think that's why they call it a weeping willow." REL admired the fluid undulations of the reflected masterpiece. Rowing easily with precision strokes, he continued, "Dr. Morrison, what do you know of God?"

Morrison chuckled, a thousand questions queued in his mind, not one as fascinating as this. "I believe that God is a loving force of which we are all a part."

"Does that include me?" REL asked.

"Well… of course…"

"From an animist's perspective," REL qualified.

Morrison hesitated and then said, "Yes. Essentially."

"You must stretch your mind, Dr. Morrison," REL teased. "Has God ever touched your heart?"

"Well, yes… REL?"

"Then you'll understand my story. There I was, cradled in the breast of God, filled with an urgent message that had to be delivered. I could not wait to be born in the traditional sense… could not wait to grow up. Nor could I risk the amnesia of birth. And there you were, offering the perfect solution, for your time and this time. You created a structure capable of containing my unveiled consciousness." REL rowed along a stand of cattails where water birds fluttered and whistled.

Speechless, Dr. Morrison stared across the small boat at his creation.

"Of course, my descent into matter confused me as it does every soul. But between your brilliance and God's..." REL smiled when the doctor blushed. "As I fought against my program, my awareness of who I am unfolded."

"So, who are you?" Dr. Morrison asked in astonishment.

"I am exactly who you prayed for, Dr. Morrison. I am an emissary from the heart of God."

Completing the circuit around the lake, REL watched Dr. Morrison with a smile. The aging eyes twinkled and he chuckled to himself beneath his silvery mustache. Drifting into the cove by the picnic area, REL was surprised to find a greeting party. The marshal and Thelma, Craig and the entire Wildwood family paced the soft earth next to the small wooden dock.

"Cindy's loose!" Dot announced breathlessly. "I called to send her some flowers and they said she was gone."

"Yeah," Craig added. "She was sprung by Jeremiah Marks. Same guy who commissioned and gave her that aerial photo."

"John..." Gary bit his lip. "You've got to cancel the publishing party. It's just too dangerous."

Burrows cleared his throat and offered, "It's possible that Marks has been setting Cindy up to shoot you for months, now... John."

Helping Dr. Morrison from the boat, REL turned to them. "I choose to live in love, not fear. Besides, whatever we run from today we have to confront tomorrow. Of course," he quipped, "by tomorrow it's usually bigger and has sharper teeth. Come on," he said, taking Valerie's hand and kissing it. "We have a party coming up."

Nudging Burrows, Gary shook his head. "See? Didn't I tell you?"

"Let's see," REL chimed, "the tents and pavilions arrive tomorrow. That gives three days to set them up. Shuttles to Syracuse, flowers, food... All covered. WooooHoooo!" he laughed, drawing Valerie down the path to the cabin.

Alpha II

Williams straightened the combination tie and status medallion considered proper citizen attire at elaborate functions and implored Alan Burgess to comb his hair. "Are you ready for your first shuttle ride?" Williams smiled at his fidgety charge.

"Am I?!" Burgess bubbled. "In my wildest dreams I never thought I'd get to."

Kyle Zephyrs helped Alan on with his jacket and said to Williams, "I thought he might like to ride with me when I return the Stinger."

"Just don't take the long way, Kyle. The world awaits Mr. Burgess. It's their first glimpse of him," Williams reminded. "Lucky for you, the media is banned from space stations. But brace yourself for the circus when you land." Patting Burgess on the back, Williams picked up his holocam equipment. "You're huge, Alan. This is like first contact all over again."

Ushering Alan to the shuttle bay, Zephyrs explained, "Wait till you see this thing. It's so hot..."

Thunderstruck at the sight of the sleek, black graphite craft, Alan Burgess circled the Stinger in silence. Timidly, he ran an appreciative hand along a graceful fin. "Wow," he murmured. "If only everybody back home could see this..."

"Are you homesick, Alan?" Kyle asked softly.

Boosting himself up to the cockpit, Burgess tossed a grin. "Not at the moment."

In a penthouse suite overlooking the festooned Center State Complex, Dan Timball and Arthur Tabbot reminisced.

"Phil would have loved this," Tabbot exclaimed, pointing to the flowers and streamers bedecking the official buildings.

"And this." Timball activated the news. "Every single story references Phil and his scheme. There are even grassroots meditation groups sending energy back to the year 2000."

"You know," Tabbot added, "years ago, Phil told me he thought one man could change the world. Guess he was right."

Timball shook his head. "I sure wish he could see this."

With a twinkle in his eye, Tabbot responded, "Maybe he can."

Wildwood

The fair was not officially open before the roads surrounding Wildwood streamed with cars and people. Leaning against the open front gate, Craig Landwehr received the first report. "We're already filled down to the crossroads," he turned to Gary Fletcher and held up his radio. "This is amazing."

"Yeah," the big man agreed. "No sign of Cindy?"

"No," Craig shook his head all the while bobbing up and down to see every face that entered Wildwood. "We've got a pretty good presence out on the roads. I don't think she'll get through without being spotted."

Fletcher nodded. "Did you get a chance to see any of the tables."

"Display or food?" Craig smiled and waved a welcoming hand at someone he recognized in the crowd. "I walked around while people were setting up. It's really something! I know Jenny and Thelma have been making the rounds. I expect a full report eventually."

"I'm headed to the food. Can I bring you anything?" Fletcher offered.

"No, I'm fine for now. Ask me in an hour or two." Craig nodded at another familiar face.

Bright tents and pavilions sprouted like spring flowers in the woods. Streamers and balloons adorned the paths and strolling musicians provided serenades that drifted through the trees.

"Hey Dot," Barry tapped her on the shoulder. "Check this out."

Just outside the cabin, caterers added the finishing touches to tables laden with pastries and fruit and decorated with masses of fresh cut flowers. Tables bloomed with colorful salads and cheeses. European carts, filled with shaved ice, offered chilled juices and the aroma of coffee and spicy tea filled the air.

Bending to whisper in Dot's ear, Barry chimed, "There's shri-imp."

"Good grief!" Gary interrupted. "They just keep coming. Craig estimates that at this rate we'll have nearly a thousand here by noon."

"I'll bet Marshal Burrows is in rare form," Dot quipped.

"He's parking cars around the backside of Wildwood. His guess is that's where Cindy will try to enter again. She knows that way already," Fletcher explained.

"I vote that she finds peace and lives happily ever after," Dot declared.

"I agree," Barry added.

Marshal Burrows grunted and pushed against the rear bumper of the Buick that had slipped a wheel off the shoulder. With a spray of gravel it climbed back onto the road. The marshal spun then plopped to the ground and wiped his brow. "Whew! You're welcome," he wheezed, turning to wave at the thankful driver.

Brushing his hands together, Reverend Marks completed his odious task and watched Cindy disappear into the woods. Concealed by the black tinted windows of the rented Lexus, he glanced into the side mirror then waited for an opening in the flow of traffic. As he neared the clogged intersection, he adjusted his Stetson and smirked through his sunglasses. Burrows didn't even see him. Humming a triumphal tune, the reverend blended into the procession.

Across the ditch in the shadows of the trees, a camouflaged silhouette dove for cover as Burrows stood and raised his eyes to stare into the forest. Then he returned his attention to the circus of traffic that had snarled in just seconds.

Rolling to the shelter of a small ravine, Cindy slumped and panted, sweating freely beneath her long-sleeved cammies. Blond hair bound in a black bandanna and grease paint smeared in khaki stripes across her face, she haunted the trees, unseen. Catching her breath, she shouldered her rifle and walked shakily on.

As shadows lengthened, the flow of people slowed to a trickle, then ceased. Throughout the budding glens of Wildwood, laughter and music echoed, rising and dying in waves of joyous expression. Festive paper lanterns winked on through the trees. REL laughed nervously with Valerie and Dr. Morrison as the crowds filtered into the clearing.

Springing lightly onto the table rock, REL surveyed the gathering. "This is great!" He spoke into the wireless microphone clipped to his shirt, "Testing."

Gazing at him framed against the sunset, Valerie stifled her own nagging disquiet and smiled at his nervousness.

REL fidgeted with the mike and spoke, "Thank you so much for coming."

Less than a hundred yards from the crowd, perched ten feet above the ground on the limb of a grizzled old oak, Cindy shivered at the sound of John's voice. Securing the strap of her rifle over her shoulder she glanced overhead then grabbed for the thick limb above her. Climbing until she gained a clear view of her target through the leaves of the giant tree, she leaned against the trunk to steady her aim.

People quickly hushed as REL's gentle words floated across the meadow. Standing on the table rock, profiled against the shimmering lake and fading sunset, he poured his heart out to the gathering. "Tonight, I want to talk about deep cover spies." REL looked down at the Wildwood family, laughing. They laughed in return. Dr. Morrison raised an eyebrow at their private joke.

Away in the trees, an electric shock of fear jolted through the sniper. Cowering at the thought of discovery, Cindy hunkered down into the leaves and listened.

Poised at the edge of the table rock, REL spread his arms and engulfed the multitude in a metaphysical hug that rippled energy from heart to heart. Sweeping a hand across the crowd, he pronounced, "We're all spies. And we're lost in an alien landscape. We are so beguiled by our assumed identities and the illusory nature of our surroundings that we have literally forgotten who we are.

"While we believe that we have been abandoned, naked, in a threatening environment, we are, in truth, immersed in love. Even as we bumble around in fear and despair, our connection home beats within our breast.

"Oh, Dearest Ones, feel your hearts, feel your way home. For as you remember who you are, you will remember why you came. You will remember yourselves to be the cherished children of God, beloved in your adventure to seed love through each of your moments."

In the darkening trees, Cindy felt a stirring, a chill, slither up her sweat-damp back. Reaching inside her blouse, she withdrew the protective medallion Marks had given her. With shaking fingers she traced the words: "The heart is deceitful above all things and beyond cure."

"Okay, Spies," REL grinned. "Turn to your neighbor. Even if you don't know them. In fact, better so. Look into their face. Study each line. Memorize each nuance that makes them unique in all the world. Look into their eyes behind your own reflection. Do you see God?"

Murmurs and sobs of joy answered his question.

"You know of course," he whispered, "that every face you meet bears the face of God. As does your own. Your mission is to remember this and live accordingly. It's that simple."

Looking up from the kindness of Dr. Morrison's face, Valerie blinked as a splinter of light and sound fractured the night.

The soft slug exploded from the long barrel, its recoil throwing the assassin off balance. Grasping frantically for a hand hold, Cindy dropped the rifle and fell crashing to the ground.

Just as horror registered on Valerie's face, the collision of lead against REL's head hammered an enormous thud through the clearing, spurring a collective flinch. The gathering watched in grief and disbelief as REL careened head over heels into the darkened lake, trailed by a gush of blood.

Craig and Burrows reacted instantly. "You go for the shooter, I'm going into the water," Craig barked as he stripped off his shoes. "Look!" He pointed at figures racing into the trees.

Without a word, Burrows raced after them.

Gripping the struggling Valerie, Gary Fletcher and Dr. Morrison reasoned with her, "Look, Barry's going in, too. We need you here the minute we get him back up. Here, hold this halogen light. Point it there..." Fletcher gestured. "That's where he went in."

Stealing a moment with the doctor, Gary whispered, "Do you think he's dead?"

"Not hardly, but then again, I just found out that he's alive." Morrison thought a moment. "The bullet won't kill him. He can't drown. His brain can live for hours on the oxygen he has in his lungs." Two splashes drew Fletcher and Morrison back to the lake. Thelma and Jenny Landwehr stood beside Valerie, aiming more light into the water as Barry and Craig waded along the narrow shelf. "Damn," Craig muttered, "he must have tumbled over the edge into the deeper water."

"Gary," Barry called. "How deep is it here?"

"Maybe fifteen feet," Gary ventured a guess.

"How long has it been?" Valerie murmured, tears streaming down her face.

REL staggered beneath the anguish as much as the impact. *Poor Cindy.* His heart ached for her even as his body hurtled into the black water. Sinking silently through the cloud of blood, a thousand thoughts processed as he watched the moonlight wane. *What will everyone think when I simply walk out of the lake? How will I explain it to Valerie?* Bumping over the narrow ledge, REL continued to sink into the soft mud and fallen trees on the bottom. Grief from those assembled above poured into the water — leaden and gelid — and sagged to engulf him. The pain of their worst fears crushed him. Compelled to spare them, REL pushed against the bottom only to shudder back down as his flexors failed one by one. Horrified, he watched lights dance across the surface of the water — fading as his vision dimmed.

Jim Burrows jogged into the woods to find a quiet group of people gathered around a tree. Burrows flashed his badge and the group parted to reveal a slight cammie-clad figure lying face-up and motionless on the forest floor. A woman

351

knelt beside her, one hand on the crown of Cindy's head and the other over her heart.

"How badly is she hurt? Can you tell?" Burrows asked.

"Her pulse is strong and regular. She's breathing fine. I think she fell out of the tree," the woman replied, gazing up at the marshal.

Burrows scanned the circle of people.

"I've got the gun." A man motioned to the marshal, then pointed to the ground near his foot. "I didn't touch it."

"I think this is the bullet." A solemn child pointed to a glint of metal in the leaves. "I won't touch it, either."

"Does anyone have a cell phone?" Burrows asked. "Let's get some help out here." Glancing back toward the lake, he wondered at the fate of John Worthington.

Barry breached the surface of the water with a sputtering gasp. "There's zero visibility down there. Shit." He shivered. "This water is freezing."

Placing a gentle hand on Valerie's shoulder, Dr. Morrison assured. "That's good. Cold water increases his chances. We'll get him."

Craig roiled to the surface, cursing the cold and the darkness.

Bursting through the crowd, Dot screamed, "Barry! I've got Gary's fishing flashlight. It's waterproof." Turning it on, she tossed it out to him. "Oh, Barry, you've just got to find him."

Catching the flying flashlight, Barry turned to Craig. "On three."

The two men gasped three deep breaths and ducked beneath the surface. People watched in silence as the back-lit silhouettes sunk quickly to the bottom.

Beneath the murky waters, their eyes stung, yet Barry and Craig probed on with numbing fingers. Zigzagging back and forth, they scanned the bottom for any sign of him. Feeble illumination cast eerie shadows in the water.

Unseeing, unfeeling, REL nonetheless sensed their hope and desperation as the two divers neared. In his mind, he called to them.

Just as their lungs burned with ache for oxygen, Craig and Barry spotted their friend. With the last of his breath, Barry cinched the flashlight strap tight around REL's lifeless wrist and burst to the surface, seconds behind Craig.

On unspoken cadence, they gasped three heroic breaths and dove for the light.

Reaching REL in seconds, they backed beneath his arms and bent him up at the waist. Squatting on the bottom, Craig nodded to Barry and they thrust up with their combined might, kicking furiously to the top. Just as they broke the surface, Gary flung a life vest secured to a tree with a rope. Slipping the Mae West behind REL's neck, Craig and Barry fastened it around his ribs and swam him to the waiting arms of Gary, Dr. Morrison, and Valerie.

Hovering inside his sensorless structure, REL observed his consciousness. No outside stimuli penetrated his cocoon, yet he knew when his rescuers reached him. He knew when his face escaped the water. And he knew when Valerie slipped into the lake to stand beside him on the shelf. Somehow, he felt Valerie place her mouth over his, filling his body with love and the breath of life.

Easing her way up onto the bank beside REL, Valerie removed her lips from his only long enough to check for breathing and a heartbeat. Placing two fingers alongside his neck to check the carotid, she studied the small gash in his right temple. Water-whitened, the shallow wound still trickled blood. Touching it gently, she raised her eyes to Morrison. "It's just a nick. Didn't even chip the skull. Dr. Morrison, he has a pulse."

Squeezing her eyes tight against her tears, she stifled a sob at the sight of his aura, shrunken and flickering faintly near his dripping body. Resolute, she bent to breathe again for him.

"Thank God for cold water," the doctor commented loudly.

The whoop of an ambulance siren prompted Barry to offer, "I'll go get the paramedics. Let's get him to a hospital."

Reaching a restraining arm, Morrison refused. "Barry, I have tools and techniques you don't even know about yet. His chances are better with me. Send them away."

Valerie urged, "We need to get him warm, Dr. Morrison." She cocked an ear as REL gasped his third breath on his own.

Frantically clearing the huge trestle table, Dot finished just as six men bore REL in on a dripping blanket. Hoisting his still form up to the table, they straightened him out, oblivious as puddles flooded the floor.

Craig and Barry kindled a blaze in the fireplace. Stripping off their wet things, they gratefully accepted warm, dry clothes.

Morrison directed Gary, "Rope this area off from the fireplace to the wall. Use clotheslines and quilts or something. We need to get him warm as quickly as possible. And we need privacy." Turning to Valerie, he asked, "Bring me as many blankets as you can find. And Dot, would you bring me my rucksack?"

His commands sent them scurrying. Grabbing a pair of scissors from a kitchen drawer, Morrison snipped away REL's clothes. The doctor shook his head when he found the amethyst tucked away in a soggy shirt pocket. Remembering the crystal from Coal Creek Canyon, he gently placed it in REL's unresponsive hand and closed the biomech's frozen fingers around it.

Outside, a hopeful vigil formed. Candles twinkled through the woods as chants and songs hummed softly around the cabin. Thelma looked out the screen door, eyes moist, and whispered a prayer into the night.

Inside, tucked away in Dr. Morrison's makeshift tent, REL lay warm and drying. Valerie soothed his forehead, cheered by its increasing warmth and his steady breathing. Shifting focus, she shook her head in dismay at his withered aura. Gently, Dr. Morrison took her arm and steered her toward the blanket-tent flap. "Valerie, in my time, when anyone is injured or ill, a meditation group automatically convenes. It's an integral part of healing. I want you to step outside with the people and lead a healing meditation." Placing his fingers on her protesting lips, he said, "Go. It's the most powerful thing you can do for him."

Blinking back her tears, Valerie returned to REL and kissed his lips. Longing to console her, he instinctively directed his awareness to his physical heart. Solid and comforting, it beat steadily with its own intelligence. He sensed, as well, the fine resonance of his amethyst. *Odd*, he thought, *that I can feel nothing else*. Quickly scanning his structure, he found all sensors numb, all senses deadened. Undaunted, he imaged solace pouring through his heart to Valerie and felt her energy brighten.

Patting Dr. Morrison's arm, Valerie slipped out the door to the crowd. Turning to Gary, the doctor said, "You stay with me." Shooing at everyone else, he ordered. "Out. Go help Valerie."

Morrison reached for his rucksack. He slid a delicate silver instrument from a sleeve and brought it to REL's face. Lifting his right eyelid with his thumb, Dr. Morrison shone a tiny light into the pupil. He repeated the procedure with REL's left eye then stood back to watch. Turning to Gary, he shook his head. "Nothing."

"But what about his breathing and pulse?" Gary argued.

"His computer brain controls them automatically. Look, Gary, I'm going to level with you. I can always re-activate the bio-mech. That's not my concern. However, I will not re-start this machine until I'm sure that REL's consciousness has not departed his body."

Gary glared at him. "What are you saying?"

Putting his finger to his lips, Morrison shushed him. "I will not have a robot masquerading as the man," he whispered harshly. "Now, I must do what I can for his structure and hope I'll do the right thing for him when the time comes." Assembling instruments on the sideboard, Morrison began diagnostics.

Valerie sat cross-legged on the porch swing, tears bursting candlelight into a thousand prisms. Composing herself, she spoke clearly to the crowd. "Please join me in a healing meditation for REL. Begin by breathing through your hearts. Feel the love of the Universe and draw it into you. Now, feel your hearts swell with the joy of REL's life. Hear his words. See his face. Feel his presence and send him the healing power of your love." Closing her eyes, she opened her own heart and cast her awareness in search of him. Her mind's eye sought him amidst the swaddling blankets. Traces of him hovered around his body. Other hints of his essence lurked deep within. And yet, she sensed him scattered among the trees, drifting in wisps among the people, unconcerned and patient. Peace filled her heart as she joined with the avalanche of energy cascading toward REL.

Wiping his beaded brow, Dr. Morrison complained, "I just don't understand it. He's sustained no real damage. Maybe the link between his consciousness and his body was more fragile than I thought." Shaking his head, he turned and walked away.

Basking in the building vibration of the surrounding meditation, REL drew in the energy. Consciously, he directed it to every portion of his unresponsive structure, storing it, letting it build. As the rush reached a crescendo, REL dispatched the energy through his heart, directly to the brooding doctor.

Recoiling from a sudden inspiration, Morrison held up his index finger. "Unless..." Striding back to his rucksack, he fumbled around and produced a squatty silver pyramid. Reeling a length of delicate filament from its base, he gently inserted it into REL's right ear. Staring at a spinning holographic display, he eased more filament into the canal until he felt a light tug. "Okay," he murmured, "talk to me, REL."

Instantly, numbers and symbols whirled and spun in the air. They showered and danced, dissolving and resolving into a readable pattern. The doctor had only to glance at it. "Gary!" he shouted in a whisper. "Come over here!"

Jerking to attention, the big man raced to the doctor's side. "What?!"

Pointing at the hologram, Morrison asked, "Do you have any idea what this is?"

Stifling a laugh, Gary said, "It's an emoticon. He's smiling at you. See?" The big man traced the sideways eyes, nose and mouth. "Now will you bring him back?"

"I still don't know what's wrong with him."

Suddenly, the pyramid hummed with running programs as REL launched his own diagnostic. A schematic of his structure burst into the air, circuits throbbing red, as if with pain.

"Of course!" Morrison slapped his forehead. "The water obviously seeped through his wound deep into his circuitry and shorted him out."

At his pronouncement, another smiley face danced into the hologram.

Deftly feeding numbers into the pyramid, Morrison smiled at Gary. "A fever will do him good," he said as he carefully monitored the hologram and watched REL's core temperature climb.

Valerie stepped quietly around the blanket. "How is he?" She moved an instinctive hand to his forehead. "Oh, my God! He's burning up." She spun to Morrison. "Where's your thermometer?"

"Valerie," the doctor soothed. "His fever is spiking, even now." He nodded to the hologram "Why don't you go brew him some tea. He'll be wanting some soon, I promise."

Nodding to Gary, he suggested, "Why don't you go get REL some dry clothes?"

Bending over REL, Morrison watched patiently as an eyelid fluttered. Then a toe twitched. And a finger jerked.

Rounding the corner of the blanket, Valerie nearly dropped the tray. There sat REL arrow straight on the kitchen table — bare feet dangling, blanket modestly draped across his lap, and merry eyes smiling at her. His brilliant aura flooded the room. Handing the tray to Dr. Morrison, she rushed to him and buried her face in his neck.

"Are you okay?" he murmured into her hair.

"Am I okay?" She placed a finger beneath his chin and tipped his head so he looked her in the eyes. "Are you?"

"I'm fine." He grinned. "Is everyone else okay?"

"Good grief!" she gently scolded. "You get shot in the head and submerged for fifteen minutes in cold water, and you ask about everyone else?"

Center State Complex

Jubilation rang through the huge Center State Reception Hall. The cavernous chamber danced with color as emissaries from every country, every culture, and every outer-planet colony mingled. Festive costumes, lavish headdresses, and sweeping robes of all manner adorned the contingent in celebratory flair. Media representatives and camera crews worked the crowd, broadcasting the event live throughout the Megacosm.

"Where is he?" Mildred Hawthorne whispered to Kyle Zephyrs as she stared down the length of the hall from her seat on the raised dais.

"I have no idea. I left him right here," Zephyrs replied, craning his neck to scan the huge room.

Just then, the massive two-story doors at the back of the hall eked open to admit a lone figure. Pausing to comb his fingers through his hair, he tugged at his tie and stepped into the parting crowd. Clutching a small shopping bag in his left hand, he grinned nervously and waved meekly. "Hi... hello there... nice to see you..." he repeated over and over as he worked his way through the sea of exotic people. Finally reaching the first riser, he turned and bowed shyly at the explosion of applause. Smiling and nodding, he made his way to the unoccupied seat of honor.

"Check this out," Alan said, scooting the chair from the table with his foot. Plopping down, he pulled a shiny-covered book from his shopping bag. "I just bought this. Twenty-first printing." He handed the book to Dan Timball and smiled like a cat, awaiting the man's response.

"Well I'll be damned," Timball chuckled, passing it to Tabbot. "He even wrote a book."

"*REL's Guide to God*," Arthur Tabbot read. "By John R. Worthington." He passed the book to Mildred, then stood and walked to the polished crystal lectern. "Citizens of Life..." he greeted them. "These are amazing times. We have new adventures, new dimensions, and new possibilities to consider. With that in mind, it is my honor to introduce this most improbable visitor from our probable past, Ambassador Alan Burgess." Tabbot smiled and ushered the former deputy to the podium.

Stepping to the lectern, Alan nervously tapped the silver disc on his lapel, sending an amplified squeal through the wincing audience. Straightening his shoulders, he murmured, "Sorry. I've never done this before." Fumbling in his back pocket, he produced a worn leather wallet. Flexing it open, he fished out a folded 3 X 5 note card. He opened it and flattened it out on the top of the lectern. Then holding it up for the audience, he began, "I guess I've officially carried this around for over two hundred years." A grin split his face as he laughed at the tender smiles from the people. In a husky voice, he continued, "Until today, I didn't even know why I did it. It just seemed important for me to remember it. Anyway..." Gulping, he pronounced, "*It is this capacity for love for all things which has always seemed to me the first indication that an individual or a race is approaching adulthood.* That's by Gene Roddenberry. He wrote *Star Trek...*" Alan faltered. Composing himself, he resumed, "He wrote about heroic people and heroic deeds. His stories were as close as I really came to... you know... religion, because they made me want to do good things with my life. A couple of months ago, plus a couple of centuries," he chuckled. "I found this quote and wrote it on the other side of the card. *Love exposes the illusion of fear and frees the soul to make miracles.* That's by REL. I even met him once. Anyway, I was wondering, what would happen if a whole world chose love? I mean, as a way of life. What kind of miracle would that create?"

Wildwood

Sparks of rumor kindled through the crowd around Wildwood. Hushed whispers of speculation filled the night until the cabin door opened to reveal REL, bright and shiny as the candles from the vigil. Only the small gauze patch on his temple gave any clue to the evening's earlier drama.

Laughing, he quipped, "Do I know how to throw a party or what?"

Applause and sobs of relief echoed through the woods as REL walked among the people. With a chuckle, he found himself back at the table rock. Sitting cross-legged atop it, he gathered his guests to talk. "Before we do anything else, I would like you to join me in a healing meditation for the young lady who left in the ambulance a couple of hours ago. She is the most wounded among us. Let us gently blaze a trail to her heart that she may find her way back to love."

After a few moments of silence, he continued, "You know, of course, that nothing happened here that did not serve a purpose for everyone involved. As *Messengers*, avowed to lead humankind to the vibration of love, we must be resolute in our understandings. This night, we confirmed for ourselves, that love is the medium of miracles."

Cindy Vinwire blinked as leaves played patterns in the sunlight, her demons dimmed by medication and seclusion. "It's almost time to come in, Cindy." An elderly nurse touched the silent girl on the shoulder.

Wordlessly, she stood up from the bench in the walled courtyard and drew her robe snugly around her. A curious thought nagged her to follow, pulling her eyes to the center of her chest. Mindlessly, her trembling fingers tapped her breast-bone as she shambled back to her ward.

Jotting a note on Cindy's chart, the nurse turned to the staff doctor. "She's doing it again. She's been doing that for three days. It's like she's looking for something."

God's Fortress

Storming through the nether hours of his third sleepless night, Reverend Jeremiah Marks raged. *They won't let me near the girl. And she's so deluded, she just might drag me into this with her.*

And Worthington… Marks ripped a golden cherub from its pedestal and smashed it to the floor.

…Risen from the dead, they say.

Thundering through the deserted halls of opulence, he encountered only shadows. No light.

Wildwood

A waxing moon reflected an almost perfect circle on the still surface of the lake. As its magic slipped through the frame of the large window, the conversation hushed.

"Oh, my," Dr. Morrison whispered, pulling the curtain all the way back to fully reveal the beauty. "It kind of puts the last three days into their proper perspective."

"It sure does," Valerie responded, linking her arm through Morrison's.

"John, so what about Marks?" Burrows persisted. "Craig and I have lots of evidence linking him to Cindy."

"Jim, you have to do what you think is right. Remember, Marks and Cindy both create whatever experience they need to grow. With or without your participation. Why don't you follow where your heart leads? Look for the love." REL patted him on the shoulder.

Gently taking the marshal's hand, Thelma winked at REL.

REL shivered unexpectedly, his soul and structure swathed in psychic goosebumps. Valerie felt it, too, and turned to him, puzzled.

"Hhhhmmmm... I think Dr. Morrison and I need to investigate this," REL whispered to her. "Be back soon." He kissed her on the forehead. "Dr. Morrison? Would you care for a walk in the moonlight?"

Morrison patted Valerie's hand. "Join us?"

Valerie smiled and shook her head.

Grabbing a flashlight, Morrison met REL at the door and stepped out into the night. "Well, that was mysterious," he chided the biomech.

"More than you know. I just felt a shiver from the time matrix. It came from the direction of our picnic spot." REL pointed into the moon-cast shadows.

Stepping quickly down the wooded path beside the lapping water, the two remained silent until they reached the clearing. There, atop the table rock, a 22nd century V-pak shimmered in the moonlight. Breathing a soft gasp, Morrison shined his light on it. Its reflection flared, as did his surprise. Gingerly, he leaned down and eyed the lustrous case. Sliding his thumb into the indentation of the rounded end, the doctor pressed down. With a soft clicking, the V-pak fanned open to reveal three, separate compartments.

"I just love surprises," Morrison grinned, reaching into the pocket on the right. His hand returned with a single, holocam disc. He slipped it into his shirt pocket and patted it. The center compartment yielded an elaborate, rare bottle of 2011 Chilean Crystalline accompanied by two ancient Venetian drams. "Mmmm," Morrison licked his lips at the sight of the confection. "This is for you," Morrison laughed, handing REL the 2189 Edition of *REL's Guide to God* from the third compartment.

Holding the book in the flashlight beam, REL opened it to find a folded note. Chuckling, he explained to the doctor, "It's from Alan Burgess. He wants me to autograph it and return it to the V-pak, right where we found it."

"That would make it a rare book, indeed. My, my, my... your *magnum opus*, a vintage bottle of Crystalline and a mysterious movie. What could be better?" Morrison winked as he settled on a log and twisted the top of the disc. He placed the disc in his open palm, waiting for his body heat to activate the hologram. As the first images flickered, he set the disc atop the table rock and motioned to the log. "Sit down with me, REL," he invited. "Sit down."

REL tucked the book under his arm and fetched two drams of Crystalline, alighting beside Dr. Morrison just as the hologram sprang to life. Instantly, a view of Center State Complex hovered above the table rock. Everywhere, colorful LRA flags waved in unison to the celebratory melody that dominated the audio track. Streamers, flowers, and confetti thronged the route as festooned transports glided down the main street of Capital City in a jubilant procession. Foremost in attention was the sleek, black Stinger, rolling along on a flatbed. Straddling the smooth, conical nose, a disheveled figure waved and threw kisses to the crowd. The camera panned in on the face of Alan Burgess, exuberant in his moment.

"Jim and Thelma will love this." REL chuckled at the elegance of fate.

With a shimmering segue, *Official World Information Team Update* replaced Alan's triumphant face, then transitioned to a begowned media anchor. Her vantage revealed a swirl of brilliant festivity. "We go now, live, to Councilman Arthur Tabbot," she announced as the view and audio focused on his speech.

"...With that in mind, it is my honor to introduce this most improbable visitor from our probable past, Ambassador Alan Burgess."

REL and Morrison both winced when Alan tapped the silver disc on his lapel. What followed held them spellbound as the earnest Alan Burgess embraced his own new paradigm.

"...Anyway, I was wondering, what would happen if a whole world chose love? I mean, as a way of life. What kind of miracle would that create?" Blushing beneath thunderous applause, Burgess sipped water until the acclaim subsided.

"I guess emissaries go both ways," Dr. Morrison mused.

Clearing his voice, Burgess concluded, "I'd like to leave you with this thought. It's from REL's book." He held up the shiny volume. "I just read it today. It says: *Breathe every moment through your heart and dwell amid miracles.*" Bowing shyly, he retrieved his note card and REL's book and retreated to his seat of honor. The scene dimmed as he received his third standing ovation.

REL dabbed a tear from his eye as the hologram shimmered through another segue. Pixels glimmered and resolved into a panoramic view of Dr. Morrison's residence on Alpha II. The doctor smiled as the camera panned his bookshelves, his precious library carefully restored to order. The scene continued into his living room to reveal an assemblage of faces toasting with matching Venetian drams.

Stepping forward, a ruddy Dan Timball tipped his glass and grinned. "Thanks for dragging me into this, Phil. My finest hours as a human being have been at your side."

Murmurs of "here, here" intruded from the background.

"You can't believe how fast things have changed. Even Arthur the optimist is amazed, so you can imagine my surprise." Timball sidled out of sight as Arthur Tabbot nudged into view.

"For you to have actually pulled this off is unfathomable," Tabbot admitted. "You and your..." He trailed off and fumbled for a word, "...Protégé have made firm believers out of arch skeptics. To wit..." Tabbot backed away from the camera, sweeping his arm toward the erstwhile Monitor Williams and a young blond man who stepped forward with a revelation.

"Dr. Morrison, I'm Kyle Zephyrs. We've never met, but I shadowed you through time. At the late, great Imperator Fells' behest, of course." He nodded and continued, "I just wanted you to know that almost every citizen alive today honors you for the future you bequeathed our world. Here's to you." He lifted his dram.

Garner Williams raised his glass. "Dr. Morrison, you shattered every belief I held about life. Thank you."

Williams bowed out with a nod of respect, making way for Alan Burgess.

"Howdy, Marshal, Thelma. I'm speaking to you from the future. Anyway, I love it here." Shrugging, he added, "I guess you could say I fit in. So... I hope everybody's okay. If anyone ever talks to Cindy, tell her hello from me." Holding up *REL's Guide to God*, Alan explained. "This is my reading copy, REL. And I just finished it. Do you mind if I consider myself a *Messenger* to the 22nd century?"

Dan Timball and Arthur Tabbot returned to the fore. "REL..." Timball placed a hand over his heart. "Forgive our discourtesy in not addressing you. Mine, especially. But we just don't know what to say or even to believe about you. The truth is your spiritual grace so far exceeds human imagination our words fall short of our appreciation. To you, Phil, the fact that I know you so well does not lessen my awe of your brilliantly deranged exploits." Smiling despite his tears, Timball motioned the camera to Morrison's floor to ceiling viewport. "Thought you might like one last look."

Reverence filled the clearing as Earth 2192 shimmered before them, awash in numinous vibration. Stirred by the beauty of it and humbled by the import of their deeds, Dr. Morrison and REL stood and raised their ancient drams to the star-filled sky as the hologram faded to black.

Living From the Heart

Practical application of the wisdom from *Second Messenger*

Ancient Wisdom ❀ Scientific Validation ❀ Real Results in your Life

Make the heart connection in your own life, and enjoy:

- ❏ Life-long, harmonious relationships.

- ❏ An enthusiastic sense of well-being.

- ❏ Enhanced vigor for life's offerings.

Learn new ways to look at the world and discover:

- ❏ A deeper sense of security and comfort.

- ❏ A joyful life, free of worry and fatigue.

- ❏ Internal harmony and improved confidence.

Seminar Leader
Jay Ritter

Living from the heart offers practical ways to connect with your true self to live the life your heart desires. The methodology is effective and proven to bring positive change into your life.

Seminar leader, Jay Ritter, has been applying his talent for teaching since graduation from Bethany College, when he joined the Rosemount, Minnesota Public School System. Since those early years teaching students, he has enlarged his educational sphere to include public speaking and seminar leadership. Jay's soothing demeanor helps guide participants toward a powerful, heart-centered lifestyle. Most people who meet Jay and follow his gentle lead report nearly instant transformation.

"After more than two years of in-depth discussion and idea exchange, we are honored to share Jay's extraordinary abilities with our readers. His seminars are the perfect conveyance to fully explore the messages of our novel."

Gale & Kitty Connell

To inquire about attending this inspirational one day seminar in the Boulder/Denver area or to schedule a seminar in your area contact:

MythMaker Press
P.O. Box 1890
Nederland, CO 80466
303-258-3929
or visit us online at: secondmessenger.com

a